THE DESTINY MAKERS

GEORGE TURNER

An AvoNova Book

William Morrow and Company, Inc.
New York

THE DESTINY MAKERS is an original publication of Avon Books. This work has never before appeared in book form. This work is a novel. Any similarity to actual persons or events is purely coincidental.

AVON BOOKS
A division of
The Hearst Corporation
1350 Avenue of the Americas
New York, New York 10019

Copyright © 1993 by George Turner
Published by arrangement with the author
Library of Congress Catalog Card Number: 92-2414
ISBN: 0-688-12187-X

Library of Congress Cataloging in Publication Data:

Turner, George.
    The destiny makers / George Turner.
        p. cm.
I. Title.
PR9619.3. T868D4 1992   92-2414
823—dc20   CIP

First Morrow/AvoNova Printing: February 1993

AVONOVA TRADEMARK REG. U.S. PAT. OFF. AND IN OTHER COUNTRIES, MARCA REGISTRADA, HECHO EN U.S.A.

Printed in the U.S.A.

ARC   10   9   8   7   6   5   4   3   2   1

For
Russell and Jenny Blackford
who have done so much
for Australian
science fiction

Contents

Part I

Fine Upstanding Copper

1

Ostrov: Policeman's Lot

From Commentaries; *Decay of the Family Nexus:*
"The psychological shortcomings and emotional
unrest of 'Harry' Ostrov are echoed today as par-
ents, with the best intentions, strive to rear their
offspring in the straitjacket of their own ideas of
right and wrong. In any culture with rapidly chang-
ing values it cannot be done. The lectured and
pressured children rarely rebel; they simply fail to
conform."

There has been too much stupid talk about what
went on in the Manor in those last days of Beltano's
premiership; there was melodrama enough without the
idiocies propounded by the channels and the amateur
psychologists. I can tell you exactly what happened. I
was there.

I was born into the mid-greenhouse generation, when
the big weather problems were understood, and to some
extent under control. The food situation was easing, and
no more than two thirds of the world's nine billions

were undernourished (or starving outright) at any given time. If the population growth could have been halted then, in 2039, we might have come through the century relatively unscathed, but even slowing the growth, so simple in theory, seemed impossible in application.

We kids didn't realize why this should be so until our body's hungers came to plague and exalt adolescence, but we were born with population warnings in the air we breathed and we accepted them as part of life. There were too many people in the world, and we had to put up with them. That they also had to put up with us was their worry, not ours.

Being kids, we played "cull" games. (That word was already being spoken as a prophecy of some distant future but not as a present threat.) In our games one side was picked to be culled and was hunted down by the "real Aussies." Those to be culled were called by the most offensive names we knew—Chinks, Wogs, Nignogs. The names had little real meaning save as denoting outsiders, non-Australians. Our own black, brown, yellow and mixed nationals (about half the population) were "real Aussies," no matter what their origins, but Chinks, Wogs and Nignogs represented the rest of the world, that place somewhere outside, full of people to be got rid of someday. In that way we prepared a chauvinism that bided its time to come home to roost.

All over the world kids played cull games like ours, games dreamed up from odd scraps of parental conversation in the home. Kids, though they may not absorb the words properly, hear the hates and fears behind them very clearly. And sublimate the uneasiness in games. Games keep the fears at bay, trivializing them. We "real Aussies" could never be the culled ones. As we grew older the hardening of familiarity set in, and as adults we didn't talk seriously about the cull at all. At any rate, not in public.

In public we made black jokes about it—

I have begun in the wrong place. Already I am caught up in ends rather than beginnings.

I am a policeman, Detective-Sergeant Harry Ostrov of Melbourne, Australia, a fairly ordinary sort of policeman whose promotions have come through attention to detail rather than through professional brilliance. It may have helped that I never let myself fall into the traps of easy corruption that elevate some to shaky heights and put others into jail with their seducers and victims.

I was brought up the old way, with strict ideas of good and evil, right and wrong—

Another false start, but there has to be some background.

My parents met and married in 2039, at the end of what social historians have dubbed the Dancing Thirties, that last decade of nonsense and thin-ice gaiety before history tightened its grip around the human race.

Perhaps my mother, Arlene, and father, Bill, had reason, along with everybody else, to throw their caps in the air and their brains after them and see life as a ballroom where the dancing would never stop. Everything was on the up-and-up, wasn't it? Man had the greenhouse effect and the ozone holes under an endurable measure of control, had damped down pollution to manageable levels and tamed the environmental vandals, had developed weather forecasting to the point of keeping crops and destructive shortages a step ahead of the brutal fluctuations of rainfall and storms and the complex temperature variations of the oceans. The planet let out the breath it had held for forty years and gave itself a party. (There were doomsayers, but who listened?) That generation seems to have been a meretricious lot whose gaiety was too often nit-brained inanity, but their party was a wingding while it lasted.

I was two months old when the earthquake that had slept for a century tore Tokyo apart, leveled its stock exchange and destroyed the most powerful financial empire in history—and tossed the dancing planet down to penury in its wake. Overnight the full bellies of the major powers became as close to empty as were the tormented guts of the Third World billions. The world learned, the hard way, what it had always known but refused to face—that shares, investments and IOUs, those computer records and pieces of paper pushed around the world by economists and financiers are not, when all the debts are called in at once, wealth. They may be "money," though even that is doubtful, but they are not wealth. Wealth is what your country can provide to satisfy its people's needs; surplus wealth is what you can trade with. When the spree was over and there were nine billions to provide for, who had surpluses? Money became again the solid stuff you grab and hold; creative exchange of paper promises died for lack of resources to back them.

Australia, that perennially lucky country, as usual suffered less than many others because it was able, by way of a grinding austerity, to feed itself at a borderline sufficiency and by the late sixties was in a condition of penurious stability. We were by then living a good life in comparison with many other nations, but in fact our standard of subsistence would have shocked our grandfathers. Or would it? We had the necessities; what we hungered for were the unattainable extras.

As a child I resented the rich and could not forgive their existence. It takes time and education to learn of the failures of communism, socialism, anarchism, and all the other fantasies based on egalitarian concepts that cannot exist while human IQs vary over a range of more than a hundred points and individual needs can't be measured on a common scale. So we are stuck with basically capitalist systems with all their faults, and the rich are always with us.

The rich have always been, in one way or another, the rulers of the world, and I had my day among them— which is how this story happened for the telling— though it was a short day and a humiliating one. I didn't ask for it to happen, just as I didn't ask to be a policeman or to be seconded to the Jackson job or even to wear the damnfool name my giddy parents wished on me.

What parents they were, still are! In the thirties they both had jobs, the world was a fun park, and they frolicked with the minor glitterati of their day. They met, married, and raced into having their permitted child (the new procreation laws were a prescient warning that nobody took too seriously, a temporary restriction until the planet sorted itself out) whom they named, with rhythm, rhyme, and a heady giggle, Ian Juan Ivan John. Their friends applauded the whimsy. Tacked on to the family name of Ostrov it made me sound like a multicultural stew.

Even the Ostrov was, if not a whimsy, not quite genuine. Bill's Ukrainian great-grandfather had adopted it for political reasons when he escaped to Australia by the skin of his gritted teeth. It was an anagram of his birthplace, Rostov.

If my parents sound featherheaded they were only reflecting their time, but when the Tokyo crash caught the working world knock-kneed in the face of sudden poverty they showed mettle. From the mild affluence of two jobs they dropped to no jobs and a hungry boy. Arlene, who had been a secretary, found servant work in the households of those who could still afford the hire of status symbols at Scrooge wages. Bill had been an emporium sales supervisor—in his own description, a "superior counter-jumper." He spat on his hands, bore with his blisters, and made do with sporadic laboring jobs in spite of a slightly crooked spine that had not troubled him until he became a manual worker.

They clung to the fetish of education as the road to success and pushed me down it as far as their tight purses could allow. It was their luck and mine that I was what theatre folk call "a quick study" who could soak up information with minimum effort. That is only a minor talent; it does not equate with high intelligence.

From their thirties gaiety they retained a deliberate, strained cheerfulness that drove me half out of my mind in surroundings that rarely included enough chairs to go round, clothes to wear or food to eat. My four variations of the one name were considered a risible affectation by my school ground peers until at age twelve, in a fury of domestic rebellion (a single outburst, never repeated) I reviled my parents for their unthinking cruelty in a storm of yelling, stamping and foul language.

My mother, instead of smacking my scarlet face, put a hand to her lips and murmured, "Oh, you poor darling." My father, more alive to tactics, asked what name I would like to be called by. I had not planned so far ahead but reached for the first available fantasy and produced the name of a favorite vid cartoon character, Harry the Kung fu Mouse, and Harry I became without further fuss. They really were good people. The kids at school took more convincing, but I grew solid and strong and able to make my decisions stand.

In the middle fifties, when "recession" began to seem a permanent condition, my parents learned the bitter lesson that the world belongs to the young; "too old at forty" was the reality. They stopped pretending that tomorrow would ever come. We became Wardies, the sour-joke word for those who became "wards of the state," our income the Sustenance Payment, the monthly dole, the Suss. I think that Minders, as a description of the administrative classes whose supposed social responsibility was the welfare of the less fortunate, came into jeering existence at the same time. With use its spiteful edge became dulled and it passed into the language of social description, establishing "us" and "them" and the gulf between.

Then, at sixteen, I passed the Grading Paper of the General Employment examinations. Rejoicings, chez Ostrov! A working son, even an apprentice, would render the logistics of housekeeping less inhuman.

I knew what I wanted to do; age sixteen had it all worked out. When I was given my Career Choice sheet I wrote in the Preferred Training section, "Electrical and computer wiring and installation," confident that my excellent marks in math and manual skills would guarantee acceptance. Installation and wiring cannot be wholly automated even in the age of computerized handling; a specialized manual skill was tantamount to a job for life.

The selection board approved my qualifications. Then it checked my physique, read my genetic print, calculated my ultimate physical development on an optimum diet—and offered me a police training course.

Received Wardie wisdom was that Police Are Bastards. We hated them as Minder menials.

I protested.

The board pointed out that the apprentice lists were crowded with applicants as well equipped manually and intellectually as I (a blow to vanity), whereas my projected strength, physical fitness, learning speed and unusually wide general knowledge (the damnable gift of cultured parents) qualified me for a physically and mentally demanding profession.

The board reminded me, too, of comparatively high wages and a pension entitlement (pensions were a rarity) and of the fact that my parents had made sacrifices, etc. . . . and didn't I think they were now entitled to my support?

Yes, sir, but I can support them as well on an electrician's—

The board feared that times of national exigency made it necessary that capable men and women be allocated to the niches they could best fill, and that I . . .

Outside the interview room I had the last and worst crying fit of my adolescence, then went home and told my Wardie parents that they had a copper in the family.

Bill—I was calling him Bill by then—cried, "Chin up, Harry boy! You're made!" My mother, closer to social issues and neighborly attitudes, said little.

The neighbors gave them a rough time for a while. Cops were bloody lackeys to the bloody Minders; justice was for the wealthy, and Wardies never got a fair go because the coppers were corrupt and vicious; no good ever came of associating with . . . then they realized that some good might be squeezed out of knowing a rotten bloody copper who just might do you the odd good turn if you kept on the right side of him. After all, it wasn't the Ostrovs' fault if they'd reared a bad 'un, was it?

The pressures on Mum and Dad relaxed, and the unruly natives treated me with expectant civility.

At the Police Training College it was pointed out to me that my initials were I. J. I. J. and I would not be known as Harry, so I began with hatred in my heart.

Fate laughed, of course. Manipulated by instructors who knew just how I felt (hadn't they been through it?) I walked headfirst into their traps of ego building and indoctrination. By the end of the first month I and my whole intake group were in love with the service and with ourselves, gentled and jollied into proud, elitist,

one-for-all-and-all-for-one police tribesmen, dedicated
to the protection of a graceless, ingrate public.

Later I saw that it was not all crafty psychological
cat crap. We did become a welded, supportive group;
we did learn disciplines, official and social, that gave
us small behavioral advantages in a depressed society;
we did learn pride in ourselves and our service.

In time we were parceled out to stations to join the
rough and tumble of no-nonsense fellow cops who had
had street wisdom beaten into their often bloodied
heads and now served it back to us good and hard.
That, with the sickening and wholly realistic view of
the truths a policeman finds behind the facades of bland
family lives, refashioned the world for us.

Some of us grew unpleasantly tough, some went rotten, some went under. Most of us grew an extra skin,
tried to stay sane and not be the bastards off the job that
we often had to be on it; we compensated resentments
with a snarling pride and a steadily hardening sheath
over the mind. I thought myself an averagely good,
honest copper and learned to distance myself from the
corrupt (of whom there were enough to tar all of us) and
keep to the code of shamed silence that binds men and
women whose lives may depend on group loyalty.

I was twice tempted to marry and twice surprised
how little heartbreak endured when the romances fell
through. I decided on a single life until seniority
should lift me out of the daily rottenness and into
the calmer air of administration. Time enough then
to seek out love and father the child we would be
allowed.

I found that I could not talk of my work with my
mother. To her it was all "horrors and nastiness." She
loved me no less, but what she loved was her conception of me, the "nice" side of me.

I could talk with Bill, who brought me up standing
at times with perceptions I had not suspected in my

old-fashioned dad—as when he said, in one private moment, "We're all born bare arsed, boy; it's putting on fancy clothes that dirties our hearts." I knew better than he what lay behind the triteness. A policeman grows away from the public he serves, tends to stand above it, looking down. And a policeman's friends tend to be policemen. Everything conspires to separate him from society and identify him with an official viewpoint that sees moral questions in terms of legal right and wrong.

I could not afford, for my soul's comfort, to admit to myself that I looked forward to the day of retirement when I could be reborn, bare arsed, into the humble world where a man could hold to a morality uncompromised.

I told Bill, long after the Jackson affair was over, that being aware of secrecy, corruption and manipulation is not enough. You deplore it in conversation, tut-tut suitably over the revelations of skulduggery on the vidnews, even play your part in apprehending the despicable and the villainous; but it registers as wickedness only at arm's length, as the rottenness of others—until the day you find your own self trapped in the web of lies and hidden actions, enmeshed without warning or chance of avoidance.

I was thirty when the Jackson job came up, a detective-sergeant with a safe future if I kept my nose clean. (That is harder for detectives than for simple coppers; the temptations are constant and great and the rewards can be breathtaking.)

In December 2068 volunteers were called for a one day special testing stint with the College of Psycho-Biology—testing meaning "guinea pigging." I was doing routine relief in a small, unbusy station on the city perimeter and, in what I took to be the local practice, was chosen to "volunteer."

It was not the local practice. I was sought, pinpointed and chosen, but that was later knowledge.

The test was done in an indoor stadium. I estimated three hundred guinea pigs, male and female, in definable classifications—police, high-IQ students, longtime jobless Wardies, professional athletes, subteen children, over sixties and one lot that appeared to be mentally retarded. Whatever happened, we could be sure of one thing, that the tests would be free of danger or side effects; otherwise criminals would have been used to avoid compensation claims on a bankrupt Treasury.

The psychs and biochemists—there seemed to be a regiment of them—told us, without too much technical fiddle, that we were part of an experiment in hypnotic suggestion.

We police exchanged glances and sighs. The force had discarded hypnotism long ago; its occasional helpfulness was outweighed by complications and opportunities for error. Almost anyone can be hypnotized after a fashion; the problems lie in the questioning. You can't tell, until you have wasted a month chasing false leads, whether you have been eliciting genuine memories, associational responses or mere subliminal garbage.

It seemed, however, that here was something new. What they were about was not hypnosis (so they said) but the effect of a combination of drugs designed to modify selected functions of the brain while sharpening others. There should be a temporary—no more than fifteen minutes—alteration of some facets of the personality, measured by reaction to key words and phrases.

We police at once suspected thought control; if that was in the wind we had better know about it. It sounded like hypnosis no matter what the boffins said, at least a pseudohypnotism, mind management on a measurable basis. It raised spectres of possible use by criminals—but that aspect would have to be weighed

by the lawmakers and only then by us ordered-about
lawkeepers.

The usual questionnaire occupied most of the morning until each group was computer sorted into sub-
groups for the action of the drugs to be observed on
variously capable intellects. Not a really significant
statistical sample, it was admitted, but a useful initial
guide.

In the afternoon we were given our injections and
interviewed briefly while "under the influence."

My interviewing psych was of Southeast Asian extraction—Thai, Cambodian, Vietnamese, you can't tell by
looking at them. I thought myself culturally unbiased
and had a high opinion of the Asians in the force. Outside the force, they were, according to the statisticians,
a brainy addition to the cultural mix who did well in
the humanities and sciences; according to us they were
a brainy addition who created occasional havoc with
ingenious variations on old rackets. On the whole they
were no better and no worse than the white majority,
who could be wicked in anyone's language. This one got
down to business without any fake reassuring palaver
and for most of the time kept his eyes on a telltale board
which he could see but I could not.

The effect of the drug cocktail felt like no effect at
all; I thought that perhaps I might be a natural immune.
The psych asked seemingly pointless questions while
I wondered what the telltale told about my answers.
I was not sure that the test had actually started, but
it had because the psych said, "That's all; you can go
home."

While I was still feeling surprised he raised his voice
with a sudden sharpness. "Look at me!" With the habit of responding to command, I stared into his eyes,
expectant but unsuspicious. "Do not discuss this test
with anyone!"

The tone was to an insulting degree peremptory.

Feeling pretty uptight, I told him that I could accept an instruction without having it screwed into place, but psychs are not impressed by their experimental animals. This one said, "Sorry, but it is important," with his eyes back on the telltale board. He added, as a throwaway, "I don't imagine you will want to discuss it."

I wasn't going to waste ill temper on a state automaton whose attention was on dials and needles and who had no interest in the reactions of a state guinea pig—or so I thought as I got myself out of the building to simmer down in the open air. How wrong you can be.

I crossed the road into the Exhibition Gardens and sat on the lawn as I experienced a moment of light-headedness. Aftereffect of the drugs? (It was in fact a rebalancing of functions as the injected cocktail wore off.) The next moments were disastrous.

I discovered with a slow sickness why the psych had said I would not want to discuss the test.

In his few scrappy minutes he had turned me inside out with drugs that had split my self-awareness into unrelated strata. My ears had taken in what he asked and my mouth had spilled the terrible answers, but in the process my brain had failed to understand what was asked of it; I had been subjected to a pressing of mental buttons and the painless extraction of the secrets of a lifetime. He had taken from me the things that exist in all of us, hidden and suppressed and often unknown to our conscious selves. He had learned, with the ease of breathing, that overt love for my parents overlaid an impatient resentment close to contempt but never admitted to myself, that I had wept in the darkness of my bed when the more obscene pressures of police work became unbearable, that there had been in adolescence—and beyond—episodes of powerful homoerotic feeling endured in frightened silence and shame at the truth of what passes for hero worship, that I had occasionally stolen unimportant trifles simply because they were available and had not realized that such actions lodged like thorns in the complex mental paths between public and private morality, and that (somehow this seemed infinitely demeaning) I had an inborn fear of spiders and would break out in sweat at the approach of one—

And some other things I don't trust myself even now to put in writing. I don't want to look at them.

Under a hot summer sun I shivered in the horror of exposure, naked as a worm, to the mind of another. That secrets were surely safe in the doctor-patient relationship counted not at all. Were they indeed safe, or would they wait in some "protected" computer file, to be one day resurrected for prurient discussion by the judges of my career, my promotion, my future?

In the end I collapsed into helpless anger—at the man who had unfairly leeched truth out of me, at myself for harboring such meannesses in the corners of my mind and, at last, at the state system which had submitted me to such self-hatred without explanation or pity.

I sat there for two hours before I recalled the end of the interview and the cynicism of the psych's final order. He was right; I could not even discuss self-disgust with my shuddering self.

Nobody, literally nobody, is proof against the secrets of his own heart.

It was late when I made for home, the huddling place, the refuge.

Mum had always made herself deaf to mention of anything more than the routine of my job, refusing to dip her mind into the human sewers, but Bill liked to get me alone and dig for drama; nothing could cure him of the delusion that I must have access to untold facts behind the cases on the vidnews. This time he asked, innocently enough, about the day's work and my immediate impulse was to unload some of the angry jumble from my mind.

Secrecy provisions are expected to apply to family as well as to all others but in fact are often flouted in the home. It is a commonplace that policemen talk carelessly to their wives and policewomen to their husbands; authority knows this, has always known it and put up with it as a prohibition that cannot be enforced.

My lips were parted for a snarling complaint about invasion of privacy before I realized that complaint would involve giving reasons that I would not, could not give. Just living with self-knowledge is bad enough.

I said, clutching at words, "Nothing much," but I was shaken badly and so, in another way, was Bill who, staring and concerned, cried out, "For God's sake, boy, you're sweating!"

So I was; so would have been anyone so shamefully hurt in secret places.

"Was it that bad, Son?"

My father's worry was acutely shaming to my harshly revealed secret contempt for him. I could only evade. "Was what bad?"

"Whatever it was. Something unpleasant?"

"Nothing unpleasant, Dad. Just a day."

Bill gave me the father-to-son I-know-better grin. "Secret stuff, eh?"

While Mum clung to her fairy floss view of life that ignored and in some fashion sublimated the dreary facts, Bill had buffered shock and disappointment by retreat into romance; he could shunt me into some hypothetical Secret Service with a flip of the mind. For once I was thankful for a father who could invent my lies for me.

At the station next morning I waited uneasily for someone to ask me what the guinea-pig job had been.

but nobody did. I had prepared such a battery of off-handed replies that this was nearly a disappointment though I had no intention of telling anyone of the existence of an interrogation aid that reduced all previous techniques to nursery games. It seeped only slowly into me that the station staff had been warned that the testing carried high order secrecy and that I was not to be questioned.

It followed, then, that high order secrecy was indeed involved, and it might well be that my participation was not finished, that I was on ice until wanted. The idea did nothing for a sullen temper that could not be released; they must have found me hard to bear with until I came to appreciate that this minuscule prohibition made no real difference to my life. There was something purely private that I had to keep to myself. So what?

The ill temper retreated to the back of my mind but did not go away; the sense of unwarrantable invasion persisted like a nagging toothache.

Six weeks later I was called to City Central Station for interview, reason unspecified, and ushered into an interrogation room—chair and table, bare walls—to see again the nameless psych who had tapped my secret mind. He sat across the table from me, and the face that had then been so uninterested surveyed me now with a hint of curiosity.

The duty constable ostentatiously switched off the recording gear and left us; there would be no record of the interview. My buzzer gave no tiny hum in my ear to warn of secondary bugs, so I knew that the psych was not wired. I took immediate advantage to spill stored anger on him. "What do you want now, Peeping Tom?"

It was wrong, childish and did not touch him. He nodded his yellow-brown face gently and in a light, soft voice commended my restraint. "Some men might have been immediately violent."

"Cracking your skull would only buy me a dishonorable discharge."

The soft voice took on a touch of primness. "I would not dream of laying a charge, whatever action you took. I know your feeling very well; I took the test myself in order to know."

"I hope you suffered."

"If it helps your mood, I did, but the thing is less significant than your anger imagines."

"You speak for yourself."

"For you, too. Are you prepared to listen?"

"To what?"

"Absolution." That was unexpected. As he leaned over the table I saw that he was older than he had at first seemed, age masked by the smooth Asian skin that collapses so suddenly when its time comes. "I promise that it will help."

It seemed that the functionary had a soul of sorts, but I was not prepared to concede much. "Go on."

"Will you take offense if I tell you now that your psychological profile is uninterestingly normal? Many don't care to be told that; they want to be strange, exotic, fascinating. They are usually bores. Your useful variation from the norm—and everybody has some variation—lies in a personal integrity expressed as a strong preference for moral concepts of right and wrong over legal definitions—despite occasional confusions. Does it cause trouble with your superiors?"

"Sometimes. So you're telling me what a good bloke I am. Get on with the rest of it."

The answer seemed to please him. "The rest of it is the clutter pushed out of mental sight as too shameful for contemplation. Your personal clutter is average in about ninety percent of men and women. Even your arachnophobia is common in one form or another.

Snakes and toads are frequent incarnations of inchoate
fears, also cats and grubs and even blowflies. I have to
force myself to endure the presence of cockroaches.
Foolish? You know better. We despise the phobias of
others and hide our own, not knowing that so many of
our shames are commonplaces. Homoerotic feelings, for
instance, are present at some juncture in the majority of
both sexes. I feel mild distrust of people who seem to be
wholly without them; I sense an inner coldness. Homo-
sexual temptation is common in adolescence, tends to
regress in maturity and sometimes returns in middle
age. A feeling is not shameful; what you do about it
may be—if you act against your nature or experiment
stupidly."

He paused for my comment, but I would not help
him. He shook his dark head. "It is you I am talking
about. I am sure that you know these things intellectually but do not stop to apply them to yourself. Why do
we all think ourselves so especially wicked when we
are only dithering with juvenile hangovers?"

"Face. You should know about that."

"I do; although I am third generation Australian, I
do not pretend to be free of a cultural weakness. That
is not as stultifying as fearing it. The matter of your
thieving, for instance. A policeman must be aware that
all humans are thieves of some kind at some time.
Stealing material objects brings punishment, but we
also steal time—and knowledge—and the contentment
of others—and we plan cunning tricks to steal a march
where we may; we are all dishonest where there is no
retribution. You deal harshly with those whose depar-
tures from the venal norm disturb the public peace, but
that does not entitle you to scourge your conscience
because you see your peccadillos as reflections of the
criminality you punish in others. You are a morally
average man. Be content with that; don't try so hard
to be an interesting sinner. There, now!"

"Should I cry, Hallelujah, I'm saved? So far it's only words." Then I had to give some grudging fair play. "They may sink in, given time."

"They will because you wish it so. Unnecessary guilt is a station on the road to the psychiatric hospital."

Impassiveness stripped emotion from the words, leaving meaning bare and stark.

"Maybe. Still—" One barb remained embedded, and he would not have forgotten it. Referring to it would cost me a sour effort of will; best let it lie.

"Still?"

It was not to be allowed to lie. "There were questions about my parents."

"Yes. That influence is always paramount, for good or evil. Yours are good people. Good to you."

"Yes."

"And you are a good son." A statement.

To be contradicted? "I try to be." That was the best I could do at that moment.

"But?"

The effort had to be made. "When you questioned my relations with them I was caught in—" I floundered and came up with "—caught between answers."

"It was noticeable, an ambiguity. You resolved it by giving both answers, love and contempt."

"You can't have it both ways."

"Why not? A relationship has many aspects; one does not react equally to all of them."

I was not sure whether that was a placebo or made good sense. "I won't let it make a difference."

"Indeed you will!" He came alive, became a person, emphatic, dictatorial; a man with a mission shone through the professional who measured and weighed. "You will see them with wiser eyes and a better understanding of yourself. All children revolt against their parents but are snared in the culturally inculcated sense of duty; some fight for their identity, others repress resentment to justify to themselves the role they feel called upon to play in public. Animals settle it much better; they turn the cubs out of the lair as soon as they can hunt. Humans stay together too long and have to make adjustments. You will make them and be happier for it. End of lesson, Detective-Sergeant Ostrov."

This was all possibly good for my mental welfare, but here was a twist that needed straightening. "Those questionnaires were coded; where did you learn my name?"

"Your commissioner told it to me after I had sorted through several hundred mental profiles to find the man to match the profile I needed for testing."

"Needed? Why me? What do you want of me?"

"I acted, you might say, as a talent scout. You have the qualifications for a particular role." His voice, level again, made nothing special of it. A man had been required; a man had been found. Yet I felt that this was not so much coolness as a carefulness with words.

"Role?"

"I cannot tell you much yet; the project is still a little in the future, but it will involve surveillance and protection on a high level. A very high level."

"And you selected me that day from all the hundreds tested?"

"No; I had already chosen you after a more usual mode of investigation and summation. Your test was for nailing down what I already knew and for flushing out anything relevant that I might have missed. The other test subjects were part of a genuine psychological comparison of effects on various physical groups."

I felt like a rat in a trap baited with rotten cheese.

"Are you a police psych?"

"No. Let me explain: The work will involve some training as a ward orderly, really only an extension of your police first aid capacities, enough to provide verisimilitude and make you reasonably useful in the hospital where you will begin."

It sounded thoroughly distasteful. "If I begin."

"You have been detailed by your commissioner on my recommendation. You cannot refuse."

"I can, you know. Just like that. It might cost me a little seniority—"

"There are those who would see that it cost you your livelihood." The smooth face showed a real sensibility that might have been distaste for what he was doing. "I had to make a choice, and your professional and psychological profiles suit the requirements. It is an important undertaking. Be complimented."

"Then I'm complimented." I was not; I was afraid. To be tipped out of the force would mean unemployment for life. I could face that in the way you can face anything short of destruction, but Mum and Bill were another matter. More than ever I could not abandon them now that I knew the paradox in my feeling for them. No doubt the psych knew all that. "Tell me about it."

"As much as I am permitted. If all goes well an old man will undergo surgery. His name will be Jackson, an incognito. Your brief will be to see that he comes to no harm, in the hospital or later. It sounds simple. It may not be. In time you will receive detailed instructions from other people."

That sort of thing disgusts a professional. "The 'need to know' principle! It smells of amateurs—people with fancy ideas playing at some stinking little intrigue. What does this one stink of?"

"Would I tell you that? There is another thing." With his eyes on mine he said, "Do not discuss this matter with anyone not already familiar with it."

"How will I know them?"

"They will know you."

"Secret society nonsense. That sort ask for betrayal

with every clumsy cover-up. They make loyalty a burden."

"Your resentment will pass. Have you more to ask?"

"Yes. Boiled down, your requirement is for a man
whose total silence can be depended upon, nailed
down by a threat of lifetime poverty for himself and
his parents. The threat interests me. I smell crime."

He smiled politely. "I have mentioned the highest in
the land; do you bracket them with crime?"

"Why not?" I treated him to a touch of Ostrov grim-in-
interrogation mode; it had frightened good men before
this. "A policeman is coerced into abetting crime. That's
what it is, isn't it? Crime?"

If the performance impressed him he did not show
it.

"Your part will not be to commit or abet, only to
protect an aging man in a position not of his seeking."
He stood. "Now I must go. I did not choose a fool for the
work; I chose a man of notable moral steadfastness."

Despite his smoothness, the lightest of emphasis
made moral steadfastness sound like a weakness which
happened, improbably, to fit this special task. He held
out his hand. "Good-bye."

"Go to hell."

As though I had not spoken, he said, "One does not
choose indiscriminately when singling out a man who
will be responsible to the premier of the state and to
no other."

Premier? The highest indeed—but it is a truism that
real crime starts at the top; what goes on below is, by
comparison, a desperate thrashing about.

Within the week I was attending medical orderly
classes by night and learning hospital routine, on the
job, by day. Three weeks of that saw me shifted to a
seventh floor convalescent ward in the State Biophysical Institute which was not, strictly, a hospital but

was rumored, among police as well as others, to carry out work that often required hospitalization—very private hospitalization—of the subjects of biophysical research.

By then my anger had slipped into a habit of mood rather than emotion, an almost token resentment; it did not interfere with my daily life. In fact, my curiosity began to look forward to the appearance of the aging Mr. Jackson who was in a soup not of his own stirring. On the day I first saw my charge, the premier's daughter sat weeping on a bed in a back room in the rundown suburb of Balaclava on the other side of the city. I did not know this at the time and, because he was in Canberra, neither did the premier.

Which, as Bill might have put it, showed that the devil has his own techniques for giving the pure in heart a run for their money.

2

Mrs. Blacker:
Love and Food Coupons

From Commentaries; *The Psychology of Poverty:*
"This harassed woman, concerned only with the
welfare of her son but beset by untrustworthy
neighbors, pursued by the fear of punishment
and tormented by the cruelty of what she saw as
socially correct behavior on her part, was typical
of the powerless. The mores of hapless masses are
always torn between the commands of law and
the imperatives of survival. There are never clear
solutions."

I must have been bloody well insane to let that half-
witted bitch into the flat. Sixteen and prissy mannered
up to the neck but with all her Minder schooling she
was ignorant of what a Wardie kid knows that's had
her education in the gutter. I ask her, "How long are
you gone?" and she doesn't know I'm talking about
her belly. She knew enough to get Fred but not a thing
about what happened after the getting. Or so she'd have
you think.

She couldn't stay here. I couldn't keep feeding her on family coupons.

I should have made Fred take her back home and dump her, but if the truth's told I got sentimental and stupid and wanted to protect her, laws or no laws.

No, it was Fred I had to protect. He's all I've got . . . not counting his pisshead father that's a waste of time and good food. . . . Fred's all I'll ever have under these stinking laws.

What if all the women got pregnant at once? What could the Minders do about it? Abort every woman in Australia? We ought to— No. They'd let us bear the kids and then they'd say, "There's no food ration for this outlaw child. Can't issue you any coupons, lady. Sorry and all that." Except it wouldn't be "Sorry"; it'd be, "Chuck it out with the garbage, why doncha?"

What could I do about Fred? In love, poor young bugger. I knew he'd played around before, but this time he'd fallen bad and there was the baby coming and his head full of all the bull about being a father to this wonderful kid.

But I couldn't hide her in just three rooms from all the stickybeaks in the other flats. If I'd told them to stay away, they'd've known I was hiding something and just about busted the doors in to find out what.

It wasn't as if she was just a nobody that I could give a kick up the arse and tell to get out. The premier's daughter, for Christ's sake! There was no Mrs. Premier or whatever they call the wife, so that made her the top lady of the state—at sixteen years old and five months up the duff! And she sat there all day in Fred's room in our falling-down shack of a flat, waiting for him to come home and not game to come out because I'd've cracked her silly mouth if she'd tried it.

How in hell did it happen? Fred was the head gardener's odd-job boy—but he got off with the boss's daughter, for Christ's sake! How did he meet her?

Where did they go for their bit of fun that turned out serious? He wouldn't have chatted her up; he wouldn't have been game. It must have been her. He's a good, solid boy and she took a fancy. That must have been the way of it.

I couldn't get a thing out of them. Fred carried on like the lovesick kid he is and she just looked like she expected me to hit her, which I should've. All I could find out was that when it got too uncomfortable to hide any longer she told Daddy. And Daddy Beltane, the premier of the state, told his daughter she'd have her bloody abortion like any other careless thickhead, and so she ran away.

She wanted the kid.

Well, that's natural enough; I would've, too.

The thing was, she didn't give a curse about Fred; she pretended, but she didn't fool me. She wanted a kid and she snared a strong, nice-looking boy to give it to her, but she didn't care what trouble it made for him. Maybe never thought. I told her the law, and she looked as if she didn't hear me. He'd get punished for unauthorized birthing and have his fathering right taken from him, but she'd keep the kid and Daddy'd fix it so she got away with it and my Fred would never see them again.

She said she never let on to Daddy that Fred's the father, and that had to be true because he still went to work of a day. He had to or how could we live with Johnno too sick or too pissed to do even half a job if it was offered to him?

I didn't know what to do. I should've said no, right away.

That's why I saw Barney about it. He's a sly old brute, but he's got some sense.

I didn't give Melissa any warning; I just took Barney to where she sat on the bed with her legs under her and said, "Dr. Barney's going to have a look at you."

She squeezed back against the wall, all suspicious I suppose because Barney's part Abo. A good doctor all the same. She said, "What for? I'm not sick."

She was nothing to look at—a bit too big for her age and too podgy for her proper size, but that was an advantage because she was one of those who don't show for months—but you could see she was on the way when she took off the tight corset she had on at first. (These Minder bitches wear corsets for their figures!)

Barney put his old leather bag on the chair while I was telling her, "He'll work out what we got to do about you."

"Do?" she says, silly as they come, and I let out a bit of spite.

"Yes, do! You don't think you're going to drop it on the bed here, do you?" I had to tell Barney, "She's that slow on the uptake it's getting me out of temper. I'll leave youse to it."

I could only go into the kitchen, of course, so I didn't miss any of what went on.

Barney was saying, "Will you please take off that overall?" in his educated voice that could pass for Minder if he wanted. I suppose he is a sort of a Minder though he works amongst us here.

She said, like an idiot, "It's Fred's overall. My dress is being washed."

"So?" says Barney. "Please take it off."

"I'm not sick."

I knew what was upsetting her. Barney always looks dirty. His shoes are never polished (whose are in the Wards?), he wears this old, shabby jacket and his trousers are always rumpled and stained. Add his dark skin to all that and to her it said, *filthy*. In her world doctors look like the dummies in the vidplays; she couldn't recognize a real one.

He says, a bit sharpish, "You're worse than sick, girl you're illegal."

She knew all that and gabbled how Daddy would look after the law side of it. He'd have to when he got over being angry and found she'd run away. When she went back he'd be so glad he'd do anything for her.

Barney put a skewer into that right away, telling her that Daddy mightn't be all that ready to help. He knew who her Daddy was and a by-blow grandchild to the premier of Victoria might be more scandal than enough for him, even if she married Fred. And Daddy mightn't be too pleased about that idea, either.

She sounded a bit guilty, as though she'd thought about it, when she said, "I can't marry Fred. Daddy has people picked out to choose from when I'm a bit older."

If that wasn't cool! Bloody slut, slut, slut!

"With a bastard child for a wedding present?"

"Daddy will find a way. There's always a way. Daddy can do—"

He cut into her like a terrier. "If Daddy has any sense he'll disown you! Now I want to see if abortion is possible, so get that damned overall off."

"Abortion!" She half screamed it. "No!"

She meant it. She didn't want Fred (but when would he wake up to that?), but she wanted his baby. His baby? Anybody's baby as long as it finished up hers. God only knows what had got into her. Besides Fred, that is.

"You want this baby?"

"Yes!"

"Why?"

"My business."

He didn't go on with that; it was a brick wall. "Mrs. Blacker says you're five months pregnant. Correct?"

"About that."

"I'd better check."

"Why?"

I took a peep through the crack of the doorjamb and she was still scrunched back against the wall.

Because, Barney tells her, she obviously knows nothing about mothorhood or how to look after herself or how to give the baby a chance to be born healthy. Cunning old Barney! He went on, inventing like mad because she was too ignorant to know it was nonsense. Things can go wrong, he told her, like her mental state could affect the baby's development and so could her change of diet to Wardie food. He couldn't advise unless he knew the state of her pregnancy and her physical condition.

She was quiet for a bit as if she was just about convinced. Then she said, "But you're dirty," and I wished he'd hit the stupid bitch.

Not Barney, though; he'd rather give her a lesson. He told her how Wardie people are suspicious of good clothes and people trying to look better than the rest. You could even get spat on in the street by some of the rougher kids. Then he showed her his hands. "Look! Are they dirty?"

I knew they'd be scrubbed clean, the pink-brown skin almost shining, the nails clean and white tipped. Better than mine. Better than bitch Melissa's, for that matter. His shirt would be clean and when he put on his white coat he would be as presentable as you could want.

He must have got through to her because he said, "Come, come, no tears. A mother has to be strong. Strong enough to lose her child if necessary."

"I won't lose my baby!" It was a bit of a squawl now, mixed with sniffling. "You can look at me and tell me what to do, but I won't lose my baby!" Then she said, as if it was terribly important, "I've never undressed in front of a man before."

What about in front of Fred? Maybe in her world Wardies aren't people. Undressing for them don't count.

It was all quiet for a bit and he must have finished his examination when she said, "What do I have to do?" and he came back to the fight to say, "Get rid of it."

"No!" I peeped again, and she was beating her hands on the bedclothes. "No! No! No!"

"Do you realize what this can do to your father's position?"

"What do you mean? It isn't his baby."

Barney really exploded then, saying he didn't believe anyone like her existed! No premier's daughter could be so ignorant of the facts of political life. Or of sexual life. Or of any damned thing he could ask her or tell her. "Didn't your mother ever talk to you about—" He must have remembered then that the mother had gone off years ago with some boyfriend. "Don't you have a governess of some sort to tell you the things you need to know?"

"I go to boarding school. I have a maid at home at weekends, but she's only a kid."

Kid! Twelve or thirteen, maybe, and pig ignorant.

"Boarding school?" asks Barney. "Nuns?"

"No. We're Protestant."

"Different but not necessarily better. Doesn't your father ever talk to you about intimate things? Sex and boys and the population laws?"

"No. I don't see him that much."

"And do they tell you nothing at school?"

"The girls talk about it. We know all about it."

That was a laugh. They'd have a giggle about the dirty words somebody scribbled on the lavvy wall and that'd be about all.

"In God's name what do they teach you at that place?"

Barney was near to busting, and she couldn't see what was wrong. "Just the usual school things. Why are you so angry?"

"Not with you. With the world for being such a sink of stupidity. Don't they teach anything that matters?"

"You mean dressmaking and hairdressing and those things? Why should they? We aren't people who will have to work. It's an expensive school." Oh, dearie bloody me! Then she thought of something important. "I do bookkeeping because it will be useful when I'm married and running a big house."

I nearly took a fit, laughing. She was hopeless. A Wardie kid of ten knew more about the world.

He said, "You know nothing, but you must understand that your child cannot be born." He tried to make her see that what she wanted didn't count against Fred being punished because of her. Once he'd had a child the law would never give him a second chance. And his parents might serve a jail sentence for harboring her. He finished up, "And it's no bloody use crying."

I could hardly hear her whispering and gulping through the tears, "I'm going to have my baby."

Barney said with a sort of despair, "You'll bring the government down before you're through. For the present, don't leave this room. Nobody must know you are here."

I don't know what she said to that; all I could hear was the sniffling.

Barney came out to me and said, "She has no mother and no effective father and nobody gives a damn about her. What little she knows is just imitation of the brats at her school. She's swinging in midair with only a pregnancy to cling to."

He kept his voice down and we moved over to the outside door, which was as far as we could get from Melissa without being where the neighbors could listen in.

I wasn't going to be taken in by any of his psych stuff
and I as good as said so. "She's a born trollop that gets
around amongst ladies but doesn't know enough to be
one thing or t'other."

He tried to tell me what it is like amongst the Minders where the gap between them and us has got so
deep that they go on like a separate kind of people.
They have this big idea that they're born to lord it
and we're born to put up with it, and they have different manners and a different way of talking and all
sorts of things you don't say in front of the children
and foolishness like that. Don't they know what kids'
minds are like? Little sewers is what they are and what
you don't tell them they invent and look what's happened to Melissa. I remember he said something like,
"When historical circumstances repeat themselves, the
attitudes are repeated, too. They're having a touch of
the Victorians up there in cloud land."

That could be, but I didn't know what it meant.
Anyway, I wanted to keep to the main thing. "She's
got to have the abortion no matter what she wants."

He agreed with that, but said we had to remember
who she is. "It has to be kept absolutely quiet; five
months is late for a backyard type of abortion and I
can't do a clinical abortion in the surgery because I'm
not equipped for it. I'm just a Wardie GP, remember,
with only the barest means of treatment."

That was bullshit. I knew his real trouble would be
getting rid of the evidence. The way they can trace
things today you can't just drop it down a drain. You
couldn't even boil one down to broth without somebody smelling it and getting curious. But that was his
trouble; mine was her.

I said, "She's got to get out of here, then."

Straight away he said, "She's too important to be
tossed out like some useless Susser. Keep her for a
couple of days while I work something out. I'll try to

get her back home. Keeping Fred's name out of it is the important thing."

I smelt he was up to something. I didn't really want to throw a pregnant girl on the street, but what could I do else? She was all right in the back room so long as nobody saw or heard, but you can't stop accidents. Then there was Frod, up to his ears in calf love and there'd be trouble enough with him, let alone her.

Well, first things first. "I can't keep on feeding her. We've only got the Suss coupons and Fred's wage money's no good there. You can't buy coupons."

That was a try-on and he knew it. He said right away, "I'll bring you some cash-free coupons in the morning." He looked straight at me and said he had a few to spare.

Nobody has coupons to spare, but a lot of whispers said that Barney would take black market coupons from some who couldn't raise cash for treatment and now I knew it was true. He didn't have to be afraid of me letting on; if anybody split on him there would be roundabout ways of seeing they got lumbered for passing illegal tender above their Suss ration.

They talk about honor among thieves, but it comes down to being careful of each other.

So I was going to keep her for a few days and precious few it had better be. I didn't know what Barney was playing at and didn't care so long as I was out of it and my Fred's skin was safe.

3

Ostrov: A Case for Tender, Loving Care

From Commentaries; *The Dilemma of Longevity: "Populations supplied with rigidly calculated rations are healthier than those with unlimited quantity and choice. The fact was noted as early as 1942 in an England with food supplies restricted by war; in the twenty-first century it had the unwanted effect of increasing life expectancies, already an embarrassment, to the point where ageing was a greater population growth factor than the birthrate. Outright termination of all on reaching a predetermined age was still emotionally impractical (do not imagine, however, that it was not discussed) but general practitioners were encouraged, at first furtively, then more openly, to deal only cursorily with the elderly or moribund. It was an easy step to active bans on certain life-preserving procedures. . . ."*

Senior Surgeon Cranko took me to the seventh floor (which consisted solely of one-bed wards for reasons

I preferred not to ask about—and wouldn't have been answered if I had) and introduced me to the matron, a jolly-looking woman old enough to be my mother and probably as hard as a boxer's fist.

"Orderly Ostrov," says she brightly. "So you're the silent cop."

I was furious. With no pretense of deference I asked the surgeon, "How many people know I'm under cover here? Half the staff? Or all of them?"

Cranko was conciliatory when he knew he had no real authority to flourish over me. "Only the people who need to know, Harry. Matron here, Jackson's hypnotherapist and myself. Come along to the ward."

We escaped down the passage from a suddenly not-so-pleasant-seeming matron, past closed doors from which no sounds emerged, while he said, "I'm afraid the silent cop joke was mine. It was a kind of traffic regulator in the old days, wasn't it? A sort of hump in the middle of an intersection?"

I had no idea but said yes, to put an end to it.

We stopped at a small room which he called the cubby, the orderly's office. It contained, in the smallest possible space, table and chair, folding bed, sink with running water, first aid cabinet and—

I asked, "What's that doing here?"

"That" was an ordinary tabletop vidscreen with a very unordinary console.

"You know what it is?" He was surprised.

"I know a Spy-eye console when I see it. It's supposed to be secret military equipment." (But the police had a few installed in places where they would frighten the hell out of the occupants if they knew.)

The surgeon, a long streak of a man with large and beautiful hands, answered from an oblique angle. "Haven't you been informed about this institute?"

"I've been told it's a group of experimental laboratories, and that's all. Everything's on a need-to-know basis, so it's like feeling around in a fog. I don't know what half the departments in this building are for or even where most of them are."

He looked apologetic. "It isn't for me to tell you much more. Take it that we do a lot of regular biophysical research here, stuff that we publish in the usual journals, but also a certain amount better left under wraps. I won't tell you about those and you're better off not knowing."

"More of the same! What about the Spy-eye?"

He chose words with care. "There are, um, operative subjects" (My mind heard "victims" and my imagination turned a little sick.) "who need constant observation but should not be conscious of it. You will find it useful with Jackson. Shall we go in to him?"

The ward was white and bare of all but necessities; the bed stood central against the back wall like an excrescence. Biophysics gave no sign of being a caring discipline.

It is difficult to judge the height of a man in bed, but I guessed him to be about my own height, one of those big-boned men with a narrow frame that renders wrists, knees and knuckles as knobs. He appeared to be in his early sixties, but the forearms exposed on the sheet were smooth fleshed and unwrinkled . . . extremely well preserved sixties. He lay on his back, asleep.

I checked the progress board at the foot of the bed— name, temperature, pulse rate, all the usual . . . "Date of hospitalization isn't entered."

"No, and the board and chart will be destroyed when he leaves. He won't appear in the registrar's records."

"I should have guessed that." Secrets! I listened to his breathing and felt his pulse. "He's not in normal sleep and I don't think he's drugged. What goes on?"

"Hypnotherapy."

"That junk discipline?"

"It has its uses. Drugs can lead to complications where induced-sleep therapy allows normal healing."

"Healing from what?"

"There has been some facial surgery."

"No sign of it. No scars."

"I would be upset if there were. There is art as well as craft in the profession."

"What else? Something internal?"

He asked, "Do you wear a bug alarm?"

"When it seems needed. Not here."

"From now on wear it all the time. There are too many people interested in the work of this institute. This room must be inviolate while this man is in it."

"I really love working in a haze of half truths and evasions. Now—something internal?"

"That's one way of putting it." He turned back the sheet and opened Jackson's pajama coat on the torso of a healthy man. "He is ninety-three years old. A few weeks ago he was in terminal decrepitude, a skeleton in a bag of wrinkles, a shaking, dribbling wreck after twenty-five years of Alzheimer's disease plus general senility."

I let astonishment settle before I said, "Age reversal is supposed to be impossible. Something about compounding of errors in intracell processes as you grow older. Irreversible. I read it somewhere."

"Now you know differently. This building is alive with the unlikely; it exists to test the improbable."

"You have accomplished the illegal—giving extension of life to the terminally ill."

"Quite so. The illegality is fully stated in the Population Containment Act Amendment of forty-seven."

Telling me the institute made its own laws.

"I'm a policeman. I don't condone lawbreaking. I know there's a popular idea that we are all corrupt and buyable, but it isn't so. We know why the laws are how they are and most of us uphold them. I uphold them."

He said to the air, "And I know that you can't do

a damned thing about it, even report it. Best not to
worry, Detective-Sergeant. Besides—" he turned a dis-
turbingly speculative gaze on me "—the circumstances
are strange; you may find your righteous reservations
easing as you learn more about the case. Law and morality can be strange bedfellows."

"I know, but my instinct is against it."

"Does it trouble you?"

"After a dozen years of respecting the law, yes, it
troubles me."

"Then I suggest you talk to Nguyen about it."

"Who is he?"

"Dr. Nguyen—Nguyen Donh Minh. He's Jackson's
hypnotherapist. He says he has met you."

It seemed I would find little pleasure in this assign-
ment. "That's his name, is it? Yes, we've met. I could
do without him around me."

"He's a very good man. Like you, he has reservations,
but he knows how to handle them." The air between us
was growing steadily cooler. "Is there any more I can
tell you?"

"Whatever you can. A great deal, I think."

Cranko spread his hands. "Less than you think, but
what there is may abrade your reservations. This man's
name is not Jackson; it is Beltane, but to us he is Arthur
Jackson. He is the premier's father and he was operated
on here at the premier's insistence. Why, I have not
been told, but that is something your Spy-eye may
discover when the son visits in a day or two. For the
rest, he should come to full waking tonight or tomorrow, and not even Nguyen can hazard a guess at what
his mental condition will be. Be careful what you say
to him. Try not to upset him; the first hours may be
crucial in deciding whether he is competent or mentally disturbed past handling."

As he left he said, "Your patient has been fed intravenously and there's a catheter in his penis. You won't have any revolting discharges to deal with."

His parting smile regretted that a moralizing copper would not have to dabble in excremental reality.

I studied Beltane's—*Jackson*'s—still face, but faces rarely tell much of the man behind the image. He remained a delicate illegality requiring protection and tender, loving care. I hoped he was worth it.

The premier's father . . . that might explain but did not justify what had been done to me by Nguyen Donh Minh, himself likely a puppet on some other string.

Now I needed some facts to set Jackson in focus, but there was no general information terminal in the ward. I went to the matron's office to ask about reliefs and was told that I would be on call on a twenty-four-hour basis. While I slept Jackson would be checked every quarter hour by the duty nurse and I would be wakened at any change in the patient.

"To do what?"

"Observe. Learn about him." She was brusque.

"Where do I sleep? In the cubby?"

"I'll have a bed shifted into the ward for you."

I had a request, but my welcome had not been promising. "I need information on Jackson, background stuff. Old news files and vidwires would be best, but I can't leave here to track them down. Can you suggest something?"

She surprised me with a smile, forgiving the humble pleader and knowing his need exactly. "I was curious, too, and we have a good library here." From her desk she drew a fat volume and indicated a protruding bookmark.

It was the *Dictionary of National Biography,* compacted edition, and fell open at Beltane G. F., a shortish, single-column entry. "Thank you, Matron. I won't keep it long."

*   *   *

DNB entries for the still living are based on material supplied and approved by the subject. Old Beltane had been miserly with information. (Uninterested, or merely careful to leave no clues?)

Arthur Jackson had been born Gerald Fitzgerald Beltane (what a smell of olde worlde upper class was there!) and had lived what seemed to the prying mind of an ordinary, suspicious copper a dry, almost marginal life. Perhaps the lives of the mighty tended to dryness behind the facade but surely not to the marginal, shy of limelight.

Born 1976—English father and Australian mother of Scottish descent. An only child. Education via state schools and a university scholarship. (What, no money, with that name stinking of lineage?) MA degree.

Became secretary to Melbourne Ports branch of the Labour Party in 2005. (An MA in Labour politics? Well, why not? Socialism had been in a short revival at the turn of the century, despite the Russian upheaval.)

Son, Jeremy, illegitimate, born 2006. His mother, Estelle Lily Broughton, had died in childbirth. (Had birthing still been troublesome then? Mothers did not die save under exceptional circumstances. An odd case, perhaps.) Child reared by foster parents. (Sensible, if no wife or female relatives available.)

Married to Mary Mavis Hogan, 2009. Entered state Parliament as member for new seat of River West, 2010. (Married for that purpose? Electors preferred their members respectably married. Why? Did they think respectability ruled out a possible rat behind the wainscot?)

Long and influential parliamentary career though never achieving ministerial rank. Seemed to have actually preferred the back benches. A "numbers man," a valuable henchman to four state premiers in different administrations. (If valuable why unrewarded? Or was he? Check the meaning of "numbers man.")

Claimed son, Jeremy, 2021. (Because no children by wife, Mary?)

Separated from wife, 2022. (One year after claiming. Difference over boy?)

Raised son to be a politician until Jeremy Beltane entered House as member for Melbourne Ports, 2030.

Retired, aged seventy, in 2046, on ground of ill health.

And, of course, the missing entry: *Cheated death by illegal rejuvenation, instigated by son, 2069, after years of Alzheimer degeneration and senility.*

Why?

As a curriculum vitae it was empty space with publicly known tether spots here and there. I needed a more intimate account, but perhaps none existed. Truth, the whole truth, is told only of the dead. There would be journalists and ancient relics of politicians who knew more, but what reason could I advance for prying?

I returned the book to matron and asked her what a numbers man might be. She, being twenty years older, might know the term. She thought it meant someone who continually sounded the ideas of individual party members so that support for or disapproval of proposals of cabinet or premier could be assessed in advance—a very useful man when a spill threatened or a stab in the back was to be averted.

"What they call now a 'weasel'?"·

"Something like, but today the faction weasels within the party try to outsmart each other. Politics must be a filthy business."

I asked, on impulse, "And the institute—is this also a filthy business?"

Short-lived goodwill faded. "A policeman will know that there's dirt under every carpet, even his own."

"Score to you, Matron." She did not smile.

*   *   *

Jackson was restless through the afternoon, small movements easing limbs that had lain too long in one position. Once I thought he had opened his eyes, only for a moment, and sunk back into unconsciousness. I called the day nurse who said, "This may happen a few times. Don't call me unless he remains awake, but stay near in case he tries to get out of bed."

My bed was brought in from the cubby and I settled down to read and, when the night nurse came on, to sleep.

I caught two more false wakings before I dozed off and then was myself awakened by a burst of snoring. Jackson lay on his back, fingers twitching in time to his raucous intakes.

I tried the old married-couple remedy of resting my weight gently on his shoulder to trigger a change of position which would roll him off his back. Instead, he sat bolt upright, fighting me off with flailing arms. I slapped the service bell to bring the nurse, folded him against my chest to calm him and laid him back on the pillow. "There, old feller, there. Take it easy. Everything's all right."

His eyes tried to see me, screwing the lids in search of focus. "Who're you?" Voice like a creaking gate.

"I'm looking after you."

"Why? Why?"

The nurse came hurrying, spray hypo ready. "Roll up his sleeve, please."

I pushed up the pajama sleeve as he closed his eyes, said, "I'm sick of bloody nurses," and went back to sleep.

"He won't need that now."

"It's just a relaxant to keep him quiet now he's out of induced sleep." She pressed the nozzle to the skin and squirted the drug through the flesh. "That will hold him for eight hours and Dr. Nguyen will be here by then.

You can get some proper sleep yourself now."

Far from it. I suffered beginner's nerves and dozed in snatches, expecting always to hear the thud of Jackson falling out of bed.

I was in the cubby, eating breakfast with half my attention on Jackson in the Spy eye and a newscast murmuring in my earplug, when Nguyen came in. He was indeed the man of my test, and I would have to make the best of it. A private war on the other man's ground would be less a running battle than a running defeat.

"Good morning, Sergeant. I see the patient is still sleeping."

You would have thought I had never insulted him. "Yes, Doctor."

"Then I shall wake him. Nurse gave him somnoline at eleven-ten, so it should be fully absorbed by now."

"Do you need me?"

"I think not." He had answered offhandedly, his attention taken by the Spy-eye console. "That is an unusual keyboard. Why are the keys arranged on the faces of a cube?"

"To facilitate finding different points of view from above and from all sides."

"Has it sound also?"

"Yes. Turned off at the moment."

"Turn it on. Watch and listen, but I should not need assistance." He went silently out on soft shoes.

A strictly business association made good sense, but I had a question for him, one better asked this morning than later on.

His dark head moved into the screen, bending over Jackson. I switched the viewpoint until I was watching from the other side of the bed, seeing both faces in profile. Nguyen, satisfied, woke the man gently.

Jackson scowled at him, looked about him and asked

mutinously, "What's this place?" He seemed to be in a poor temper.

"A hospital."

"I can see that! What bloody hospital?"

"The Biophysical Institute."

"Never heard of it."

"It is a recent structure."

Bright, shrewd eyes surveyed Nguyen without grace. "Is it, now? Since when did the government have money for recent structures?"

The question belonged to the circumstances of a past government, but the situation in 2069 was no different. The old brute had wakened with a vengeance, cleareyed, clearheaded and on the ball. I heard Nguyen soothing placidly, "As a politician you will know there is always money for what the government wants."

"Even if nobody else wants it." He was ready to take on the nearest, whether or not they agreed with him. He asked, "What's wrong with me?"

"Very little now. There will be a minor weakness in the legs and arms, needing practice in walking and stretching. A matter of days only."

"Weakness from what?"

Nguyen said with some care, "A form of wasting disease which affected your memory of events."

Jackson peered closely at him. "Wasting? Memory? I remember some things. I remember quite a lot. I remember—" He broke off, rubbing his hands uneasily. As if he had suddenly seen too clearly, he raised them to his mouth in a gesture of shame and shock. Old brute gave way to nervous child.

Nguyen waited, watched, said nothing.

Jackson's hands slipped down to the sheet. He began to say, "I was—" but his voice cracked. Nguyen put a hand to his wrist and had it smacked away. "Don't baby me! I was out of my mind, wasn't I?"

"I would not say that."

"Well, I would and who the hell are you to contradict me? I know how I was."

"It seems so, and I am surprised that you recall even a little." He said casually, "You exhibited mainly the genetic type of Alzheimer's disease. It is mentally debilitating, but we don't class it with the insanitioo."

That shocked him; it was enough to shock anyone, but his mental resilience was amazing. He asked, with arrogance muted but not gone away, "Am I well now?"

"I see nothing wrong. Your apparent recovery exceeds expectation."

"Apparent, eh? We wait and see, do we?" He was quiet for a while. Nguyen waited silently. A large part of his performance seemed to lie in strategic waiting. Jackson said at last, "It is a disgusting condition."

"But it is over."

"Not recurrent?"

"There is no reason for recurrence. The genetic defect has been corrected."

"And you're my doctor?"

"Not your medical doctor. I am a hypnotherapeutic psychiatrist."

"Ah." Another pause. "I don't think I need you."

"On present evidence, nor do I, but there is always the unexpected."

"Is there? It gives you an excuse to keep sniffing at my mind, I suppose. I could do with some breakfast."

"It will be here fairly soon."

"Good. You can go away; I've things to think about."

To my surprise Nguyen said, "Of course; I'll just look in now and then," and turned away.

Jackson called after him, "Some great ape woke me in the middle of the night. Who was that?"

"When he brings your breakfast you can ask him yourself." Nguyen's smile was faint but relishing.

"I will. And you'd better get a message to my son. Tell him I'm better."

"He knows."

"Then where is he?"

"In Canberra, I believe."

"Why Canberra?"

"For a meeting of state premiers and the PM."

"Premiers? He's state premier?" His narrow face split in something more than a smile, a great, gaping triumph. He bounced gently in the bed, clapping his hands together and chuckling with delight before saying with a wistfulness that had seemed totally absent from such a makeup, "I have been too long gone. I was not here to see it happen."

But Nguyen had left him.

He slipped into the cubby laughing, actually laughing, like a human being. I said, "That wasn't much of a VIP consultation."

"There is nothing urgent to be done, and, as the stage folk say, always leave them laughing."

"You think he's OK mentally?"

"No. Nobody is. Not even you, my little-bit-starchy policeman." That was a new tone from this bland man. "He is an aggressive man, at his best in confrontation; while he questions and distrusts circumstances he will try to ride over them with energy, but other qualities will surface as unpleasant truths come to him. That may be the time for tinkering and adjusting. He spoke of memory. He probably has flashes of recollection rather than continuity. Do you agree?"

"Why ask me? You're the tinker." My surliness disturbed me; I amended, "It sounded bitty."

"Good; we agree. This is important. Alzheimer types lose a great deal of memory, and he was seen to be in mild deterioration for over ten years, followed by severe recession for fifteen. In clinical terms, he has little right to be alive. A man who has been absent from a changing world for some three decades will need time to establish a place in it."

"An unjustifiable and unlawful place."

"See? Starchy cop! Illegality does not alter facts. We deal with what is. The law is your concern rather than mine since you will be his mentor and guardian."

"After he leaves here? I'm not trained in any but pretty generalized criminal psychology."

"And that is no training at all. For psychotherapy, you will call me; for his safe introduction to present realities, I will depend on you. Who better than the man who will be as close to him as a twin to show him the world? Who better than a policeman to show him what lies behind its self-justifying face?"

That made sense of a kind, but I was suspicious; the psychs have never been popular with the law. "So you only oversee, in standby role?"

"First lesson in therapy, Sergeant: Don't undo what is not knotted. He is what he is, and for that has been brought back. Who will thank us for curing him into somebody different? Now, he wants his breakfast."

"It won't be here for ten minutes or so."

"Then we have time for small talk." He tapped the Spy-eye screen. "Tell me about this, please."

On it Jackson was sitting up, frowning and moving his lips; an indecipherable mutter came from the speaker. He looked like one stripping an enemy for torture. "What do you want to know?"

"Why did my detector not respond to the presence of camera and microphone in the ward?"

"No camera, no microphone, no electronics to detect."

Nguyen was impressed. "Am I permitted to know how it operates?"

The question indicated that he was not a regular member of the institute staff; biophysicists presumably had little use for psychiatrists. "The principles

are on patent file; they can be inspected. Encryption
and decoding are the secret stuff. The lens, if you call
it that, is a coating of the entire room with a light-
gathering varnish of the same color as the walls and
ceiling. The light is siphoned to this end by thousands
of glass fibers embedded in the plaster; no light is
emitted, only gathered, so you can't see them, but the
Spy-eye screens their input selectively at this end. The
electronics are here, not there."

"And the sound? Without microphone?"

"The optical fibers are fixed loosely and they vibrate
to the sound; a computer here measures the vibrations,
sorts them, suppresses the noises we don't want and
turns what's left back into speech. It's just a high-tech
application of available material."

"Now nobody is safe."

"I wouldn't worry. It takes a building team and a
gaggle of technicians to install it after they've torn out
your walls and ceiling and rebuilt them." There were
less wholesale methods, but he didn't need to know
them. "Now, I've got a question."

Nguyen's thin smile mocked. "I will make a bet with
you. It is a question you should have asked that day in
the police station."

"If I hadn't been too angry to think straight."

"But now you have thought of it and you can talk to
the psych bastard without wanting to hit him."

You need preparation for these needle-pointed ex-
changes. I grunted, "Near enough."

"The question is: You know that professional integrity closes your mouth on dangerous knowledge, but
what closes mine?"

"You hinted but I didn't follow up. For all I know
they simply trust you." I did not believe that; nobody
is ever *trusted* with official secrets.

Nguyen had started this hare but now was diffident.
"This is difficult for me, but I feel I owe you a tit

for tat. Mine is a pure-blooded Vietnamese family; we have not married outside the—the blood—in our three generations in Australia. We have standing among the unassimilated Asian families—*face,* the word you used to me. Do you understand what it means?"

"Pride? A sort of unsullied appearance? Front?"

"Those and more. The reverse of face is shame and it affects every member of a family. Senior administration understands these things. Listen: I open my mouth, I tell what I know—and my license to practice is withdrawn without reason or notice. My capacity to earn is gone and my family and I are nothing; we are Wardies, eaters of food coupons, anthill dwellers without a future. I am not a tradition-minded man; I could bear it. But for my parents, my wife, my children, the social descent would be ultimate disgrace. Theirs is an artificial and fragile world, but it is the world they live in; I could survive manufactured shame, but they might not, and who am I to destroy those whom I have made what they are? So my tongue is still, and those above me know it. There are pressures other than chemical cocktails."

Emotional blackmail is the most common kind and the most effective; even children practice it. Yet Nguyen's situation had its sardonic aspect and my nursed anger was not about to drown in easy pity. "I'm glad I don't sweat alone in the political steambath."

His mouth grew tight. "I have not used you for jest, Sergeant. I have given an earnest confidence."

I hesitated, conceded, backed down. "OK, I'm sorry; I shouldn't have said it like that. But there's still a question: Who controls us?"

His expression eased a little; it was hard to know his real mind. He gestured at the screen. "The son must be the ultimate controller."

Jackson still sat upright, desultorily exercising his shoulders and arms, staring angrily at the wall.

"The premier? He has probably never heard of either of us."

"Be assured that he has. He knows who we are and what we are."

The screen buzzed an alert. From an ancillary speaker the day nurse called, "Ostrov?"

"Here, Nurse."

"Mr. Jackson's breakfast is ready."

"Coming."

Nguyen walked beside me down the corridor. "You will have noticed that I did not address Jackson by name."

"I noticed."

"It is for you to tell him his new identity."

"Why me?"

"You are the answerer of all questions, his guardian, keeper, nurse and friend. You shelter and protect him. You know his secrets—"

"I don't."

"You will and he will depend on you. Make yourself the one person who understands and cares for him. He was an arrogant man in public life; you must be the one to whose integrity and knowledge he defers. Let him dominate and your position will be impossible. Answer his questions when you know the answers and don't send for me unless he becomes unmanageable. Now, good morning, Sergeant Ostrov. Happy nursing!"

He went quickly round a corner and out of sight.

I took Jackson his breakfast, and he looked murderously at the single bowl on the tray. I asked, "Will you have the tray on your knees or just hold the bowl?"

"The bowl." He lifted the lid. "What's this? Infant gruel? I'm hungry!"

"It's a specially prepared breakfast food with a lot of calories, vitamins and trace elements packed into it."

"Do you always talk like a traveling salesman?"

"No, I can do stand-up comedy and I take off the matron a treat."

"Oh, God, the life of the party and I have to get it!" He waved the bowl at me. "Get me some food! About four times as much as this."

"You wouldn't eat it. You've been on intravenous for weeks and your stomach has shrunk. It does, you know."

He threw the sheet back and opened his pajama coat as I grabbed the bowl from him. He examined his flat stomach, pinching the flesh between his fingers as if testing its genuineness, his face a study in puzzled calculation. Seeing that I watched him he covered himself and reached for the bowl. He spooned up an unwilling mouthful and found it edible, which was as well, for I wouldn't have put it past him to spit it over the bed.

He chose now to ignore me. The way to treat a childish tantrum, as Mum taught me until I learned not to sulk, is to leave it alone to die of inanition.

I left the room and watched him on the Spy-eye.

He wasn't able to finish the gruel. He glared furiously at it, put the bowl down on the side table and looked about for someone to blame. I would not be forgiven for being right. He examined his belly again, threw back the sheet to survey his bony but smooth-skinned legs, pulled back a sleeve to check his forearms and felt his cheeks and jaw.

Then he thought for a long while before he took a last angry look at his unwrinkled skin and banged his hand down on the bell push as though force would bring me like a bullet.

I took my time answering and earned an insult. "I remember you. I saw you last night. You're the ape that woke me up."

It was time to establish the parameters of our relationship. I said conversationally, well below his stand-over level, "And you're an ill-mannered old bugger."

"Oho! The underdog stands up for his rights, eh?"

"Under-ape. Stick with the metaphor."

"Educated under-ape!" He was pleased with me for standing him up to swap punches. "What's your name?"

"Orderly Ostrov while you carry on like a brat, Harry when you're feeling human."

He grinned, though not especially nicely. "All right, truce. But don't make a habit of it."

It had not only gone off better than I had expected, but I was sure now that half his projection was playacting, each role discarded as a more effective one presented itself.

I said, "You rang, sir. You want something?"

"Come off it, man. Unbend."

He didn't do the hearty-fellow persona half as well; it was possibly too distant from his real personality. I wanted to see a genuine reaction, so I said, "If that's what you want, Mr. Jackson."

"You've got your wards mixed, young feller. My name's Beltane."

"No, sir. Your name is Arthur Jackson."

"Some silly mistake—"

"No mistake, sir. Look here." I unhooked the progress board from the foot of the bed and put it in his hands.

"An administrative error. Get it sorted out."

"No error, sir."

He went dead quiet, and the quickly controlled twitch of his mouth was fear. I hadn't wanted quite that, and now it struck me hard how closely he had examined his body and seen that it was not one he remembered. God only knew what fantasies he was beating back.

I said quickly, "It's an alias. I know you are Gerald Beltane, but you must be Arthur Jackson for a while."

"Why?"

"Because as Arthur Jackson you are one more among

the millions of the city, but Gerald Beltane would be an illegality flung in the public's face."

He said harshly, "Explain!" Then he took a deep breath and said, "Please explain."

"I can only tell you what has happened. I can't explain it; I'm not in the confidence of the movers and shakers. You had a terminal disease and have been cured of it some twenty or more years after the onset."

He put up a hand to stop me. "Does the law say the old must be left to die? Have they got round to that while I was—out of the room, so to speak?"

"No, that hasn't happened, but it's more or less what actually occurs. People taking years to die are an unaffordable surplus population; the state can't afford them. We haven't got round to actually killing them yet. Many take a euthanasia option."

(Oh, but we talk tough, don't we! We recognize necessity and try not to recognize that it is a financial necessity, the outcome of something humanity invented for itself. We learn to live with it because we must, to speak of it—when we must—with all emotion tied back and gagged. The aged hope that their final illnesses will be short and painless. The young refuse to think of the day when they will see Mum and Dad dying before their eyes and know there is nothing they can do, although supportive treatments are known—because the supportive treatments will not be given by a Health Service whose funds are cut to the bone and into the marrow, and whose capacities are throttled by cold legislation. We know, endure, talk tough and refuse to think. And yet . . . this was the condition of all humanity throughout most of history. We are reliving the basic facts of existence.)

He said, "You're no sentimentalist, are you? Killing them may be law when your own time comes. Think of that!"

It was all too likely. "But treatment of the terminally

ill is forbidden by law; only analgesics are allowed. Alzheimer's is recognized as terminal. How you lasted to be ninety-three I don't know, but I'd guess that your son's influence had a lot to do with it."

"Ninety-three? So long?" He shifted unhappily as if easing the body might ease the assaulted mind. "There's not much memory."

"Not yet, perhaps, but the doctors have got your brain working again. I guess they've reestablished lost neurone pathways, but it's only a guess. I think it hasn't been done before, that you're a first up."

He thrust his plump, unlined hands at me. "More than that, much more. Look at those! Ninety-three?"

The hands shook badly. I took them in mine and suddenly he began to cry, all the time glaring fiercely at me as though I should not observe his weakness, but he did not pull his hands away.

I told him, "It's rejuvenation, Mr. Jackson. They've given you back about thirty years." I picked up the progress board from where he had dropped it. "Look here—date of birth, twenty-oh-six. Gerald Beltane was born in nineteen seventy-six. I know; I looked you up. This is twenty sixty-nine, so Arthur Jackson is sixty-three years old. And that is about the age he looks to me."

I didn't have to tell him that rejuvenation techniques were illegal; that had been so back in his own time of functioning.

"Your face has been altered a little, too. Not too much, but enough to be sure no one will look at you and suddenly remember old Beltane who should be dead. That makes you a sort of secret in full view."

He pulled his hands away. "Harry, get me a mirror." He remembered manners and grinned wickedly. "Please."

That wasn't an easy commission; a hand mirror seemed to be an item considered unnecessary in a

ward. In the end I lifted one off the wall of the staff
toilet, but when I got back to Jackson he was asleep.

He had been awake for just over one packed hour.

I laid the mirror on the bed table and left him.

He slept through most of the afternoon, and I dozed
in the cubby. Policemen catnap when they can. I might
have missed his waking if the watching Spy-eye hadn't
brought me to with a clatter of something dropped and
sounds of frustration from the ward. He had tried to
pick up the mirror, but his arms, too long unused, had
misjudged the effort and let it slip back onto the bed
table.

He cursed unintelligibly and breathed hard as he
lugged it back onto his lap, propped it against raised
knees and examined his face. It's as well we never see
the selves we display when alone; pugnacious old Beltane would never have let anyone observe the startled
and petulant child who hated and rejected the face in
the mirror.

Compared with the portrait accompanying the bio in
the *DNB* it wasn't an unpleasant face, but it wasn't his;
I suppose his reaction was natural although there were
scraps of the old Beltane to be found, overlaid and
redesigned with sharp, bold strokes. Jackson's wrinkles were younger and shallower, less gouged, and his
flatter cheeks highlighted the bones to present a hun-
grier but less forceful character; a narrower jaw had
been strongly sculpted and the scraggy fold below the
chin had shrunk to a small slackness. The designers—
carvers, makeup men—had given him more hair, flatter
to the skull than Beltane had worn it and darker than
his fading mousiness.

The changes were not sweeping, but they hid him
effectively; across a gap of memory no one would make
the connection. The doctors had given him back thirty
years and done it handsomely but I wondered how

long the glands, hormones and vital cells would labor to preserve the forgery. Years? A month? Days?

And would the new face change the man behind it? That was not psychologically impossible.

He pushed the mirror off his knees and lay back to stare at the ceiling. Once or twice he shuddered and I thought of him confused and doubting and fearing the future in a strange new world. There was anger there, too, but that would be a psyching-up response to new challenge. It was no surprise that he banged the flat of his hand down on the bell as if he would summon hosts to his bidding.

All he got was me, and he squawked in his rusty voice, "Take this thing away!" I smiled, pacifically I thought, as I took up the mirror, but he said, "You grin like that biblical dog that runs about the city!"

Seeking whom it may devour? Old bastard! "The new improved version doesn't please?"

It was the wrong thing and I should have known better, but weeks of battened down annoyance had their day out.

He yelled at me, "Watch your tongue, you hospital flunkey!" and I reacted without thinking about an old and bewildered man not properly in control of himself. At any rate I followed Nguyen's advice to grab the upper hand, and I must have looked as angry as I felt about the whole damned underhanded business (and I haven't the gentlest of faces at any time) because he looked at first surprised and then almost submissive as I laid down the law.

"I am not a hospital orderly or anybody's flunkey. I am a detective-sergeant of Victoria Police assigned to your protection, responsible for your safety and possibly for your life. I may well be all that stands between you and an expedient euthanasia, which is not impossible in the annals of political bastardry. I know you are in a frustrating position and I don't know how to relieve it any more than you do, so make it easier for both of us by behaving yourself. You are not a human being in trouble—you are a job I could happily be rid of. I would rather deal with someone prepared to watch and wait and not make enemies in a situation he doesn't understand—and which could turn out to be lethal."

Such words to such a man could see my career ended and myself back on the Ward streets, but he had no legal right to complain or even a wholly legal life. Technically, he didn't exist.

To my surprise he apologized, and very persuasively, too, but I hadn't worked off all my ill temper. I said grudgingly, "You politicians turn it on and off like a tap."

Saying it, I reflected with irritation that I had alienated every person I had dealt with in the hospital and had small right to resent another's moods.

Be that as it might, Jackson smiled, not too easily as new muscles creaked in a new face. "We understand each other." It was generous. Then he said, "I have had too many shocks too quickly; I must get used to being sixty-three in a strange land."

That I ought to keep always in mind. I said, "You're taking it better than some might have."

He did not answer that brash guesswork (how we flounder, trying to comfort in another's territory) but went off at a tangent. "It would have to be Jem, wouldn't it?"

"Wouldn't what?"

"All this: face change, rejuvenation, you, all of it. Illegal, you said, so who else could have arranged it?"

That was treacherous ground for a serving copper, and I backed off. "Maybe. How would I know? Nobody tells me Minder business."

"But the real question is, why? What does he want? What is there in me that he needs?"

"Does there have to be something? Down in the Wards they do things for love. Not all the time, because love's like money—never enough to go round—but quite often. Have Minders got rid of love the same way they've got rid of pity for Wardies?"

He answered more gently than I deserved, "We've got rid of nothing, Harry. Jem and I were close, but the most loving son could hardly be expected to carry his affection through decades of senile drooling, could he, now?"

It was a nasty picture. And yet . . . "Perhaps he carried it better than you think. He kept you alive and on prophylactic treatments all that time, didn't he? Otherwise you'd pretty certainly be dead."

That simple reminder raised his spirits amazingly; he really glowed. For a moment I was his dearest friend. Still glowing, he said, "Go away for a while, Harry; I want to think."

Under the circumstances, who wouldn't?

He had half an hour to himself before I was back with his evening meal. He said, "Feeding time, Ape?" but I had determined to shrug off heavy whimsy. His inspection of the food said clearly that it was a bowl of cat crap fit only to poison good relations, but his voice said, "In the name of truce between us, no comment."

This time he got it all down.

When I called back to collect the bowl the afternoon was about over and the evening's twilight storm swept across the windows with its usual tropic suddenness. The short remnant of day vanished in racing cloud; thunder crashed, lightning blazed and the rain came down in waterfall sheets.

Jackson was taken aback by the unheralded violence. "I thought it was summer. Have the weather patterns gone mad again? What time of year is it?"

"Mid-February. Rain month. All that sunshine today was exceptional."

"March used to be the wet time. Floods and storms in from the ocean."

"The pattern is spreading back towards Christmas. Winters are getting drier."

"Is that good or bad?"

"Mostly good. Genetics has come up with some dry-winter cereals not subject to hot weather fungus and UV."

He said, "I must catch up with change," as if that would be as easy as changing his socks.

I waved at the wall screen. "News, current affairs, talk shows."

He seemed not to have noticed it before. There was a selector on the bed table, but he waved it away. "I wouldn't understand half of what I'd see."

"It wouldn't be as bad as that, but I can get you printsheets if you'd rather."

He snorted, "What do they print, news or placebos?"

"News mostly. Was that unusual back then?" Had news dissemination altered in a quarter of a century? There are gradual changes that you scarcely notice.

"Very. Kept up to date, are you? Tell me!"

"News is real because things keep happening that can't be hidden—famine and food chemistry, small wars and big weather disasters. I don't mean that anybody tells all the truth, or even Minders' truth slanted to policy, but facts grow too big to be sat on and bits keep leaking out. I suppose government pretends it's opening its heart by letting us have stuff when it's too late to stop it."

"Wardie cynic! Do you believe that's the way of it?"

"I'm a policeman, Mr. Jackson. I know it's so."

"Then you've told me quite a lot: that the police and public information services are being taken more into official confidence than before, which means that ever so slightly the balance of power has shifted towards the people. Truth has made a small gain. Now, what about the world scene, the overriding problems?"

"Food again. Or still. Always will be, I suppose. Twelve billion people—"

He broke in, horrified. "Such increase, so quickly!"

People didn't waste good horror on the inevitable; it was hardly worth small talk. I gave him the current catchword: "Sex is the sport of the unemployed, Mr. Jackson. The problems don't change: enough food produced but no knowing just where it will be needed, no knowing what new corruption will steal it or whether the distribution links will stand the strains put on them."

That would be no news to him after twenty-five years or a hundred years. He asked irritably about, "Genetic improvements? Sturdy cereals? Fungus crops?"

I heard myself talking like a vidnews headline reader. "New varieties spawn new ecologies to cope with the unforeseen changes they introduce—insect plagues and insect extinctions and bacterial imbalances. Like the Harmony Cultists say, Man proposes and Gaia disposes. Our grandfathers shook the balance and every correction we make shakes it further. Too many unknowns in the ecology equation. Then there's the sea . . ."

I hesitated because I was venturing on uncertainties there, but he asked, "What about the sea?"

"This is hearsay."

"So is most of history. Go on."

"Fishery police say there's a big increase in poisonous species, down the chain as far as plankton. Survival of the fittest, could be—the best protected. Nobody fishes for poison." It very well could be so; nature (all right, Gaia if you like that sort of thing) uses dirty weapons to hold its own. "It may be we're losing the war. In some parts of the world nutrition levels are falling and that can't be kept quiet. Factory foods look the same and taste the same as ever but don't have the same value; it's faked-up to hide the shortage of staples. Just not enough arable land per head."

Jackson grunted, "Nothing new in doom and devastation, Ape. We always survive. Tell me a real shocker."

That was the Minder attitude as we saw it from underneath. Bugger you, Jack; I'm all right. So I gave him a shocker. "Global statistics lists the weight of newborn babies as an average eight percent lighter, worldwide, than twenty years ago and the average height is down nearly three centimeters on the last century."

He didn't have a dismissal for that; looked at closely, it wasn't to be dismissed. "Look at me, Mr. Jackson. A hundred and seventy-eight centimeters and ninety-two kilos. I'm no giant, but I'm bigger than most, and I'm ready to bet my kind will go out like the dinosaurs. Dr. Nguyen is the model for tomorrow."

That was one of my personal thoughts about the future. Other species faced famine by ceasing to breed, but humans seemed unable to follow that road; a dozen regimes had tried different forms of restriction and all had failed after initial success. Survival of an overall smaller species would be some sort of stopgap alternative to mass sterilization. Reduction of the biomass would buy time. Men and women were no healthier for being bigger and no less healthy for being smaller. The day was past when sheer size was a survival factor. When you've wiped out the opposition your advantage ceases to matter, becomes a useless property.

Nguyen, now . . . about a hundred and sixty-five centimeters and fifty-five or so kilos, sinewy and trim and limber, neither overbulked nor underdeveloped, capable of doing whatever a man might reasonably need to do. Heavy laborers are often comparatively small men with less brute strength but endless stamina. A race of Nguyens would use less protein, need fewer calories and less of the precious arable land per feeding head. However, starving the hulks and preserving the

lightweights would not be a proposition to lay before
the world's Minders; they were themselves apt to fill
the tallest and heaviest ends of the population spec-
trum because they were the best fed and best tended
and would have no high-minded desire to eliminate
themselves for the greater good.

Their conception of the greater good had long ago
refined itself as, Keeping the bastards quiet.

Jackson said, "That's a constructive idea, Ape. All
you need is a willing world and a slimming diet."

Back to persiflage. "We might get the diet soon enough
without waiting for the willingness."

"True," he said, and closed his eyes.

I took his bowl and left him to sleep again.

Nguyen came through a little later and I told him briefly what had passed. He was happy that the awakened
brain operated so well and went through to the ward
while I fed my curiosity on the Spy-eye.

Jackson woke and grunted at him, "What do you
want?" as if he had been pestered all day.

The Oriental face is as expressive as any other, but
that impassivity you hear about came down like a curtain as Nguyen said, "To look at you, to listen and
decide."

"Decide what?"

"Whether or not my time is wasted here. Perhaps you
have no need of me."

The old playactor heard the warning and became
gracefully polite. "Not at the moment, perhaps, but
there may be shocks coming to me that will need
buffering."

"You have uncertainties?"

"There's no comfort in an illegal existence."

Nguyen smiled thinly and got in a smart rap of common sense. "You would prefer to be dead with your
legal standing intact?"

Jackson backtracked. "What's done is done and I'll make the best of it, but I'll remain uneasy until I know where to look for danger."

"For the present leave that to Harry."

"My ape policeman?"

"A trained man who knows the dangers and is better equipped to evade them than you are. Does he answer your questions?"

"Well enough. Are you Vietnamese?"

"No. Why do you ask?"

"I like to place people. It makes them easier to talk to."

Nguyen let his face unfreeze. "Talk? Why not? I am Australian though my grandfather was born in Vietnam."

"Last century? Boat people?"

"Something of the sort; he did not speak of it. It was for him a time to be forgotten. He was a paddy farmer there. He came here that his children might grow up as human beings with room to live."

"Room! My detective nursemaid thinks we should all diet down to your size and take up less space per hungry stomach."

"Don't underestimate him; he has honesty, doggedness and loyalty."

Take a bow, Harry!

"And an untethered tongue."

And now a black mark, Harry!

"Use it! How many tell you the truth at all times?"

"None, praise God. There's a limit to how steadily you can gaze at the facts of a decaying world."

"Asia reached it long ago. Its people are not cheek by jowl but may achieve that any day."

That was a definite subject stopper. Jackson changed tack. "When will Jem be here?"

"Jem?"

"Jeremy. My son."

This seemed to take Nguyen's interest. "I understand that his conference will conclude tonight." He took Jackson's wrist, felt the pulse, consulted his watch. "He may return to Melbourne in the morning; a busy man will not stay away too long."

"I need him."

Nguyen dropped the wrist. "What are you afraid of, Mr. Jackson?"

"I?"

"You control your face with the ease of a lifetime's practice, but your shoulders stiffen slightly, your breathing slows and only an adept can control the pulse. I read tension and anxiety."

Jackson surrendered with a sigh of martyrdom; he couldn't let a word pass without milking it. "My son and I have been very close. Perhaps unusually so."

"Those who remember say so. A team."

"Some do remember?" He allowed himself a flash of satisfaction before making a confession that must have galled his pride, but he did it smartly with no pussyfooting. "I became a burden to him, undependable in the House and in public—and then a fumbling and forgetful nuisance, a relic to be hidden in a back room. I don't remember the worst years, but I can imagine the mumblings and spittings and the smell of incontinent age. Can a son's love survive that?"

"Harry told you it could."

"Oh! You check with him?"

"Naturally."

"He was guessing."

"Guessing well, but he was not to know that your son is as much afraid as you are and with better reason."

That silenced the father with its unexpectedness.

"Consider! You have received treatment so radical that only parts of it have been confirmed in laboratory testing. Your son asks himself will he confront a robot with all memory gone, not knowing so much as its name? Or a miracle returned to physical competence but with his brain obstructed by a disease which has gone away but left its ruin behind, rusting in disuse? Will his act of love be repaid by empty eyes and a wordless mouth? He has had no communication with the medical staff because no message is safe in an electronic society. He does not know yet whether the end is success or failure. He is the one to be afraid and I know that he is afraid."

All that I should have worked out for myself.

Jackson said, with a pain that rang genuine, "I am a self-centered old man."

"You are a convalescing, youthful sixty-three, gathering together the memories and faculties which I believe will return completely. Until then your first care must be yourself."

"Jem has always been my first care."

"Then be gentle with your frightened son. I must go; I too have a family waiting for me."

Jackson called after him, "What are all the premiers doing in Canberra? What is Jem involved in?"

Nguyen turned his head to say, "In discussion of the population question. That old trip wire: how to restrain birthing. Or perhaps"—his face betrayed nothing at all—"how to expedite dying."

The old politician was at once back in control and making a speech: "Forget the drama. They only talk and make useless proposals and then go home until next talk time. Those unresolvable arguments have circled the globe for seventy years; in the end they throw up their hands and let humanity go to hell at its starving leisure. Any biologist will tell you that no species endures forever, so who's next? That's the real question. Given a million years to heal its wounds and let evolution heave into action like the incompetent old lady it is, Gaia should be able to produce something solidly armored against recurrent fate. Something with built-in endurance. Something tried and tested. The cockroach?"

Nguyen smiled politely and left him.

That was Wednesday afternoon. On the Thursday Premier Beltane visited his father, so early and at such short notice that I was nearly caught unready.

Matron's voice came from the speaker as I got back to the cubby after giving Jackson his breakfast (besides his gruel, a small peach to keep him happy and help stretch his hungry stomach), telling me that the premier would be here in ten minutes, coming direct from his plane with only barest warning. I was to see that the old devil was shaved, brushed and sweet-smelling for the royal visit.

Matron could not eat me alive as she would another undutiful orderly, so I let Jackson have five minutes to swallow his breakfast undisturbed. He was finishing the peach when I picked up his tray, wearing the grin of a blissful child at a treat and wiping it off as soon as he saw me. "How many days of this sick-kitten diet?"

"A couple. A bit more bulk each day."

"Any news of my son?"

"He should be here in a few minutes."

It was too sudden; he bounced around the bed in desperation, demanding a mirror, clean pajamas, a shave.

"I shaved you only half an hour ago, you silly old bugger. It's only your son, not the pope."

"Only!" As they say, If looks could kill! Then he played his trick of reversing his emotional state in a tick of time. "A mirror, Harry. Please! And a comb."

"It's too late to rip a glass off the toilet wall." I used my pocket comb to smooth his hair for him. "You don't want to look too lively; you're supposed to be sick and in need of sympathy."

"Just go away, Ape." But he remembered to smile.

In the cubby the vid comline was ringing. It was Nguyen. "I'm told the premier will call at the hospital on his way home."

"He's on his way."

"Can you record from that Spy-eye machine?"

"That's what it's for; it's an information gatherer. Sound and picture on wire, every imperishable performance preserved forever."

"Please, this is not a joke. Harry, I want a record of the whole of this father and son meeting, every word and action."

That was certainly no joke; it was more like snooping. "Do you have authority, Doctor?"

"No, Harry, no authority, but I have a patient whose mental welfare is my commission. These two men are dissemblers; little they say or do is without its subtext. If I am to understand them I must take this chance to observe them as it were mentally naked to each other."

He had a point, but there is a limit to prying. I might have demurred if he had not added a rider, "So should you."

I wanted to see for myself what this relationship amounted to, for reasons I told myself were professional, and his were at least as professional as mine.

"OK, I'll make a chip for you."

I switched on the Spy-eye and headed for the main corridor to escort the premier to his father's bedside, but I had used up the ten minutes and a few more. The head of state was already leaving the lift outside matron's office.

He called to her, "I know where he is," which told me that he had visited the comatose man's bedside before my tour of duty began. He passed me as though I was not there and in three paces stopped dead like a parade ground soldier to spin round and ask, "Are you Ostrov?"

Nguyen had been right; he did know. "Yes, sir."

"Good." And he was on his way, not quite running.

He was smartly turned out, trim as a pin and carrying his sixty-odd years with ease, but his face wore the dead expression of a man to whom intense strain was his way of life.

I returned to the cubby. Would he have said *good* if he had known of the Spy-eye?

Perhaps he did know.

What happened in the first minute of that meeting told me that he did not.

The screen lit up on a still life, an unnaturally posed, unpainterly framing of the bed with Beltane at the foot and Jackson upright against his pillows, both under tension like fighters in their corners, urgent to move but held by an invisible timekeeper.

I started Nguyen's recording. What in his psychiatric cookbook would he make of this?

I had time to think that no one would identify them as father and son, and the reason was not only Jackson's facial surgery. The father was narrower in every measurement, a thin man; the son was inches shorter and broad, square skulled and built like a small bull. I recall thinking that his vid appearances must give him extra height by low camera angles and careful placing, and wondering what manner of mother had so impressed her genes on the son as to smother the father's physical characteristics. There are statistical chances about that sort of thing, but I could not remember how they operated.

Beltane moved first, just in time, it seemed to me, before whatever barrier lay between them became impassable. He took two steps and pulled Jackson forward into his arms with a kind of hungry ferocity.

Jackson wept, not quietly as he had done before but noisily, without reserve. In a moment, as if at a signal, they pulled apart, laughing relief at some fear overcome, then Beltane leaned forward again and kissed his father on the mouth.

It is not easy to convey all my reaction to that. It lasted perhaps two seconds and was over, and it left me feeling voyeurish, intrusive. There are fathers and sons who preserve the kiss of greeting into adult life, habitual to the point of meaninglessness, but it was a gesture I could not imagine myself making. Upon which I at once recalled that when I gave Bill a casual hug after being away for a week or more, he would brush my cheek shyly with his lips and this did not disturb me; it said all the things left unsaid. Mum usually offered only her cheek and I could not remember her kissing me since adolescence save on a birthday or some such occasion.

It may have been that both men being in their sixties—one actually and one apparently—lent incongruity to the action. Surely something did.

Beltane said, "I was afraid," and his father, "So was I," and that was the end of it.

As surprising and unsettling as the kiss was the way in which the greeting was suddenly over, as if so much time had been allotted for sentiment and both had obeyed the stopwatch. Jackson dried his eyes on the sheet with no attempt to hold on to dignity and demanded, as roughly as though a combat signal had sounded, "What the hell do you imagine you've been doing?"

Beltane sat himself on the edge of the bed. "Getting you back into operation."

Jackson watched him evilly, calculating. "You realize what you've done, what will happen to both of us if this becomes known?"

"I have thought about it; that's why we decided on the facial changes."

"We?"

"The senior surgeon and I."

"And?"

"Stop it, Dad! Nobody knows you after thirty years and nobody will know you now. Be glad of stolen time."

"Oh, I am! Did you get tired of having a dribbling scarecrow in the house?"

It was as if they had picked up some ancient quarrel at the word where it had left off.

"No, I didn't." He took Jackson's hand and shook it gently. "Affairs reached a pass where I needed you, need you now, badly." Beltane trying to convince, to make his point, was a more lively man than the one in the corridor with overburdened eyes.

Jackson asked, "For what?"

"Advice. Guidance. Assurance."

"You have a goddamned cabinet for those."

"They're no use to me."

Jackson screwed his face into mixed suspicion and unbelief. "You've alienated your cabinet? They're about to topple you? Is that it?"

"No. They know that the Wardies want me and so do the armed services and the police. Cabinet can put me out—and watch the people put me back in."

"Armed services! Police! This is medieval. Are you dreaming of assuming personal power? Dictatorship?"

"No!" He threw the word out as though the suggestion frightened him. It may have done, because he muttered, "I've enough trouble without blundering into autocracy."

Jackson lay back, watching his son as if for two pins he'd strangle him. "Tell me. Make sense."

"You taught me all I knew. That may have been a mistake."

I had their faces fairly large in the screen and thought that for a quick second Jackson was first insulted and outraged and then alarmed. "Go on."

"While I had you with me, steering and arranging and

bringing off the little coups that kept me in the public eye, everything went well. But I was your puppet."

"No!" Affronted and ferocious.

"Yes, Dad. I thought and so did you, that I was my own man, learning the game. Then you . . . went away . . . and I had to carry on alone. There was momentum; I was on my way up and not to be stopped, but I had to make my own decisions and little by little they became my decisions and not those I knew you would have dictated."

"That's natural."

"I tried to be the one honest man instead of swaying and bending as you taught me."

"Honest! I didn't teach you to be a bloody idiot! Honest, in that cage of snakes!"

Beltane winced, made a small, placating gesture. "It worked, worked very well. It got the people behind me and it got me the premiership. This is my third term. And I'm falling apart. All the tub-thumpers and bureaucrats who came up hanging to my coattails are waiting for the mistake I can't recover from. Oh, I have friends in the House, even amongst the ministers, but I can't talk to them. They tell me either what will suit their own advantage or what they think I want to hear; my friends will topple me for their own purposes as fast as the others will dance on my bones. I have decisions to make and I can't face them and I have no one to talk to, to ask an honest question of, to tell a truth that won't be twisted, misinterpreted and misused."

"In the House," Jackson said, "you rarely did have—you or anybody else. You can have only allies and fellow travelers. Friends are too dangerous; they're up close before you see the knife. What has changed?"

"The nature of the decisions to be made."

Jackson understood an implication that evaded me. "This Canberra conference?"

"Yes. They're closing in. The talking is over."

"Taking sides? Picking the teams?"

"That's done; they're at the tactical stage."

"And you?"

"I can't accept any of it." Now that he had reached his statement Beltane ceased to be upset or confessional; he said, as though exposure had reduced the trouble to a matter of simple planning, "There are actions to be taken, words to be spoken, and I recoil from all of them."

Jackson grimaced; he seemed to grasp exactly what the conversation was about. "What do you want of me?"

"Just that you be here."

A plea for moral support? A confession of dependency? An attempt to shift a load?

He said without emphasis or emotion because it was part of their lives and needed no stress, "You are the only confidant I ever had and I've been lonely long enough."

"And for that you have ruined yourself."

"I shouldn't think so."

Jackson waved his arms. "This—all this! This damned institute and Nguyen and the surgeons and that bloody policeman somewhere down the passage! How many people know what you've been doing with me?"

"Just four—matron, Ostrov, Nguyen, the surgeon. Their mouths are stopped."

He said that as though the stopping of mouths was routine procedure, and I felt a prickle at the nape of my neck. It was the sort of thing the coppers joked about when a case against a Minder collapsed for lack of some item of evidence that we knew had been collected and now was mysteriously missing; it was no longer a joke when I heard corruption spoken aloud by the head of the state, with my own mouth among the stopped.

"Until," Jackson said, "the unthought-of happens and you can't coerce them any longer. Think of this great ape of a copper with his smarmy conscience aching in his guts—how safe from him will you be?"

"He's safest of them all. Integrity is his conscience and his prison. He does the job given him."

"Without question?"

"In spite of question. A morality wedded to duty. Nguyen found him for me."

At that moment I thought very little of this Beltane who made himself a white knight to the people but who, when trouble loomed, moved heaven and earth, right and wrong and downright criminal, to run to Daddy. And who held trustworthiness in contempt. I felt that Jackson, tantrums and all, was a better man than his son.

Jackson was saying that he would need convincing because the ape ran off at the mouth like a washerless tap.

Ah, well . . . as others see us. Policemen take more abuse than most—and try to pretend that it does not bruise or fester.

Beltane took him—and me—by surprise by bellowing, "Shut up, Dad! You can't guess at the circumstances and there's no time now for long explanations. I have a cabinet meeting at eleven and I need to bathe and change and eat. For God's sake defer making up your mind about anything until—" He seemed to become aware of raucousness and snapped his mouth shut.

They glared at each other, beloved father and beloved son, until Jackson completed the sentence with gimlet spite: "Until my decrepit mind falls into agreement with your errors and flailings."

They observed a half minute's silence.

I can think of no other way of expressing it. They turned their eyes away from each other and sulked at the walls. I supposed it must be some family quiddity, some time-tested custom of stopping before they came to blows, comparable with Mum's stamping out and slamming the kitchen door or Bill's dealing himself a hand of patience while he spilled the cards in shaking rage.

How they judged the moment I could not tell but Beltane said, in high good humor, "You'll be coming home tomorrow night. There will be a car for you and Ostrov—after dark; you'll have to be smuggled out. Try not to quarrel with him; he was chosen with care."

My precious charge told him, "We bicker amicably, but I do as I am ordered and he hasn't actually struck me yet."

Amicably . . .

Beltane stood up to go and Jackson grasped his wrist. "There are gaps in my memory, Jem. Big gaps. More gaps than memory. I see . . ." He ran down like an exhausted clockwork, groping for something that escaped him. It was in fact a name. "She is only four or five. And sometimes she is older. There are sequences like scraps of film and I know she is my granddaughter but her name has gone right away from me."

For the first time I found some pity for him, as distinct from understanding of his plight; I slipped a little distance into his confusion and grasping at what might be memories or might be imaginings, inventions of a mind sliced into glimpses of its fragmented past.

"Melissa, Dad."

"Yes! I think somebody else told me, but things come and go."

"She will be home to meet you."

Jackson simpered like a doting old fool, an expression I wouldn't have believed possible to him. "She won't know me."

"No, she won't. But she isn't a silly girl; she will understand. After all, she's sixteen."

"So old?"

"They grow, Dad. Now I have to go."

I half expected another scene of family sentiment, but

Jackson only nodded, swinging from past to present in the flick of an idea. "Till tomorrow night, then."

Beltane gave him a smile and a sketch of a wave and walked off. I had never met two people like them.

Prescience—it can have been nothing less—made me cut off the Spy-eye, switch in a news program, whip Nguyen's chip out of the recording slot and slip it into my pocket.

The premier tapped on the cubby door and walked in.

I got to my feet as he said, "You will be leaving here with Mr. Jackson tomorrow night. A car will be provided. I don't know how long your tour of duty will be; it will depend on circumstances."

"I understand that, sir."

His eyes were on the screen where a newsclip showed highlights from a soccer match of the previous afternoon, then they slipped past it to the distinctive box-shaped console. I was sure he knew what it was though his square, still face gave nothing away. He asked, "Is that the news? What did you think of that stupid riot in Paris?"

Riot? Paris? A trick question if ever I smelled one. I said, "I haven't seen that. I just switched on."

"Ah."

He came right into the cubby and placed his hand casually on the frame of the screen. "Warms quickly, doesn't it?"

I said nothing. You can only lose by protesting when you are already in the idiot seat. He flicked off the news program and cut in the Spy-eye, to see his father scrabbling for something in the drawer of the bed table. He switched it off again. "I'm not sure I approve of these things, but what the security services want they usually get." He moved to the door, turned and gave me the uncommunicative stare of a man confident of his power. "Never lie to me, Sergeant Ostrov, and never be afraid to tell me anything—anything at all. There must be trust."

He had delivered himself up to my resentment. "Trust, sir? Why, then, there is something else I will never do: I will never forgive you."

He appeared at first not to understand; it was some small thing that had slipped his mind. When he grasped the point his eyes livened with interest and I knew that on impulse I had said something right which had been absorbed and evaluated.

He said, "I ask your pardon for the action of a frightened man who sees too much betrayal and loose talk. I had to be sure of you. You must have heard it said that it's lonely at the top; it can also be terrifying. That is why I brought my father back."

"It was unwise."

"A wiser man might not have needed him."

He left me to think over what I had seen and heard, to see that all of it amounted to confessions of private weakness, that mine field area of the soul where defenses do not exist and which brings us all down in the end. I liked this secondment less than ever.

The Canberra conference had been on population control; that much was common vidnews.

It is disquieting now to recall the jokes about the Big Squeeze, dreary jokes without humor, betraying the underlying anxiety: "They've passed a law banning sex." "Great! I've always fancied a life of crime."

We made jokes about everything in a gray world recovering from the greenhouse onslaught only to be faced with unstoppable fecundity.

Many refused to think of the squeeze at all because the prognosis was the stuff of nightmares; they joked about the food problem instead—but not, I reckon, in Asia or Africa or South America where the nightmare was already a dreadful century old. "Did you know that all the basics for protein can be drawn from the atmosphere?" "Fine, but what happens when they've recycled all the air?" "They recycle our shit into atmosphoro."

Soggy and sad and sick.

I was no better than most others, no more overtly concerned, preferring to get on with living while the good times rolled. (Good times! Our grandparents would have been horrified.) After that curious father-son dialogue, however, I chased round the vid channels to discover what the newscasts had to say about the Canberra meeting of premiers.

They had little to say beyond the official handouts indicating that they had discussed peripheral subjects, mainly a rehash of a topic that rose every so often—the creation of forced-food farms on floating islands of vegetation in the Indian and Pacific oceans—but this time covering a slew of new techniques for holding such fragile constructs together in the teeth of subtropical storms and for recycling pollutants to maintain the purity of the seas. (If you can't stop the birthing, at least feed the bastards!)

As usual the meeting had come to no firm conclusion; further reports had been called for from the Solomon Islands base; CSIRO had been asked for a more searching analysis of nutritive value per square meter deliverable as food for immediate consumption. . . .

I could have written the handout myself from a lifetime of hearing that further investigation was required, that imprecise items needed clarification . . . that, in fact, the scheme was just another carrot dangled a finger's width from the donkey's nose.

What interested me more was the presence of observers from Canada and the United States and Israel. Observers at a meeting of state premiers? Observers commonly attended only major power conferences.

Had they been scientists their attendance would have made some sense, but the United States man was the president's personal aide, and I remembered one of the Israelis as having high military rank. Reasons for their interest might be plain to the newshounds and pollie watchers but not at all to a simple copper who badly wanted to know just what brand of decision making Beltane found intolerable.

I didn't know until later that something was happening elsewhere, something that would influence events. I insert it here to keep the timing in order.

Some seven kilometers on the other side of the city, in the run-down suburb of Balaclava, a down-classified doctor named Barney Fielding had decided to take a fling at rehabilitating himself by turning the criminal stupidity of a couple of kids into political blackmail.

4

Barnabas Fielding:
The Social Ladder

From Commentaries; *The Political Scene: "The sheer blatancy of the political machinations of the period is an indication of the moral breakdown of the Minders and of that indifference of the masses which amounted to a malaise, an absence of concern in a future without hope. The self became paramount.* Now *mattered; tomorrow was of little interest."*

I have never been a schemer, a maker of plots. From the beginning of my meddling I muddled, fell into error.

I should never have left the girl in the care of that inconstant woman, should have known that the moment I turned my back she would have second thoughts and third thoughts until fear of the clacking tongues of neighbors rattled alarms in her head and every step on the broken cement outside her door became squads and posses of police seeking her arrest. She would be taken for a dozen dire offenses . . . harboring criminals,

81

implication in birthing fraud, concealing knowledge of a crime, food coupon malfeasance, conspiracy against the public welfare. . . . These people, whose minds are so acute in their daily encounters with embattled neighbors and the exigencies of remaining bearably alive, fall into confusions of guilt and punishment when they contemplate the admittedly loaded scales of justice.

Still, that block of flats is a festering snake hole of prying eyes and poison, sheltering at least two known criminals, one of whom doubles as a police nark (God help him if the others ever suspect) and one psalm-singing cult family who would shop Jesus himself in the name of righteousness. She had cause to worry.

I should have smuggled Melissa away after dark of the same day and kept her in the storeroom behind the surgery while I made up my mind.

But—there would have been trouble from Fred. He would have been in and out, cow eyed and putty souled over the Minder mistress who had dropped into his life to make an everlasting summer day. More like an eternity of sour regret, had his brain been geared to thought.

She didn't give a tinker's curse for him. She wanted a baby and Fred was handy. It happens that Fred is good breeding stock—if he harbors no inimical genetic recessives, which I am not in a position to determine—well-shaped, strong and sensible enough if only some crisis would stir his brain out of its peer group somnolence. But, to be "one of them clever bastards" is a social sin in the Wards, matter for ostracism and the odd beating up just for the hell of it.

By what criterion Melissa chose Fred was unimportant; she wanted a baby and the mystery was, why? I felt, more by intuition than deduction, that she was not motivated by any premature maternal compulsion but that for some reason she *needed* a baby. Her determination was combative rather than helplessly emotional. She needed a baby as a fanatical philatelist will all but kill to possess the one stamp coveted to complete a set.

When I left the Blacker flat on the Wednesday morning I had it in mind to probe this peculiar need, but that was secondary to another project sprung full-born into my head. Melissa Beltane, here under my hand, out of the reach of father and protective security personnel, was a uniquely valuable property for disposal in a civilized but gainful fashion. I was not the fool to dream of a ransom demand, which is a sure way to deadly pursuit and ultimate destruction; I did not dream of rolling in Minder money and the wasteful stupidity of wealth. I longed for, and still long for the only thing worth coveting in an unstable world: personal security, that syndrome of small things—a respectable position in Minder territory, if only on the outskirts, an income sufficiently greater than the statistical average to keep want at arm's length, with access to good music and sophisticated company. These do not demand great wealth, only the trifle more than is needed for decent survival.

My problem in disposal of the goods was, how to obtain a reasonably payable price without resorting to blackmail or major crime. Minor infringements there had already been and more were inevitable; therefore the purchaser should be one with influence to protect me as well as himself. He or she must protect me as part of our common interest in freedom; it would be better still if we shared some other interest, some ambition or other trait demanding solidarity . . . other trait . . .

There the obvious rose up and smiled at me.

We mixed breeds do not love each other with any racial closeness but neither do we betray each other lightly. Our instinct is to protect where possible, swinging as we do between worlds, regarded as doubtful allies by both in spite of a century or so of multiculturalism. Black and white lie down together more readily than the olive brown with either.

Therefore I thought of Dick Kenney, Richard James Kenney, one quarter white Australian and three-quarters Koori, not pale enough to "pass" and not dark enough to disguise his white heritage. His mother had been a black poet and a good one, his half-caste father an Anglican clergyman. His parents had given a good education to a smart brain, and the issue of their love was a son who had cared for them dutifully in their old age but in his heart resented the accident of birth that left him generally respected but finally close to no one. That, at any rate, was the summing up of the mixed-blood population; as one of the few of us among the Minders he has done well, but the outward success decorates an achievement that leans, on the surface, neither to black nor white. Leaving only his own kind . . .

He was known for a very astute man though too honest to be a wealthy one. He was also, then, the shadow minister for Internal Affairs on the Opposition benches of the state Parliament, and that was what mattered to me. I had never met him. At my most affluent, before my trouble (an illegal birthing that went unpleasantly wrong) I had not moved in his circle, nor could have—but he was human and fallible and a politician. The politician is doubly fallible. Honest or not, he would pawn his Liberal soul for knowledge that would spread an oil slick under the feet of Labour's Beltane.

There is nothing like a sex scandal to start parliamentary skeletons rattling—with fright.

I followed the habit of a lifetime in taking a day for consideration before acting in so delicate a matter. On the Thursday morning I set the affair moving.

In an age when no electronic communication is entirely safe and every politician's words are subject to eavesdropping by interested professionals as well as by merely mischief-making amateurs, there is a recognized method of doing what I was about. I called the Liberal party headquarters and told the answering voice that I possessed some 062 information. The voice replied, as I had feared it might, "You are not oh-six- two."

"Of course not, but she will vouch."

"Arrange it, then call again."

I had hoped to manage without dragging the woman into it. 062 was then a prostitute who once, in the pursuit of her calling (she was no street drab but a cultured "home entertainer") received, as part of the attentions of a South American diplomat, a mutated worm infestation which could multiply furiously under the skin and create a spreading nuisance difficult to control in its ease of transmission. It was more a pest than a danger, but it brought her by circuitous ways to my Ward surgery rather than to her Minder physician, whom she did not trust to preserve a still tongue.

From my surgery she took the first vidcall step towards relaying to a relevant contact the news of the diplomat's infection, which in his homeland would be regarded as proof of his association with the diseased peonage of his country. It was blackmail material and was at once used as such in the polite world of international pressures.

She did not care that I, a disgraced and demoted doctor, could identify her as a "party tattler"; my opinions would not be canvassed by Minders. She was amused when, instead of charging her for the visit, I asked that she pay the debt in kind if someday I should call on her. That is a common enough arrangement for communication between the Minders and twilight dwellers like myself, who are socially neither one thing nor the other but try (in general, hopelessly) to keep lines open. Throughout history the flesh trade has been a useful linking duct.

The time had come to call her and, when she answered with her screen dark, I let my face flash for a second or two before I cut the visual. Her voice was wary as she said, "I remember you," and waited. She understood at once that no names were to be used between us.

"I have used your number to make a contact."

A moment stretched in a hiss of breath and an arctic silence before she spoke again. "That was an impertinence."

"Had I asked, you would have refused permission."

"Surely."

"So I used it and now I tell you."

She thought about it. "The contact refused a man's voice?"

"I told them you would vouch."

"So sure of yourself! And of me!"

"I am sure of my material. And you owe me."

"I don't need reminding. Have you thought that you may compromise my status? I may agree to vouch— after I have considered the material."

Nothing for nothing in this world where the payment of a debt can be made ground for further extortion. "Time is short."

"Meet me for lunch." She named a city restaurant, a civil service rendezvous. "Have you suitable clothes?"

Bitch! Yes, a closetful, unworn for years. "Enough, but I can't afford that place."

She succeeded in injecting a smile into her voice. "I can. Information is worth paying for."

She cut off. Now I had the thankless task of explaining to my half-trained, semiofficial assistants that they must cope, for a few hours, alone and as best they might, with the odorous queue in the waiting room.

Dressed for once in clothing that could attract unwelcome attention in these pitiless streets, I slipped out through the rear laneway gate and drew only a few more or less friendly catcalls from old patients.

In the restaurant the lady called for a Privatent, and so we dined and talked in the safety of an electronic screen which, so far as I know (but who really knows thoɔo thingɔ?) oan bo piorcod only by a powerful array too obviously visible for use in a public place.

Over lamb cutlets whose bone proclaimed them farm grown rather than sliced from the monstrous protein mass in the Yarraville factory, I told her what I proposed to do. At first she thought it dangerous, an adventure into territory where Dick Kenney's vaunted probity was a hazardous unknown. I had to convince her that political power is a greater magnet than money and that probity is to be measured by its breaking strain; also, that if the move paid off, the status of 062 would be enhanced while, if it did not, she could disown me as a paranoid fake. In the end she agreed to vouch for me and did so over the vid while I listened at her elbow.

Complex arrangements for the meeting were made; I had only to do as I was told and be spirited from point to point as possible observation was circumvented.

And so a chance infestation by an exotic worm entered history, but the lady's name must remain out of it. She has sharpened her skills to become a discreet, almost "society" madam whose establishment is noted for the outrageous accomplishments of a gifted staff.

I met the shadow minister that night, not at his home but in the home of friends of his family, people unconnected with politics, ideal cover for a casual encounter. How I reached the house is his business and mine. With newsbugs and scandalcats sniffing after every public figure, it would be graceless of me to reveal how these simple objectives are so simply achieved.

I was ushered into a library and told to wait. I waited for quite a while, sure that my public and private files were under examination and discussion.

This was a rich library, a collector's library; many of the books were old, leather bound, gilt embossed and locked behind glass. There were paintings also, minor works from the Impressionist period. That they were minor did not mean that their value was small, and it seemed to me that such works should be in the public galleries, that this private hugging of wealth is more reprehensible than vulgarly open display. Do not misunderstand if I say that I took little pleasure in examining these things; I was merely murderously jealous of their unknown owner, as though I were personally denied so that he might wallow in possessions. The class war had long been a dead issue in the face of global necessity, but I could have fought it afresh that night, face-to-face with the private sequestering of a planet's heritage. Despite the silliness of old Marx, there are circumstances in which property is theft.

Behind me a voice said, "You are Barnabas Fielding, a registered medico of the third grade?"

That was only a warning that my background had been inspected. I corrected, "Second grade."

"Third," the voice repeated, politely, "after demotion for professional infringement."

"I am still a qualified second."

"Yes, yes, we have our pride. What is the nature of your information?"

"I will tell the shadow minister. You are not he."

The man moved round in front of me. Well dressed and well spoken, he was yet no secretary or confidant; he was a hundred kilos of broken-nosed thug. "We like to guard the shadow minister against wasting his time. Just a general idea, please."

"Ask him does he know where Melissa Beltane is."

The heavy face brooded over me. "Should he care?"

"He will care greatly when he knows where and in what condition."

"She is not at home?"

"Far from home."

He meditated. "You are a doctor and you mentioned 'condition.' Two and two make—what?"

"Between three and five. That is enough."

Without ceremony he hauled me upright with great butcher's fingers clutching my shoulder, holding me one-handed while he searched me with an expertise that spared no privacies.

"My apologies, Doctor, but there are many methods of deceiving the doorway detectors. I will tell the shadow minister what you have said."

Kenney did not keep me waiting. He came quickly into the library, shut the door behind him, skirted the large desk, sat down across from me and said, not making a great declaration of it, "Remember that above all considerations of race and color I am an Australian. The part-Koori bond takes no precedence."

That was unpromising, even menacing, but I had not come all this twisted way to have the initiative stolen from me in a few words. I replied as casually, "You are a shadow minister of the Opposition. I favor the Opposition or my information would go elsewhere."

He said as though he had not heard, "You hint that the premier's daughter is missing."

"Yes."

"Where is she?"

A haggler's bargain must be struck before information is divulged, but I fancied that huckstering would not go far with Kenney. He was a thinnish man, lighter colored than I despite his extra quarter of Koori blood, but still carrying his heritage plainly. He was also a man of palpable self-assurance, no simple fish to be played on a line.

I fenced carefully. "She is in private quarters not far from my surgery in Balaclava."

"Not actually in your charge?"

"Effectively, she is. Her hostess will be relieved to be rid of her."

He gave a short, startling neigh of amusement. "I can imagine it. Balaclava tramp society entertaining a princess! A featherbrained princess, as I remember her." The merriment ceased abruptly. "To Belcher you mentioned her condition. What condition?"

"She is five months pregnant."

"Stupid of her. How old is she?"

"Sixteen."

"And the father?"

"Seventeen. One of the premier's Wardie gardeners."

"Holy God! And the premier knows?"

"The boy's identity? No. But she confessed her pregnancy to her father and he behaved ferociously. Unreasonably so, I gather. So she ran away from home."

"To her boy-love's slum?"

"It isn't quite a slum. A seedy block of flats—"

"I don't want the address; the family need not be involved. You plan to perform a clinical abortion?"

"No. She wants to bear the child."

His sallow face lighted in comprehension. "So that's why she flew the coop. When?"

"Last Sunday night."

"Yet Beltane took off for Canberra that same night."

"He may not know yet that she is gone."

He smacked his hand lightly on the desk. "Now, there's a situation for you!" My doubts eased; he was eyeing the bait, no matter what his scale of honorable commitment. "Can you bring her here?"

"I can remove her from the boy's family. Bringing her here unseen might be more difficult."

"Arrange it through that grubby underground woman, once you have the girl. Tomorrow morning?"

"It can be managed."

"Good. I shall expect her in the course of the day."

All this had passed in the manner of cronies talking over inconsequentials. I had expected if not drama at least some of the tension with which romance invests intrigue in high places, but I might as well have been selling him a bag of potatoes. Skulduggery seemed unnaturally dull—and still my side of the exchange had not been mentioned.

I asked, "What do you propose to do with her?"

Kenney pursed his lips, spread his hands, made a spectacle of playacting indecision. "A Minder child cannot be left unprotected in the Wards."

Rubbish; many visited there for the frisson of mildly perilous dirt. "A population law breach could be a scandal loud enough to unseat the premier."

"Grossly handled, it might." His manner was still gossipy, but now he spread his hands again, the pink-brown palms towards me. "Look, Dr. Fielding, clean hands!"

I think I preserved dignity in spite of the blow. I had misread him, found for myself the one incorruptible politician. Kenney would do no more than see the girl safely home. I was trapped; there could be no shopping for a more amenable schemer, for I would be under watch to head off such a move. It remained only to put a courteous face on defeat and leave politely.

Kenney said mildly, "You should have taken her home, shouldn't you? There would have been some reward, I think." His face changed to a startling likeness of an animal, teeth bared and lips snarling. "What do you want, you filthy thing? Money?"

To the pure in heart all things are filthy. I said, and I think I managed it equably enough, "Gifts of money are for wastrels. I can earn money. I want my grade two surgeon-physician rating restored."

"A thinking criminal, eh? Not just a greedy grabber. But what you want is not easily given. There must be evident reasons for such action on my part, and what reasons are there for elevating such as you? Money is a more transient but more certain reward."

"No."

He stood, frowning and angry, then strode round the desk and past me towards the door. He spoke from behind me. "I suppose there must be baksheesh of some kind to shut your mouth, but I make no promise of what you ask—only that I will see what can be done." I heard his hand on the doorknob. "Don't make the amateur's error of not bringing her; there will be no alternative market for your goods."

He slammed the door behind him.

In a few minutes Belcher came to guide me through the sly passage out of there and on my way home.

I spent a bad night. Kenney's contempt had bitten, but some things cannot be bought with money and if my return to grade two had to be paid for in private shame, so be it. Blameless morality is for those who can afford it.

Friday dawned gray and drizzling. It was the season of hot, humid rain, of ill temper and restlessness and short-fused violence amongst the youngsters on the streets; for me, too old and slack muscled to break knuckles on some unoffending jaw, it was the season of sour depression.

I rose early because Kenney had murdered my sleep, and so I heard the vidnews at dawn. No studio scream-er made vocal headlines of Melissa Beltane. The pre-mier was home by now, so the matter was being hushed up. If he was bending before the potential fallout of a birthing scandal, then bargaining might yet bear fruit; surely he would act in my favor, guilt calling to guilt.

I could not get the girl from the Blacker flat until young Fred had gone to work; a scene with the wor-shipping lover would be unbearable. I listened to commentators driveling about the Canberra meeting of state premiers, praising some food initiative and deploring lack of progress on the planetary population level while I drank cups of the disgusting factory-spewed tea which is the only kind covered by the coupon issue. I remembered real tea, but today's Asia has no room to devote hectares of precious hillside to a luxury plant. The Minders—and not all of those—have what little leaf tea there is.

At eight o'clock I went out into the dreary day and trudged round to Inkerman Street. Strangely, the Blacker flat was silent while all the others were yelling music or talk shows as breakfast was cleared away and the drudgery of housecleaning begun.

Putting my head inside the kitchen door, I saw Mrs. Blacker disconsolate at an uncleared table, drinking the same rubbish as I had done and staring, by habit, at a cracked and dark vidscreen. When she saw me she began to cry, silently, without so much as screwing up her face; tears trickled from wide eyes while mechanically she lifted the cup and sipped at it.

The misery of the hopeless is as real as cruelty; they deny it, refuse to speak of it, but it cannot be hidden. The only kindness is to stick to practicalities, to not intrude too far, so I nodded at the wrecked screen and asked, "Your husband again?" He was alcoholic, prone to destructive hysteria, but he seemed not to be home. He was not one to stay with another's grief.

She put down her cup and said, "It was Fred."

That was hard to believe. Fred, for all his intellectual nonentity, was the quiet, dependable one of the family, the center of what stability existed there. He was a fighting man because in that neighborhood he had to be, but he was never hot without reason, and a fortglass vidscreen is not easily smashed.

"Drunk?"

"You know he don't drink."

"Something to do with the girl?"

Defensiveness burgeoned into a deliberate, worked-up hostility. "It was your fault!"

She needed a whipping boy, and there was I. "How so?"

"You said you'd bring coupons and you never come."

Yes, I had promised and, fizzing with my own plans, had forgotten. "I'm sorry. I'll bring them this afternoon. That's a promise."

She was not listening, bent on my damnation. "You never brought them and I got worried because we're nearly out, what with her to look after and a week to go yet. You don't know what it's like with two men to feed and I was frightened we'd finish up with scenes and noise and the other flats listening to everything. Me old man can't control his drunk's tongue, he'll say anything and soon everybody'd know we'd got Fred's bitch here and then the trouble'd really start."

It would indeed. She broke off to wipe her eyes, but kept her blaming gaze on me. "So I said she had to go, I wouldn't have her no longer, and Fred blew up. The way he yelled at me you'd never think I was his mother. Then that old slag next door has to poke her head in to see what's going on and I just had time to push the girl into the back room before Fred abused next door for a muckraking slut. Next thing her husband's here saying Fred has to apologize, and Fred pushed him through the vidscreen." She said, with incongruous satisfaction, "He's a good protector, my Fred. But I couldn't have her here anymore. You can see that!"

Her tone said that I'd better see it or be the focus of another yelling scene.

"So I said to Fred he had to send her back home and she heard me and started crying. He just looked at me and went in to cuddle her and calm her down. And when I got up this morning they was both gone."

She pushed a scrap of paper at me, the wrapping of a soap packet carrying Fred's farewell on the back of it in careful schoolboy hand. *Dear Mum Good-bye Sorry Fred xxxx*

She said, weeping again, "Now see what you've done!"

No use protesting; she had her scapegoat and reason would not shift her. I strove helplessly to think where he might have taken Melissa. Home? No; he wouldn't dare. They had gone secretly because Fred did not intend to be found and it is easy to become "lost" in a city of ten million people, of whom a million or more are street kids or vagrants or addressless petty crims.

I don't think I said good-bye to her; all I had in mind in that sweaty, overcast morning was Kenney's face, moving from contempt to rage and vengefulness when he found that I could not produce the girl. Almost worse was the dread of confessing the failure, but it had to be done; I could not hide in shame only to have Belcher or some other remorseless brute hammering on the surgery door, demanding that I make good my word or suffer the reward of a fool.

I thought of 062 because I could not bear to face Kenney as a cheap schemer and a bungler. I told her what had happened and left her to do what had to be done. She was unpleasant about my having smirched the dependability of her number, and that was quite bad enough. This world offers no sympathy to the luckless.

There was worse to come, when Kenney had me hauled forcibly to the Manor to face Beltane.

Part II

The Private Life
of Politics

5

Ostrov: The Players in the Game

Nguyen came in on the Thursday afternoon, ostensibly to check Jackson's mental condition, actually to collect his chip. I told him that it would replay on any commercial vid and for God's sake not to let it out of his hands; it would be best if he viewed and erased.

"I will view and consider."

"It's my head that will roll if you're caught with it. Beltane knows I watched but not that I chipped him."

"He was angry?"

"Maybe, but he made the best of it. You'll see that he has other worries."

"His daughter?"

"Why her? Jackson driveled about her, but there was no fuss."

"She has disappeared."

"Nothing on the vid about it." Teenagers deserted home every day and made nuisances and often criminals of themselves on the streets. Only the police cared greatly, but Beltane's name would have the newsbugs circling for honey.

"There will not be. Police have been informed but nobody else. They are combing the city for her."

I said that combing the Melbourne labyrinth would take an army. Nguyen agreed and said that the thing had to be kept quiet because the kid was pregnant and even the police had not been told that bit.

That certainly made it more newsworthy. "Did Beltane know about it this morning when he visited the ward?"

"No. That news greeted him when he reached the Manor. He collapsed."

"That wasn't reported either. How do you come to know about it?"

"I was sent for. I am his psychiatrist."

"The hell you are!" I should have guessed as much. "You seem to have some connection with every little thing that happens."

"That is fortuitous; I am nobody. Like you I am caught in a web. We must keep this from Jackson; meeting his son was disturbance enough."

"He and I move to the Manor tomorrow night. He asked after the girl, so he'll have to be told."

"Perhaps. We may concoct a story—a short holiday. Or, she may be found by then. Either way, the premier now has another secret operation to manage and another group of mouths to close. He is beset on every hand."

"He bought it; let him worry. What's the story about the girl?"

"Last Sunday evening, before he went to Canberra, she told him she is pregnant and he lost his temper with her. His self-control has been uncertain for some months and her confession triggered an outburst. He admits he was unreasonable, that he yelled at her and threatened her and she ran out of the room. Later, she could not be found. The housekeeper thought she had returned to school as she always did on Sunday evening. She attends boarding school during the week and returns home each Friday afternoon. The school seems to have thought nothing of a short absence— some minor indisposition, not worth bothering the premier about—but when she failed to appear on the Wednesday a class mistress rang the home and started a stampede. She had walked out of the house and vanished in circumstances guaranteed to prevent anybody noticing anything unusual."

"Who's the snake in the cradle?"

"The boy? Nobody knows. Beltane says she refused to tell him. I'm not sure that he actually asked her; he seems to have behaved like a madman."

"There goes the only good clue, already out of reach. Just searching the Minders' homes is a near impossibility with a limited force."

Nguyen had a small, reserved smile which came and went as he contemplated disaster; it came and went now. "Why only the Minders' houses, Harry? Sex is classless."

"If she's run away with the butcher's boy, God help them both. And God help Beltane when the Opposition gets its teeth into the story. They'll blow it up until it looks as though he threw his pregnant daughter out of the house when the housekeeper could have fixed the girl with a knitting needle."

"Not at five months."

"Five months and nobody knew?"

"That is possible, given the girl's tubby build and a corset."

It seemed that on Friday night I would be guarding Jackson in a madhouse.

I began to wonder what the arrangements for leaving the institute might be. Beltane had said only that a car would be sent, and that might be as far as he had thought. He was a man removed from gross detail, in a position to say, *Do this,* with no need to think how it could or should be done—somebody would see to it. We police were competent to carry out such moves, were we not? What, he might ask, did I think I was there for?

I checked with matron, but she had not then been notified of the imminent discharge and it took several minutes of argument to convince her that I should be allowed to speak to the senior surgeon.

He knew but had given the matter no further thought. Why, he asked, should he?

Because, I told him, we had to get Jackson into his home without any not-so-innocent bystander asking himself why the premier's limousine, with state insignia, should be collecting someone from an institute which the general public regarded as a place where unspeakable experiments were carried out. It would be a question worth repeating to the news channels for a small gratuity.

I might have known he would say, "You will have had more experience than I at this sort of planning."

I snarled that my job was arresting criminals, not planning their getaways. We parted without warmth.

I scouted round the entrances and goods delivery intakes of the building, decided how the removal should be made and told the surgeon I wanted Jackson taken out in an ambulance. Since I had the premier's authority to appeal to, he agreed that an ambulance would be provided and even suggested that he drive it himself rather than make a regular driver privy to secrets of state. I thought he saw himself, like my dad, as an intriguer in high places, a cloak-and-dagger type.

Next came the business of making contact with Beltane. He was still at home, preparing to leave for the previous day's postponed cabinet meeting, but the name of Ostrov cut no ice with his staff of secretaries until in desperation I howled into the screen that I had word of his daughter. That brought him smartly, stuttering in my ear.

I had to explain that the lie had been a necessary stratagem to get his attention. He was furious and so would I have been. When he had done with telling me that the ruse had been an indecency practiced on a distraught father (true enough) he came round to the idea that I had done it for a reason, perhaps a good reason. I explained why the Jackson transfer should be done my way and why he should order affairs at his end as I suggested. Once he grasped the idea that he had to do a little more than toss orders in the air for others to catch, he became apologetic and willing.

That accomplished, the next thing was to get Jackson on his feet and moderately mobile. He should be capable, in emergency, of some degree of self-help.

Jackson had decided this for himself. I found him sitting on his tail in the middle of the ward, halfway between the bed and the window, while the day nurse tried ineffectually to help him to his feet and he cursed her between bouts of telling her to "Call the ape! Get Harry! Get a bloody man on the job!"

I told him to shut up, lifted him over my shoulder and dumped him on the bed. "Now apologize to the nurse."

And so he did, charmingly, making me look like a musclebound thug who did not appreciate the emotional stress on a sick, confused old gentleman.

Life among the Beltanes might be criminal, noisy and passing the understanding of a bedeviled cop, but it would not be dull.

Jackson's trouble was partly stiffness, partly inability to manage the growth of new muscle and partly a fear of making a doddering fool of himself—which he had done on his first attempt to walk unaided, collapsing flat on his behind and alarming the day nurse, who had come running and scolding.

She thought he should stay in bed for at least another day, and I was less than tactful in putting her right about that. She vanished in the direction of matron's office, hissing that I had too damned big an opinion of myself. What happened down there I don't know, but there was no further opposition to my arrangements.

Jackson, entering into the memory of his old public persona, which involved acute consciousness of dignity, wanted me out of the ward so that he could practice stumbling alone until he mastered the new art.

"Arthur!" I had not used the first name before and he glowered at the impertinence. "We're going to be too close to be suckered by each other's pretensions."

That hadn't occurred to him, living as he did in the instant minute while trying to assemble a coherent life. He snorted and cursed and accepted the idea and clutched my arm to slide off the bed and stand up.

"Now, listen. A person loses about a third of his musculature in old age by failure of cell replacement; you lost nearly all of it in years of inactivity, but the bio boys here have given you a new lot, modeled on the old physique but only guess accurate, so you'll have to experiment to discover what the muscles do and how well they do it. You'll have to assess what is a comfortable pace and what your energy expenditure limits are, like getting down on your knees and deciding just how to go about lifting your weight upright again—"

"Or punching your impudent jaw to see whether or not you fall down."

That was only repartee; he was inspecting the idea of interdependence with someone other than his son and seeing some advantages in it.

We started off across the floor, a matter of four or five meters from bed to window, with him leaning very lightly on my arm, just heavily enough to ensure balance, too obstinate to let me see that he really needed mo. He muttered, "I was dizzy the first time." That excused the bruises on his behind, but he knew what was required and set himself to do it and established a fair amount of muscular control in the short stretch.

At the window he leaned on the sill and looked out over the city. The institute had been built on the triangular block just across from State Parliament House, so his view was from the northeast corner of City Center, that square mile that had once been the commercial heart of Melbourne, with towers and canyon streets funneling the wind.

"Nothing different," he said.

This was true. The tall buildings, empty and useless in the long collapse of trade and finance, had been torn down while he was still a functioning M̃P and replaced by the low, energy-saving structures of a culture governed by thrift. He could see across the Yarra and the Botanical Gardens to the square-cut landmark of the Shrine of Remembrance (we had lost any real idea of the war it commemorated, over a century away in dimness) and over the suburban roofs to the waters of the bay, gray under the seasonal rainclouds.

"Except this. This building." He made the institute sound like an eyesore. "We must be five or six floors up." Such height, he implied, was reprehensible.

"Seven," I told him, "with more above."

"Why? What's gained? What are the running costs in lifts and ducting and maintenance?"

"I don't know."

"What did people say when it was built?"

"Nothing. Since when was government accountable to the people?" I had shocked him. He leaned on the sill, sucking at his lower lip.

"So it's come to that, has it? How long since?"

It was an impossible question. We are aware of big changes that offend and discomfort us but only vaguely of the small ones imposed gently over a long period until another right, another freedom has gone as though it had never been. I did not know when the relationship between government and governed had changed its face. It would have been happening gently from some time in my youth. It could be that even Jackson, at the heart of things, had not noticed the insidious creep.

"I was still a kid when you were bowing out, Arthur; I don't remember a time when government explained itself. Did it ever?"

He surveyed me with troubled eyes before he turned and stepped out in the direction of the bed. I grabbed his elbow, but he pushed me away, fueling his progress with anger. "Of course it did, Harry! If it didn't, the people had their own ways of forcing explanation from it and secretive governments tended to have short lives. Have the people forgotten how to be individuals? Don't they care?"

It seemed to me that we didn't care very much but that we remained individual. Individuality was the big policing problem, the me-first syndrome behind nine tenths of crime; it was individuality in the struggle to exist in a world of shortages and small opportunity that kept the eyes on the self and regarded government only as a source of regulations and laws to be paid lip service but evaded, flouted or, in the last choice, sullenly obeyed. We didn't think much about government; like night and day and food coupons, it was there.

I tried to explain this to him, haltingly because I had never tried to sum up the situation in a few words and was now looking at the citizenry—and myself—from a fresh angle.

He said, "Your lives must be very gray."

"For most, yes." I was not sure about my own; a copper's life is lively but not on that account colorful or lovable.

At last he said, "My legs are trembling," and sat down. "Let me have a spell and we'll try again."

I found some thin oil in the cabinet and, failing anything better, gave him a rubdown with that. The new muscles were stiffer than I had counted on. We tried another walk in the evening after the meal and did appreciably better. I made up some simple exercises for him and checked with the nurse for her approval. She looked me over, stone faced, and said, "Just don't tire him out." I gathered that she no longer cared what I did so long as she was not called on to clean up the mess.

In the evening Nguyen came for another check on Jackson but stopped at the cubby to ask my question a fraction before I could voice it: "What do you make of them?"

In truth I made very little. "People who understand each other so well that they don't have to explain themselves. One starts a line of thought and the other answers as though all the spaces had been filled in."

"Good. And the kiss?"

"Not my line of country. Did you notice that it wasn't sentimental yet it wasn't perfunctory?"

"Yes. Well?"

"It was like recognizing something that needed no words. It made me uneasy. It was—" I cast about for a word and found only a poor one. "—unhealthy."

That caught his interest. "Do you know that a century ago people called relationships 'unhealthy' when they were too genteel to refer to sexual deviation?"

I hadn't known and deviation had not crossed my mind, nor did it impress me now. "No, but it was just a salutation and they went straight into business after it. In fact they went into a quarrel."

It was my turn to ask what he had made of it.

"No more than you, but a psychiatrist's reactions are apt to be clinical and your gut reaction might have shown me a fresh one. It did not. What about Beltane's reason for having his father cured and returned to normal life?"

"Genuine. Their father and son thing had been so strong all their lives that there must have been an almighty big hole left in Beltane's existence when he had to carry on alone. I can imagine that."

"You feel sympathy for Beltane?"

Was it the moment to be outspoken? I thought it was. "None at all. He's as weak as piss. Jackson's worth six of him, temper and all thrown in."

Nguyen smiled at that with his fleeting, semisecret flicker of the lips that might be mockery or might be approval; it was most likely satisfaction that I had formed a positive attitude towards Jackson. I took the opportunity to tell him of the arrangements for Friday night and he said only that it was as well that I had taken the planning on myself and that I should not push Jackson's new musculature too hard. Then he asked, "What about Canberra?"

I hadn't thought about it; that was Beltane's mess, not mine. "He sounds as if they want an agreement or a concession he isn't willing to give. Perhaps the other premiers ganged up on him and he's stalling for time."

"He has weathered that storm before without crying for his father. The subject was population control."

"The newscasts say they talked about food. There are a dozen conferences around the world every year and they never come up with a useful control idea. The range is pretty limited, and they've all been picked over like a lousy singlet, so they concentrate on feeding us until next time."

Nguyen said thoughtfully, "Limiting family size was the first consideration, back in the nineteen seventies."

"Didn't work then and won't work now. People want children, particularly when they're told they mustn't have them. As well as the biological urge, it rouses defiance in them. Besides, the need is to reduce the population of the planet, not to only stall it."

"Deliberate neglect of the old, the useless and the terminally ill."

"That goes on, but it's a drop in the bucket. No effect worth counting."

"Why, then, something more basic, like contraceptives in the drinking water."

"Scuttlebutt says it's been tried, but I don't believe it. Some strains have to be preserved and wholesale sterilization isn't selective."

"So we come to selectivity. Preservation of an elite, eh? A meritocracy ploy."

"How do you decide merit? It would turn out to be preservation of the rich and powerful—sure to be the most useless in a world reduced to basics."

"So a plague would be unsatisfactory?"

He was homing in on something, so I played along. "Too hard to put boundaries on a plague, even if modern techniques weren't good enough to stop most plagues in their tracks."

"Here, yes, but how about in Africa and Asia and parts of South America? Those couldn't stop an outbreak of stomachache."

"Still too risky. They'd know the big powers were doing it to them and they'd loose off some of the nukes they've got stowed away against the day somebody thinks they can be taken off the board. Then we'd all go in a nuclear winter."

He suggested, "Efficient diplomatic meddling could start brushfire wars and keep them fanned."

"Hot enough to kill five billions or so? Nothing much less would be of any use. Out of the question. And unselective."

"Back to that. Do we really think in terms of 'us' and 'them,' of who is to be hit and who spared?"

"Of course we do. Everybody does. When it comes down to bared souls it's always, how will we do it to them? not, we all have to take our chances. Hell, Doctor, we know all the answers to all the questions. Why should Beltane go to water over it?"

"Something new, perhaps?"

"Such as?"

"How should I know, Harry? But I would very much like to know what sort of decision is too repellent for him to embrace."

He did not add, *And you will be next to him and his, in a fine position to find out,* but the thought was clear behind the bland eyes.

He changed the subject abruptly. "He feels he holds the Wards, the army and the police. If the Wards knew about Jackson, about their well-beloved premier breaking some of the most emotion-rousing laws for his personal benefit, would they continue to support him?"

That was tricky; I had to sort out the probabilities before I spoke. "They might. If the rabble-rousers got to them with the idea that Beltane's example gave them the right to demand easing of the population laws, they might stick with him to make him do what they wanted."

"Demonstrations, marches, mobs in the streets, anarchy and unnecessary bloodshed!"

"They always finish up killing some poor harmless bastards."

"And the police?"

"Would do nothing if it got too big. We couldn't handle demonstrators by the millions; we'd be dead if we tried. We'd be guarding special people, I suppose, and keeping communications open."

"The army?"

That was not so easy. "I'm guessing, but I think the

federal corps, the permanent army, would fire on the Wardies if they were ordered, but the duty men doing their obligatory two years might jack up. They aren't real soldiers, they're Wardies in uniform; they might stick with their civilian families and friends."

"So, soldiers fighting soldiers might be the end of it. I think, Harry, that the premier's secret had better be well kept."

With that he went to pay his pointless visit to Jackson. I didn't bother to switch on the Spy-eye; I was too much concerned with a mental queasiness over the monstrous ramifications emanating from a son's act of love for his father.

Or, had it been a purely selfish act, the instant soothing of a need, a desire, a comfort?

All love is touched with selfishness. It is the lover, not the beloved, who races to embrace his obsession.

On Friday morning Barney Fielding's plan had fallen apart and my own worst mistake of the entire affair had already been made when I took it on myself to arrange the Jackson transfer in orderly fashion. There's no profit in asking now, what if? By Friday the chaos effects were unstoppable.

In the morning Arthur was early out of bed, stretching his legs while he clung to the bed table, making tentative forays and at last walking fairly steadily to the window. The doctors had given his comatose body the usual course of isometric exercises so that he was, you might say, factory-fresh for normal usage and needed only a short running in. He should be reasonably capable by nightfall.

When I took in his breakfast he told me of his exploit, peacock proud, passing it off as a mere nothing to a determined man. I congratulated him with a straight face, and he passed the day wandering round the ward and then the corridors, making longer and longer expeditions and complaining of the silence and the locked doors.

The arrangement was that we would leave in the ambulance at ten o'clock that night, not only because it would be full dark but because there would be few pedestrians around the area, which was mostly gardens and public service buildings; even the small risk of a passing observer was not worth taking while newsbugs were a questioning pestilence in the city. I would ride in the back with Jackson, wearing a gun under my white orderly's coat. The rest of my gear fitted into a suitcase; I had not brought a police uniform to the job.

Going to collect and pack Arthur's gear, I found that he had none, none at all; not so much as the toothbrush was his own. Matron said he had been brought in by ambulance, wearing only a pair of pajamas which had been burned at once because of his incontinence on the trip. "His home is only three kilometers away but you can't outguess their bowels when they're in that condition."

In the event of an emergency he should be fully dressed, but matron could not supply clothing. There was nothing for it but to call the senior surgeon, who hemmed and hawed and would see what he could do and I should come down to his office in half an hour.

I had not paid much attention to Hugh Cranko. Senior surgeon or not, to me he was just another doctor around the place, but his appreciation of the necessity of having an insider drive the ambulance had displayed a little personality, though the impulse had been romantic rather than realistic. He was a nondescript, fair man of early middle age whose conversation seemed always a touch vague minded, but he had a public reputation for brilliance on the job and could afford an affectation (if it was that) of offhanded-ness. Perhaps I should have taken more interest in him, but my general dislike of the whole Beltane business stopped me bothering with anyone who did not actually get under my feet.

When I went down to him he gave me a clean overall which should fit Arthur, a singlet, underpants and a pair of old sandals. "The best I could do, Sergeant." His best was good enough.

He said, "It's only a short trip. Where will we make the changeover?"

"Not all that short. We'll move right out of the city for the swap."

In a city of ten millions, especially in summer, islands of privacy can be hard to find. My plan was to move right out of city limits, along the Ballarat Road and past Digger's Rest, a few kilometers into the forced-pasture country where there were still empty stretches and little-used side roads and not much night traffic. There Beltane's car would meet us.

I showed Cranko the spot on a road map and he said the job made a nice change from the humdrum. A surgeon's life had not occurred to me as humdrum, but I supposed that after a while one sliced-up interior would look much like another. To a butcher a carcass is only meat.

During the evening I gave Arthur his clothes and would have assisted him to dress but he waved me away. He seemed to have taken fairly good control of his body though he swayed and made two attempts at standing on one foot while he lifted the other to get his leg into the overall, but I was satisfied that he could make a quickish move if he was pushed to it.

After that we could only wait. At some stage he asked, "What the devil is biophysics? Some new branch of biology?" I had never heard of it before entering the institute and I still did not know. "Do you mean you haven't asked?"

"Why should I?" If I sounded surly it was with myself for not having done so. I had accepted the term as indicating some special area of biology with which I was unlikely to come into contact.

Arthur said, "You could translate the word roughly as life measurement. Does that make sense?"

"Why not? Exercise factors, relation of muscle mass to stress positions, effects of internal and external temperatures—all that sort of thing."

"Nothing new in that."

"No."

"So why a special institute?"

"I don't know. Let's do what we have to do tonight and ask questions later."

We were fidgety by the time Cranko called us down to the parking bay. There he was, posing by the white vehicle in an ambulance service uniform and hugely pleased with himself.

I was not so pleased. "Is that getup from the institute store?"

"Of course not; we don't supply the ambulance people. I had to chit them for it."

"On indent?" In my mind's eye I saw a trail of documentation as evidence of our movements.

"No. Does it matter?"

"Do you mean that you asked the ambulance service for one of their uniforms and they just passed it over?"

He gave me a smiling, incredulous stare as if I were ignorant of the facts of life. "I *asked* for the correct size; I *demanded* the use of the uniform. You're a jewel, Harry; you really don't know what authority the institute wields, do you? I suppose not many outside our senior staff do know and we don't keep the police force informed of our daily despotisms. Life is easier that way."

Jackson, leaning against the open rear door of the

ambulance, listened with plain dislike. "The premier will be interested in the arrogance of privilege."

Cranko's amusement did not falter. "He knows, Mr. Jackson, he knows. Shouldn't we start?"

He settled himself into the driver's cabin and I holped Arthur into the back, where he lay on a stretcher. I sat up; anyone looking through the rear window would see only a paramedic in a white coat.

At exactly ten o'clock Cranko lifted us on the air cushion and backed out of the garage.

Jackson was interested. "A hovercraft ambulance! It doesn't sound economical."

"It comes cheaper than maintaining good surfaces over thousands of kilometers of country roads."

That shocked him. "Is the country so poor?"

"Every country is poor. There are too many people to feed and clothe and house and too much necessity to conserve all natural resources. And I mean all, Arthur. We don't have anything we don't need."

He fell silent. Cranko took us around the northern end of City Center, through the decaying western sub-urbs and on to the Ballarat Road. There he cut in the turbobooster and the screeching siren and we belted up the highway, an ambulance on its mission of mercy to some call from the countryside, its balance system holding it level on a road so neglected that it would soon have wrecked the suspension of a wheeled car at any decent speed.

He drove fast and when he slowed and stopped, still suspended on the air cushion, I checked my watch and opened the sliding hatch to the driver's cabin. "You're three minutes early."

"Doesn't matter," he said, "because they're here."

They were indeed. Looking slantwise through the hatch I could see the red nose of a car alongside us and heard the doors slam as people got out of it. It was a wheeled vehicle and I thought they must have started very early, driving slowly and carefully on the ruined road, to keep the appointment. It would be a slow trip from here on, but at least Beltane had had the wit not to send one of his official, blatantly identifiable hovercars.

I helped Arthur to his feet and was reaching for my suitcases when somebody hammered on the rear door and yelled for us to hurry up and come out.

What prompted me to murmur to Jackson, "Answer him," while I shifted the gun from its belt holster to the right-hand pocket of my white coat is not easily pinned; the mind works faster than it can trace its movements. The sense of wrongness could have been born of the thought that staff from the Manor would not hammer and bawl but be discreet and polite. Be that right or wrong, I was alerted and it is a firm memory that I recognized at once what the wrongness might portend and whose would be the responsibility.

Jackson called, "Coming!" and undid the double door. As he pushed one wing open I hissed, "Stand aside," but he either did not understand me or was bewildered. I caught a glimpse of an orderly's white coat like my own, but the rest of the man was obscured as Jackson hesitated on the sill, hesitating because he saw what I could not, that the man held a gun.

The gunman yelled at him, "Come out of it, quick!" and gestured with his gun hand so that now I glimpsed the weapon, too.

I dragged Jackson out of the way with my left hand and shot at the gunman through the pocket of my coat. I did not expect to hit him with a hurried, half-aimed round, only to surprise him for a second while I freed my gun—but hit him I did. He stepped back, clutching his side, tripped on the rough road surface and sat down hard, dropping his gun.

There was no time to think because he was not alone and the second man was moving to get a shot at me

through the open door. The luck went my way; my gun
was free and firing before he was sure of me, and that
shot was better aimed. It took him in the throat, in the
artery.

I jumped down to the road and kicked the first
thug's gun away from his scrabbling fingers before I
peeped cautiously round the side of the ambulance to
see Cranko sidling the length of the bus towards me.

Behind me Jackson said, with no sign of panic, "I'll
get that gun, Harry. You carry on." A tough old bird in
every way.

I called to Cranko, giving nothing away, I hoped, "It's
all right, Doc. Enemy dispersed."

In the light from the ambulance he was white to the
gills and had every right to be. He glanced at the dead
man, saw there was nothing to be done for him and
looked to the other who sat glaring at his own weapon
as Jackson covered him.

"Kidnap job," I said.

He answered shakily, "Yes."

"Incompetent. They should have sent you to open
the doors."

"Me?"

"Their bad manners made me suspicious."

He breathed deeply and some color seeped back into
his face. "I'd better see to this one."

"Do. Keep him alive to regret it."

The ambulance had been, through all of this, resting on its hoverjets. Now, without warning, it moved
sharply away, gathered speed and shot down the road,
leaving me to gaze after it like a slack-jawed nitwit and
howl, "Christ! There were three of them!"

Cranko had known it. And knew now that in failure
the driver had abandoned him.

The runaway lifted the hovercar over the post-and-
wire fence and into the empty field where the wheeled
car could not follow. I put three useless shots through

the windscreen as it swung past me but probably hit
nobody; the resilient glass would show only little round
holes, no impediment to the driver's vision. The ambulance headlights vanished round the hump of a low rise
and that was the end of the snatch.

Cranko spoke, in the tentative voice of a man who
must speak though he has nothing useful to say. "Did
you think of the possibility of this, Harry?"

"Of a planned hijack? No." I had nothing to say to
Cranko just yet; later, a great deal. I noted the registration number of the red car though I did not imagine that
its owner's name would tell us anything save perhaps
that it had no history. I asked Cranko, "Can you drive
this thing?"

"I don't know. It's one of the old hydrogen burners
with a gearbox. I don't think so."

I wasn't sure that I could drive it either.

Jackson said he had driven the same type in his
younger days but never on a road surface like the mess
we were stranded on. He wondered about the ambulance: "A very distinctive vehicle for a getaway bus."

It was perfect for the job; it could go almost anywhere unquestioned; the driver could dump it outside
a hospital and simply walk away. "And the doctor
here will have to account to the ambulance service
for it."

Cranko looked round from his bandaging of the
wounded man's side. "Beltane's responsibility, I'd
think. This man may have a broken rib."

I said, "You can be lucky," meaning my shooting as
much as the victim of it. He was a smallish ratface
of the typically undernourished breed that swarms in
some areas as though the state's balanced diet did not
work with particular people. He made no attempt to
protest or complain; he would be most conscious of
his duty to his employers, who might well be far more
fearsome than we. He would know little of any use,

would have been hired for the job and told only what he needed to know—almost nothing—and was philosophical as Cranko ripped his shirt off his back and tore it into a pad and bandage. After all, my wild shot could have killed him as surely as the next round had slaughtered his mate.

Then a brilliance of headlights swept out of the distance and in a few minutes the premier's distinctive hovercar (he had not been so longsighted after all) pulled alongside us with two men peering from the cabin. The driver called out, "Have you seen an ambulance anywhere along here?"

Jackson's tensions erupted in temper. "Yes, and so would you if you'd been on time!"

The driver was indignant. "A couple of bloody minutes is all! Who the hell are you, anyway?" Then he spotted the two hijackers laid out behind us and dug furiously at his mate's ribs. "Look, Gus! Look there!" He yelled at us, "What's been goin' on?"

That was the panic sound of a peaceable man confronted by violence and wanting no part in it. A wounded man and another with his blood spreading black in the headlights, fronted by two men with guns, was enough to unnerve a quiet citizen. He told his offsider, "We're gettin' outa here, Gus," and the car edged backwards.

The headlights dazzled vision, but I thought that the offsider hit him with a swinging open hand and reached for the controls. The hovercar settled to the roadway with a sigh of failing air. The offsider jumped down and came towards me, watching the gun rather than myself.

He was a tall man, fortyish, wide in the shoulders but flat chested and stringy, one of the long-boned types with no fat and little flesh. The immediately noticeable thing about him was the gentleness, verging on sweetness, of his narrow, bony face. It sat poorly with the gray uniform of a private security firm with a reputation for toughness.

He stopped two meters away. "That's a police issue gun you got there. What's your name?"

"Detective-Sergeant Ostrov."

"ID?"

I showed him and he called back to the car, "Come out, Willy; they're on our side." He counted us and looked round to see there were no more. "We got to pick up two. Who's the freeloaders?"

The driver came cautiously near. "Is one of you Mr. Jackson?"

"I am and I have no documents. I can't prove it."

I said, "I vouch for him." The Jackson face wakened no recognition in the Manor servant. "You can take us all to the Manor."

"Mr. Beltane said two."

"And the copper says all of us."

He looked sideways at the dead man. "Not him."

"He can go in the boot."

"Not in my boot! You don't have to clean up after."

A spasm of glee took the gentleness from the face of the security man; the reverse side of his nature was enjoying itself. He returned to benignity to ask what had happened and I told him, briefly. He stared at Jackson. "What'd they want him for?"

"Tell me and we'll both know."

His face flickered to hard suspicion; he did not believe me. He was not your usual eight-hour shift, disinterested operative. "Not my business, eh?"

"Not yet," I said. It sounded like a half promise of confidences later on, enough to soothe for the moment. "Give me a hand with this bloke."

He took the dead man's feet and I the shoulders, letting the blood stain my coat rather than his uniform. As we dumped him in the boot we could hear the driver complaining that he was a chauffeur, not a bloody commando. Gus, the security man, winked happily. "You ought to see the blood 'n' guts vids he watches."

"Home, James," I told the driver as we climbed into the passenger compartment. He slew me with a look but got into the cabin and started to lift.

We had a superbly comfortable ride, all of us but Ratface. Cranko's bandaging was less efficient than his surgery and the stripped shirt leaked blood onto the upholstery. Poor Willy!

The hovercar was a work-on-the-run model with folding seats and tables for conference, a panel vid with a capacity for direct communication worldwide and a soundproof glass shield between the driver's cabin and the passenger compartment. Willy was competent once his mouth was shut; apparently holding the map in his head, he went cross-country to hit the city limit in ten minutes, then ran us sedately along the urban roads.

I thought it best not to challenge Cranko immediately; if he had a gun concealed and was fool enough to use it, the results could be disastrous for all in a moving vehicle. He sat still and silent; for a man who must know that he was now a sacrificial goat he was remarkably calm. I watched for recognition between him and Ratface, but there was none. In good planning it was unlikely that they would know each other.

I asked him, as much to end the silence as from curiosity, "What is biophysics?"

The question surprised him; he had been expecting anything but chitchat and he had to think himself into the sociable mode. "The application of the laws of physics to biology. You gave a couple of basic examples to Jackson."

I had forgotten that an ambulance driver's cabin has microphone connection with the casualty compartment. "So it's nothing new?"

"Quite old, a nearly useless term not often heard."

"Good for naming an institute. Yet who needs a ten-storey tower to measure muscle tension or heat dilation?"

"Nobody, Harry, I'm sure."

All right, I was being laughed at. "So?"

"That's privileged information which I won't give you." His smile was frankly malicious.

Jackson listened but kept blessedly quiet.

The hovercar slowed and turned left into Royal Park. We were within minutes of the Manor, and now Cranko made a last show of impudence. He snapped on the intercom mike and said, "You can put me down here, driver. I'll pick up public transport. The premier is not expecting me."

My turn to smile. "No! Dr. Cranko will stay with us."

"Mr. Cranko," he corrected gently. "I am a surgeon."

"Mr. Cranko knows he is needed."

He sighed elaborately, "One has to try." He looked out to the lights of the Manor. "Do you know," he asked, "that once the state premiers lived in their own homes instead of in these high-tech palaces?"

I did not know. He carried on: "The rise of ultra-sophisticated electronic eavesdropping techniques and the consequent employment of ever more expensive countering equipment made the protection of private homes impossibly costly, so each state built itself a single high-tech luxury prison for its premier and con-gratulated itself that the secrets of official intrigue, cor-ruption and skulduggery were safe from newsbugs and Wardies."

He cocked an eyebrow. To a born playactor I could only feed his next cue. "And the moral of that is?"

"That nobody and nothing can protect the man with a death wish. All the wizardry of the world's protective devices could not save Beltane once he set a course no technology could smother or disguise. Brain or no brain, he's a born idiot. The question for all of us is: How many will he drag to destruction with him? And you, his faithful hound, can't do a damned thing to help him."

"Mr. Jackson's faithful hound, not Beltane's."

"Of course, Jackson's. That could be worse. Don't let loyalty hobble your feet when it's time to run."

No tour of duty had ever taken me to the Manor, and in the night I gained only an impression of extravagant spaciousness with few lighted windows in long, low walls. The wide lawns were floodlit, but the lights were strategically aimed to dazzle the incomer rather than to reveal the building. All there was to see amounted to dimness and size.

The car swung round the house and halted at a back entrance. The driver's offsider came to open my door. I said to Cranko, "It is not yet time for you to run. Don't do anything to alarm me. I'd enjoy shooting you—in the knee."

He came cautiously after me, keeping his hands in sight, but made an effort at jauntiness. "I didn't really need to escape. Nobody in this fool's paradise can harm me."

He was wrong about that; I was capable of harming him very badly if it could gain me anything. We have good policemen and bad ones, talented men and misfits, the overrighteous and the corrupt, but we all respond identically to an insult to our professionalism, and Cranko had no idea of the illwill I bore his treachery.

Jackson came out behind him and murmured to me, "First time I've ever seen the back door—that I remember."

I told glum Willy to leave the corpse in the boot until we had decided how to deal with it. "And both of you keep your mouths shut to the rest of the staff. Not one word. Not one!"

Willy shepherded us through the Manor passages,

radiating sulky resentment, and ushered us into a large room, part lounge and part office. I glimpsed a sound-screen strip in the lintel and felt the familiar *cluck* in the ears as we passed through the door. Premier Jeremy Beltane sat morosely behind a desk, facing two mixed bloods, both of whom I recognized.

The driver grasped at his moment of safe spite. "There's four of 'em, sir, not two. And there's another one, dead. The copper shot 'im."

The mixed bloods stared, not understanding, while I silently cursed the gabbling ass.

Beltane gave no sign of hearing him. His dull eyes livened as he surveyed his disheveled father; he smiled and nodded, then controlled himself and turned to Willy, as if the chauffeur had said nothing untoward. "Very well. Good night." To the security man he was more civil. "Thank you for your assistance. You can return to your duties."

6

Ostrov: All Through
the Night—

The three-parts Koori, Richard Kenney, a shadow minister in the Opposition, I knew only from print photos and the occasional vid talk show; he was best known for his moral integrity and his political antipathy for Beltane, whom he had once described as "not worth the snot of his father's sneeze." The speaker had suspended him when he refused to withdraw the remark. So, what was he doing in the premier's home? Labour and Liberal members were said to drink together in the House bar after sessions of invective that would disgrace a gay whore's pimp, but I could not imagine it of Kenney and Beltane.

More peculiarly, what was either doing in the company of Barney Fielding? Fielding I had run across three, four years earlier when attached for a while to the Balaclava station, and I knew him for one of those fakes with so many false faces that he no longer knew which was real. He was a doctor, downgraded for malpractice, who worked now (and, admittedly, worked well for a dog's income) among the Wardies, looked

and dressed like a Wardie, talked like a Minder and
dealt industriously in forged food and clothing coupons. The local coppers knew it but left him alone
as long as he did not exceed a reasonable limit of
criminality and because he was often good for useful
information with a minimum of arm twisting. He was,
at bottom, a self-important twit with little nerve.

Strangely Kenney, with a much greater inheritance
of Koori blood, was the lighter skinned of the two;
you had to look twice to see the legacy alive there.
Fielding, much darker, showed his one-quarter heritage
more plainly. The genetic dance plays tricks.

Accepted wisdom says that the mixed breeds stick
together, having little feeling for black or white but
much sorrow for themselves as swimmers in limbo.
Like most accepted wisdom it is only half true, but I
could think of no other reason why these two should be
together; Kenney's ferocious honesty would not waste
spit on the dishonored doctor.

I had to wait a little while for answers, because Beltane asked them to excuse him while he dealt with
an emergency, meaning us, and summoned a Manor
security man to escort them to another room.

If they were a puzzle, Beltane was a disaster; he
crouched at his desk, arms flat on the surface, fingers
rigidly bent as if to claw the wood, shoulders drooping
and startled eyes crying out bewilderment and despair.
There was nothing of the little bull in him that night.

He gestured to all of us to sit down and asked Jackson,
"Are you all right?" At Jackson's "Yes," he turned to me.
"What happened?"

When I had finished he swung like a dead-weary
man between thankfulness and anger. "I appreciate
your quick action, Sergeant, but there was a lack of
forethought—"

Jackson broke in on him, an outraged father berating
his son. "You are ungrateful and ignorant!"

"Am I? If you say so, Dad. Perhaps I am. I am also harassed by human rats."

I told him, "You had one right in your nest." I indicated Cranko. "Him."

Cranko had been tense; now he relaxed, with the first and greatest revelation over.

"Dr. Cranko? But he has—" He shut off whatever had been on his tongue and shook with a psychic fever, clutched his arms across his chest like a man about to crumble in bitter cold, but fell suddenly calm to say in a wondering voice, "My father taught me that betrayal always comes from a friend. I should have remembered."

Cranko said coldly, "Indeed you should," and there was nothing vague or offhanded about him now.

Beltane asked, "How do you know, Sergeant?" and I told him how Cranko and only Cranko had known our route plan and known it early enough to alert an ambush.

Cranko grinned at me, not as a friend. "And who gave me the knowledge, Harry? I wouldn't be in your smugly virtuous shoes for a fortune."

He would keep; his score was mounting for payment.

Beltane said to him, "Shut your trap until I want you to talk," but he was out of his depth. He asked me, "What must I do with him?"

"Hold him here. He has questions to answer."

"Hold him? That is for the police."

"I am the police."

"Yes. But—"

"You have a private security force here. And rooms with locks, surely? Realize, sir, that you have had a secret stolen from under you and Cranko is a link in a chain of thieves. Also, there's a dead man to be accounted for. We must control damage as much as possible by letting no word escape from the Manor.

These two may earn their food as hostages to keep wagging tongues outside from giving you away. So keep them!"

Beltane turned to wounded Ratface for the first time. "Who are you?"

Ratface, whose side must have been an aching torment, pulled his jacket gently round his shoulders. "Name don't matter."

"He'll tell me," I said, "when I'm ready to ask him. Won't you, son?"

" 'Spose so. Lotta good it'll do yers."

True; he was a nobody, probably a stray gun picked up for the job.

"Lock him up, too, sir, but keep them apart."

Beltane said into his desk console, "Will the chief security officer please report to the Small Office."

Through all of this Jackson had sprawled on a sofa, gaze darting like a hunting wasp from face to face. Now he said, "I gather my incognito is broken to some person or group, but what are those two Koori doing here?" To Beltane's stare of helplessness he persisted, "You're open to political blackmail now, aren't you?"

"Yes."

Cranko laughed.

"Well?"

Beltane said slowly, "Nothing is well. I've had two severe blows and my brain has slowed to a halt. Dad, please do something for me."

"Isn't that what I'm here for?"

"Then go to bed, Dad. Please!"

Jackson bristled like an enraged terrier; I fancied the hair rising behind his ears. "To bed, is it? Knowing nothing! Your plans fall apart and you tell me to go to bed!"

"When I can, I'll tell you everything I know. Just now I'm not sure what is truth and what is confusion. Please, Dad!"

Something of the implicit understanding I had observed at the institute seeped into the angry space
between them, and Jackson quieted, accepting a need
for him to shut up and agree. He gave a surly, "Very well,
then," and to me, "How much do you know, Harry!"

"Not a lot."

"Your job involves keeping me informed, doesn't
it?"

Sneaky old devil. "Where necessary."

"When you feel like it, eh? Do you also want me in
bed and out of the way?"

"Yes, sir."

"Bloody Ape!"

I recognized Beltane's chief of security when she
came in. Like so many private security people she was
ex-police, working for better wages and conditions than
the regular service could earn her, and I remembered
seeing her here and there in the past. Jeanette somebody or other; I had forgotten the surname.

Beltane asked was Jackson's room prepared and she
said it was. "Then please escort him to it."

I said, "Seeing what has happened tonight, he had
better have a guard on his quarters."

"Besides yourself?"

"I also have to sleep sometime."

He told Jeanette, "See to it, please. Also, I want these
other two locked in and guarded—most securely guarded. Separately."

Escorting Jackson out, she paused by me, scowling.
"So you're the undercover man. I remember you."
She said to me what she could not say to Beltane:
"Please keep in mind that my manpower is limited,
fully employed and entitled to be paid overtime for
additional work."

I didn't bother to answer. Overtime might be written
into their contracts, but they would be lucky ever to see
the cash; their jobs could be filled too easily.

Beltane called to her retreating back, "On your way, please ask the two Koori gentlemen to step back in here."

She sent two standard issue plug-uglies to take Cranko and Ratface away. Cranko went with the insouciance of one who thinks himself untouchable, Ratface with the resignation of the recidivist who has seen it all before.

When we were alone Beltane said, "I apologize for trying to put blame on you. You had no choice but to depend on Cranko." The words came slowly, as sad discoveries. "You could not have suspected him."

Rankling, I said, "I should have suspected everyone."

"Don't beat your breast; there's no time for it. And it smacks of self-righteousness."

That again. And here it was surely unjust. (Or was it? Later. To be thought about later.)

He asked, "What sort of man are you?"

How do you answer such a question? "I do my work."

"Including killing?"

"Tonight? That was unusual. I had to act. Your father's life and perhaps my own . . ."

"It worried you?"

"No time for worry, sir. I just did it."

"I did not mean the risk to your life; I meant the act of killing. Did that worry you?"

That one certainly hadn't. "No, sir. Should it?"

"A life snuffed out, by your hand, and there is no reason for you to be concerned?"

"No, sir." He expected a specific response, but what? I plucked a rationalization out of memory. "My father tells me that when he was young there was talk of the sacredness of life, as if it was to be treated as a . . . as a precious thing . . . like a work of art perhaps. But the fact is, it's more like a disease on the planet. With five times too many of us now, what does one less matter?

It matters to me if I'm the one to be made less, or my mum and dad, but who else cares? So what does it matter if one gets knocked off? There's twelve billion more infesting the place."

He had listened with close interest. "Do all the Ward people think like that?"

"They don't think about it at all. Death is just something that happens, so they make the best of what little life they have and don't give a bugger about the people next door! I'd think the Minders are much the same. Life's basically selfish."

He did not answer but explored my face with an unsettling intentness, as if from within him a Martian was examining his first Earth human.

When he had done surveying me—or perhaps himself—Beltane said, "First things first. My daughter has disappeared and I must find her quickly. Very quickly. Last Sunday—"

"I know. Nguyen told me."

"Did he, indeed? I wonder why."

"So that I might not work in a vacuum. And perhaps he thought finding her might be a job for me."

Kenney and Fielding came quietly in and sat down.

He nodded aimlessly at his hands stretched across the desk. "Why not? This man—" he nodded at Fielding "—had her and lost her. He is a doctor."

"I know him. He is also a manipulator of forged coupons and an occasional police informer. Poor stuff."

Fielding looked through me as if I were not there.

Beltane was unsurprised. "Then he has manipulated beyond his capacity. Mr. Kenney here is a member of the state parliamentary Opposition. He is, within his limits, an honest man. He is also a politician who sees an opportunity to apply pressure—but his lever has vanished into the Wards and his conscience is restless."

Kenney said mildly, "I would have brought her to

you, J.B.; I am not a hostage taker. The weapon was my knowledge of her condition, not the girl herself."

"Don't expect understanding and fair play from me, Dick, while I suffer abduction, treachery and blackmail. Sergeant Ostrov, I need my daughter back in this house; these two are all the information I have and I do not know how to use them." He added in a meandering tone, "You come highly recommended."

He threw himself back in the chair, folding his hands in his lap and watching me as though I might answer with a blaze of Holmesian deduction. Feeling like an actor pushed on camera without a script, I delivered the first apposite line to come to my head: "Who is your daughter's boyfriend?"

The three of them said together, in varying degrees of disapproval and prurience, "Fred Blacker." Fielding pursued with a small man's malice, "The gardener's boy."

"Your gardener, sir?"

Beltane smiled sourly. "A junior in the vegetable section. I can't say I have ever seen him."

Why should he have? Every home has its vegetable patch as a matter of necessity, but I didn't imagine the premier helped with the watering and weeding.

"Where does he live? In your area, Barney?"

"Yes, but he's gone off with the girl. And just remember, Sergeant, I haven't done anything wrong." He reconsidered. "Nothing criminal. I'm not going to be held responsible for any of this."

"Not if you can wriggle round it. What did you do?"

His account was probably truthful in pinpointing Mrs. Blacker as the silly complicating force . . . but not so silly when you know Wardie life. You have to live in that condition of tribal, hand-to-mouth wretchedness, knowing there will be no improvement in your lifetime, before you can understand and condone the wrenching tug of loyalty versus self-preservation that bedevils their actions, in eternal fear of the mindless, pitiless law.

The most revealing thing he said was that Melissa didn't give a damn for the love-blind Fred but was hell-bent on preserving his baby. No, her baby, the father didn't come into it. Barney thought she had got all her sex knowledge from the other girls at school—and knew just enough to fall into trouble without knowing how to avoid it or enjoy it.

"Where do you think she went, Barney?"

"If I knew where I'd be chasing her myself."

"How old is the boy?"

"Seventeen."

"Does he run with a gang?"

"You know better than that. They push 'em out when they take a job."

True. A working man's responsibilities make him undependable.

"How long has he been working?"

"A year or so."

"And before that?"

"He ran with the Handspikes for a while."

I had to think quickly over what little I remembered of the Handspikes while keeping Barney thinking I was a jump ahead of him. "They ran a bunch of teenage prostitutes. Headquarters in the disused railway cutting through Alma Park. Good place for a pregnant girl to hide out. You would have thought of that." A tiny facial tic flickered and twitched as he considered denying contact with the local gangies. "You would, wouldn't you?"

He caved in resentfully. "They said they don't see Fred and they've never heard of Melissa."

"They wouldn't tell you if they had, particularly if she offered them money—real Minder money that buys things coupons can't get."

He had been stupid to go near them and knew it. "Maybe."

"Did she have money?"

"How should I know? If she did, Ma Blacker would have had it off her quick smart."

Possibly, but I guessed that Ma Blacker would have thought twice about rough-handling her son's beloved. He was the family provider, by Barney's account.

I thought the Handspikes might be worth another visit.

I turned to Kenney, more from curiosity than with any expectation of extracting a clue from him. "Tell me about your end of the transaction, Mr. Kenney."

Kenney rounded on Beltane. "Is he really a police-man, J.B.? Are you out of your mind? Why not make the girl's condition public while you are about it?"

Beltane said, "I thought that was your intention; I want to forestall it. The police are searching for her and for young Blacker but do not know of the preg-nancy. Sergeant Ostrov knows but will not betray a confidence."

"Can't," I said, reminding him that loyalty can be an artificial condition.

Kenney did not understand the subtext but needled where he could. "A private commission, J.B.? Your own personal copper, bodyguard, hatchet man? Have you come to that?"

Beltane sounded tired to death. "Please, Dick, just tell him what you can."

So now I heard how bumbling Barney tried to bar-ter the premier's daughter for respectability and how Kenney dragged him to the Manor to confess that his ineptitude had lost her.

Barney opened up his store of spite. "You meant to blackmail the premier by threatening to expose the pregnancy. Premier trying to cover up a birth! It'll sound fine on the vid and in the House, won't it? And fine in the Wards, too, where a concealed birth brings jail sentences and a dead child! The Wardies'll love finding out that their hero thinks he's above the law."

Beltane seemed unmoved, but Kenney observed him with a faint contempt.

I said, "I think they'll sympathize." There was an almost physical sensation of Kenney switching his attention to me. Which was what I had wanted.

Barney sneered, "Then you don't know the Wards."

"I was born and raised in them."

Kenney asked, "Are you saying, Sergeant, that the Wards will not turn against the premier if they see him as conniving at an illegal birth?"

"Wardies live on emotion more than reason. They like a premier who has diverted funds to their food and clothing instead of setting up projects that mean nothing to them—scientific research, road repair, higher education—the things they regard as Minders' perks. They see him on their side, giving them something, so they'll forgive him for getting into the kind of human trouble they get into themselves. If they didn't like him they'd call it a Minder crime and yell for his blood; but he's a mate, so it will be just a peccadillo."

"Interesting." Kenney, frowning and thoughtful, became suddenly all Koori, remote and concentrated, "thinking black" as the Wardies call it. Then the white politician in him returned. "I was born Minder; we don't understand the Wardie thinking as well as we should."

"How can you if you don't talk to them?" I knew the conventional answer to that: Give the Wardies a decision-making responsibility, and in the ten million–voiced argument nothing will ever get done. It might have been the right answer, but historically democracy has been successful. I suppose each age has its own givens.

"So you think I have nothing to bargain with?"

"You might make it stick in the House, but I think

not in the Wards. There you might get demonstrations and blood in the gutters." I decided to lean on him a little. "Besides, you weren't bargaining with the premier, were you? It was blackmail, wasn't it? What did you want as the price of your silence?"

He said only, "Prove it."

"I will if I'm pushed to it."

"Manufactured evidence?"

"If the premier agrees that it was moral blackmail, some form of proof can be found."

"Do you think you can frighten me?"

"Yes."

He turned to Beltane. "J.B., will you get your leech off my back?"

"No. Why should I? He's right." The unexpected support had enlivened him. Kenney retired into his Koori fastness to consider his position as attacker under attack, while Beltane called again for Jeanette.

He told her to take Fielding away and see that he was watched. "Not with Cranko," I interjected. "We don't want him picking up clues about the hijack; he talks too freely."

Barney put on his Minder front as an insulted gentleman but had more sense than to object. She shepherded his dignity briskly out, raging at her multiplying surveillance problems.

Kenney returned from his far country. "I agree that the less that fumbler knows the better for everybody."

I pointed out that I also had no true knowledge of the situation between himself and the premier.

"Better that you don't, Sergeant."

Beltane disagreed. "He needs to know a little. I have to make a decision, to throw my weight for or against a certain proposition. Mr. Kenney thinks to control my decision by holding my daughter's pregnancy over me. Be sure that he will not do so, one way or the other. It is a decision which will affect . . . people . . . outside as well as inside Australia." He paused before he added, with a stolid refusal of emotion, "It is more than should be required of one man."

Remembering his conversation with Jackson at the instituto, I had a hazy and unpleasant idea of the scope of the decision but not its precise nature. I did not want to know that; I did not want to be locked with Beltane in some secret that ate at the roots of nations.

Kenney said, "I think you will live through it, J.B."

I was less sure. Beltane needed his father, that old pragmatist who would return the world snarl for snarl and carry the son with him. He asked, "Would it be of any use to inquire, Dick, where you obtained your information on the subjects discussed at Canberra?"

"Just ask who wants your job."

"All of them, even the talentless."

"And treachery begins at the top, as usual."

"Don't offer me pity, Dick."

"That I will not. The Koori, to whom I should belong if I did not carry a white smell with me, are not a pitying people. In their universe all things have their place and proper behavior; a man fails because of something less than a full recognition of his place in the scheme. That does not command pity."

I found that less than comprehensible, but Beltane seemed interested. He said to me, "Go and talk to Cranko, Sergeant; see what you can get out of him."

"If you insist, but he wouldn't have been left behind if he knew anything useful. I'd rather take a turn round the house; I need to know the layout if I'm to guard Mr. Jackson."

"Do what you need to do." He had more on his mind than the routines of a Wardie copper.

I looked in at nearby rooms to find Cranko placidly reading a book, Fielding sulking and frightened as imagination magnified brutal possibilities, Ratface asleep and comfortably snoring. One of Jeanette's men sat, bored stiff, outside each door.

The huge house was quiet as a museum, but in a sort of communication-center-cum-armory that they called the wardroom I found some off-duty security guards playing poker for food coupons—probably forgeries but, under the circumstances, not worth making a police fuss about. I introduced myself; they were all retired coppers or time-served soldiers and received me with resignation. Private security groups have their extralegal methods just as police have theirs, and the private men have no wish to be dogged by the force with bigger boots.

Only Willy's hovercar offsider did not sourly resent me, so I asked him to give me a guided tour of the Manor, and he threw in his hand without complaining. Just then, Jeanette returned from settling Jackson for the night, and she was furious. "I have exactly four men for each operating shift, Sergeant, and you now have one complete shift looking after your police affairs! If you need more, call on your own department."

You can't argue with an angry woman, especially when she is in the right. I took my guide and escaped.

First I wanted to know where Jackson was, and he led me straight there. "He's asleep," said the security man at the door. I looked in to note the relevant details of the room, but there was nothing to query or object to, so we moved on.

Kostakis (like half the population, he was second- or third-generation European) knew what I wanted and led me very efficiently round the doors, windows and ducts. There were, he told me, sixteen security men on six-hour shifts of four, one indoors on each shift and three patrolling outdoors; all doors were fitted with metal and explosive detectors, all windows shielded against high-frequency radiation and sound-snooping. . . . . "All the usual junk," he said. "Only better quality and more of it."

His threatening, gravel voice contrasted coarsely with his peaceable, kindly face.

I had expected the Manor to be expensively appointed, luxurious as one of the "great homes" preserved by the National Trust but, save for its size and the proliferation of communication gear and computerware, it was little more impressive than any average Minder home. When you stop to think about it, the difference between a Minder home and a Wardie tenement is that one has enough of everything and it is all in good condition, while the other has just enough to get by on and the place is usually falling down around its dwellers. Nobody these days is really loaded with treasure on Earth, but Beltane seemed to do with less than he could easily have had.

The only relief in all the functional blandness was the pictures on the walls. The corridors and rooms were hung with them, not in great numbers but with enough to bring a fresh one into view at every turning. I found Beltane's taste frustrating and dully modish.

"Does Beltane own all these or do they go with the Manor?"

"They're his. All the regular Manor stuff went back to the art galleries that lent them."

"So there's an expensive private investment in this lot?"

"Nah! I don't reckon he's got much to spare while he's keeping an absent wife in style. She lives better than him. These are all repros. Good repros, though."

He spoke as though he appreciated the stuff; to me it was wholly uninteresting. I have never been able to whip up a taste for collages of scraps of cloth and paper or infinitely receding depictions of a hand drawing a hand drawing a hand down to a microscopic blot,

or even the surreal, cubist and impenetrable works of
the previous century. My taste comes to a dead stop
somewhere about nineteen hundred, in the recognizable world.

I said, "They mean nothing to me."

"They didn't to me at first."

"Now they do?"

"Some of 'em. You see 'em every day and they start
to get meaning. It's—what's a word for it? It's elusive,
as if it was peeping from behind a door and would duck
back if you didn't cop it right away."

The grass-roots Wardie art critic is a satirist's commonplace, but Kostakis's language struggled for expression without pretending to knowledge.

In a long corridor hung with a dozen of the irritating
things but otherwise unfurnished, I stopped at a fan of
graded blue tints, all anchored to a single yellow eye
from which a drop of blood fell infuriatingly upward.
"Does that mean anything to you?"

"Yersss. I don't like it much but it means."

"What?"

"Nah, you have to see for yourself. It'll mean something different for you because you aren't me; you're
somebody else. You've got different eyes in your soul—
or whatever."

I began to warm to Kostakis; I have a soft spot for
the oddities that turn up in commonplace exteriors.
"Doesn't he have any ordinary pictures—paintings of
scenes of people or such?"

"You mean representational?" I was sure he had discovered and polished up that word for use on the occasional willing listener. "Have a look in his bedroom,
right here."

Bedrooms breathe in personality from their users, but
this had none, unless you count plain utility as a positive statement. The furnishings were a three-quarter
bed, a desk, a chair and a small vidscreen. Opposite

the door was the bed; the other two walls were glass-
fronted cupboards—one a wardrobe, the other a reposi-
tory of massive bound books.

Kostakis pivoted heel-and-toe in the middle of the
room, playing the tourist guide. "The whole man's here.
This is what he is. Start with the bed."

"Three-quarter. Nothing unusual."

"Single bed for loner, double bed for married man,
but three-quarter bed for a lonely bloke with an occasional short-time visitor. In, out, see yer later!"

Crude psychology, but probably near enough for a
man deserted long ago. The library cupboard was
daunting—Hansard, law, sociology, legal history and
philosophy, the sciences—and, in the bottom right-
hand corner as if ashamed of its frivolity, a complete
Shakespeare in single annotated volumes.

"Works here at night. Gets up all hours and plows
into it at the desk there. Doesn't sleep enough."

Yes, this was part of the man who had come to the
institute in the early morning; he could be equated with
this. I said, "No pictures."

The gravel voice chided, "Should be ashamed of
yourself, Sergeant, not noticin'. Black mark!"

Indeed I should have noticed what was not a normal
fitting, the rectangular outline of a flap flush with the
wall and the same color, some three meters long and
twenty centimeters high. Only hairlines betrayed it but
I should have noticed.

Kostakis lifted it up and small lights came on, one for
each of the fifteen small pictures revealed. I recognized
the subject because van Gogh is one of the few artists
whose peculiar techniques seem not at all peculiar to
me, whose despairing expressions of himself call as
loudly across a couple of centuries as on the day he
rammed the thick paint onto canvas or board or card
or whatever he could afford.

They were fifteen self-portraits reproduced as small,

cheap prints and hidden in a premier's bedroom. I knew them all, knew them well; they told me how Vincent felt, lost in a world with no understanding of him. They spoke to me because I sometimes woke in the night with all my misapprehensions of the world astride my chest like a black dog, reminding me that all I knew of life was its visible face, while the deep truth of it lay in signs I could not translate, perhaps not perceive.

These were all painted during the tormented last two years of his life, when insanity came and went, and unhappy clear hours alternated with the furious times of power and twisted vision, so that he painted Vincent normal and gentle and almost colorless in his sane self, and Vincent flame haired and bare boned and brute eyed in his insanity. The degrees of his madness can be traced in the swirling-flame backgrounds to his haunted heads, at its worst when the flames flow out of the background to eat at his face and clothes.

This was what Beltane hid in his bedroom as others hide the pornographic wishes of easier needs.

"That's the boss," Kostakis said. "That's him all right. I've been five years here, watchin' him as things go right and go wrong, and that's him."

"You think he's mad?"

"Nah! Not him, never that. Just lost. I reckon it's all too much for him."

That was surely true of the crisis of the moment; perhaps he shouldn't be blamed for wanting to throw himself in Daddy's lap.

I had seen enough; I had a diagrammatic idea of the Manor's exits, entrances and defenses. "Let's go back to the office area." On impulse, perhaps because the man showed a quirky brand of insight, I asked Kostakis, "Would you like to help me with an interrogation?"

He was wary. "You mean the two-clowns act—you nasty copper, me good bloke?"

"No. Just be there and put in your coupon's worth if anything suggests itself."

"Anything you say, but I'm just professional muscle; I'm not up on political shit."

I could not picture his skinniness as a strong-arm bouncer, but there can be deflating surprises in these gangling types. "Who mentioned politics?"

"That's all there is in this morgue."

Perhaps, but they were entwined with more mundane matters of which I needed independent opinion. We moved into the corridor, where I could see anyone approaching, and I asked, "What sort of a lad is Fred Blacker?"

"Why him? What's about him? All right, all right, it's your business. Young Fred—gardener's assistant, good build on him, good manners—surprise, surprise— easygoing but not a lot of brains, not so they show, anyway. Good kid if he can keep out of trouble."

"What sort of trouble?"

He hesitated a split second too long; his answer was relevant but not the answer he first thought of. "Fred's just out of the teen-gang stage, and they can call on old members if they need them for something—like a big gang stoush or special talents or whatever. You know what it's like in the Wards—don't let your old mates down, remember they looked after you, you may be off strength because you're workin', but you still live here, you're still a gangie at heart, Freddo. It's a load of shit, but it gets to them."

"Did he tell you he was a gangie?"

"You know they don't tell. They swear an oath on the arsehole of a dead chook or some stupid thing and never to break it, so strike me dead. But when a sweaty boy wears a shirt in the sun instead of UV barrier grease it's because he's hiding something—like, say, the gut tattoo some Wardie gangs wear round the navel."

"What else would get him into trouble?"

"How do you mean?"

"What were you going to tell me before you changed your mind?"

"Clever bastard, aren't you?"

"Not very; just well trained." I had no idea how much was known by the Manor staff, but experience suggested that they kept a gossipy eye on more private matters than their employer imagined. I asked, "Would it be possible for Fred to be having it off with Melissa Beltane?"

Kostakis did not pretend surprise. "Having it off? I didn't know coppers used nice language for common habits. That pair have been fuckin' like rattlesnakes for half a year. Talk about little innocents! They thought nobody knew what they were at down behind the vine trellises. Everybody knew, even the bloody cook's offsider."

"Everybody except the girl's father."

"If you was a servant here, would you have put him wise?"

"I suppose not, but why didn't he see what everybody else could?"

"Because he's no sort of a father. Sees the girl at mealtimes of a weekend, lets her have what she wants, sends her to visit her mother on Sunday and gives her a kiss for hello and good-bye. And that's it. It isn't only her; he's the same with all of us. He doesn't know the names of half the staff; he's a working politician and that's all he is. He's got eight gardeners here and he never walks in the garden; there's an orchard and he wouldn't know a tree in it. He's got a daughter and doesn't realize she's growing up. Or he didn't until a couple of days ago."

"He certainly knows now. He was told about Fred tonight."

That upset Kostakis. "Poor bloody kid, that'll be the finish of him. He could stay jobless for life because the boss can't spare time to look after his daughter."

"I think the premier may see reason before it's all over."

"Reason!" He shook a bony finger at me as though I had offended him. "The Wardies say Beltane's a good bloke, but I tell you that all he ever sees is what goes on inside his own head."

It began to seem that quite a number of Jeremy Beltanes found shelter in that single skull.

"Come on; we'll talk to Cranko."

"That's the doctor?"

I should have known that the security crew would have been sniffing around the prisoners; they had the excuse that strangers were their responsibility. "Yes."

"You going to fill me in?"

"I can't tell you anything about him."

He misunderstood me in the true spirit of a vidscreen copshow. "We play it by ear? OK by me."

We walked into the room, and I told the guard, "We won't need you for a while. I'll call you."

He shrugged, holstered his gun slowly and marched out with the clear implication that his prisoner had been in good hands and coppers weren't needed round the Manor.

Cranko laid down the book he had been reading (it had a large gold crucifix embossed on the cover) and asked pleasantly, "Would you agree that the doctrine of the transubstantiation of the host has a genuine psychic attraction for the worshiper?"

Aside from its being a pretty clumsy demonstration of cockiness, I had no idea what he was talking about.

Kostakis had. He grunted, "Only for a cannibal."

The instant put-down flustered Cranko unreasonably. Snide intellectualism cut from under him by an obvious product of the Wards left him mentally flat-footed, and I moved straight in on his disheveled thinking.

"Some questions, Mr. Cranko. We aren't interested in crossed identities, so—"

"So why should I answer at all?"

I had expected that. He had taken the point that Jackson's identity was not to be revealed to Kostakis, and of course, he wouldn't reveal it. It was his ace in the hole for bargaining with Beltane, but he had had to try the gambit. I carried on as though I had not heard; persistence is a good eroder of confidence.

"What did they offer for delivery of the man? What coin do they pay in? What does a high-tech Minder want that has to be cheated and betrayed for?"

He protested raggedly, "I'm not some cheap informer, Harry! I'm not for sale."

I was about to ask was he playing for some holy personal conviction when Kostakis took two quick paces and leaned over him like an avenging fury, his gentle face twisted with a viciousness that seemed to rise out of his depths. "All Minders are for sale, 'specially the brainy ones. They're the ones that want things different from other people and twice as much of it."

Cranko flinched away from him, appealing to me, "Who's this animal, Harry? This isn't right."

Kostakis slapped him hard and painfully across the mouth and bent closer until he could have spat down the man's throat, and screamed at him, "Don't call me names or I'll tear the fuckin' face off you! What was the price? A big promotion? Or maybe permission to do a really nasty experiment? How about that? Or won't some Minder woman say yes till they twist her arm for you, eh? Or maybe little boys! How about little boys?"

Accusations beaten in with brute force don't have to be true, only terrifying; they frighten because the rattled mind has been jolted out of reality into a void where innocence has no force. Cranko's resistance collapsed in shock. He pleaded, "Harry, you can't allow this! I'm not that sort of—"

Kostakis cut him short. "Sort of what? Forget Harry; it's me you're answerin' to!" He clutched Cranko by the shirtfront and with one hand lifted him clear of the ground and shook him. I would have counted myself as having twice Kostakis's strength, but I could not have done that; the man grew more extraordinary by the minute. Now he kept needling murderously into the frightened face held level with his own. "Picked it right, didn't I? Little boys, eh? You turn over the bloke they want and they keep up the supply for you!"

Cranko must have thought he was in the grip of a maniac; he whined, "Harry, please!"

I gave him a cunning, amused grin, and he howled.

Kostakis hissed, "You want Harry, do you? Do you? Well, I'll give you to him, you bastard!"

Still holding with one hand he turned on his heel and threw Cranko at me. From two meters the surgeon struck me hard enough to stagger me and then nearly brought me down by clinging for protection. Over his head I saw Kostakis breathing hard as he collapsed onto the couch where Cranko had sat. He gave me a shattered, conspiratorial wink, and I sensed vaguely the nature of the exhibition I had seen. He might be useless for the next ten minutes.

I pushed Cranko into a chair where Kostakis was out of his line of sight. He looked round at him once and did not turn his head gain. I had seen police violence often enough but never anything as fast and effective as Kostakis with homicidal mania in his eyes. Nor had I ever seen the miracle of the total strength of a narrow, lanky body channeled into a single, limited effort. Kostakis was an unsettling phenomenon.

I said, "Tell me about it, Doctor. Who, how, why."

"I don't know who." Cranko looked fearfully into my

eyes, willing me to believe. "It's true, Harry; I don't know who the people are."

It took me half an hour to turn him inside out and discover that he knew almost nothing of any use. Once, when he verged on indiscretion, I had to steer him away from revealing Jackson's identity, and he stammered in the knowledge that Kostakis could have it out of him in two seconds flat. He clung closer to dependence on me, ready to spew his whole brain up if I asked for it.

None of what he told me seemed to be of the slightest use in identifying the kidnappers; he was a pawn, bought at second remove and told nothing. His motive seemed to be sympathy with the political Opposition.

Towards the finish he regained some confidence, enough to remind me obliquely that the premier would protect him rather than have Jackson's identity made public.

Behind him Kostakis made his first statement since he had sat on the couch. "It's my curiosity you've got to worry about, Doc. What if I want to know sometime when Harry's not around?"

That possibility had to be scotched. I said, "Come on, Cranko; we have to talk to the premier."

Kostakis would have come with us, and I had to tell him, "Not this time. This is between the premier and us alone."

Another aspect of the man surfaced. He gazed down while his foot scuffed the carpet, the picture of a disappointed child, protruding lip and all. He muttered, "I reckon you owe me."

He didn't mean money and, uncomfortably, I reckoned so, too; that daunting exhibition had earned a payout. I reckoned also that I did not want that sharp man prying into dangerous matters, for his own sake and mine.

Playing for time, I said, "We'll talk about it in the

morning." He lifted a face full of suspicion that I was only fending him off. Which I was. "I mean it."

I would think of something by morning. And so, as it happened, I did.

Kenney was gone from the premier's office; Beltane sprawled behind his desk, one hand at his lips, eyes blankly on the ceiling, away in his thoughts. I coughed and he straightened with an expression of ambushed guilt. I'll swear he had been sucking his thumb.

He nodded to us to be seated and said to Cranko, with more disappointment than contempt, "What a reptile you've made of yourself."

"I think not." Free of Kostakis, Cranko came rapidly into form, smoothing his clothes, adjusting his face to remote superiority and making a fair attempt at a steady voice. "You have your loyalties; I have mine."

"I persuaded cabinet to approve the backing that had already been refused for your work at the institute." So one item in Kostakis's mad accusations had been near the mark. "You accepted it as payment for your silence."

"Not so; my silence was never mentioned. There was a most gentlemanly agreement between us; my response was taken as read, but it was not spelled out. You understood it so; I did not."

"I see: It was not written in the bond."

That stirred a memory of home, of Bill reciting scenes from the plays—and of the Shakespeare in the premier's bedroom along with the van Gogh portraits. Beltane was a man of moods, secret affinities and solitary fears.

"Not written," Cranko agreed.

"And if it had been?"

The surgeon laughed. "Then I should have had to betray your trust."

I said, "He'll play word games all night, Mr. Beltane. Let me tell it."

What had taken half an hour to extract, check and recheck from Cranko I told in minutes. Most of it was, anyway, common gossip in the slandering streets.

The network of informers (such as that 062 mentioned by Barney Fielding) had developed from casual fellow-traveling contacts and sources into something similar to the police system of informers, where each constable or detective knows and deals with his own snouts and there is no poaching by other coppers; it is the only way to preserve the essential secrecy.

In politics the criminal element, alerted more than once by House members themselves (once again: Corruption begins at the top) moved in to take charge of the sources and through them to squeeze the members, who paid through their two-timing noses for the information that could turn parliamentary debate into hucksters' trading. The crims covered themselves by the ancient and effective "switch" system whereby contacts were made anonymously and the same contact man was never used twice between source and buyer. The member got his information and paid for it without knowing whom he paid. He knew of but rarely met his informant, and everyone beyond that point was a shadow.

The system had pinpointed Cranko as malleable material. Somebody else, he assumed, had alerted Beltane that the surgeon was his man for clandestine work.

Cranko had not appreciated the full scope of the plan until "they" told him they wanted not only the information but also the rehandled man; they wanted the flesh to parade before the vid cameras. Snatching Jackson from the institute had been the most ticklish part of the operation until my too cunning caution gave them our route and the spot for exchange several hours before we set out; "they" had had all the time in the world to set up their hijack of the ambulance. Beltane, they knew, would not dare any move against them that might reach the public ear; his staunchest party supporters would run for cover if a population law scandal broke around him.

There Cranko's knowledge ran out, but I had little doubt as to who had "alerted" the premier; he might also have suggested the reconstitution of the decaying father in the first place. Beltane had been trapped through the old man; Melissa was an unplanned complication, but one that could be dangerous in its own right.

(But—what was the nature of the swinging decision required of Beltane? Required by whom?)

Beltane held his head for a moment with both hands. "I should sleep, but I don't think I can."

Cranko gave a small, satisfied grunt. He would have done better to have sat quiet.

Beltane asked. "Is there more to be got from him?"

"Not immediately. He had a good squeezing; it ran out of him like juice."

Beltane grimaced a decent man's disgust at what he conceived to be police methods but could not forbear asking, "What did you do to him?"

"I, sir? Nothing at all. He begged me to listen to him." Quite true.

Cranko's professionally superior air slipped away, or it may have been delayed shock that set him squalling, between a stutter and a howl, that I was a liar and a monster who had set a homicidal sadist at him and had stood by enjoying the show.

Beltane, perplexed, doubted that I had so easily procured a homicidal sadist at that hour of night.

To enlighten him as to his ignorance of the world of his own home, I said, "One of your security men."

He was hard to convince. "They've all been screened and found thoroughly steady types. Highly dependable."

Cranko hissed, "Oh, Christ!"

"Name of Kostakis; a rather gentle bloke who claims to understand modern art."

Cranko insisted, "A raving maniac!"

Beltane was no longer interested in Cranko; he was affronted by the idea of such an anomaly on his staff and grumbling that he saw them around the Manor but did not know their names. Why should he? The secretaries dealt with them. I gathered that someone would pay for this. He saw my incredulity at his isolated incomprehension of his surroundings and only half understood it. "These people are here to look after me. That's what a staff is for, man! For God's sake, do I have to be aware of individuals every time a foot falls or a door opens? I delegate. Others are my hands and eyes and ears. I have a state to run, not a bloody household."

No doubt there was reason in that, but it was hard to believe in a man who could not call his staff by name. He said, still fuming over this new upset, "Can't we let Cranko go? I don't want him around me."

"Not yet, I think. Let your security men look after him for the night."

He did not contest my decision nor ask a question; he was used to being looked after. He fingered his desk console and ordered, "Send a guard to the Small Office."

It was not Kostakis who arrived, which was just as well; Cranko might have collapsed and I would not have blamed him. Beltane said nothing, waiting for me to give the orders; when he delegated, he delegated completely.

"Put him somewhere for the night. Lock him in and see that he doesn't get out."

The security man shot a querying glance at Beltane, who nodded slightly. My standing was established.

When we were alone I prodded him for action. "Your

daughter, now. I've no Jackson to guard, so I'm free."

"The police—"

"Forget the police. If they find her they'll get more truth out of her than you want. Let me do it."

"My father—"

"Your father is safe, asleep, locked in and guarded. Your daughter matters more, surely!"

For an unguarded instant his face told me I was wrong, that the priority was otherwise. I saw and he knew what I saw. The instant passed and the blandness returned, but he had made a decision.

He climbed out of the chair like an old man and came round the end of the desk to plant himself squarely before me and say, "I'm assured you won't repeat what you hear in this house. Is it true?"

"Yes, under moral and emotional blackmail. I promised you I would never forgive you for it." Let him keep it in mind!

"So I can't depend on you either."

"You can. How I feel doesn't matter. I am a policeman and I will do the job that was handed me."

"Yes, there was something like that in your profile—loyalty before self. I suppose it's rare enough."

Somewhere in my mind a small voice murmured, *Self-righteous?*

Beltane went back to his chair. "So I can tell you the truth and in effect be talking only to myself."

It was an aspect that had not occurred to me, the role of confidant and emotional shock absorber; it might not be an appealing role, as such, but the opportunity was too valuable to pass up.

"You could say that." And what a two-faced form of assent that was.

"Then here it is: I need Dad badly, badly. I need him here, to know that he is safe, unharmed. I need his advice, his decision. I need him."

God forbid that I should ever suffer such a binding relationship; love is enough without groveling. I said, "But you must have your daughter home first, because you neglected her and abused her for a trollop and because of it she ran away. Can you live with that?"

I thought he could, but, "No. She must be found." It was a dismal and dishonest admission, but even heads of state must bow to conventional moral imperatives. He added, "You may regret too much freedom of speech before you're through."

"Then I'll regret it when the time comes. Until then, a question or two. One—Was it Nguyen who suggested you put your father in Cranko's hands?"

He mulled over that as though the answer was unclear. I had to prod him. "Who beside Nguyen knew how much you missed that dribbling old man in the back room?"

"Nobody. Nor did I ever confide in him."

"You didn't know you confided. He would have built up the picture piece by piece from stray remarks and simple deductions. And maybe some hypnotherapy. He set you up."

That must have hurt him badly. A patient places great trust in his psychotherapist; that's the strongest weapon in the rat's armory.

He said tightly, "You have another question?"

"Why is the institute the tallest building in the city?"

It was not the change of direction that caused him to hesitate. Secret information is still secret even from a mute. I think he decided on a half answer that would keep the other half hidden. "Because it is built around a central shaft ten meters or so in diameter and forty deep. It is a simulation chamber which can model, on a small scale, atmospheric conditions in graduated mixtures of temperature, pressure, wind speed and the rest of it. Now are you any wiser?"

I thought I might be. "That's the shaft that puts the physics into their biophysics."

"More or less."

"So if I have a shaft set up for all sorts of conditions for different heights, like simulating what happens in the air between the top of Mount Everest and sea level . . . Can it do that?"

"I'm no scientist to understand completely." He had decided already that he had said too much even to his mute. He watched me as though I had sprouted a third eye and seen too clearly.

"Then you could drop a handful of very special bugs in at the top and monitor what happens to them all the way down—how long it takes, how many die, that sort of thing. And especially, how wide an area they would disperse over. Like that?"

He chose to laugh it off as if pleased with the toy confessional that could actually talk back to him. "I wouldn't know. Science is not a politician's field."

"But the results are, and I think I know what you were really talking about in Canberra."

The laughter broke up in harsh, hurtful breaths, and he bent over with his hands at his chest as if to quiet it by force. When he had calmed a little, he said, "Oh, no, you don't. You don't know that at all."

He lifted his face and he was crying. "Leave me alone! Go after Melissa, go to bed, go to hell if you like but leave me alone! You don't know a damned thing!"

7

Ostrov:
—And into the Morning

A man in decay becomes confused between trust and discretion. Beltane could tell his mute about the shaft in the institute, which was dangerous enough knowledge, but not about the Canberra discussion, though that was equally safe with me.

They had talked life and death in Canberra, no two ways about that. The institute might be at the crux with its plotting of place, time and dispersion areas.

A reasonable guess: The other six state premiers had agreed to trials, and Beltane had shuddered away from them. Now they were pressuring him to say yes because he had the institute and the bug—bacterium, virus, whatever it might be—and time was running out in a planetary flood of birthing. The prime minister also must be waiting uneasily for this decision.

I could think about this coldly; most people could. The apprehension of some manner of cull had been with us for generations, until familiarity accorded it the mental equivalent of a shrug and a philosophic, *But not just yet.* Given time, human beings can get used to any obscenity that doesn't have to be faced up to right at this terrible minute or may, with luck, be deferred until someone else will have to do the facing.

Beltane had become suddenly the someone else, and he was not strong enough. In the same case, would I be? Nobody knows what his brain can bear. I had lived too long with the idea as part of the fabric of the world; it had lost the terror of nearness.

Or, was I wholly mistaken? Had I misjudged what had taken place in Canberra? Those overseas observers had been present. Why? What was in it for them? A watching brief for the experimental run?

Or had my guessing fallen short of something beyond the old, waiting fears?

Now, about Melissa . . .

I went back to the office, and Beltane sat there yet, hands clasped behind his head, his short bull body painfully vulnerable as he gazed at nothing. He spoke without moving: "I told you to leave me alone."

"I'm sorry, but I have work to do that won't wait and there are two things I need from you." I rode over his gesture of impatience. "First, we need a line on your father's would-be kidnappers, so can you get Mr. Kenney back here by nine o'clock?"

He straightened as though he saw me whole for the first time. "You begin to sound genuinely sure of yourself. By tomorrow morning?"

"This morning. It's been a long night." It was in fact after 2 A.M.

"That will need arranging. He is of the Opposition party; he can't risk being seen to enter the Manor."

"He did it last night; he can do it again."

He thought about it, turned it over, sighed and said, "I can't command him, but I'll manage."

"Impress him with urgency. The other thing: I want one of your security crew as a personal assistant to help me find your daughter."

"Take whoever you like. See their supervisor."

Such things, his attitude said, arrange themselves. It was hard to accept that anyone could live on so remote a plane. I had to insist that he call Jeanette from his desk console.

"A particular man," I said. "Kostakis."

He ordered it and asked, "Is that all?"

"Yes, sir. Good night."

"Good night, Sergeant."

In the security common room I received no welcome at all. Jeanette had been hauled out of bed by Beltane's call and was not friendly. I remembered her as a tough, unmotherly type.

She complained that her men were privately employed. "We aren't government goons; you've no right over us."

"Tell it to the premier."

"I will." She might—and he would tell her to see one of the secretaries.

"Where's Kostakis?"

"For Christ's sake, you don't want him right away, do you? He's gone to bed."

"Then I'll get him out. Where is he?"

She gave me terse directions to the warren of staff quarters, then relented enough to shout after me, "Gus doesn't wake happy."

"Touchy?"

"Call it looney."

"Then why is he on a high-trust watching job?"

"Because any prowler that runs into him will come out of it near dead. He breaks bones."

"That could be a virtue." She grinned nastily, seeing my bones splinter. I asked, "What does Gus stand for?"

"Gustav. Norwegian mother. That makes him a good Australian mongrel." Greek-Norwegian. Mother might account for his paleness.

I found his room, knocked gently and called his name but heard no sound. The door was not locked; I pushed it open quietly, felt for the lightpress and lit the room. Kostakis had been in bed but the sheet was turned right back as though he had risen quickly in a single coordinated move. The sheet was still warm, so I stood still and spread my empty hands out from my body.

From behind the door he said, "Good boy; you learn fast. I had to break a couple of fingers to teach the fellers not to play jokes, but some never wake up to theirselves."

"I was warned."

"I'd think twice about wreckin' a cop, anyway." It sounded more like soothing syrup than truth.

He was birthday naked, and without his clothes he was cat skinny, too finely built for the lift and throw he had used on Cranko. At a closer look he carried a fair amount of muscle on slender bones, which can be a deceptive mixture, but it did not explain his lifting some ninety kilos, one-handed, by the shirtfront. I was not sure I could do it myself and then throw it away.

He sat on the bed and waved me to the only chair. "What now?"

"Get dressed. You're seconded to me and there's work to do."

He did not question the secondment, merely looked slyly pleased as though he had forced payment from me. He was a clothes-on-the-floor type and found his singlet and shirt by stretching an arm down for them. He was half dressed before he checked his watch. "At this hour!"

"The best hour for where we're going."

"Such being?"

"Where young Melissa is."

"You know?"

"I've got a line."

"Like?"

"Handspike."

"Gangies?"

"It's probably what young Fred has tattooed on his belly. It's the brat gang that hunts the Balaclava district."

"I've never worked that side. That Fielding rabbit thought Melissa might be with them."

"How do you know about that?"

"The boys have got him on ice in one of the bedrooms, and they get curious—you know. It took about two minutes for them to get the story out of him, and they told me all about it when you went in to the boss. Do you know she's up the duff?"

"Is she, now? Tell about that."

And so he told me all Dr. Barney's stupid tale and freed my tongue to discuss it with him. There was a way round the information embargo by nudging the listener's ideas until he revealed how much he knew. If he knew enough, my freedom to talk was that much enlarged.

I told him, "Barney Fielding is a self-satisfied piker and as sloppy minded as they come. Of course Fred took her to the Handspikes. Who could do a better job of hiding her than a brat gang that knows every hole in the Ward? What other friends would hide her just for the hell of it, to cock a snook at the law? Everybody else would be yelling that they didn't want to be involved. Barney knew that and tried to get them to admit they had her, because as a doctor he looks after their bruises and breaks and has a little bit of privilege with them. But—he'd already threatened her with abortion, the idiot bastard, and of course their first loyalty was to Fred, so they denied all knowledge."

Kostakis stood up, fully dressed and gentle eyed, incapable of hurting a fly. "And you reckon she's still with them?"

"It's a place to start."

"The only place you've got. But will they truck with a copper?"

"Maybe, maybe not. Some of the older ones might remember me from three years back; I always gave them a fair go. The thing is, she'll know you and perhaps be willing to talk."

"Could be." I thought I detected a sudden uneasiness there, but he covered it quickly. "What then? What if she won't come home?"

"We play it by ear. Ready?"

"Sure." He patted his shoulder holster. "You got transport?"

"No problem."

I vidded the CIB at City Center, identified myself and asked for a car to be sent to the Manor; I didn't want an all too identifiable Manor monster. The super complained, mainly for effect and, knowing I was on a Manor job, tried to wheedle out of me why I wanted it; failing, he cursed the premier's inconsiderate use of privilege and sent the car.

The hovercar arrived at ten to four. By ten past we were as close to the Handspike hangout as innocent parties could get without raising the bratpack alarm. The police driver whooshed off into the night, leaving us alone in the not-quite-silence of a city never wholly still; streetlights were doused to conserve power in the early hours, but the sense of eyes and covert movement was never doused. Kostakis and I headed for Alma Park and the railway cutting.

The signs are that Alma Park was once a recreational area with a cricket ground, but now it was grass grown and weed grown under shrubs and trees, with ragged outcrops of asphalt where paths once had been. It was, like all the neglected old parks around the city, a place to skirt by day and stay well away from by night, a haunt of fugitives, thieves and violence. Its only decent

use was as a refuge for the city's small birds and animals; even teenage gangies had had enough ecological
sense thumped into their arrogant skulls to let the wild-
life alone. The park's attraction for the Handspikes was
the ancient railway cutting that ran through the middle
of it, thirty feet deep and overgrown, the rails long ago
torn up and recycled for more urgent use. Somewhere
in its three hundred meters the gangies would be gathered, most of them sleeping but with sentries posted.

The rule is: If you must go into a park at night, go in
as if you mean it, standing upright and walking a direct
line. Weave and dodge and try to avoid detection and
the night life will be all over you from sheer need to
know what you are being careful about. We marched
straight along the line of fence posts, most of them
broken and rusted, that still guarded the edge of the
cutting though the protective wire had been stripped
for reuse long ago.

After twenty meters or so I said to Kostakis, "Talk.
We aren't skulking; we want to be seen and heard."

Said a young voice from the shrubbery ahead, "Well,
I seen yers." And so he should have; the moon was
bright enough through the cloud cover. "So stop right
there."

From behind us another voice, female, said, "An' no
reachin' for the pockets, neether."

The first one carried on, "Yers wantin' somethin'?"

"Some talk," I said, "with the Big Spike."

"Who are youse?"

"Tell the Big Spike that Harry Ostrov's here. Someone ought to remember me."

Beside me Kostakis giggled softly. "Big Spike! Fancies himself, that one."

The sentry whistled and someone came grunting and
stumbling up the steep side of the cutting; after a short,
whispered colloquy he snorted and stumbled down
again. Then there was more scrambling as a group

climbed to ground level. Four or five, I thought; the
Big Spike was taking no chances.

With increased numbers the air smelled of sweat
and unwashed flesh. They were a scruffy lot, clad in
the usual unimaginative junk they thought set them
apart from and superior to the law-abiding "shitheads";
narrow chests pretended breadth and depth under the
cover of fluffed-up imitation fur shirts, knobbly teenage knees peeked from patchwork kilts; shaven scalps,
painted black, made the latest in terror announcement.
They all looked as though they could do with a good
meal, which they probably could; most of them were,
after all, street kids, whether or not they had homes
to retreat to as a last resort. These stupidities made
them no less dangerous when reason, never their strong
point, snapped. They could be hysterically vicious,
murderous.

The Big Spike pushed past the sentry and came right
up to us, making a show of bravado for his watching gangies, and he had a gun in his hand. He was
about fifteen. Before he could speak, I said, "I reckoned Ronnie'd be the Big Spike by now." That stamped
me as familiar enough with the gang to be worth a
hearing.

"Ronnie's copped it." Somebody had probably slit
him up and left a vacancy for an up-and-coming young
vandal.

One of the retinue said, "That's 'Arry, all right. 'E
wasn't bad for copper shit. Don't know the other one."

The Big Spike asked, "Who's yer mate?"

"Name's Gus. Not a copper. I'm not a copper now,
either." All right, omnipresent listening God! So I was
detached on a civvy job, wasn't I?

"So what yer want?"

"Fred Blacker and his girl."

"Never 'eard of 'em."

"So you told Barney."

"That old shit! Wouldn't tell 'im nothin' anytime."

"But tell me. Fred's your old gangie. You'd help him out."

"Maybe we would, maybe not." After an impressive silence while the great man pretended to consider all sides of the matter, curiosity won out. "All right, they're 'ere, but they got sankcherry."

"Let me talk to Fred. He's in trouble and maybe I can get him out of it."

A runner was sent for Fred. More stumbling and slipping.

The Big Spike shoved his gun into his rope belt, a swagger to let us know he had no fear of us, but other guns glinted in the moonlight, keeping us covered. (Their guns were mostly for show; half of them would be jammed for lack of proper care or useless for lack of the ammunition so hard to get in a world largely stripped of small arms. But which half?) Big Spike asked, "You got guns?"

He should have thought of that earlier; he was new in the hot seat. "Think I'd tread the park without?"

He didn't try to take them from us; that could have been for him a bad move in the shadows and half light. "Then both of yers put yer hands up an' keep 'em there."

We did as told and stood in silence, feeling foolish for an age before Fred came.

He was a big lad, strongly made and not at all bad looking as the popular models went; he would have had a successful pick-and-choose sex life before Melissa hooked him to destruction. I recalled him as a one-time nuisance in the area, steadier looking now.

He studied me closely. "Harry Ostrov. I don't owe you."

"I wouldn't say that. I've kicked your arse and sent you home when I could have slammed you in the nick."

"All right, then, what do you want?"

"To take Melissa somewhere safe."

"She's not leaving me." He said it as something settled, inarguable; she was his responsibility and he had
accepted it. This was rite of passage time for Fred when
he was growing up too fast to see reason outside his
protective manhood. And, if Barney's observation was
correct, too besotted to be frightened by his situation.

I made up my mind on the spot. "You can come with
her." Beltane might rave and call down the lightning
but a concession would be in order.

"Where to?"

"To her home." I did not name the Manor, hoping
that Fred had retained sufficient sense not to reveal the
girl's true background. Apparently he had.

"She won't go there. Her father called her names.
And he'd make her have an abortion. And what do
you think he'd do to me?"

"To you, nothing. He has his own troubles. He'll be
glad just to have her back."

"She won't go home."

"I tell you she has nothing to fear from her father."

He said morosely, "I still think I have. And what
about the pop laws? She wants her kid and so do I;
it's my kid, too. That bastard, Barney, frightened her
with abortion talk like her old man. She won't go."

"Will you let me talk to her?"

"Does she know you?"

"No."

"Then what's the good?"

Playing by ear was getting me nowhere. Fred was not
belligerent, merely stubborn, while the Big Spike and
his train were showing signs of boredom.

Into the pool of silence Kostakis dropped the coupon's worth I had hoped from him. "Fred, boy, tell
her Gus from the house is here. She might talk to
me."

Fred came closer to examine him. "Gus! I couldn't see you properly in the dark. What are you doing here?"

"Just friendly interest, boy. And I got an idea where she can go instead of home."

"Where?"

"Not so fast. That's for her to hear."

"Why would she listen to you?" I heard suspicion and jealousy; this was love on a quick trigger. Poor kid.

"Because she knows something you don't, but I'll tell you now. She knows I was awake up to you two all along, but I kept it to myself and I reckon that was friendly of me. She ought to give me a hearing."

Would that bring her? Had she, perhaps, a secret with Kostakis, a debt he could call in? A policeman's suspicions don't exempt his allies.

Fred said reluctantly, "All right," and started down the cutting.

Time dragged and my arms ached; I locked the fingers behind my head and that helped a little but I felt uncomfortable and silly, bailed up like any sucker by a pack of brats. But they were murderous brats and Gus and I were the weak force. I noticed that Gus's hands were raised as high as mine but did not touch his head; he kept them there, unsupported, and still seemed at ease.

After an age of silent stress the girl came through the shrubbery. She was a big girl, nearly as tall as Fred, and she had nothing in the way of a figure. She was not dumpy in the rolls-of-fat sense, just straight up and down, shapeless, with nothing much wrong that exercise and some mealtime restraint wouldn't cure, but her face was sullen and short of the signs of burgeoning character that should be visible at sixteen years old. My immediate thought was, What did the boy see in her to land himself in this mess?

The possessiveness in his bearing as he led her towards us said he saw much that I could not. In a less fraught situation it would have been touching.

She said with only a touch of suspicion, "Gus," and stood still, gazing and puzzled. "Why did he send you?"

"He didn't. Daddy doesn't know about this little jaunt."

She took a half pace back into the safety of Fred's solid presence. "Then what are you here for?"

"To get you out of trouble."

"I'm not in any trouble."

"Not yet, but your boyfriend is."

"Fred?" She turned to look closely at him in the half dark as if he might be a fresh complication. "Fred isn't afraid."

That was a shocker. To her it was a matter of plain fact, needing no discussion; almost certainly she had never seriously considered the danger to him of his involvement. Barney Fielding had been right; to her Fred was just a useful appendage, a bodyguard and comforter.

Kostakis said slowly, clearly, as to a child, "Then Fred can start being afraid right now."

The boy answered him, loudly and aggressively, "I can take care of Melly."

"Like hell you can! Listen, you two! Barney Fielding will be squealing to the coppers by morning to save his own skin for not reporting a pop law evasion. What happens to Fred then? And to his mum and dad that harbored his girl? What about them, Fred?"

Fred, stupid with love and gallantry, said, "I stick with Melly."

"She'll be all right; Daddy will see she doesn't cop a penalty." Then Gus shot the bolt he had saved for last. "But who'll look after the Handspikes?"

The Big Spike and his sentries had been acting sophisticated boredom, above all this shop talk, but suddenly they were in the middle of the exchange.

The Big Spike said quickly, "Nobody knows she's 'ere."

"That's what you told Barney and what he told us, but me and Harry came straight here just the same. You know why? Just in case you didn't trust Barney any more than anybody else would, is why. And the coppers will think exactly the same way. Eh, Harry?"

"That's right," I said, and picked up his lead. "And all you Handspikes won't last ten minutes with your little pistols if the cops decide to clean you out. They'll gas the cutting and pick you out with copter claws, and don't you know it!"

The Big Spike was not slow on the uptake when his skin was in question. "You reckon they'll care that much? About her?" He believed; danger is always believable when you live on the thin edge. He turned on Fred. "Who is this bitch of yours? Maybe she isn't just a Minder bitch lookin' for a Wardie thrill." He shoved his face into Melissa's in the half light, and her eyes were frightened as he accused her of the worst thing he knew. "Is your dad a copper, is he?"

I put in quickly, "You could call him the head man of all the coppers."

The Big Spike pulled Melissa out of the way and confronted Fred in fury. "You never said that! You never told me! You never said her dad was the top copper!" I have to say for Fred that he stood his ground although he was as close to a gangie payoff as anyone would ever want to be. He grabbed the terrified Melissa and held her close while the Big Spike howled in near hysteria, "I oughta spill yer rotten guts on the grass, yer bastard! Yer put the whole gang in the shit!"

Kostakis raised his voice. "Not if we take her away with us."

Melissa became hysterically noisy. "I won't go to Daddy! He'll take my baby away!"

"Shut up, yer stupid bitch! I don't give a fuck about yer baby. I got my gangies to look after, an' you don't mean nothin'!"

Kostakis said before she could start squalling again, " 'Course you can't go to your daddy. We'll take you to your mum's place."

"She'll only tell him."

"You reckon? She doesn't like him all that much and she'll listen to us when we explain. She'll look after you just to spite him. I know your mum; she'll listen to me." Melissa also seemed to listen to him; he added, for good measure, "She'll look after Fred, too."

At last Fred was interested.

The Big Spike strode close to Kostakis. "You dinkum?"

"I'll get 'em off your hands, and Harry'll stop the coppers looking. That's all you got to worry about. Right, Harry?"

"Right. I can stop them; I've still got contacts."

"Then get 'em outta here!" He turned to Fred and Melissa. "Get goin', the pair o' yers! And don't you never come near us again, Fred. Brother'ood's cut, right now!"

Because my shoulders were now aching like centers of rheumatism, I said, "For Christ's sake, let's go. Come on, you two."

We backed away a good twenty paces, the gangies watching us with guns up and ready. Fred came after us, half dragging a crying Melissa who seemed now to have believed nothing said by anybody. When the gangies at last took a couple of backward paces and vanished behind the shrubs I was able to lower my arms, with shoulder joints grinding.

We reached the comparative safety of Alma Road before Fred asked, "What about my mum and dad?"

"They won't be touched."

"How do you know that?"

"Because I'm not an ex-copper; I'm a serving detective-sergeant, and I'll see they aren't pulled in."

"Jesus!" said Fred and I don't know whether he was awed, gratified or dismayed. He asked, "What about you, Gus? Are you something else besides a security guard?"

"Not me, boy. What you see is what you get."

Privately I doubted that.

Melissa, still full of a fugitive's suspicions, asked, "How would a man like you know my mother?" and seemed unaware of insult. That school of hers must have been an outpost of aristocracy operating on a closed circuit.

Kostakis was cheerfully uninsulted. "Never seen her in my life. Now don't start bawling again; if she won't play we'll find someone else."

And so, I thought, he probably would. Choosing him had been a stroke of idiot genius.

At 5:15 the streaks of dawn were livening in the east and the Balaclava police station was within ten minutes' walking distance. There we picked up another car after a reference to the Manor stopped protest in its teeth. I hoped it might be possible to fit in a short nap before the morning conference with Kenney and Cranko.

Mrs. Ivy Beltane lived in the Dandenong foothills, which meant either that she had private means or that Beltane could afford to keep her in lush style; it also meant a longish trip, with my short nap as a casualty. From the Balaclava station I vidded her home and waited while she failed to hear or was slow getting out of bed. Then a male voice answered without clearing the screen at his end; he sounded very much at home and out of temper.

Melissa said crossly, "That's Val. I don't like him." She pushed past me to the microphone and said, "It's me, Val. Get Mummy!"

"Melissa? At this hour? What the devil's up with you?" I thought he didn't care much for her, either.

She repeated, "Get Mummy. I'm in trouble."

"You could have picked a better time for it. Hang on."

I asked, "Who's Val?"

"Oh, you know . . . he lives there."

One of the consolations of loneliness.

A woman's voice spoke, still without clearing the screen. "What's wrong, Melissa? Is it something serious?" It was a pleasant voice, concerned but not flustered.

I butted in. "Police here! I have your daughter with me and I want to take her to you right away."

"What trouble is she in?" No panic there.

"Not very much, Mrs. Beltane; I think we've cleaned up most of it. Could you let the details wait until we get there? She hasn't been harmed. I'm ringing to make certain she will be welcome."

"Welcome? My daughter? Are you out of your mind? Of course she must come here. Why should you think I might not want her?"

Best to make it short and sharp, because Melissa's time of secrecy was over. "She is pregnant."

Melissa began to cry again and Fred whispered in her ear. The mother was silent for a while, but we could hear Val muttering in the background, sounding like a spate of objections delivered at speed. She hissed at him to shut up and spoke to the vid again. "Why can't she go to her father?"

"Best to keep him out of it for a while, I think."

Her tone changed. "That I can imagine! It would make demands on his time, keeping it out of the news. Bring her here." She was no Jeremy fan.

"And the boy, the father? I have him, too."

"My God, you've got a nerve!"

"It may seem so to you, ma'am, but I'm sure you realize the political implications. It would be best to have both of them out of sight until other arrangements can be made."

Ivy Beltane began to say, "She'll have to be abort—" and Melissa shouted over her, "I won't! I won't! I want my baby."

There was desperation in her voice, but somehow not the urgency of a mother fighting for her child; the determination was loud and clear, but something other than maternal love gave it strength. I saw that Kostakis watched her with head cocked and teeth closed over his lower lip. Only Fred seemed in his normal state of unquestioning devotion.

The mother said in no motherly tone, "We'll discuss that when you get here. I will be waiting for you, Officer."

"About half an hour," I said, and she cut the connection while Val still argued in the background.

Melissa returned promptly to hysteria, and we left her to Fred to deal with; his loving patience cared beyond any sympathy I could feel for her just then. It took him ten minutes to calm her to the point where we were ready to leave in the police hovercar.

I put the pair of them in the front with the police driver and switched off the communicator so that Kostakis and I could talk privately in the rear. As we slipped over the road to the Dandenongs I told him that I felt I owed him a debt for his performance in Alma Park.

He said, "Reckon I'm paid."

"How?"

"Workin' with you. That's what I wanted."

Another romantic? They come in all shapes and sizes. "Do you think police work is all like tonight's game with a bratpack? It isn't."

"Better than walking the Manor grounds six hours a day fighting off intruders that never come."

"Makes a nice change, does it? You earned it, thinking of the mother."

"Should have thought of her yourself."

So I should have. "The truth is that Melissa is a side issue. All the time I'm thinking of something much more important than her."

"About the one who nearly got pinched off you?"

"What do you know about him?"

"Nothing really."

"You and your mates deviled a story out of Fielding; what did you get out of Cranko?"

He put his hands up defensively. "Fielding's only shit, but Cranko's got status and influence. Nobody was going to put the scares up him. That was all right while you was backing me but he could be real bad news afterwards if security tried it on."

"Is that all you know?"

"That's all."

"Sure?"

He was upset. "You'll learn I tell the truth, Harry."

"Except when a lie smooths the way, as in telling Melissa you know her mother."

"That wasn't a lie, Harry; that was a stratagem."

Mockery was barely audible. My father would love this one; I would have to take him home someday. "Gus, do you think she'll make a good mother?"

"Melly? She wouldn't know which end pisses. These Minder girls are brought up pig ignorant. They learn how to be society hostesses and that's about it."

"She knew enough to get Fred."

"They learn that off secret porn vids and lavatory walls and think they know it all. Then the real thing knocks 'em for a screaming loop because it wasn't like that in the vidplay." He eyed me distrustfully, having more to say and weighing my acceptance of it. "She got me before young Fred. And I wasn't the first."

That was not the surprise it might have been for some. In my years in the force I had seen too much of sexual ignorance displaying itself as easy access. "Who started it? You?"

"Fair go, Harry! I'm not in the kiddy market."

He sounded honest rather than outraged—within his uncertain definition of honesty. "So?"

"She just walked up one day and put her hand on it and said she'd yell for help if I didn't give it to her. She might've. I wasn't going to risk her doing it."

"That from a sixteen-year-old?"

"Fifteen then. And she was no virgin."

A fresh and unlovely portrait of Melissa emerged; Beltane's lack of interest in his daughter could be a political rope to hang him. I was haunted by the false note I had heard in the girl's voice. "Do you think she might have been trying to get a child by no matter who?"

"I think so now, but it wasn't me that filled her up. I take the pills."

"You think so now? You think she doesn't sound like a loving mother-to-be?"

He concentrated, frowned and said, "You know what she sounds like when she starts yelling about having the kid? She sounds like someone seeing all her hard work go for nothing. It's got nothing to do with Fred; she don't give him a thought unless she wants something."

Similes are never quite right but this one had a homing-in ring to it. She could not bear the thought of the prize being snatched from her.

Mrs. Beltane was dark, much younger than her husband—say, forty-fiveish—and good looking without being a beauty; her figure was what Melissa's should have been with attention to exercise and diet. She was

also self-possessed, direct and intelligent; Beltane had
been a fool to lose her.

To Melissa she said, without preamble, "It was delib-
orate, wasn't it? I saw it coming and gave you pre-
ventive pills, but you didn't use them. Later you will
tell me why; for the moment we must think what to
do."

Melissa said nothing at all and for once did not
crowd poor Fred for comfort; he seemed overwhelmed
by his surroundings and afraid to move. Mrs. Beltane
assessed him in a deliberate, slow summation and
seemed to decide that her daughter might have done
much worse. "I suppose that the rule is: If you must
throw yourself at a Wardie, pick a good-looking one
and hope to God." After that she paid no attention to
him though he flamed lobster red down to the chest.
"Still, there's a price to be paid for stupidity. The two
of you can sit in the kitchen while I talk to these
gentlemen."

Being treated as children, as a problem to be solved
by responsible adults, had an effect. There was not a
peep out of Melissa, who showed a wary respect for
her mother; she went in silence with a dazed Fred
trailing behind, surprised eyes trying to take in his
surroundings with a sort of cowed envy. Ivy Beltane's
house was nothing special as Minder houses go, though
a dozen times better than anything I was likely ever
to live in. Like all Minder places, it had too much of
everything—or so it seemed to me—too many pieces
of furniture serving only to fill up space, too many
decorations on walls and shelves, too many hangings
where a single blind or curtain would have done, so
much of everything that it looked like an exhibition
of what can be got for money. Don't think I was contemptuous; I would have given a slice of my life to live
under conditions as clean and convenient and easy to
look at, but it would have taken me years to get used

to them. Fred was shaken and a bit frightened by what
may have appeared to him real grandeur; he had probably never been so far as inside the back door of the
Manor. Though I knew this was only what they call
middle class, it left me uncomfortable, too.

When they were gone, Mrs. Beltane said, "I knew she
had hot pants and God knows I lectured her enough,
yet she even made a play for Val."

Val, a little middle-aged and a little portly and not
wholly at ease in his role as man of the house, said, "It
was embarrassing. One did not know what one should
do."

"You knew exactly what; you told me before worse
happened."

There was no doubt who wore the trousers, but Val
had his eye on legal safety as well as on his lady's love.
"She must go back to her father, Ivy. She can't stay
here. You lay yourself open to a harboring charge."

"Harboring? I'm her mother! You'll go before she
does. In any case, Sergeant Ostrov is the police and
he brought her here for me to harbor."

I said, "Temporarily, ma'am. Until the premier gets
his affairs sorted out. I assure you that he has matters
on his mind more urgent than an illegal birthing. Your
daughter is better out of the way for a while."

Val gave an I-have-done-my-best shrug and content-
ed himself with listening. Mrs. Beltane was more upset
than she allowed us to see. "She would have been
better off with me all the time, but I agreed to let
him have her while I took the blame for our sepa-
ration in order not to foul his political career. The
honorable member had to be stainless in the eyes of
the electorate! I could tell them a tale! Do you know
why I left him?"

"No, ma'am; it's no business of mine."

"I have sometimes wondered if the police knew—or
the secret service, whatever that may be." She pressed

a bell push. "You could do with a cup of tea, I suppose? Real tea from New Guinea?"

A nondescript male servant appeared and she ordered, "Tea for four. And give the children something in the kitchen; at their age they'll want breakfast." He disappeared and she continued with no change of tone, "I could throw Jeremy to the dogs if I opened my mouth—and his disgusting father after him."

Then she switched to small talk with no sound of social gears changing. The business session was over. We drank our tea from ridiculously flimsy china, feeling like clumsy gutterbums, and left.

Minders also, it seemed, had their home dramas— just like the sillier vidplays.

The police hovercraft dropped us at the Manor just before seven o'clock. It had been a long night and the new day was no tonic for me.

Gus, insultingly fresh, asked, "What now?"

"Breakfast. A quiet nap. I've a meeting at nine o'clock."

"Do I come to it?"

"Not this one." Perhaps my subconscious was performing better than my tired, rest-needing forebrain, because I changed my mind. "Yes, you can be in on it. I'll pick you up when we're ready."

His gentle, infinitely deceitful face lit up with unspoken thanks.

Beltane was not in the Small Office. Asleep at last, perhaps, despite his cares. Or because of them. I needed an hour on the spine for myself; thirty-six-hour stretches were not unusual on intensive cases and I had learned to snatch at opportunity.

I told security that I would be on the couch in the Small Office and that I should be wakened at 8:15.

They accepted my authority with resignation.

I fell asleep in the middle of a thought that I stank of a night's sweat and tension.

A guard woke me on time and told me where my own bedroom had been prepared. He said, straightfaced, "Chauffeur Willy's having fits over a body in the boot of the limo. Did you forget a little thing like that?"

Yes, I had forgotten the damned thing in the piling up of events. "Tell him to ferry it to the police morgue in City Center for identification and to tell them I'll make a full report later in the morning."

"Your job, I'd think."

"You an ex-cop?"

"So what?"

"So for Christ's sake try to help instead of standing on your civil rights. The Manor's in crisis."

He eyed me with personal hostility. Crisis in the Manor was a security affair, in his book, but he hadn't the nerve to carry it through. "OK. I'll do it."

My case had been taken to my room. There was a shower recess; by eight-thirty I was in clean clothes and looking for Kostakis.

Whether he had slept or not, he looked daisy fresh. I asked, "What time's breakfast?" and he told me, "When you want it. This is the ever-flowing trough."

"Now?"

"Me, too."

He took me to the security wardroom, which was for once empty, and buzzed the kitchen for food.

While we waited, I quizzed him. "You'd be a bad man in a brawl, I'd think."

He became at once reserved, noncommittal. "Can be."

"And stronger than you look."

"No. Just ordinary."

"I'd put Cranko at ninety kilos. You don't throw that around 'just ordinary.' "

"Some special training." The peculiar man was bashful.

"As in how to concentrate and coordinate mind and muscle to get the effect of hysterical strength."

"Something like that."

"Tell me about it, Gus. Give out."

He mumbled as if it was all a terrible embarrassment, "Can't keep it up, of course. A big effort, then I have to rest up. You can only use what's there, but all at once instead of a bit at a time."

"The energy equation is conserved."

"Eh? What's that?"

Gus was purely a practical man, without theory. I suggested, "Oriental stuff?"

"In a way." He capitulated. "Look, Harry, I had to have some self-respect. Physically, I mean. Better than the next bloke."

"Why?"

"Well . . . because I don't love this security work, but I'm not much good for anything else. And who wants to be a Wardie on Suss? I wanted to be an artist, but I got no talent, only thought I had. I like poetry, but I can't even remember to speak proper English. So I got this job where you don't need to know much except what you're told, and still I was with blokes who could run rings round me when a brawl come up. I felt useless. Then this Asian psychiatrist spotted me as delivering less than a full dollar on the job and got to work teaching me how to use what I've got instead of whining about it. Lot of concentration and pinpointing your intention and all that, but it works."

Kostakis as a bruised soul! I didn't dare laugh. "From what I've seen, it surely does. Nguyen?"

"Yes, but why'd you pick him?"

"He turns up in everything connected with my job here, and I don't trust him."

"No?" He reached across the table to grab my hand. "I don't trust anybody all the way. Not even you."

I pulled my hand back. "What's against me?"

"Nothing. We're just different people. There's always some point where nobody can trust another person."

There seemed no end to his oddities. "For example?"

"You killed a man last night."

"If you'd been me, so would have you."

"But I would have been sick all night afterwards."

"Why? He would have shot me."

"It isn't about right or wrong; it's about feeling. There's no way you can feel right about killing someone. A man's alive and then, all of a sudden, nothing. Think of it happening to you!"

I had had this conversation during the past night; Kostakis was carrying on with the things Beltane had left unsaid, as though I were under fire for . . . for what? Righteousness? "Thinking about it wouldn't help. It might make me hesitate and then I'd be dead instead of him. And once I was dead it wouldn't mean anything at all to me, would it?"

"But you shoot first to stay alive, don't you?"

"You mean life is precious? Mine is—to me."

"And the other bloke's isn't?"

That was the stopper. *No* would have been a not quite true answer, but the other man's life wouldn't bother me too much. Kostakis had a point, but it was in fact a matter of right and wrong. Getting sick over death was meaningless. When a thing was done, what did regret achieve?

Kostakis was saying, "Jeanette says you're hard in the head, a right-and-wrong man. But nobody's hard all the way through."

His persistence became an irritation. "For Christ's sake, Gus, everybody needs somebody else, but he doesn't have to need the whole goddamned population!

You're like Beltane—" I stopped dead there because I began to see the nature of Beltane's problem—not the problem itself but the idea of intractable choice. I caw why I had put it aside as one I did not want to share. Now my moral ground was in question as a right-and-wrong man.

Instant psychology was averted by Jackson in dressing gown and slippers and a full morning grouch.

"I've been looking everywhere for you! What's been going on all night, Harry? Why am I shut out of what's happening?"

"You aren't shut out, Mr. Jackson; you're a linch-pin—"

The PA system shouted suddenly, "Vid for Detective Sergeant Ostrov."

There was a screen in the room, but I could not guess who might be calling. I said into the mike, "I'll take it in the Small Office."

The Small Office was empty, and the miniature desk screen was alight with Ivy Beltane, both frightened and angry. She cried out, "Val's gone! We went back to bed, but he got up again when I slept."

I did not jump to the connection that was obvious to her, and she shrieked into the screen, "He was afraid. You saw that! He was afraid of a harboring charge!"

"He'll go to the police? I can fix that."

"Not them! He's taken his clothes, so he isn't coming back. He's a mean spirit, and he'll want money. It's all he ever wants. He'll sell the story to the channels. They'll pay a lot for it."

They surely would! I had a vision of her home invaded by the merciless vidpress; there would be no right of privacy, no pity or mercy. "How long has he been gone?"

"I can't tell. At least an hour. Maybe more."

"Pack a bag. I'll send a car for you and the kids. Quarter of an hour, so be ready! You've got to be out of there before the newsbugs get their claws into you."

"Where to?"

"The Manor, of course. They can't get in here."

She seemed distraught. "Jem won't have me in the place—"

"Oh, yes, he will! Get moving!"

I cut the connection before she could waste time with protests and uncertainties, and put out a PA call for Jeanette, who answered at once. "Do you have a security car available? Not a Manor car."

"Yes." She sounded, like her men, resigned.

"Please, this is mad urgent. Get Kostakis to pick up Mrs. Beltane and bring her here with Melissa and Fred."

"And Fred? You said Fred?"

"Explanations later. He has to get there before the newsbugs find them." She began to say something but I talked over her. "Gus is in the wardroom. Please, just do it!"

By the time I reached the wardroom Kostakis was already gone, my breakfast was on the table and Jackson was drinking tea—real tea in the Manor.

"Is it any use asking questions, Ape?"

I checked the time. "In just seven minutes we'll get the nine o'clock news and perhaps more answers than anybody wants." They would work as fast as that to get a hot scoop on the air before others smelled it out.

I switched on the room screen, and we were at once in the middle of a brutal lead-up. Third Channel had it; it had been my guess that hungry Val would go for their standing "story of the week" offer and the channel had seen it as good enough to deserve a promo.

The little cartoon, Snoop Monkey, was parting the bushes with lickerish expectation and swinging his camera up to catch something just out of view, while the voice-over belted out a promise of titillation to come: "Have we got something for you on the *Nine*

O'clock News or have we got it! Just a hint to whet your attention so you can grab your crotches and hold on for the porno feature of the century! What you like in the Wards is just the same as what they like up in the society lovenests, and this item is as high up as you can get! Just five and a half minutes left for drooling until Third Channel brings you the hottest love story since Samson trashed the temple—and maybe there'll be somebody important rocking under the pressure when this roof falls in on him."

Jackson heard it with glowering distaste, unaware of worse to come. He exploded, "And those disgusting animals squawk about the 'public right to know'! Bedroom crawlers! In my day that snake would have been sacked on the spot for such a performance!"

Would he? Had vidcasts changed so much in a couple of decades? Overseasoned hype had become so common that we scarcely heard it; it was just noise preluding a story that nine times in ten would be an innocuous beat-up. But this was the tenth time. I hoped, felt like praying, that Kostakis was a criminally fast driver.

Then I realized what Jackson had said.

"Please remember not to say things like 'in my day.' Say it a few times and people will be puzzled, and puzzled people ask questions."

He snapped, "We're alone, aren't we?" then conceded ungraciously, "I'll remember." The screen was now displaying some harmless fill-in oddment, but he continued to glare. "Has public taste found its level in the gutter at last?"

"It was never far above it."

"There are limits to public barbarism. Jeremy should have it stopped. Does nobody complain?"

"Those that don't like the mass communicators tune to First Channel. That's the one for propriety and art shows and good English grammar."

"Then shift to First Channel."

"I think you should listen to this news; this may be the only channel to carry it."

"Why should I?"

For all his abrasiveness he was at bottom an old man, lost and afraid and covering fear with pugnacity—and due for a considerable shock. I thought of my own dad, never quite recovered from the collapse of his world, and had no courage to brief Jackson beforehand. Besides—and it was true that I could never forget being a cop who wanted every scrap of information—it was necessary to know exactly what had been told to this squawking public vidmouth.

The Third Channel fanfare blared over the logo, and the screen faded it out as it faded in the head and shoulders of Ivy Beltane's decamped lover, Val. He stared doggedly into the camera, unhappy with the publicity (had he imagined the channel would let him get away with anonymity?) but seeing it through because Albie Aldridge, the "Wardies' communicator and great good mate," allowed him no choice. Albie's face appeared, with its soundtrack *ta-da,* in the top right corner as he gave the wink that meant "all the news that's fit to tell and just a whisker more," and launched into his spiel.

"See this gentleman, all you good citizens, and be glad there are still a few like him—men who will stand for the truth when truth needs to be told. This is a pop law story and a political story and a sex story, and I can tell you right now that Mr. Val Frewby is the top contender for our regular bonus for breaking the story of the week. A bigger story would have to be a war."

Beside me Jackson snorted disgust. The screen switched to a view of a big, rambling, old-style house set among trees and lawns. "This is the Fitzhugh Ladies' College and School of Culture, where the girl children of the wealthier Minders—the super-Minders you might say—go to be educated. Educated? Curious word, that.

They go to learn how to make polite conversation and do the old-time waltz with icy elegance and choose the right spoon for oysters—or is it a fork for oysters? But it seems they also learn a few things not on the ostensible curriculum. Like, for instance, sexual behavior. You see, one of these highborn young ladies has got herself pregnant—or, as they say in the Wards, up the duff!"

Val's head and shoulders surfaced again. "Tell us about it, Val." *Sing for your supper, Val.* "When did you see the little lady, Val?"

"This morning. The police got us out of bed, saying they had these two kids and the girl was pregnant."

"Cops? Why the cops?"

"Because she'd run away and they'd been put on to finding her."

"And find her they did, pregnant and all. But what's unusual about that? The little lady takes her blue pill and it's all over. So what's different here, Val?"

"She didn't take the pill when she should have."

"And so?"

"So she's five months gone and swearing she won't have an abortion. And her mother's on the girl's side. She's taken her in to look after her."

A rat and a half, Ivy's Val. He'd run like a rabbit from the mere suggestion of harboring and run straight for the money.

Albie said sweetly, "The little lady is just sixteen, not married or engaged to be married and so has no legal right to birthing. Correct, Val?"

"Correct, sir."

"Well, there's still time to fix it all up—but both mother and daughter say, No abortion!" With a wild change of emphasis he screamed, "Who the hell do they think they are!" His face expanded to fill the screen, the face of the fighter for right and truth and the underdog! "Who are these Minders who think they are above the law, think they can assume the

sacred privilege of parenthood at their own arrogant
wish and thumb their high-class noses at decency and
deprivation? Would you like to know who, you Wardie
millions? What would happen to you if *your* daughter
was illicitly pregnant and you parents were not merely
harboring but conniving? Doesn't bear thinking about,
does it? So, who are they? Well, here's the daughter."

On the screen appeared a street snap of Melissa, tak-
en a couple of years earlier and not easily recognizable.
Jackson, at any rate, did not recognize her as the tiny
girl he remembered in flashes.

"Know her? Of course you don't. You Wardies aren't
society; you don't get to meet such people. But some of
you may remember Mama."

He had a fairly recent picture of Ivy Beltane. Jackson
made a sound of glottal shock, and I put out a hand to
steady him. He trembled violently.

"This is Mrs. Ivy Beltane, wife of our much-respected
premier, Jeremy Beltane, from whom she separated—
amicably, so it is said—well, so it is said—a dozen
years ago. And the daughter is Melissa Beltane, their
one and only child. And Daddy is liable to be grand-
daddy pretty soon unless justice is done. But will justice be done? Well, now . . . if Val Frewby hadn't done
the honorable thing and blown the whistle on this
family setup, and if your Third Channel watchdog, old
Albie, hadn't seen at once that you had a right to know
of these top-flight shenanigans, justice might well have
been thwarted. If you have money and position you can
get away with most things—until you are found out!"

With an obscene switch to virtue (and an escape
route) he carried on, "Don't think I am maligning Premier Beltane, the people's premier. We don't know yet
what he has to say, or even if in some fashion this
has been kept from him." Yes, old Albie's arse was
kept clear of the firing line. "You can be sure we will
be seeking comment from the premier as soon as he

is available. In the meantime one question remains unanswered. Who is the father? Do you know, Val?"

Val reappeared, more confident now. "I've seen him, Albie. I don't know his name, but I could tell by his speech that he's a Wardie kid."

Albie exulted, "A Wardie kid; people! The princess and the pauper, eh? There's a phrase the girls learn in their highfalutin finishing schools—*nostalgie de la boue.* I looked it up only just now. It's French so maybe my accent isn't quite right, but I can tell you what it means. It means, they still like rolling in the mud! Well, the princess may come out of it smelling like a rose, but God help the boy from the mud!"

Jackson pawed helplessly at my arm. "Take me to my room, Harry. Please, Harry." He couldn't see for tears.

"I can tell you the premier didn't know. She managed to hide it." A kind lie, I hoped.

He whispered, "It will be the finish of Jeremy. A pop law scandal is the end."

Perhaps, but I saw worse to come. As I guided him through the passages I tried to explain to him why, in spite of the trash-stirring Albie and his like, Jeremy might still come through.

He shook his head. "Somebody knows about me, too."

"I think we can head that scheme off."

That is, I hoped we could.

I got him into his room and onto the bed before I recalled that I was late for the meeting I had set up myself.

Kenney was there, calm and neat and collected. So was Fielding; I hadn't asked for him, but he might be useful.

Beltane waved me to a chair. "I know why you're late. We've seen it."

He was unbelievably sprightly, nothing like the man who had been up most of the night, bowed under shock and strain. He was the kind, perhaps, who faced up poorly to the gathering storm but came together as a fightor whon it brokc.

Kenney nodded coolly to me; Fielding stared at the carpet.

"I'm told you have sent for my wife and Melissa and the boy. Thank you for moving quickly, but you should have brought the youngsters here in the first place."

"She needed sympathetic understanding."

His face became very still. At length he said, "Yes," and after another pause, "that was proper thinking. We'll deal with the situation when they get here. You will have heard that vidlouse say he would try to get a statement from me. He'd better have one or he'll speculate worse things. He's survived enough defamation actions to know his limits, but he still spits poison."

Kenney said, looking at me, "The truth should do. Why be complicated?"

I could only agree. "Your daughter was not pregnant to the eye; you knew nothing of it until, say—late last night. She left home under pretense of going to school and the police have been searching for her. You will see her later this morning. That's enough."

"And what then?"

I had no ideas but Kenney had. "Wait until your statement has been vidcast, then get the First Channel pollsters into the Wards to sift opinions. The analysis the sergeant gave last night may be correct. At least you'll know, one way or the other."

"Thank you. I wasn't expecting help from you, Dick."

"Just a suggestion. And that Aldridge disgusts me. Besides, I also need to know."

How to fight dirty while maintaining decency.

Barney Fielding was still rancorous over his own stupidities, still wanting to hurt someone, anyone, if he could do it safely. "Albie told the truth, didn't he? He told it in the people's language. They like him."

Kenney said, "The people are sheep."

That stirred a little venom in me. "Of course they are because that's what you and your kind have made them. They're bound up in their personal affairs because just staying decently alive takes all their attention; they've none to spare for your political caperings until you do something that hurts them. Then see how sheeplike they are! The people have a nasty way of looking straight at the truth while you argue ideology. Treat them like sheep and you'll finish up trampled by bulls."

Fielding grinned. "Sergeant Ostrov for the grimy people! All red and bothered about them."

Beltane's console buzzed, and he picked up the earpiece, listened and grimaced. "The channel. Put them on. On the big screen." On the left wall of the Small Office a painted hanging rolled up to uncover a wall screen, already lighting to show a half-length of a smallish, bald-headed man in shirt sleeves sitting at a desk. His eyes were furious, but his voice under control as he said, "Good morning, Premier."

"Good morning." Not frigid but barely interested.

"I am the chief news editor for Third Channel, and I offer the apologies of the channel and myself for the embarrassing news release concerning your daughter and yourself on the nine o'clock roundup."

He paused expectantly. Careful people, even premiers, treated the channels with respect and kid gloves. Beltane said, "Rubbish! Get on with it."

The news editor's eyes were feral, but he was under orders to placate. "I am instructed to ask if you have any statement to make for the ten o'clock 'cast. This should have been asked of you before the original announcement was made. It certainly would have changed the nature of Mr. Aldridge's delivery."

"Would it? Can you teach an old hyena new tricks?"
The editor waited, hating. "Well, yes, I have a statement. You will notice that I deliver it in the presence of
Mr. Dick Kenney, a shadow minister from the Opposition benches. He will, I think, vouch for my honesty."

So much for the secrecy of Kenney's visit. Beltane
was not above taking advantage, and Kenney could
explain to his party as best he might. Beltane gave
his statement much in the words I had suggested. To
the editor's questions he replied that he had nothing to
add until he had seen his daughter, who had not yet
arrived home.

The editor had a final message. "Your statement will
be on air at ten o'clock. I am instructed to tell you also
that Mr. Aldridge is to be severely disciplined for gross
violation of news channel ethics in not contacting you
before his 'cast. Good morning, sir."

The screen blanked. Beltane asked the air, "Now
what was that disciplinary nonsense about?"

"Reassuring you," Kenney suggested. "Letting you
think the channel will soft-pedal from now on."

"Which it won't, if that man's eyes give a straight
message. But why take it out on Aldridge?"

I had an idea about that. "Somebody high up in the
channel administration is venting spite. A bigger blast
was being readied, but Aldridge hadn't been consulted
and he got in first with the wrong story. Now they're
committed to testing the wind on the premier's popularity before they let loose with the big one."

Fielding asked, "What big one?"

I said, "Get him out of here. He's not in this." A
security man was summoned to march Fielding out.

Kenney mused, "I am in this, am I? Well, then, what
big one?"

Beltane told him: "About twelve hours ago the kidnap failed. I am sure that by now the Opposition network will have got round to telling so senior a member

as yourself that the Cranko ploy had gone astray."

Kenney played at thinking it through, pursing his lips, shaking his head, crossing and uncrossing his legs, enjoying the stretched-out moment. When he was ready he said, "Yes, J.B., I would like to see your father in his new guise. Last night's 'Mr. Jackson,' I take it?"

His imperturbability needed shaking. "Presume what you like, but you can't see him. He's in distress." Beltane cocked an eye at me, considering how much of me he would continue to put up with, and I said to him, "Jackson's my responsibility, and I want him properly recovered. It's him we have to discuss—and not to his face while half of his knowledge is still unrecovered. From what I hear of you, Mr. Kenney, you wouldn't dirty your political fingers with kidnapping for blackmail, so just when did you hear of the kidnap plan?"

"Do you propose to arrest me?"

"Whatever for?"

"Then I will not answer questions."

"You will, Mr. Kenney, if I have to beat answers out of you."

Beltane made some horrified interjection that passed me by, and Kenney sat up straight in his chair. Beyond that he did not seem too greatly disturbed. He said, "You wouldn't be such a fool."

"Jackson is in my care and your loyal and honorable Opposition threatens him. In turn I threaten you—with personal violence."

"You won't dare."

"I will dare, and you will tell me what is necessary and you won't do a solitary thing about it because to do so would entail explaining publicly your party's involvement in criminal activity."

"Then both sides of the House would fall together."

"If the public has to choose between a sentimentally foolish premier and an Opposition that calls on crooks for its dirty work, which will it prefer?"

I didn't dare look at Beltane. Aside from the personal criticism, this was politics at sewer level. Kenney retired into thought, made his decision and said, "About three hours ago I was given a bare outline of what had occurred. I knew nothing of the plan until that moment. I strongly disapprove of the whole affair."

"Your reputation says I should believe you. What matters is: Who told you?"

"I don't know."

"I suppose that's true in a way. We know how the system works and your network contact would be that lady, oh-six-two."

"Whom I would not recognize if I saw her."

"No matter. Fielding knows her and will talk like a gusher. Then there are Cranko and Ratface, still here and with no convictions to have the courage of. They will talk. The system being what it is, none will know very much, but in total they'll supply unrelated driblets of fact and guesswork that will eventually add up to a picture of sorts. We'll get there in the end, Mr. Kenney. Then, there's the evidence of the man I shot."

"You don't imagine I know his name, do you?"

"No, but the morgue will identify him, and that will give us the network of his immediate associates. And so on. You see how it builds."

He said nothing.

I turned to Beltane. "You might as well send him home now. His knowledge of Melissa has been pre-empted by the Third Channel, and his immediate business will be to stop his party making any move against you while we hold Cranko and Ratface."

Beltane said to him, "Yes, go away." Like sending a bad child to bed.

Kenney stood. "You've come down to taking orders from your hired gun."

"In his area of competence."

"He's a hoodlum at heart. Be wary of him."

"I know it and I am."

That rankled but did not surprise. Beltane trusted me within certain limits but did not approve of me as a human boing. I, for that mattor, thought littlo of him. We moved in different worlds. I preferred mine.

Kenney said, "Good morning to you, Premier. Happy grandfatherhood," and as he passed me, "Your kind wins police medals. The citation: He gave his wasted life to brutishly insensitive loyalty to a myth."

I would not give my life willingly for any loyalty. People build too much on a personal impression.

In the silence of his going there seemed little to discuss. Beltane fiddled with papers on his desk. After a while I caught him looking at me.

"Thank you," he said.

For all the grudging tone, it was more than a copper usually gets for making a bastard of himself to a mixed-blood gentleman who I suspected was basically worth more, in human qualities, than either of us.

When Ivy Beltane came, she came with banners flying, followed by a grinning Kostakis. She stormed in, crying, "Your damned driver should have his license canceled!"

Kostakis mimed apologetic grief. "The boss said to hurry. Had to hop a few fences."

Behind him Melissa and Fred crept in like frightened mice, whether overwhelmed by circumstances or simply terrified by Kostakis's driving was hard to say. Corner cutting by hopping fences is one of the few maneuvers capable of overturning a hovercar.

Beltane faced his wife—for the first time in years if the gossip was true—with a blank stare, but she, thoroughly upset, was ready to hit out at anyone and he was a given target.

"I didn't ask to come here! I don't want to be here, and it's certain that Melissa has lived here too long. You are not a fit father!"

Beltane answered like a statue giving voice, with honesty but without heart. "I don't want you here but for your own sake it is necessary that you remain. Unless you prefer to be thrown to the vidhounds. I bow to your judgment about Melissa and my fitness as a father; my neglect has brought this situation about. Now, if you will sit down and we can cease quarreling, we may be able to decide what's next."

The sheer bloodlessness of his answer took the hostility out of her. Besides, she was in my view an intelligent woman who could have her moment of spitefulness and at once retire into firm sense. She sat on the nearest chair and said bitterly, "Not quite all your fault. I hadn't many illusions about Val, but I didn't think he was quite such a cowardly bastard."

Kostakis explained, "There's a miniscreen in the security bus, and they saw the vidcast. We only made it out just in time, Harry. The channel copters were coming in all angles, so they know we headed for here."

Beltane was unmoved. "This place is safe from bugging. Any channel attempting it will be put off the air. The important thing is that no public statements be made by anyone but myself." He looked at last with tightening lips at Melissa, then surveyed Fred with a frankly inquisitive stare before nodding obscurely to himself. Perhaps he approved of the look of the boy. He waved them to the couch.

They sat down gingerly and Fred put out a hand to hold the girl's, but she pulled away.

Mrs. Beltane asked, "And what position do you propose to take?"

"We must decide that here and now."

"In front of strangers? This is a family matter."

"No longer. It may be a national scandal before it's over. And these two strangers have so far been our staunchest helpers. What they know is safe with them."

That was handsome; at least he didn't waver over a decision once made. He turned to Kostakis. "You must not confide these affairs to your colleagues or to anyone else at all."

"Understood, Boss . . . sir."

The premier returned his attention to the couch. "You are Fred Blacker?"

"Yes, sir." His voice was strong but strained, a touch too determined not to be overawed.

"And you wish to marry my daughter?"

"Yes, sir!" No strain about that.

Melissa said, "No!"

Fred regarded her with astonishment, not quite believing . . . some error . . . some misapprehension . . .

Beltane, faced with the unexpected, waited. His wife, better prepared, said quietly, "You have two choices, Melissa: You marry the child's father or—" She checked and asked the obvious question, "This boy is the child's father, is he? Are you sure?"

The implication brought Beltane's head sharply up.

Melissa said, "Yes."

Her mother asked, "How can you be sure?" and Beltane's expression I can describe only by a word you don't often hear these days—scandalized.

There is a phenomenon you come across occasionally in kids in their mid-teens, a vacillation between the grotesque ignorance that leads to so much of their idiot behavior and an uncanny assumption of adulthood and dignity. It is as though in the midst of juvenile chaos some promise of the man- or woman-to-be shines through, and for a moment you are dealing on an equal footing. I had seen Melissa, up to this instant, as a plump, self-absorbed, sulky little bitch; now, suddenly, she was a woman facing unpleasant facts and ready to deal with them, older and gravely sure of herself.

She said, "I got frightened with the others and took those pills. Then I saw I had to go through with it and didn't take them after Fred. So it's Fred's."

Fred's baffled, horrified gaze was fixed on a stranger, someone he had not dreamed existed. Beltane retreated into stony blankness, his politician's tactic for covering fast reappraisal. Then he asked what seemed to me the wrong question because shock overtook thought. He asked, in startlement, "Others?"

"Three others." She made it a fact, not a confession.

I stole a glance at Kostakis, standing close by me, and he was in a petrified funk, eyes helplessly on the girl, waiting for the moment when she would turn her head and identify him with a collusive smile. Melissa looked only at her father; she was intent on the matter in hand, not on her incidental diversions.

Beltane remarked aimlessly, "Three!" He pulled himself back into the immediate scene. "Melissa, you have two choices: You marry Fred Blacker or you have the child aborted."

She responded with a calm precision that cried aloud of her Ladies' College training. "I can't marry Fred. It wouldn't be suitable. He will realize that when he goes home and thinks about it. Besides, Daddy, I've been thinking about those boys we discussed as possible husbands and I think we should settle on Jimmy Sinclair. He's quite nice, and his people have a lot of money."

I had never heard anything quite like the cool delivery. It pinpointed what was often said of the finishing schools: that they turned out girls who understood every twist of the social maze but not a solitary fact about the pity of the human heart. It was not the girl's fault; it was the outcome of parental neglect and an education that equated social requirement with emotional reality. She was not deliberately cruel to Fred;

she did not consider him because he was, aside from the usefulness expected of Wardie workers, outside the ambit of her consideration. One considered one's equals; others recognized their places. The old joke says that sexual congress does not constitute a formal introduction. I had seen it come true.

Ivy Beltane, more aware than the rest of us of the forces at work in her daughter's mind, recovered first. "You will present this Jimmy Sinclair with a ready-made infant? He might not be willing to forgo his right."

"I've thought about that. He doesn't have to know. Once it is born the baby can be given to some barren couple who can't have their own child."

Beltane's face was unreadable. He said slowly, "That will not entitle you to a second conception. Also, the law does not concede the right of adoption to barren couples save on the death of both natural parents of the child. It would leave the way open to concealment and illegal birthings."

Melissa shrugged. "Oh, the law, the law!"

"It decides."

Fred rose to sudden outrage. "It's my kid, too! It's my baby you're all talking about!"

Melissa half turned to him. "You can have it if you insist, but I would prefer a better home for it."

She was merely practical, in her view, unconscious of insult; she was the one talking sense in a welter of adult obstructionism.

Her mother tried to close some understanding around the girl. "You still will have used up the single permission you have in fact not yet been given. You won't be able to give your husband his own child."

Melissa's adult calm deserted her as she turned on her mother in an exasperated tantrum. "All you talk about is the law! Well, Daddy can change the law."

Beltane said, "He can't."

"Of course you can! It's only a little thing."

"It is not a little thing. Even if it were, I could not do it and I would not."

The girl did not believe him. "But you're the premier! You're the one who tells them what laws to make."

"Where did you hear that?"

She began to cry, not in breakdown but in frustrated rage. "Everybody knows that! The girls at school all know; their people know. They know you can do anything if you want to." Her voice rose to a thin squeal. "Otherwise what's the good? What are you premier *for?*"

A sickness passed over Beltane's face, and I wondered was he thinking of the disgraceful truth that had thrust itself into the open: That our society of oligarch administrators striving to maintain themselves in position had created so corrupt a system that their children saw corruption as the way of life, the norm, and never realized more than dimly what "corruption" meant. To them it represented the perks of position. They grew up knowing the true purpose of power.

Beltane said softly, knowing he would not be understood but that the beginning must be made, "Your pregnancy has become public knowledge. It is no longer possible for me to bend the law without the entire nation observing me at it. It cannot be done."

Melissa retreated directly from rage into hysteria. She threw herself screaming to the floor, beating at the carpet. The hapless Fred, still incredulous of his utter rejection, lifted her up, and she battered his face with closed fists, drawing blood. In the end I had to take her from him, clasping her arms to her sides while she squalled and hacked at me with her heels.

Beltane used the console to call for a first aid attendant, and it was Jeanette who appeared with a ready syringe. With her came a security man who carried a quiescent Melissa to her room.

When they had gone, Beltane sat still in his chair, but his hands shook. His wife tried to comfort the shattered Fred; she put an arm round his shoulders and murmured to him while with a handkerchief she dabbed at his ignominiously bleeding nose. He listened dully, saying nothing. Or, perhaps, he didn't listen at all.

Beltane said, "Now a word with you, young fellow!"

Ivy stood to face him. "You'll leave him alone. He may be the greatest loser in this unpleasantness, and you are not blameless."

They confronted each other in silent thoughtfulness. A bitter and demeaning personal battle was brewing and that was better left to them alone. I took Fred's arm and urged him out of the room. Kostakis came after us, happy to escape unscathed.

We went to the wardroom, empty while poor Jeanette scratched for men to fulfill my unreasonable calls upon her small command. I commented to Kostakis on the thing uppermost in my mind. "I've never realized the extent to which these Minder kids grow up thinking that power is the right to do as you like."

Kostakis pretended surprise. "Isn't it that? Even you believe it—a bit—in your own way."

"I don't think so."

"Every copper believes it. He knows he can get away with bribe taking and violence and that's just what he does."

"Not all of us, Gus."

"Too many of you, anyway. And you all get funny ideas, like the kids at that school of hers."

Kostakis had the mischief-making instinct of the cunning. He was fumbling for a blade to prick me with, so I thought he might as well unload what bothered him.

"Such as?"

"Such as that the law is right. And if it's right, then law and right are the same thing. But they aren't, are they? Then there's justice. That gets mixed up with law and right, but it's really something else; and between the lot you can always find a moral reason for what you want to do—just the way those kids see power is right and don't worry about who gets hurt. You get that way it seems every thought a man has should be questioned because it's hiding something else."

Maybe, maybe, but I was too tired for abstractions. "And what do you believe in, Gus, that should be questioned?"

"Me? I'm silly—I believe that having a good heart gets you further than worrying about right and wrong."

Fred lifted his head from his hands to say, "Bugger that for a sod's idea." He looked from Gus to me with tears in his eyes. "What the hell does she want the kid for? Just to give it away! What for?"

That question, lost in the crossfire, still needed answering. But not now. . . . I needed sleep.

Part III

The View from the Gutter

8

Ostrov: A Place for Jackson

I had counted on five hours sleep, but Kostakis shook
me awake shortly after midday.

Spitting and snarling as though the whole news service was an outrage, he told me how the midday 'cast
had carried the premier's bald statement and followed
it with reactions to street interviews. I stopped him
there. "What reactions? What did they get?"

"Thumbs up for Daddy, not one lousy crocodile tear
for the girl."

"That could be a matter of how the questions were
asked; Third Channel is only a garbage hunter. We'll
get First Channel opinion later in the day; they'll ask
the right questions in the right way."

"So what? Wardies don't watch First Channel; that's
for snobs and arty types."

That was unfortunately true; public opinion was
molded by the loudmouths. In the Wards, Melissa
would remain Bitch of the Season.

"There's more," Kostakis said. "They got on to Fred's
parents."

Bastards! "How?"

"That's my question, too. Only Fred and Fielding knew about them, and they've never left the Manor to be able to talk to anyone."

The world wouldn't wobble on its axis if the Blackers served jail terms. Leakage of information was the irritant. I suggested, "Your security group?"

"No chance. Beltane ordered that nobody leave the grounds or make private calls without supervision. Everything goes through Jeanette."

"Then security's tight. I know Jeanette."

"Nobody else knows about the Blackers."

"Somebody does; somebody outside. Miss oh-six-two, whoever she is."

Kostakis was glum. "The Opposition link. Kenney's. No name, so we can't find her."

"Fielding knows her, so she's a pipeline to—" I became uncertain of how much I could say and finished lamely, "the enemy."

"What enemy?"

"We'd better talk to the premier."

"What's this about an enemy? Aren't I supposed to know?" He sounded like a child told he can't be trusted with grown-up matters. This peculiar man—part lunatic actor, part failed artist, part efficient operative and wholly romantic—was readying himself to sulk. "Why won't you tell me?"

I said, "Classified. I'll pick you up in the wardroom in ten minutes."

He slouched out, convinced that I hid things from him in sheer capriciousness.

This raised the question of whether or not he could be trusted with knowledge of Jackson's identity. I saw him as one who would guard a secret to the death while he fancied himself a masterminding spider in the web, but romance can make an unmanageable hash of reality. Yet, my effectiveness could be enormously

increased by an offsider who knew enough of the facts
to act in an emergency without consulting me.

Beltane's morning recovery had come and gone; we
found him alone but harassed and gray and tired out.

He told us to sit down and had to tell Kostakis twice,
at which Gus perched on the edge of a chair like a small
boy wary of taking some disastrous liberty. Delivering the family had been one thing, but inclusion in
planning at the highest level of state was more than
a Wardie soul had dreamed of.

Beltane asked had I seen the midday news on three.

"No, but Mr. Kostakis has told me about it."

He looked at Kostakis as though aware of him for
the first time as an individual with a face as well as a
function. "Are you co-opting this man as a permanent
assistant?"

"With, I hope, your approval."

"I have other work for Mr. Kostakis. Your task is to
look after Mr. Jackson and you should not need an
assistant for that."

The next few minutes might be difficult and were
best broached head-on. "There is the complication of
your wife and daughter."

"He is a stranger to them. People stay in the Manor
for short periods—politicians, diplomats, persons of
influence in civil sectors. Mr. Jackson is known as a
visiting political aide. That is enough."

"Perhaps not, sir." I had been thinking over an aspect
of Mr. Jackson's disguise that could be difficult to deal
with. I tried a shot in the dark. "Let me ask Mr. Kostakis
a question. Gus, has Mr. Jackson ever put you in mind
of somebody else?"

Beltane was in immediate fury but contained it.

Kostakis, who had been following or failing to follow
the conversation blank faced, said, "I was meaning to
ask you if he was a relation of the old man—old Mr.

Gerald I mean, the one resting up country."

I didn't care to look just then at Beltane. "What makes you think that?"

"This morning I saw him in a dressing gown and slippers like the old—Mr. Gerald I mean used to do on his good days when he could get around a bit. It was just for a minute when he had his back to me I thought if he hunched down and shuffled a bit he could be old Mr. Gerald to the life. When you've seen people a lot you recognize them from the back as much as the front. Would he be a nephew or some such?"

Beltane said sharply, "No!"

I told him as gently as I could, "You do recognize back views. The person turns round and you see it is someone else, but the confusion lingers. Members of the household remark on it to each other and ask questions—about relatives, for instance. If they don't get answers they start to make them up, and sometimes they finish with something worse than the truth. We should—"

He stopped me with a gesture. "What have you told this man, Sergeant?"

"Nothing, sir. How should I?"

"Indeed, how should you! Yet here and now you are feeding his curiosity to a point where it must be satisfied." In anger his battered weariness had fallen away. "Are you trying to force my hand?"

Nothing for it now but boldness. "Yes, sir. We must get Jackson out of the Manor before your wife and daughter feel the first prickles of familiarity. We don't want questions—and there is altogether too much vid interest centered on the place."

He tried to stare me down as though rage might wilt me, then roared like a tormented bull, "He was brought here because I need him here! Here! He's of no damned use to me somewhere out of reach!"

I could see Kostakis relaxing, enjoying himself now,

at the heart of affairs and loving it. I wondered was I
risking a gun in the hands of a big child.

Beltane needed pushing. "You depend on me—or say
you do—but every twist makes my job harder to do. I'm
not equipped to outthink fate and accidents. If I ask for
something it's because I need it." He listened with stiff
patience, preparing more anger; I needed to jolt him.
"This whole Jackson affair has been a blunder from the
beginning."

He said, pleasantly and dangerously, "I think otherwise," but I sensed a willingness to listen. He was
not so sure of his planning as he had been. Then he
surprised me by saying, casually, to Kostakis, "Would
you call yourself an honest man?"

Kostakis looked helplessly at me, found no answer
there and settled for truth. " 'Course I would. Only a
nit'd say different of hisself."

"And what would you be prepared to die for?"

"Me?" His tone said this was unfair; a man shouldn't
be pelted with thought stoppers. "I'd die fighting for
me life, but I don't go for any guff about dying for me
mates; that only swaps one waste for another. And I
don't think much of dying for a cause, neither. You
have to live for it. You don't train a soldier to die for
his country; you train him to stay alive so he can make
some other silly prick die for his."

Years might have passed since Beltane had heard the
like; he was fascinated. He asked me, "Do you trust
him?"

"Yes."

"Why?"

There's no answer to that, no matter how well you
know the one in question. I could only shrug and say,
"You do or you don't. If you trust a man it lifts his
opinion of himself and he tries to justify it."

Beltane disregarded that nonsense and asked, "Do
you feel important, Mr. Kostakis?"

"I feel I'm being suckered by experts."

"Take my word, you are not. Sergeant, tell him who Mr. Jackson is."

I said, "Think twice."

"You urge me, then you caution me."

"It's your risk, not mine."

He corrected me, "Yours, I think. You will be responsible for seeing that he does not betray knowledge carelessly. If he does, what will you do? Shoot him?"

Perhaps he was testing me, perhaps only laughing at the bind I had got myself into. "Maybe. Maybe not. I don't know." I really did not know; the question had taken me by surprise. Calling yourself a pragmatist is a far cry from bringing a life-or-death decision immediately home to roost.

Kostakis said, "He would, you know. He's one of those bastards who thinks he knows right from wrong and which poor sap ought to suffer for it."

Beltane nodded companionably. "I know. But how about you? Do you want such dangerous knowledge?"

"Of course I do. I want to know what I'm doing and why I'm doing it."

He wanted it for the fluff-headed reason that he was having a ball and wanted every dance. And he was all too sure that he knew what made me tick. So was Beltane. Parlor shrinks should remember that a man is many men.

"Then listen carefully. My father is not, as you think, in a country retreat. He is here, in the Manor, as Mr. Jackson, rejuvenated and restructured."

Kostakis swallowed that whole—the miracles of science are, after all, only two-hour vidcast wonders—but applied a cautious test. "But the old feller—your father that is—was off his—got senile."

"Off his head? Out of it, perhaps." Quickly he told the whole demeaning story while Kostakis listened like a bright lad to a cloak-and-dagger yarn, and I wondered, with a sick feeling of having jumped off a cliff, if I had not acted with more instinct than judgment.

He told how an increasing inability to deal with some decisions (carefully he did not specify which) had caused him to consider and in the end connive at the cure and rejuvenation of his father. He needed a crutch and knew no other than the one he had been taught and disciplined by. He spoke of Nguyen selecting a bodyguard of total integrity— at which Kostakis shot me a glance of curious wonder. Or was it doubt? Finally Beltane spoke of a momentous decision he must make and deliver to a meeting of the prime minister and state premiers in the next forty-eight hours. He needed, could not do without his father's advice. He made no bones about his position of emotional dependence. At the end he said, "There you have it. No more mystery."

He mistook his man. "Beg to differ, Boss. Two mysteries still."

"The nature of the decision to be made? That remains my affair. The other?"

"Why trust me?"

"Do I? I trust Sergeant Ostrov. You are the only other person capable of betraying what I have said. If the word leaks you must be the informant, but you can easily be discountenanced as an eccentric with romantic ideas and a rich imagination. Your supervisor's description was vivid."

So he had had his own reasons for checking on Kostakis, but he was Minder clumsy with people outside his class; I saw the flash of anger on Kostakis's face, instantly hidden but undercutting his apparent gentleness in unnerving fashion. It was not something to become easily used to.

Beltane asked, frowning, "Do I wrong you?"

"No." I chalked up a plus for honesty; no man enjoys

having truth fired at him. "But I got more going for me than just some private beliefs."

"She said that also." Jeanette, I feared, would hear more about that, but I would back her to return as good as she got.

Kostakis took hold now to point out that Cranko and his connections could tell of the hospital treatments.

"Not while I can prove their association with professional crime."

"So where do I come in? What do I have to do?"

"Be my personal bodyguard, unnoticeable in a crowd."

I had to protest, "You surely don't mean to show yourself outside the Manor!"

"I am a public person, almost public property, and I have appointments to keep. I must not be seen to hide or to enter by back doors or to disappear for no good reason or to appear suddenly with an augmented police guard. So I am recruiting Mr. Kostakis on his supervisor's commendation of him as a man with fast reflexes and some unexpected physical capacities."

Kostakis didn't actually preen, but his resentments began to cancel out. He asked, "What do you reckon might happen?"

Beltane smiled, all good fellowship. "They should try to kill me. In their place that is what I would consider. Wouldn't you?"

Kostakis matched him grin for grin. "Not with me guarding you, I wouldn't."

He meant just that. Nguyen had certainly given him self-confidence.

Beltane asked me, "Where will you hide my father? With the police?"

"Good God, no! Give them a mystery and they'll drive him mad with snooping. I wouldn't put it past some of them to try drugging the info out of him."

He said something foul about police methods, and I

pointed out that people had been saying that for two centuries. "But, for better or worse, they're all you've got. Can't live with 'em and can't live without 'em."

"Where, then?"

"In my home, with my parents."

"Telling them what?"

"That they have a guest. Big secret! My father will be awed but delighted; my mother will disapprove but say nothing. She's the kind that slams doors and stays tight-lipped for a week."

He smiled grimly, admitted that he must trust my judgment and asked, "What sort of place is it?"

It was a fair question, but it scratched the class consciousness I pretended was not in me. "Poor but honest. Mr. Jackson will have a chair to sit on and a bed to lie in."

He said, "Don't be so touchy," but he looked away.

"Now I'll have to think how to get him out of here unseen. The newsbugs are swarming."

"In darkness, I presume. You can have him after midnight."

"So late?" I had already been up all one night.

The charging bull expression returned. "I brought him back for a purpose and I haven't had ten minutes alone with him! Midnight—or later if we're not through by then." He stood up. "Mr. Kostakis, be ready to accompany me into City Center at three o'clock. Afternoon suit and brimmed hat. If you have nothing suitable, see my chief secretary. His name is Collins."

He walked out of the Small Office as though he had already forgotten us. Perhaps he had.

Kostakis made a grimace of distaste. "Under all the acting he's as weak as piss. Would you believe it, hanging on to Daddy's hand!"

"I believe it, but I don't really understand."

"That's another little mystery to put with why Melissa wants a baby. It's a real hang-up of a family."

*   *   *

Kostakis went in search of Collins for clothes suitable to a gentleman mingling in the crowd round the premier. I thought he would pass so long as he kept his mouth shut.

Going to my room, which was next to Jackson's, I was hailed peremptorily by the voice of Mrs. Beltane coming up behind me. She asked without preliminary frills, "Who is the man occupying old Gerald's room?"

I told her I had no idea which had been old Gerald's room, while silently I cursed the premier's idiocy. Whatever tales he told the staff to account for the old man's absence, he should have had better sense than to allow a stranger to be put into his father's room.

"That one," she said, pointing. "You have just passed it."

"Mr. Jackson is in there. A political aide from interstate, I'm told."

"So Gerald will not be returning?" More than curiosity loaded the question—suspicion and something nasty, an almost prurient nuzzling after information. Her animus against the old man ran deep.

"I couldn't say. I'm told he is under treatment."

"Do you believe that? He has been in senile decay for over twenty years. No doctor will treat the moribund and no hospital would accept him."

I could only say that in that case I didn't know where he might be.

"Nobody knows or cares," she said. "I would not have known he was away if Melissa didn't have a soft spot for the old wreck. Thinking he might be back from wherever they took him she went to this room and was shooed away by a stranger."

"I can't help you. I've been here only a few hours."

She regarded me closely as if wondering would I respond to a blatant pass (and I might have done despite her being some fifteen years older) but instead asked, as if for a favor, "Would you please ask my husband where Gerald is? Melissa wants to know."

"Can't you ask him?"

She became harsh, "Only if I must. We speak when speech can't be avoided."

It would have been interesting then to have known what lay behind their estrangement or what in fact powered the whole unbalanced family. "Very well; I'll ask him."

"Thank you."

She would have gone on past me if I had not said, "In return, can you tell me something?"

"What is it?"

"Why your daughter insists on having her baby."

She could have told me to mind my own affairs, but perhaps she considered that Melissa's rescue from the Handspikes constituted a debt to be paid. "She no longer insists. She will submit to a clinical abortion."

After all the squalling hysteria that was anticlimax. "That will calm the public airwaves for the premier, at any rate."

"Him? Who gives a damn for him except those precious Wardies he placates with tiny concessions? My thought is for the man she will eventually marry and who will want his own child."

"And Fred Blacker?"

She bit her lip, looked undecided and then guilty, and settled for an unconvincing hardness. "A good enough boy of his kind, but he doesn't count. He'll father his own legal child when his time comes. He's been sent home. Big-hearted Jem, instead of kicking him out, has arranged to transfer him to City Parks. That will have to satisfy him."

Power solves its problems easily—a new job to massage heartbreak. *That's it, son; like it or lump it! Could have chucked you on the junk heap, you know!*

She mistook my brooding on Fred for unsatisfied curiosity. "How did I get her to agree? I pointed out that she can't go back to her Fitzhugh school after all the public foofaraw; she'll have to be tutored at home until the noise dies down, and in any case she'll be social poison to the rich bitches with daughters at the school. It took her about ten seconds to decide to get rid of it when she saw that she wouldn't have to face up to the girls at school. She said they'd know she'd won her bet anyway because of the Aldridge vidcast."

"Bet?"

She echoed flatly, "Bet. Never underestimate peer group inanity among teenagers. Our rich little sluts-in-the-making talk smut just like Wardie sluts-in-the-making but without the firsthand observation. Because ours are kept in ladylike ignorance of the obligations of the sexual contract, they fantasize on the basis of girl-ish scurrilities whispered behind their hands. Melissa has had, as well, a savagely deprived home life, for which I have to accept blame for not seeing just how deprived. She strives for attention. I've known that she exaggerates to make herself interesting, but her dormitory fancies have been more unrestrained than I imagined. She boasted to the girls that she had had sex with a man. They know her too well to believe her so she vowed to prove it by having a baby. So— three men, three failures, and up and over with the gardener's boy!"

On that savage sentence her voice broke and she wept.

In the helplessness that tears bring to a man I mumbled, "You must get Beltane to let her go."

"Let her go!" She moved from tears to ferocity. "I'll take her from here if I have to shoot him! And I hope the other old animal is dead, too. I hope they took him away to kill him."

She pushed past me, turned the corner and vanished.

Kostakis's "hell of a family" didn't cover the half of it.

I lay on my bed in preparation for another long night and drifted into sleep while pondering on Ivy Beltane's hatred of old Beltane . . . and on where Nguyen fitted into the big pattern.

The premier's appointment had not been a lengthy one because Kostakis woke me a little after five. The change in him was enough to make me say, "Clothes make the man!", and indeed he was Gus transformed into an estimable Mr. Gustav Kostakis by the outfit Collins had found for him. It was by Minder standards a simple afternoon suit, but it fitted him like a sheath and would have been the nearest thing to finery he had worn in his life. "What was the job?"

"Opening a science history exhibition. Waste of time for a top man."

"He has to keep the scientists on his side; they're a strong lobby. No suspicious characters all gunned up and aiming to kill?"

"Don't laugh. You just try personnel protection in a crowd and see how you go. We got a drill for sifting groups and vantage spots, but it isn't perfect; it's hard to sniff out a bloke who might risk a shot from twenty or thirty paces." He sat himself on the end of the bed. "Finished with the gossip? Now—there's a new twist in the story."

"Christ, what now?" I reached automatically for trousers and shirt for instant action; the job had me on tenterhooks.

"Newsbugs. Fourth Channel this time, looking for something to match Albie A.'s beat-up this morning. And it stinks."

"Tell me."

"I can show you. Did you know all news releases are recorded here for study by the secretaries? We can get a playback on the Small Office screen."

In the Small Office he fiddled with Beltane's desk controls as to the Manor born. "Boss showed me hisself!" Peacock vain but no less effective for that.

On the screen some idiot crowd idol asked with a more-in-this-than-meets-the-eye wink, "Who's heard of old Gerald Beltane lately? You oldies will remember the premier's father, battle-weight loudmouth of the House of Reps for thirty years, the numbers man who just about ran the state by conniving behind the scenes and rode his son to victory as member, minister and deputy premier and had him on the way to the premiership before he— Before he what? Disappeared from politics, that's what. Went away with no farewells, no tears, no nothing at all. Well, it's no secret what happened, but folks do forget. The old man went home to live with the genetic form of Alzheimer's disease and no memory of what happened yesterday or two minutes ago—complicated by a type of stutter-and-dribble senility. Something nasty in the family chromosomes, it seems."

The yammering icon made a meal of it, a tattler's banquet. "The old man has lived close on thirty years with a disease that usually kills much faster than that. So—has he been receiving unauthorized care, taking up medical time and talent for the dying rather than for the living? The system is plain, folks, with no room for sentiment: When you've had it, you've had it and you don't snaffle the services needed by the useful young.

"It's possible for Alzheimer sufferers to live a long time, but wouldn't you think they'd be better off dead? Staying alive could be torture. And should the useless old occupy population space on a planet that can hardly feed itself? Some people think we should stop being po-faced about euthanasia and make a law. . . .

"Well, some weeks ago the old boy was transferred from the Manor to a rest cottage in the countryside. So we were told, though in fact nobody gave a damn where he was; he was history. But was he transferred? And if so, where to? You know the public record system— cradle to grave, every move, everything except how many craps a day you have—but we can't locate old Gerald. No rest home or cottage has him, even under an assumed name. And Jeremy Beltane owns no secret properties, being a more honest man than some of his confreres.

"But how honest? Where is old Gerald, why is truth covered up, why can't an old, sick man be traced? And why make a secret of it? After this morning's keyhole peep at the premier's daughter we find some intriguing questions about her father and grandfather. What goes on in the Manor, eh? What goes on?"

It was classic smut, delivered with loads of "honest puzzlement," scratching a story out of nothing . . . save that it came out of something deadly.

"What did the boss say?"

"They jammed a mike in his face as we left the exhibition and asked where his father was. Resting in the country, says he. 'So why can't we find him?' squawks the bug, and the boss says, 'Bad staff work I reckon,' and clams up on him."

It had been the only possible spur-of-the-moment tactic. "Did the question upset him?"

"No. He just treated it like bad manners. These public men learn to handle theirselves."

In public, yes; in private this one was less impressive. "Did he comment about it to you?"

"No, but when I got a chance I said to him it was as well the old man was getting out because the bugs would be sniffing at the Manor fences to see who went in and out or even blew his nose. He just nodded."

"I'd better talk to him."

"You can't. He's with his father and said not to inter-
rupt him for anything short of murder. You can see him
maybe at midnight, not before."

"Then how the hell can I spirit the old man away
without planning? There's a gauntlet of eyes to run—
a skyful of them."

Kostakis said, "I've got that arranged."

I didn't believe him. "He told you to see to it?"

"He said he wondered how it could be done, and I
told him how and he said, 'Hop to it.' "

" 'Hop to it'?"

"Well, words to that effect."

"So tell me how."

He did, and his method was as complex as his own
personality but as nearly flawless as shooting in the
dark can be. I had to pay his ingenuity; he remained
my one piece of good fortune in this business.

After that I could only cool my heels until he should
decide it was time for us to move. He loved having me
under orders, and I was too amused—and too pleased—
to resent it.

The channel copters, five of them, circled at low
altitude, searching the area for persons entering or leaving. The Manor was protected against electronic bugging but "news observation" (an elastic term) had to
be permitted. Beltane could have had the police minister shepherd them off as constituting a nuisance, but
that would only have brought vidhowls of "What has
the Manor to hide? The public has a right to know
what happens at the residence maintained by public
money."

What they hoped to find they could not have said,
but they had started two hares and hoped to catch
one or both. As people moved in and out, the copters
dropped a camera or two on extension lines, taking
full-face pictures to vid to their head offices for identi-

fication. They bagged a score of deliverymen, political
secretaries, gardeners and outside security men—and
one channel lost an expensive camera when it swung
too close to a sturdy old Moreton Bay fig tree.

At sundown they switched in the infrareds, tuned to
body heat. That gained them nothing. Any more than
my attempts to sleep gained me anything. A broken
sleep pattern upsets my rhythms completely; I drop off
at wrong moments when I should be alert, then fail to
drop off when there is time to relax.

That night I read and dozed and read again and
squirmed on the bed until, a little before midnight, I
began walking the corridors because I could not keep
still.

So it was that I walked down a corridor and round
the corner into the main reception hall, to find father
and son alone in the huge space and at a furiously
hostile end to the meeting the son had moved science,
law and love to bring to pass.

They saw me and fell silent.

Beltane, for the instant before he controlled himself,
blazed with anger and hurt, not at me but at his father;
he presented, for the unforgettable second, a picture of
a man insulted and goaded beyond bearing. Yet with it
he was a son, a small boy who had been shamed and
humiliated where he had sought guidance and love.

The tableau broke at once. Beltane pushed silently
past me as though he would as soon have run me down.
I doubt that he recognized me, that he saw more than
an interruption closing off an intolerable scene. His
breathing hard and hoarse, he went in the direction
of the Small Office without a further word.

Jackson gazed after the retreating back with an expression of acute disappointment and distress, as if he had
picked up some familiar thing to find it tainted and
decayed. Then, slowly, his face fell apart into lines
of regret and grief. For the second time I saw him cry

slow tears that gathered at the corners of his eyes and
hung there before they slid to his cheeks and he raised
a hand to brush them away.

I asked, if only to cover the embarrassment of intrusion, "What's wrong, Arthur?"

I thought he might snap at me, but he replied only,
"This is outside your brief, Ape." I stood there, discom-
fited and helpless, until he said, closing off the scene,
"I understand I am to be shipped out to other quarters."

"Yes."

"In your care."

"Yes."

"That may be best; there's nothing left here." He put
a hand on my arm. "I need rest."

Leaning heavily as I took him to his room, he was
near to emotional collapse. As I laid him on the bed
and pulled the slippers off his feet, I told him, "We
leave in three hours or so."

"Well enough." After a moment he said, "He didn't
need me; he only thought he did." He sounded like
a man speaking from the far end of an echoing hall.
"He needed someone to agree with him, to assure him
he hadn't got it wrong. And now he is in his office,
rearranging destiny after bringing his own disasters
upon himself. And this damned resurrection has been
a total waste."

He closed his eyes, and I left him, feeling that what
I had seen in the reception hall had been something
more than the end of a lifetime's affection, the recognition that the affection had in fact died long ago. It had
been the kind of falling out that occurs when each sees
the other—and himself—for the first time whole and
undistorted by love.

That can be terrifying. As you will discover, I know
what I am talking about.

Strangely, I slept easily and woke, as I had timed
myself (it's something you learn to do) at 3:30.

*   *   *

I wakened Jackson and at first tried to help him dress, but he pushed me away with a mulish determination to look after himself. "That's all done with," he said and half snarled, " 'Richard is himself again.' "

We went down to the wardroom to find not only security but staff from all areas of the Manor gathering there.

The prelude to the movement was something close to a yelling tantrum from Jeanette, who was threatening to throw in the job. It seemed that on discovering what Kostakis intended she had taken the risk of confronting Beltane in the early hours of the morning, only to be told that the bodyguard's orders were to be followed. For once tough Jeanette had been near tears of fury and had vented some loud, unwholesome truths about hours of work and the state's unwillingness to pay overtime. She was appeased only by a rattled premier's promise that every duc cont would be paid. (From whose purse?) It had probably been the only way he could struggle free of her.

I asked her what condition he had been in, and she screamed at me, "In his bloody pajamas, of course!"

"I meant mental condition, mood."

She didn't know and didn't care, and sat herself in a corner of the wardroom in shrewish silence. Who could blame her?

What Kostakis had done was, co-opt every available member of staff in the Manor, including two affronted but press-ganged junior secretaries, to form a night search party which would spread in an expanding circle from the house (and let the ambushing spycraft make of it what they cared to) until, at a covered point, some of the thirty-two pieces would vanish from the board while the others continued their scouring of the Royal Park gardens and sports grounds. The channels would receive a garbled account of perimeter alarms being set off, necessitating an area search, though triggering had possibly been caused by a straying cat or dog or a failed circuit. An inspection would be "proceeding." They wouldn't believe a word, but they would have to swallow it.

Beltane did not put in an appearance.

As we waited, Jackson asked, almost in his old form, "Have you prepared your family for a curmudgeonly old bastard?"

"I haven't had opportunity to prepare anything, but they'll accept you as my friend."

"Friend, Ape? You? Irritant and tyrant! If father is like son I can expect a rough passage. Do you know that in all my years I have never experienced at firsthand how the other half lives?"

"You will find your needs provided but little to spare and not as much space as you are used to."

"I shall suffer cheerfully."

If his mood required me to match his own sour friendliness, it was best to oblige him. "You will find these particular slum dwellers as cultured as yourself though their interests may not be yours."

"Then they shall teach me survival philosophy and I'll teach them opportunist politics."

Which might well be how it would work out.

Kostakis came and called for silence from the chattering crew. That earned him a few catcalls, some laughter and a glance of lacerating hatred from Jeanette, but the briefing went well. He knew what he wanted and had reduced his orders to simplicity. The thirty-two of us were to work in pairs, fanning out from the perimeter on compass bearings, examining obstacles and possible points of cover as if in a genuine search. The object was to smuggle two people out undetected. He did not say whom.

"Keep search speed; that's about thirty meters a minute in open country. If a copter drops a camera, cover your face and don't get photographed. Don't talk too much and for Christ's sake don't say anything to let the channels think it's a fake exercise; there's sound pickups on the cameras. You spread out for an hour and come back when you get the call on your personal coms; otherwise, radio silence. Groups four, five, six and seven will rendezvous with me at the old Royal Park railway station on the outward move. Start time, oh-four-hundred. Questions?"

No questions. Jackson and I were group six. Kostakis came for a quiet word. "I better have your home address, Harry. Just in case."

True. I wrote it down for him. He whistled softly. "Port Melbourne, eh? Flash!"

That told me much about his own background. Port Melbourne is run-down and shabby, not as mildewed and neglected as the Handspike-infested tenements of Balaclava but in no way flash.

At four o'clock we poured out through the rear exits and the noise of circling copters was an instant insult to the ears. They saw only an erupting mob sorting itself into pairs and shaking out into a search pattern.

Their frustration would have begun immediately as they made hurried vid-links with the Manor, shouting each other down until Jeanette, sole remaining security representative, sorted them out. I could imagine it:

Why the search, lady?

Perimeter alarms blew.

But thirty-two bodies! You got that many?

Staff helping; alarm is alarm is alarm.

Looks like a prearranged search pattern.

It is. Standard security pattern.

What blew the alarms?

No guesses.

Keep your line open for us.

Too busy.

Aw, now, listen . . .

Silence. From Jeanette they wouldn't get enough for even a beat-up. In the end it turned out to be a false alarm, a technical fault. Or so they were told.

We fanned out across the park in near darkness. Cloud cover was normal for this rainy time of year, and the moon penetrated just sufficiently to plot the bumps and furrows before we stumbled over them, so I kept one eye on the old man for fear of him falling on his face. He was aware of his convalescent clumsiness and moved with care. The slow search pace helped.

A couple of copters dropped cameras on carbon polymer ribbons, but the odd shrubs and lone trees prevented them getting to face level. Losing a camera could be a heavy setback in a ready-cash economy and a few recorded scrappy grunts and curses were not worth the risk. Jackson spoke only once, to say loudly, "Shit!" and massage his ankle.

It was about six hundred meters to the old railway station, and we covered it in twenty minutes. Four, five and seven came curving in just after us. The copters gathered to see what came of our search of the building.

The eight of us scrambled onto the platform and under the ancient, rusting, galvanized iron roof. Kostakis, with seven, herded us at once into the ticket box. The copter cameras could not see us because the box faced the length of the station platform and had no side windows; they could not peek from any angle. We were safe there from any but ground-based surveillance, and they could not risk landing a man who might be taken for one of the searched-for intruders, and perhaps shot; they could only buzz in a balked swarm. Still, we kept our voices down while he outlined our way of escape under the noses of the newsbugs.

It was very simple. The disused rails had long ago been removed and recycled and the resulting bare

paths had been disguised cheaply by planting shade
trees on either side of them, forming covered walks
and picnic spots for the gentle weeks of autumn and
early spring.

So there were four totally covered ways out of the
station, two running northeast to Brunswick and two
southwest to Flemington Road. At five o'clock the four
groups would leave the station together, four and five
to move towards Brunswick, ourselves and the Kostakis
pair towards the road, under tree cover all the way to the
public transport hoverbus route, where the first dayshift
engineers and service staffs would be commuting and
cycling to City Center.

The copters would soon discover what we did but
not who we were.

When the time came we all moved together. Jackson
and I went a little faster now, with Kostakis and his
offsider keeping pace under the trees of the other track.
Our only punishment for deception was the rain. After
holding off all night in this, the wettest season of the
year, it came down without warning in the proverbial
buckets. The trees could not keep it off nor capes save
us being drenched to the knees or wincing at cold
trickles down our necks. It was a small price for escape,
though Jackson tired quickly on the rough footing and
had to take my arm.

Otherwise, the escape went without a hitch. At
Flemington Road we hailed the first hoverbus for
City Center and all four of us boarded. It was, as we
had known it would be, crowded; we were lost among
the early workers. The copters could pack up and go
home.

I was given a glimpse of Kostakis's thoroughness
when Jackson pointed out, softly, that four searchers
vanishing into the city instead of returning to the Man-
or would cause comment. Kostakis only beamed at
him. "I must of forgot to say how the Manor called

on the com and said since the night was over and the search was called off, us four could go straight off on our rostered Sunday leave. And so we did."

We left the bus at Center Terminus, all hundred or so of us, indistinguishable in raincapes, moving off to workplaces. For farewell Kostakis said, "Call if you need me, night or day." I assured his enthusiasm that I would. His companion gave us a fed-up grin, and they wandered off to find their way back to the Manor and breakfast.

Under the footpath verandah Jackson insisted on pausing to peer up and down the street through the curtain of rain. He grumbled, "There would have been a few cars still."

He was looking back thirty years. "Not now, Arthur. Nobody makes them; nobody keeps up the roads. Public transport is good and we use bikes a lot; they're just as good."

There were, in fact, quite a few bikes on the street.

He asked, "Is that what they teach you? Still rewriting history, are they? There's more to life than making do within the circle of walking distance."

I tried to see with his eyes; memory did add a time, back in the forties when I was a kid, when private cars still threaded among the streams of buses and bikes. They had been on their way out even then, part of the guzzling consumption a bankrupt planet had had to sacrifice if it wanted to eat.

As if he heard my thought, Jackson said, "I'm hungry, Ape."

"You'll have to wait till we get home."

"No!" He stopped dead, a small rock of stubbornness in the flow of a city going about its business. "Your job is to look after me. I'm hungry and I expect you to earn your pay."

Undercover work is often as petty as it can be bracing. Wind swept fresh rain in on us half-drowned rats while we argued a triviality. I asked, "Have you money?"

"How should I? Never thought of it."

"And I won't have any till I get home. And your food coupons and mine were lodged with tho Manor catering staff. What will you have? Rainwater?"

He jeered, "You didn't think ahead."

How right he was; the police mentality wasn't coming well out of this confusing exercise. "I'll see what I can do." Like Nguyen, I had face to preserve.

I took him to the City Central police canteen, where I could get tea and toast without coupons and charge them to my account. He complained that the tea was tasteless and the toast like straw. Since both were ersatz, he was right. Nobody queried his presence; he could be a witness or a nark being buttered up for questioning.

While there, I told a few lies and was able to sign for a week's supply of emergency food coupons—which would have to be repaid.

We arrived in Port Melbourne about nine o'clock. The rain had stopped and the footpaths steamed. As in the city, Jackson looked about him. There were few people around; those with nothing to do began Sunday when it suited them.

Our street was considered "class" because it had not been overbuilt with apartment blocks. Shabby and ancient though the dwellings were, a faint social clout clung to the possession—well, rental—of a family home with a patch of garden, some vegetable beds at the back and a fence dividing neighbor from neighbor. If the gardens were ill kept and the fences unmended and the walls weatherbeaten because paint was expensive and hard to get, the house dweller was still immeasurably better off than the apartment dweller; simple privacy was an enormous and envied advantage.

I asked, "Better? Worse?"

"Much the same. Years pass and nothing is achieved."

"I wouldn't say that."

"Nothing that matters. It will be so until we learn to live within the planet's means. We can't continue maintaining billions on the resources of millions."

Nothing new or memorable there, but it gave me an opening. "Is that what the all-night dialogue was about? All the long, long thoughts of political world minders?"

He snapped at me, "Yes! Need we stand here? I want to sit down. I want to think."

When Dad answered the door I pushed Jackson in ahead of me and said, "I don't want anyone knowing he's here."

Dad brightened at drama landing on his doorstep. He pulled Jackson in, nearly shut the door in my face, then threw his arms around me in the ritual hug. "Three weeks! We thought you'd never come."

Jackson mimed stunned surprise. "Somebody loves my Ape! I thought I'd be the only one."

From down the passage Mum's voice floated with an edge. "Who called my boy an ape? Mind your manners, whoever you are!"

The old brute only said, "Protect me, Harry! I'm new around here."

So my first necessity was to excuse what the cat had dragged in.

With four persons in it the lounge room seemed crowded as never before; after the spaciousness of the Manor salons it was a cupboard.

I introduced old Beltane as Arthur Jackson, and he chose to revert to his best behavior. Dad, old romantic, received him with the courtesy of a father taking pride in his professional son (a middle-ranking copper, for God's sake!), but Mum preferred cool reserve, conveying a we-are-something-better-than-nobodies impression and not quite ready to forgive the "Ape."

My mind was busy with contrasts. Ours was a semi-detached, five-room weatherboard dwelling a hundred or more years old and typical of the suburban houses of its period; it was also becoming typical of the centennial state of decay. The floorboards creaked with warps and shrinkages past curing, and the second grade paint which was all we could obtain was peeling from the inner walls as my last inept attempt at plastering crumbled under it. We had the furniture to be able to entertain friends but my Manor-fed eyes were conscious of coverings that looked like brocade but felt like what they were, stamped plastic.

One raucous putdown from Jackson and I would have been tempted to hit him, forgetting that he knew more than I ever would about being all things to all men. With introductions over I said, "I'd like you to take Mr. Jackson as a boarder for a little while."

The word confused them momentarily. The idea of boarding was by then almost extinct in the Wards; you either mucked in—share and share alike in everything—or you found yourself a solitary hutch. Mum repeated uncertainly, "Boarder?" and I told her it would be for only a few days. That meant immediate creation of fictional explanations. I drummed up a tale of interstate conferences which required participants being kept out of public view.

Dad was only too willing to be convinced; Mum wasn't. She gave me the look that promised inquisition later but said, like a careful housewife, that she hoped Mr. Jackson had been provided with state coupons. I gave her enough for three days for both of us, and she said at once, "These are police issue."

"Yes."

Politics? asked her eyes. *Police business, rather, and I do not want to know.* But she put the coupons safely away.

Jackson said, very gently, "I doubt if even three days

will be required," and the trouble in his voice told at last that he was desperately worried and trying to find resignation.

"Or maybe a week," I said.

He shook his head slightly. "Harry, you must know it is all over with him. The vultures have him trapped."

I had thought so from the moment of the failed kidnap; any observer would have thought so. If Jackson crumpled I would have to deal with it, knowing there would be no fresh miracle of rescue, and to plan for disaster.

My parents heard this exchange with the pained good manners of unintentional eavesdroppers. Mum solved her social problem by vanishing into the kitchen to make tea.

Jackson, playing his game of quick-change moods, sent a malicious half smile after her. "The housewife's unfailing panacea . . ." He let it die away.

I finished it for him, determined to allow no snide jibes, "and the perpetual poultice of the common people."

He didn't like that and shot me a look like the crossing of swords, but Dad moved in on us with gentle reproof. "There are no common people, Son, as I am sure Mr. Jackson would agree; there are only those less well equipped than the uncommonly fortunate."

That set both of us in our places. Dad was in his early fifties then, a spare, graying stick of stubbornness he could disguise with wounding politeness. Jackson, old politician and old socialite both, read the signs and capitulated; he made one of his rare, totally honest speeches uncontaminated by bile or guile.

"Mr. Ostrov, I apologize for my behavior, now and to come. I am under stress and unaccustomed to restraint on my tongue." Dad listened with the encouraging gaze of a schoolmaster with a talented pupil. "I was born to be a Minder, though the word had not its present meaning then, and I have never known any other existence. Simply entering your home has for me an element of adventure, of new experience. I am uncomfortable not only for that but because I am unable fully to explain my presence."

Mum (not one to miss a word simply through being in another room) said from the kitchen door, "I'm sure Harry will make it plain."

"Harry won't," I said, "because he can't."

"But you said—"

"I said as little as possible. I suspect that what I said is more or less true, but I don't know. And, Arthur, please don't create unnecessary mysteries."

"Mysteries!" Mum said. "We are not children, Harry."

Jackson rescued me. "Allow me, Mrs. Ostrov." He became the complete gentleman, communicating with an equal, solving her problem with courteous dispatch. "Harry has in the course of his duties been subjected to a threat which inhibits his speaking of certain matters. It was done to ensure his silence."

My parents' most notable reaction was that they did not at once question the validity of such nastiness. In sensibility they belonged to an earlier convention, but they had few illusions about this one. My father's comment was typically practical. "It would ensure Harry's enmity, if I know my son, and strain his loyalty rather than preserve it."

He had that dead right. Mum said, "I never did approve of his police work; there's something inhuman about it." And retreated to the kitchen.

No, Mum, it's all too human—at the lowest level of self-preservation.

Jackson stared after her as he told Dad, "You should be horrified, not acceptant."

"Horrified by some mean-minded expedient of power? This is the age of stopgap crudities."

"At the use to which it has been put."

Dad sat up straight in his chair. "A corrupt and cruel use?" His voice did not rise a decibel above its usual placid level. "You must be a full decade older than I as well as Minder born and bred; you must know more of immoral expediency than I who can only deduce and suspect, yet you ask me to expend emotion on futile resentment. At this lower end of the financial tree— and this house lives more comfortably than most—we see that the individual is the unit and that existence is hand-to-mouth, while the international plottings of the monkeys in the higher branches make good tribal gossip but are nearly irrelevant as fact. Premier Beltane preserves a sort of status quo in Victoria, yet still we are driven to concentrate on essentials—food and shelter. On this planet dog eats dog without gagging; our last pretense at civilization is to refrain from overt cannibalism until the alternatives run out."

Jackson was getting his fill of the Wardie philosophy he had joked about. "You can't speak for all people, Mr. Ostrov."

"Can I not? Shall I remind you of Africa and South America where sixty years ago the Western world forgave their unpayable debts and poured billions of dollars into feeding and healing and maintaining them so that they could cease destroying their environments in order to clear arable land? The debtor nations were expected to develop internally, to produce individual stability and justify the forgiveness of debts by buying from the donor countries. That was the catch in their generosity. You cease deforestation, we give you money and you return it to us in payment for our cheap goods with inbuilt obsolescence, our luxuries that you don't need but must be taught to want and the suspect pharmaceuticals banned from the shelves of our own stores! The big dogs, slavering with generosity, had the little dogs halfway down their throats! But the little dogs had learned hard lessons about subsistence; they refused to buy. They employed the largess to produce their own necessities and shut out unnecessary imports; the financial dominance of the West shrank for lack of the markets it had sought to perpetuate. The little dogs were eating the paws and tails of the big dogs because they knew all about subsistence living, while the big dogs couldn't stand tight belts and long fasts. Once there would have been a war (remember how 'all wars were trade wars'?) but that was no longer a response in a world terrorized by its own destructiveness. The choice lay between knuckling down and nuclear winter, and the outcome was that we all live in an approximation of poverty, in what I would guess has been the lot of the average citizen throughout most historical times. The world's wealth has become fairly evenly spread and, as the economists foretold, there isn't enough to go round. Among twelve billions there never will be—except, of course, among our Minders, who are 'more equal than others.' "

Mum, who had heard it a hundred times, brought in the tea tray and set out the cups. Jackson said, as if prodding a sore spot, "I fear you can't do without Minders in some form."

Mum asked, "Who can't?" but Dad said, "We're so accustomed to elitist administration that we've lost the power to imagine any other."

"At least we don't eat you."

"Only enough off each one to supply the comforts due to an intelligent and hard-worked government. One grants your necessity, with a permanent ruffling of resentment."

"So there is no cure?"

Jackson was obviously enjoying himself, but Dad surveyed him incredulously. "Of course there is a cure: Curb population growth until there are once again enough natural resources to sustain a human culture and its ecological support. That is, to allow rational behavior back into life."

Mum said as she poured, "This is artificial milk, but it's drinkable."

Jackson seemed never to have heard of such a thing, but he kept his attention on Dad. "Curb?"

Dad smiled gently. "Reduce."

"To what level?"

Dad stirred his tea and kept his eye on the cup as he answered, "Two billions? Perhaps fewer? A figure low enough to give us time to learn how to conserve population increase before it happens all over again. There will be psychological processes to learn and disseminate, all manner of cultural profit and loss accounts to be exposed and balanced. Basic biological processes are not throttled back without payment in unpredictable traumas. Two centuries, perhaps, for learning and training?"

There could be nothing new to Jackson in all this, but he thought about it and what he asked was, "Do the Wardies think on such lines?"

"Those who bother to think. Most are concerned with shelter and the next meal."

"But you—?"

"Thanks to my son's career I have leisure to think."

Career, he called it, with a straight face.

Jackson tasted his tea and nodded appreciation to Mum. "This is not substitute."

"I keep real tea for visitors." Her smile challenged him. "Snobbery from a uselessly educated background."

He said, deadpan, "But culture is preserved," and then, without change of tone, "How, Mr. Ostrov, do you propose to reduce the population so drastically?"

Dad was ready for him. "Murder."

For the first time I saw Jackson's brio stopped cold. He picked up his cup and put it down, loured furiously at Dad and said, "You're blunt—or you're not serious."

"Why should I not be? Politicians speak of it—behind their hands."

"Why should you think that?"

"If they don't, then they're fools with their heads in the sand. Even Wardies talk about it—only occasionally but not behind their hands—as something that has to happen. In husbandry it's called culling the herd."

"They talk about it?"

"Why be surprised? Subsistence living sharpens the wits to accept the obvious instead of intellectualizing it. They make jokes about it, think up wilder and wickeder ways of going about it."

Jackson set his cup down carefully. "That makes for jokes?"

"Like sitting under an axe and making good-humored bets about whose neck will get the chop."

Mum said, "I find it hard to believe that the administration is unaware of these feelings in the Wards."

Jackson twinkled at her. "It is not unaware. Nor was I. I was in some degree checking that nothing has changed radically during my absence."

"You have been away?"

"I have been . . . shall we say, absent from the public scene for many years."

He might as well have said he'd been in jail; there were few other modes of being "away" in a computer-recorded culture. Good manners triumphed over the tiny hiatus as Mum (always quicker than Dad at these recoveries) asked, "And how do the administrative classes feel about such Ward joking?"

"There is an intellectual element that abstractualizes fear, treats it as a specimen for examination. Wardies make jokes, Minders play mind games. Same thing, different expression."

Mum said, with an air of closing off discussion, "And then there are those of us who rarely think of it at all. One lives in the present, having no other time."

Dear Mum, saying in effect, Under the falling axe we preserve the dignity of life. Her flag would fly, come what might.

Foolish? Maybe, but no indomitability of spirit can erase fact, and for a moment she looked all of her years, weary with the disappointment of talent denied and the dull ennui of living just to be alive. She pulled herself together and fussed with the tea things, but Jackson observed and diagnosed. "I agree that this century will not bear much thought except as an object lesson to those who come after us."

"The survivors?" Dad asked, and there didn't seem much more to say about it.

Jackson purred at me, reminding me of duty. "Harry, I have been awake since the devil was pupped and wasted six hours in exhausting quarreling with my son. And I am still convalescent."

Quarreling about what? "You want to be tucked in and sung a lullaby?"

"So long as there's sleep at the end of it."

I put him into my own bed in the sleepout at the back of the house. He fell asleep in the middle of undressing and scarcely rallied to my rough removal of his trousers and socks.

Back in the lounge room I asked Dad if he had been trying to shock our visiting politician. He was smug. "Succeeded, didn't I? What's the story, son? What's he hiding from?"

Only professional steadiness prevented me from telling him; it would have been a relief from the endless crises arising from a weak premier's multiplying error.

The urge was still between my teeth when the front doorbell rang and Mum said, "I'll get it."

She returned almost at once, saying, "A gentleman for you, Harry."

Behind her, Dr. Nguyen entered the room. He did not wait on civilities but said, "You must get back to the Manor, Harry; the premier is in a a very odd mental condition and is asking for you. In fact, demanding."

"Mr. Jackson—"

"Will be safe here, will he not?"

At "Manor" and "premier" all Dad's dreams of my involvement in great matters came true. He said steadily, "Perfectly safe; no one will know he is here. You run along, Harry, and leave us to look after our guest."

Dependable Bill Ostrov—the smooth, suave, secret agent with never a mental hair out of place!

So dear old Dad sent me off with his blessing to the most terrible moment of my life.

9

Ostrov:
The Political Madhouse

Waiting for us outside the house was no opulent Manor luxury body but a dirty dump-tray utility with no identification—a service truck the outside staff might use to ferry waste to the recycling points. Beltane had learned common sense. Or had he?

"Did the premier allocate you this truck?"

"No; I commandeered it. It was the nearest to hand."

"And unlikely to cause comment in the street outside our house."

"That, too."

He started up, swung the truck in an inept U-turn and moved too fast towards City Center.

I yelled at him, "Slow down, man; you'll kill someone!" There were children in the streets now, always in evidence long before their parents and as likely to play on the roadway as on the footpaths. "You're a lousy driver. Why didn't you send someone with a message?"

"Would you have obeyed it? Or would you have niggled that your commission is to accompany the old man, wasted time in argument? Perhaps sent the driver back for confirmation? And would I tell a servant that the premier is unbalanced? For me you would come at once."

The speedometer was creeping up again already. "Slower, man! You're all nerves. Frightened!"

His brown eyes slanted towards me and away, but his expression did not change. "You must not try your interrogation tricks on me, Harry. Still, I am excited and a little concerned. The man whose mental welfare was my watching brief has become, overnight, my patient."

"Unexpectedly?"

He took his time answering. "Not altogether."

So he was prepared to be truthful, at least up to a point. "Did he in fact send for me or is this your idea?"

"He sent for you."

"Why?"

We were approaching City Center as he answered, "He said—and I quote without fully understanding— that he wants truth from the gutter."

He took his eyes from the road to watch my reaction and I said, "Pull in to the curb. I wonder you got to Port without an accident. Let me drive."

We changed over and he sat in the offsider's seat, sweating. With excitement and concern?

There was commercial traffic in the streets now and the usual amount of irresponsible driving of vehicles that do not respond well to turning and deceleration and are, after all, owned by the state rather than by their unconcerned drivers. I stayed in the road center with minimum ground clearance and pondered "gutter." My status was now clearer than it had been. I could be trusted, even allowed some small impertinence—but there was a gulf fixed.

Police bear with the enmity of those they serve but not easily with their contempt.

I tried a shot in the dark: "A truth to oppose the different truth his father gave him last night? A sugary truth that doesn't put action into the too-hard basket?"

He turned his head to look full at me and I'll swear the brown eyes were wide with a sort of anticipation. He asked, "What did the old man tell him?"

"How should I know? I only saw that filial affection seemed to have sprained its smile."

His disappointment was palpable. "I had hoped . . . well, we shall learn soon enough."

"The whole Jackson operation was stupid."

"Indeed, yes. Beltane raised his decrepit oracle to advise him and now wishes he had let it lie."

"But you pushed him into it, didn't you?"

"No!" Even the supposedly inscrutable East can be startled into truth when the insult is straight enough. "I am not a manipulator of shaking wills."

"You manipulated mine and it was not even shaking."

"I showed yourself to you, no more than that."

He did not claim that he had only been working under orders; that was one sign of a fairly honest man.

"As for Beltane," he said, "I did not dissuade him from foolishness."

"Such being not your brief?"

"Don't sneer, Harry. I explained foolishness to him; further than that I could not go."

"He ignored you. He was desperate."

"Of course."

"And you couldn't calm his desperation?"

He waited a half second too long to say, "There was no point of entry; it was a response to ongoing circumstances."

That was at best an evasion. I guessed that though he may not have prompted Beltane towards Cranko he had also not attempted to check the foolishness. He was at least an enemy by default.

I would get no more from him on that line. I changed
direction. "Did he let me take the old man away because
he no longer cares a damn what happens to him? Does a
lifetime's dependence reverse itself so easily?"

"Given the right disappointment, yes. The dependant suddenly sees his shackle for what it is—the tie
of his own weakness. At once he is free. And raging."

"Free forever?"

"For perhaps a day or two. The anger passes. Dependence is a most persistent emotional trauma."

"Trauma?"

"Certainly. An undercutting of the will to act, as
ultimately disabling as a lost limb."

Before that, I would have called it a weakness to be
overcome by an act of will. That's the sort of loose
thinking a man will carry with him throughout his life,
never considering closely, dismissing weakness with
contempt until someone like Nguyen lifts it suddenly
into a new perspective that fits all the parameters with
fresh understanding. "That makes him a cripple."

"Yes." He glanced at me again, smiling this time.
"And you snatched his crutch away to Port Melbourne."

It seemed that every decision I had made during these
two nights and a day had brought disaster, because in
each case I had lacked essential knowledge. But this
disaster, this leaving of Beltane alone and unbalanced,
could have been retrieved.

I said to Nguyen, "We could have brought Jackson
back with us."

His smile did not waver. "The premier is my patient;
I make the choices."

There was obscurity in that, but he would have
blinded protest with psychological science. To cap it,
he had another development to throw to me: "Beltane
has sent for Kenney. An Opposition member! Expect
entanglements."

That sounded like a friendly warning. I would be fumbling in the dark to discover what role Nguyen played behind his knowing efficiency.

As we pulled in at the rear of the servants quarters he asked, with an expression of one contemplating a splattered egg, had I ever noticed the outward serenity and peace of a mental hospital. "Flowers, lawns, spick-and-span walkways! Then you enter the wards . . . the Manor differs only in degree."

As we passed the wardroom he called to Jeanette, asking if Kenney had arrived.

"Somebody in a flesh-mask," she told him, "wearing white gloves. Could have been hiding Koori skin."

"Most likely."

I asked, "How is he smuggled in? In a closed van with a load of vegetables for the kitchen?"

"Why not? It's simple and it works."

Jeanette said, "Try the Small Office. He's got Cranko in there. Have you seen the channels?"

"Something fresh?"

"On the face of it just trouble stirring. A rumor story about old Gerald being shanghaied into the Biophysical Institute. All nudge, wink and further revelations in the next installment of our muckrake saga."

Somebody in the political network had talked. Black-mail would be in full squeeze by now. I wanted to think about it, but Nguyen hurried me on.

Then Ivy Beltane swept out of a corridor a few meters ahead, not seeing us and moving ahead of us to the Small Office with the determined stride of one with body and mind concentrated on a thing to be done. In her own home I had seen her roused from bed by police, hurriedly dressed and yet presented flawless-ly for the day. Now I saw her close to bedraggled in slippers and kimono with hair hanging wild as though she had lunged from the bed after a night of furious thinking, caught up a wrap and moved into action before procrastination should disarm her.

At the door of the Small Office she shouted Beltane's name, really shouted it in a full female baritone of hoarse anger. She found herself in the middle of a room where her husband was not alone.

Either she had immense self-possession or her anger carried her, because she launched her tirade as though she and he were solitary and private.

I would have hesitated at the door, but Nguyen muttered excitedly and stepped through. If he could count on his profession to allow intrusion, so could I.

Kenney was there, unperturbed, observing and hearing Mrs. Beltane with the well-bred, polite interest of the perfect guest. He was not inwardly calm, though; between his fingers he crumpled and smoothed the flesh-mask.

Cranko lounged across the room from him, acting insouciance but looking seedy and tired after two nights of wondering what was to become of him. Kostakis, leaning against the wall behind him, saintly faced and thoroughly alert, did not help his role-playing.

Beltane stood at one end of the desk, blindingly enraged, while his wife played virago at the other. They did not see us enter; they were intent on each other.

I caught the tail end of Mrs. Beltane's yelling that she would do just as she bloody well pleased, that Melissa was her daughter and she'd not leave her in this cesspit a day longer. "Cesspit" was the word she used.

Beltane bellowed back at her, with the unnerving resonance of the public speaker, that she should leave well alone and add no further scandal to the scum already clogging the channels. "Don't you realize what will be said if you take her away? That the abortion talk is only talk and you are conniving at secret birthing!"

She was in no mood to listen to reason. "Let them
say! I'll take her interstate and put her into a school
where they train girls to be women instead of bird-
brained harlots by default! As her mother I'll teach
her what she was never able to learn in the perverted
household of her disgusting father!"

I could not see Nguyen's face because he stood a
little in front of me, but Cranko's eyes popped and
perhaps mine did; Kenney's wrecking of his flesh-mask
halted in amazement. Only Kostakis listened placidly
as though human beings could not surprise him.

Beltane stiffened as if she had struck him, but he said
only, "You'll take her when I'm dead and not an hour
sooner."

"Then die and let her live in a normal world!"

Simultaneously they became aware that the number
of the company had grown. Beltane yelled at us, "Get
out of here, all of you!"

His wife said, very coolly now, "All their ears are
burning. Safer to let them stay while you think fast,
Jeremy. Is that little gray-yellow man the psychiatrist
Melissa talks about? What does he make of the family
history? It should be good for a scurrilous thesis."

Her coolness was venom; she had stepped over the
safe mark and could no longer retreat if she would.
I saw, with some shock, that Beltane's bull roaring
was done with also. She had returned him brutally
to a here and now in which he was afraid. His eyes
sought escape; for a moment all he wanted was to run
and hide.

The skills of a drilled lifetime returned. He stood
straight, dredging up the outlines of the practiced
smile. "You go too far, Ivy. These gentlemen do not
know the family history. I am surprised that you do.
Or do you?"

She refused the cue, turned it against him. "Your
creatures don't know? They are your creatures, aren't

they? All except the snotty Koori double-dealer from the Opposition, and he'll be here only to bid for some rottenness. But the sly little Veet and the big macho copper belong to you, don't they? What does it matter how much your creatures know?"

Nguyen cocked his head. "What indeed, madam? In my profession all communication is confessional sacred."

"Until someone pillages your files! But poor old Ostrov does what he's damned well told—or else. Why should a young girl have to live in a house of dirty secrets? What do you say, psychiatrist?"

"Knowing nothing, madam, I say nothing."

"Then what about this: two perverted old men protected by their professional lapdogs! A proper setting for a teenage girl?"

A change came over Beltane. He had heard the doors of escape slam shut around him, and he was one of those who can conduct themselves coolly enough when there is nowhere left to run. He moved round and behind the desk, settled into his chair and lay back with hands behind his head. With deliberation he set his feet on the blotting pad and said, "Go on, Ivy. To stop now would be ungracious to your audience. It would create speculation beyond the facts."

She made an exaggerated double take of unbelieving amazement. "Beyond? How, beyond? Then tell all of us, where's the dribbling old pederast you call your father?"

Easy now as a man with nothing more to lose, he did not change position. "He's elsewhere, safe from your poison, Ivy. And 'pederast' is not a proper word for him. I was an aberration, a behavioral sport."

"I don't know the sporting term for it. Boy-lover? Will that do?" She turned a little to face me. "How about that, policeman? What's the official charge?"

I schooled my voice to flat indifference. "If supported

it might refer to corruption of a minor. But that must have occurred many years ago."

"Oh, our cold-blooded Ostrov! The law names the crime without emotion. Do you reckon only by the scale of sentences and have no moral attitude to the criminal?"

"Moral attitudes can be as evil as the crimes they affect to despise."

Before the morning was out I was to remember that reply and taste it like poison on the tongue.

Now I added, trying to play down in advance the nastiness that surely must come, "After so long a time, who would care?"

Ivy Beltane hissed at me as though I had become the object of her rage, "I care, policeman! I care for my daughter caged in a moral pigsty."

Beltane said with sudden exasperation, "Get on with it, you unpleasant woman."

It sounded like simple impatience, but his voice was tensely off-key. He half raised himself to glance at Nguyen and myself, and I saw his eyes. He was running to destruction, staring into it without welcome but also without avoidance, not mad in any clinical sense but moved aside from common perception to view himself and the world from an angle denied to the rest of us. Is that madness? Close to it, I think.

Nguyen straightened his shoulders with a tiny, almost imperceptible shrug, and his head poked minutely forward. In him that was a strong sign of interested calculation.

I looked back to Beltane. He had relaxed again, but I saw him now at the edge of a high place, feeling that curious urge to leap that makes you shudder and step back before it takes over. But he had decided to leap.

I thought Nguyen should interfere professionally, but he did nothing.

Ivy Beltane, with the challenge leveled at her, became more subdued, less certain of rightness. Her peak of anger had begun to ebb. She said without heat, trying to get the thing done with, "Old Gerald is not Jeremy's father. He is his lover. That's all."

The dart fell curiously short. Perhaps the others felt, as I did, only that puzzling aspects of a long public relationship had been satisfactorily explained. It may have seemed less important, now that it was aired, to Mrs. Beltane; after all, her interest was in prying Melissa loose from an old agreement to allow her father to keep her. The rest had been dragged in on the tide of intemperate determination to have her way.

Beltane, almost lying in his chair, spoke to the ceiling, correcting her on a point of fact. "That was true forty-eight years ago but not now. He picked me out of an orphanage when he was on the edge of middle age, and Dr. Nguyen will tell you that the middle period can give rise to aberrant behavior in otherwise normal men. I think that is true of Dad. I think of him as Dad because I don't know any other. He was married for reasons of political advancement to a woman who could not give him children and refused surrogacy. He wanted a child, was obsessive in his wanting; obsession and his wife's obduracy may have combined to tangle his emotions. On a Charities Commission visit to an orphanage he saw a fifteen-year-old and fell in love. Those are his words, not mine. Do you follow, Dr. Nguyen?"

"You make the matter psychologically simpler than is probably the case, but such midlife disturbances are documented. As a case observation, did sexual advances begin at once?"

"No. He claimed me as his illegitimate son by an old liaison and was able to carry on the imposture because the shift to total registration of the population in a central data library was still in progress, with all the usual errors and stumblings and bureaucratic bumbling. In the muddle he was able to arrange a false genealogy. I doubt that it could be done today."

It certainly could not. There had been wild tamperings at that time; some were still coming to light as anomalies emerged, but nobody cared enough to make legal fuss over ancient villainies unless inheritance was involved.

"He separated from his wife, amicably he told me. And why not? I, an impressionable fifteen-year-old, was to be brought up by a personable pseudofather who very quickly claimed my gratitude and affection. He wanted a son to attain the political heights he could not. He got what he wanted."

He said it all smoothly and easily, but he would not look at us.

Nguyen asked, "May I guess that sexual advances began when he and his wife separated?"

"Before that. It was why they separated. She was quieted by money; she kept him comparatively poor."

"And pederastic contact persisted?"

"For two or three years."

"And ceased suddenly?"

"I think he lost interest. I've read that pederasty rarely persists with late-teen objects. Perhaps I turned him off; I was more acquiescent than interested. Don't imagine that affection was lost. He became a father; I became a son. The aberration was over."

Ivy Beltane said, "You're a liar. I've seen you kissing."

Nguyen interfered quickly. "So has Harry; so have I. It was not an overtly sexual kiss, yet more than filial."

Beltane became testy as though we were all missing the point. "I did not say we ceased to love, only that affection changed its nature. It remained strong; it became, also, habitual. Dad was a dominant personality; he said and I did what he said. Willingly. Note that:

willingly. He wanted me to achieve the political leader-
ship that was beyond his purely manipulative talents,
and I wanted it because he wanted it of me. It was not
simple submission to a more powerful will; I loved him
and I also wanted what he planned for me."

Nguyen said, "Past tense."

Beltane was silent as though he had not heard. Then
he lifted his feet from the desk and sat up. "Past tense,"
he agreed. "It's all over."

"Since last night," I suggested.

"Good Sergeant Harry, who sees all and says nothing!
Yes, since last night. I called Dad back from the edge
of dissolution because I needed him. I told myself I
needed his vision and advice, but what I really wanted
was his paternalism to shelter me. I recognized that as
soon as it failed me. Last night I told him the problem
that troubles me, and all he saw was incompetence
and cowardice. He found that he hadn't trained a brilliant talent; he had only created a robot that jerked to
his commands and coasted to success on a slowing
momentum until the commands died out. It's true; I
coasted on popularity until the test came and I couldn't
face it. That shocked him out of all restraint. For my
part, I saw a selfish old man realizing that his whole life
with me had been wasted effort and unable to forgive
me for it. Love is the most demanding emotion and the
most unforgiving."

Nguyen asked with clinical coldness, "What love?
You had twin illusions complementing each other and
crumbling at a touch of reality."

"You aren't usually facile, Doctor."

"Facile? The relationship died when the falsity of
its premises became clear." He turned to Mrs. Beltane.
"Basically, madam, you had nothing to fear."

She said, stubbornly, "I saw him kiss the old beast.
They didn't know, but I saw them, several times. That
was before old Gerald became altogether irrational.

Melissa was newborn and I may have been irrational myself; but I knew that Gerald's wife was still alive and I found her and told her what I'd seen. She told me about the adoption and how she found them out and what she did about it. I did the same to Jeremy."

She might have left it at that if an aspect of callousness had not tripped my tongue. "And you left your daughter behind!"

She would take no criticism from me. "I thought the police were beyond surprise at what human beings will do. Are you also bereft of any kind of understanding?"

Jeanette used to say, *If a man hits a woman he's contemptible; if he argues with her he's a fool. We'd run the world if we didn't pity the poor dupes.*

I backed off as gracefully as I might. "I hope not, Mrs. Beltane."

"I was out of love and I loathed Melissa as the issue of such a father, though in time that passed. In return for freedom and money I made promises that were easy then; he didn't want a scandal in what happened to be an election year and I wanted above all to get away from him and all contact with the marriage; so I agreed to conditions that I knew later I never should have. It seemed easier because I had met another man. . . ." Her voice faded away until she picked up again, talking to herself. "There have been other men. They pass the time." She looked up. "Time catches up with us, doesn't it, Jeremy? The actions of years ago erupt today."

His answer held an incongruous touch of pity, as though only she needed support. "Don't blame your own humanity, Ivy. We build ourselves social systems fit only for saints and are forced to live lives of deceit to preserve them." He had calmed himself into a gentle amiability. "We are sufficiently civilized to know what we should be; our problem is what we are."

Mrs. Beltane gave a faint, sour smile. "I won't be patted into acquiescence. I mean to take Melissa away."

"With one cat out of the bag and others waiting, she has served her turn of damage. You may as well take her and go. Her belongings can be sent after her. Get her away within the hour."

"Good God, but you make it sound like an eviction order!"

"It is. Go quickly, Ivy. There will be disturbances here this morning, and you will want nothing to do with them."

I wonder now if that was the point at which he finally made up his mind. I felt the tenseness of climax waiting.

Mrs. Beltane hesitated, with questions unasked, then saw that she would get no answers. She said, "Good-bye, Jeremy. We need not meet again. There can be some arrangement for you to visit Melissa. If you wish."

He did not answer that, said only, "Good-bye, Ivy."

She turned, with all of us watching her, pulled the kimono round her, said, "I must look a fright," and went.

I never saw her again. She was given a brutal time by the newsbugs when all the stories finally broke, but she dealt stolidly with them, conceding nothing; she was one with unused reserves to fall back on. She had made her mistakes, neglected her daughter and played courtesan with more energy than careful taste, but she had my respect. Not many women or men had that.

Beltane motioned Nguyen and myself to sit down. I chose a seat within easy reach of Cranko, perhaps because I would have welcomed a reason to do him harm for the treachery that had spread like a running sore. He grinned at me as though he knew it and mocked my chances.

Nguyen said, "You are clearing your decks, sir, setting your affairs in order."

"Yes."

"You have thrown in your hand." Smooth as silk, stating without accusing.

"By no means. It will be played out this morning and I'll take the last trick."

Nguyen let him have his little mystery and asked instead, "Why have you brought Mr. Kenney back here?"

Beltane answered at once, "So that he may witness the end of his and his party's meddling." He made a small gesture towards Cranko. "This rubbish also."

Cranko said sourly, "I have my beliefs to act on; you are helpless without the strength of others."

"I'll not swap spite with you; I have news to interest all of you." He was suddenly bright, brisk, purposeful. "Those of you who pay more than minimal attention to the newscasts will know that the Canberra conference of premiers held earlier in the week was attended by overseas observers. So-called. In fact, they had their own irons in our fire, axes to grind, what you will— meaning, a contributing interest in secret deliberations which were not open to the channels or to anyone else. Circumstances have so fallen out that my decision on the matter discussed will determine the outcome. My decision will be known in Canberra today."

He was blandly cool with every word predetermined and exact, in character as premier in session. The political mask covered completely the desperate and driven man. Old Gerald's training had its uses.

"One of the observers called me, at the barbarous hour of five-thirty this morning, on the direct, personally encrypted line." He flicked a glance at Kenney. "How he gained such access becomes a minor question; I will not pursue it." Kenney showed no reaction, only an intelligent interest in Beltane's speech. "The caller's purpose was political blackmail. He insisted that my decision should be the one desired by his country. His weapon was knowledge of my—of Gerald's—oh, call him my father—of my father's recent treatment in the Biophysical Institute. He threatened to make the matter public. Something of the sort has been inevitable since Mr. Cranko chose treason, but I had hoped it would be delayed a few days while the sale-of-secrets network haggled in its dirty marketplace."

Cranko made a contemptuous, dismissive sound, ending in a hiss of pain as Gus slapped him with his open hand.

Beltane said, "Leave him alone, Mr. Kostakis, unless some purpose is served. The political weapon is powerful despite Sergeant Ostrov's confidence in the sentimentality of the people but the—foreign observer—had another, to be used in case I should attempt to bank on that popularity to stand firm against his requirement. And I assure you that I will stand firm against it. His more personal weapon is knowledge of the genealogical matters and falsified data my wife has just made so unpleasantly plain to you. Add Melissa's regrettable escapade, already public knowledge, and nothing could preserve me against such an avalanche of scandal. The observer—it's best you should not know his country—will call for my capitulation at one-thirty today. He will not get it."

Like puppets on a single string we all looked at our watches. It was a few minutes after eleven.

Kenney asked, "And you?"

"No matter what public revelations ensue, my decision will be made plain at one-thirty. I imagine tomorrow's Canberra meeting will be abandoned."

Kenney showed an emotion now, curiosity. "You will go public?"

"Very public. You might say, most noisily public." The idea seemed to please him; he returned to humanity in a smile close to smugness.

Gus had been frowning over his own thoughts and asked a question as though the fact of his presence

gave him as much purchase in the affair as the rest
of us. Perhaps it did. "How would this observer know
about the adoption thing?"

"My question also, Mr. Kostakis—how? Not, I am
sure, through my wife."

Kenney said, "I have known for several days of the
data falsification."

That succeeded in rocking Beltane. "The hell you
have!"

"Indeed so. It was whispered to me by the administrator of records in an attempt to cover his own position if the news leaked to the channels and he might
then be charged with failure to protect the security of
the Limited Access files. The matter had been uncov-
ered accidentally, he said, during a routine information
search for something else. I am not one to use such
underhand information, but I promised to stand by him
on condition that he kept his mouth shut. Apparently
he did not. I suppose he wanted money."

That was in my field. I said, "Not necessarily the
administrator; more likely the search clerk who stumbled on the data."

"Possibly; I did not think of him; I'm not familiar
with the internal procedures of that department. Are
you, Sergeant?"

"Fairly well. These chance discoveries sometimes
call for police involvement; they're more common than
you'd think."

Beltane said, "Perhaps you can tell us how it might
happen."

"I can make a rough guess at it since it involves old
Gerald faking an entry fifty years back. Something like
this: The search clerk is perhaps doing a legal job, such
as a land inheritance claim that may get into equity
and division questions that go back generations. In the
2020s he comes on an anomaly. The line he is tracing
suddenly expands to take in a boy named Beltane who

makes no relationship sense. Peculiar. He traces further back and finds the kid's birth certificate faked to
Gerald and a woman who seems to have no other existence, before or after the birth. He's onto something.
Who really is Premier Beltane and why did old Gerald
pretend to be his father and who doctored the data?
He smells money. He tells the administrator in order
to protect his arse and make him equally culpable in
secret knowledge. The administrator uses the network
to contact Mr. Kenney because he thinks the Opposition will welcome the information. But he's picked the
wrong man; he's told to shut up and stay shut. Mean-
while, the search clerk is looking round for a customer.
We believe the political information networks reach
into Limited Access as they do everywhere else, and
that particular piece of dirt would fetch a high price."

Kenney grunted, "Corruption everywhere."

I told him, "You can't afford to be both honest and
ignorant, Mr. Kenney. The rats will gnaw your feet
before you can get your shoes on."

He said nothing to that. Who the hell was some
upstart cop to tell him his business? Irritated by his
refusal to acknowledge, I pushed a little harder. "My
advice comes from service in the Wards, Mr. Kenney.
After all, I was brought back here this morning to give
the premier an opinion from the gutter."

Beltane asked sharply, "Did you repeat that to him,
Nguyen? Why?"

Nguyen answered with no respect at all, "At this
juncture he's as entitled to truth as anyone else."

Beltane controlled anger. I know now that he was
saving Nguyen for shredding later. He looked at his
watch. "Perhaps. There's time for more truth than any
of you will enjoy, time enough to tell you just what was
discussed at the Canberra meeting."

I found myself sick of revelations wriggling out as
each stone was turned. I said, "You talked about the

bloody cull. You always do, here and everywhere."

He nodded. "The cull that everybody holds in mind and tries not to believe in. Not me and not today— somebody else, somewhere else, some other time."

I told him, "You don't really know how people think."

"You and Mr. Kostakis can teach me."

Kostakis, forever unexpected, put in an indignant oar. "You shouldn't've called Harry a gutter man. To me he's class." His gentle face did not change as he gave a complacently matter-of-fact datum: "I'm gutter, the real thing; I was actually born on a scrap dump. Or so me mum told me. Sometimes I think I've never got off it."

Nguyen smoothed ruffled feathers. "You've reached the Manor; that is something."

Gus grinned at him, and the effect was ferocious. "That's what I meant."

Only Cranko laughed outright. "How does opinion from the gutter smell at close range, Mr. Premier?"

Nobody answered him. Nguyen looked Gus over with an interest close to whimsical, while Kenney smiled for the first time, as if he had found a man he could do honest business with.

I wished I could have spoken as forthrightly, but constraints of duty, of respect for superiors and of the policeman's eternal need to keep his thinking to himself, kept warning my tongue. I had already thrown away strategic advantage by letting anger show.

These Minders of the fates of millions had made game of me in the last two days and nights and of my ideas of right and wrong. They could not or would not understand that my situation as a man bound by oath to carry out the duties given me had forced, the whole time, my connivance with actions that clashed with common morality. They had shown contempt for morality more than once. I had done my share of evil in this life—and writhed for it afterwards—but never with

the cold disdain for right and wrong that invested these
men of power. They did not glory in their activities like
driven psychopaths; they transgressed against decency and justice like intelligent men whose pragmatism
paid full respect to facts and none to humanity. Their
disagreements were over comparative degrees of rottenness. Even Kenney's pretenses balanced on knife-edged
quibbling as to how dirty he would allow his hands
to get.

It would have been a pleasure to walk out on them,
taking simple Gus with me, but I was a man under
authority, as the Bible has it, learning to what dirty
ends an oath of loyalty and obedience can bind.

The real monstrousness was still to come, and Beltane was about to deliver it. "These asides have their
interest, but I must keep to the point. I have something
to tell you and something to show you, beginning with
the cull. It is indeed what was discussed in private session in Canberra and not for the first time. It has been
discussed at the highest levels—as a possibility, that
is—for half a century, all over the world, by different
combinations of powers with different ends in view.
The ends can be described simply as variations on,
How can we kill off half the planet without ourselves
becoming victims? That can be translated as a universal
desire to rule the ruins."

His bluntness shocked none of us. We have grown up
with the bogey in the cupboards of our minds; having
it brought into the light for open survey was perhaps
equivalent to being told that your pet dog could destroy
you if it ran mad with hydrophobia. Well, you know
that, but you don't worry about it, do you?

"There are twelve billions of human beings on this
earth. We can feed them at a reasonably healthy subsistence level and for the most part we do, but that level
is now strained to its limit. Bulk additives are being
introduced into mass-distributed foods. Reafforestation

after the greenhouse debacle still must be balanced against arable necessity—and half the planet's topsoil was blown into the oceans a century ago; only God knows how long is needed to replace it by husbandry. The sheer processing of human waste, personal and artificial, is a problem of endless ramification as each solution breeds a new crisis. Do I have to run down the list of resources vanished or in short supply, of food plants whose basic genomes have been lost in decades of breeding for special environments, and all the rest? You know that resources are not the true problem; numbers are. Present demographic opinion—" here he actually smiled as if his punch line would bring down the house "—is that a practical cull, designed not for human well-being but to allow the planet a couple of centuries to recover at least in part, would reduce the human population to a maximum of one billion— a single thousand million."

Someone, I didn't notice who, muttered, "Eleven of twelve to be—"

He stopped, whoever he was, and into the hiatus Beltane dropped his one word with the coolness that comes of having lived too long with an idea. "Killed," he said. Then he reconsidered. "Or, perhaps, prevented from being born."

At the back of all our simple calculations had been ideas of ruthless enforcement of birth control for half a dozen generations, of placing limits on life expectancy with euthanasia at sixty or so, of denying treatment to the mortally injured or terminally ill, of by these means slowing population increase until the birthrate showed actual decline. These stringencies could be maintained while we husbanded the ruined earth back to a sane ecology. There would be an era of appalling harshness, one in which all concepts of sentiment and moral philosophy would be adjusted, not to the greatest immediate good for the greatest number but to the rehabilitation of the planet as a total environment.

Despite all statistical demonstrations of the shallowness of this approach, it was the comforting, seemingly desirable outcome—because beyond it lay the obscenity of the cull and nobody wanted to look directly at that.

Yet here was Beltane telling us that our Minders, our balancers of need against bounty, our shepherds through the valley of the shadow of want, had stared it in the teeth for years past. But why should that shock? Deep down we had known what we refused to face. *Don't look, and it will go away.* It hadn't gone away; it had gathered strength to pounce.

Beltane continued in the manner of a general laying out his staff appreciation before announcing the battle order. "Consultation always foundered on determination of method. Simple reversal of population trends by strict control was always out of the question; it could not halt the continuing ruin of the planet. Already some ninety-five percent of all known species exist only in DNA banks against the day when an emerging habitat can welcome them back. Humanity is a disease that slaughters everything in its ambit; now it must slaughter its own flesh in order to preserve a viable core. Are you with me, gentlemen?"

Kenney snapped at him, "To the point, man!"

"The point? Method is the point. Several ways have been suggested. The obvious stupidity of nuclear raids on swollen cities was discarded without discussion. Even with its back to the wall of decision, the race can do without a nuclear winter. Conventional warfare leading to mass annihilation in densely populated areas, reducing millions at a stroke, is wholly impracticable for a variety of reasons, including the fantastic outpouring of scarce resources to achieve a measurable effect. But the real argument against war of attrition is the inevitability of the killers declaring themselves.

Once the attacker is known, even the unattacked take fright; sides are chosen, alliances are made, the attacker becomes the attacked and all plans collapse in chaos. Nobody wants to leave the outcome to chance; everybody wants to be one of the victors. But how do you guarantee survival when every man's hand is against his brother? Warfare is wholly impractical. It might be said that only the need for self-preservation has kept us from each other's throats for the last half century.

"It became necessary to decide who should be preserved and who wiped out, even if the method was still to be found. Of course each alliance had different ideas about that. Blacks would dispose of whites with some sense of justice done, and who would blame them? Islam would have little mercy for the non-Mohammedan, while Hindus and a few others would cheerfully see Islam to the devil. Religion and race are only part of the problem; political persuasions enter, too, likewise possession of mineral resources and arable land—and who you can trust when it comes to carving the turkey afterwards.

"Then there's this: How do you preserve the scientifically and politically competent, or make certain of preserving people with essential primitive skills in farming, hunting, building, weaving and cottage industries? Such skills will be in demand as technology shrinks for lack of use. It will be a pauper planet until it devises new philosophies of living. So the cull is fraught with difficulties, to be undertaken only with absolute certainty of the outcome.

"Disease was an option discarded. Bacteriological warfare directed against food supplies would become a two-edged weapon. It might starve friend as well as foe because bacteria do not recognize boundaries and checkpoints, particularly when mutation occurs. Direct infection of human populations was ruled out for similar reasons; in so crowded a world area control is impossible. Even oceans are not barriers to disease vectors—insects, personnel, freight. So—stalemate.

"Until now."

He scanned each of us in turn, seeking reaction and getting little. Everything he had said had been discussed to the point of boredom by theorists from the gutter upwards. Until the last two words. His audience was attentive.

He asked, "Do I make myself clear? The difficulties attendant on direct assault have been eliminated." He paused before he added without emphasis or feeling. "The way to global holocaust is open, thanks to the Biophysical Institute."

Only that egomaniac, Cranko, had the stupidity to comment. "Ten for content, only five for delivery. The crowd failed to applaud."

From behind, Gus reached a long arm to take him under the chin, turn his face up and half around, and say, "You'll be one of the first off the drop. I promise it."

"Enough, Mr. Kostakis. I still have use for him." Beltane was amused.

Gus stepped back. Cranko had gone corpse white; Gus's face had imprinted in him a fear of hellfire—in *this* life.

Beltane continued, "I am not highly educated in the technology of mass murder, so Mr. Cranko can earn the price of his meals this weekend by giving us a clear, not too technical account of the work of the institute."

"What's this? Revenge?"

"Why not?"

"An attempt to off-load blame! You knew why the place was built."

Gus leaned over him. "Get on with it, shithead!"

Beltane signaled, *no more,* but Cranko was already in spate. "The biggest problem of the greenhouse years has been weather forecasting. With help from specialists in the mathematics of chaos it was determined that greater understanding of the effects of minor fluctuations could bring meteorology close to zero accuracy for periods of up to twenty-four hours with point predictions possible for areas as small as a couple of hectares. This meant that conditions might be safely predicted for the immediate environment of a village or a city."

It had been almost a gabble, but the gabble of a man who knew the order of the subject and the simplification of its ideas. He had given this talk before, but not to scientists. To military staff, perhaps, or satellite operation groups?

"The operational difficulty was in testing the efficiency of microcondition measurements and of the deductions drawn from them. An experimental method was projected and shown on paper to be feasible. It was costed at something like forty times the state of Victoria's annual budget." He dropped suddenly into the venom that seemed natural to him. "Your tough premier, the friend of the Wardies, took fright, didn't want any part of it, saw what the knowledge could be used for and turned his compassionate back on it."

"True," Beltane said. "I saw that in tandem with another line of research the physical uncertainties of a deliberate cull could be almost eliminated. I did not care to have that on my head."

"As gutter opinion would phrase it, the premier dogged out on the big decision. But interested people made sure that members of his cabinet knew the facts, and cabinet threatened to roll him if he didn't give the go-ahead. So he said, 'Yes, boys, have it your way, boys,' and saved his job. So much for his sentimental conscience. Since it was all done in cabinet session, the story never reached the channels. The Wards never knew that their champion could back down."

Beltane said mildly, "Cabinet would have elected a leader who would do whatever they wanted; it was better for me to stay in office and try to control events."

"But you did nothing. You *could* do nothing."

Beltane looked at his watch. "That is to be seen. Get on with it, Mr. Cranko. It is midday and we have still to hear from the Wardies present."

"What can they—" He scowled suspiciously at me. "All right, Mr. Premier, play your game out; it's all you've done for eight years. You took fright when your cabinet showed a will of its own, and you've never been sure of yourself since. It ended in crying for Daddy. Or whatever he is to you."

"You've lost the thread of your discourse, Mr. Cranko."

Cranko took a long breath and said in his platform voice, "Money was a stumbling block, so was a lack of top-level weather scientists to pinpoint the precise structures for microexperimentation. It was necessary to put out feelers in the larger world, and for once the idiotic secret service agencies were able to locate and confirm the necessary contacts without alerting the rest of the planet in their usual ham-fisted way. We were able to gather expertise and a large amount of impossibly expensive equipment from Britain, Canada and the United States. Unfortunately we had to take a scientist from Israel; he was the sole practitioner of some essential techniques."

Kenney observed gently, "A touch of racism, Mr. Cranko?"

"I'm white Australian and I know where my priorities lie."

"You're white but not Australian. Even I am only partly Australian. We are interlopers on a forty-thousand-year-old culture. But that is the condition of the world. My best friend is a Jew."

"Your taste in company is your own."

Beltane tapped the desk. "Twelve-oh-three and time flies. So the institute was built. But what is it?"

"It is a laboratory. The empty cylinder in the center is the meteorological testing ground; most of the rest of the building is devoted to bacteriological experiment; the hospital wards are for the most part occupied by patients playing their patriotic roles in these experiments. Rejuvenation procedures and other dubious favors for the powerful are an optional extra."

"Please confine yourself to explanation, to facts."

"None of you would understand them; I'll make do with approximations. The cylinder at the heart of the building is a well of empty air, but the instruments and activators built into its walls can render it a microreplica of any set of meteorological conditions the operators wish to study—conditions at the edge flows of major air currents, long-distance effects of storm turbulence, ground-air turbulence, moment-to-moment operations of heat gradients, interference by gusts and eddies . . . a thousand interacting forces not in my field of expertise. Measured and computed, they allow such exact knowledge of the behavior of a column of air that an aerodynamic missile of thin plastic, a few centimeters in length, can be launched from an orbiting satellite and landed, without guidance, within a hundred meters of its designed point of arrival. Guidance, you see, is detectable. The satellite records its regular weather observation of the target area and passes it to the institute's computers, which factor in all the variables common to such conditions and instruct the satellite when and where to release its tiny, fragile, buffetable load. The missile will strike where desired, split open on contact and discharge its contents, with a precalculated favorable wind to waft them to their point of operation. No one will know where the cloud of plague came from, save that it was carried on an ill wind. And who will connect it with a scrap of crumpled plastic rotting in a field some distance outside the city?"

It sounded disgustingly practical, and Beltane was watching us for reactions. Nguyen had retreated into his charlatan's shell of impassivity, and Gus seemed puzzled by the complexities. Kenney said thoughtfully, "In a column of air the full depth of the atmosphere and probably two hundred square kilometers in upper area, and allowing for a slanting and erratic descent, the chaos effects would be too many to formulate."

"Chaos mathematics deals with precisely that probability, and chaos effects themselves usually add up to a total observable overeffect. In practice, the accuracy is about sixty percent of effective drops, with the remainder close enough to guard against the possibility of bombarding a friend a thousand kilometers away by mistake."

"It has been tested?"

"Several hundred drops have been made. None has been detected. Why should they be? Scraps of rotting plastic!"

"Filled with?"

"So far, water."

We have become used to technological solutions to unlikely problems; Cranko was wholly believable. What was hard to believe in that moment was that we ill-assorted six sat together in a comfortable room and discussed—fairly quietly, all things considered—the fate of the human race.

Beltane asked, "Didn't you know any of this, Dick?"

"No. I suppose the party leader has it all, but it has been kept from the rest of us. Network security is strict and effective until some vainglorious ass like Fielding blunders into it. What will be the active filling of these scraps of plastic?"

"A product of Mr. Cranko's busy genius. Don't let me steal his thunder."

Cranko said with the judicious air of a judge at a cat show, "There are several possibilities. I favor a strain of nasal-infective bacteria developed in my own research area. It is airborne and therefore aerobic but can also extract its oxygen from body fluids. Its symptoms are those of the common cold, save for a slight drop in body temperature. It invades both sexes but leaves the males irreversibly infertile. Any community exposed to it in large force should see its numbers halved in fifty years and be extinct within a century."

"The common cold," Kenney observed, "shows no respect for international boundaries. It could sterilize the planet."

"Perhaps this is after all not so common a cold; it is one strain of a family designed with inbuilt instability leading to quick mutation to a harmless form. It does its work on the body in a few hours, mutates with a reduced reproductive capacity and is then easily dealt with by the human immune system. It can be spread by a sneeze or a kiss in the first few hours but not thereafter. I take some pride in such fine tailoring for its purpose."

I think Gus might have hit him again if Beltane had not caught his eye and mouthed a silent order to be still. "Whole cities!" Gus said with a child's wonderment. "He'd kill off whole cities!"

Cranko cringed away from him but in vanity could not stay silent. "Cities! Whole countries! The whole planet if they're stupid enough!"

Kenney asked, "If who are stupid enough?"

"The people waiting for the premier's decision. I don't know who they are. That is not my business."

He was resentful; genius surely deserved a seat on the councils of the great.

"You have heard who they are: Australia, New Zealand, Britain, America, Canada and Israel. All

English-speaking countries except Israel, who entered the club perforce. The smell of racism rises to a stench."

Beltane said, "That brings us to the decision-making process. Thirteen minutes past twelve and time does not slow down. Let me bring you to the nub of the matter, which is that we have a capacity to act. The question debated in Canberra is not whether we should act, but how. The situation has degenerated to that. There are several possibilities."

At this point I was not sure how to interpret what went on here. It occurred to me that Beltane was, however gently, quite mad because only a madman could discuss the sterilization of millions with such placid lack of commitment. Then, too, I was acutely conscious of his reason for having recalled me; I was a piece in a game that had turned disgusting.

Kenney addressed him now like someone gentling a confused child. "Is it wise, Jem, to speak so freely? Why not—"

"What has wisdom to do with what we speak of here?"

Nguyen stood. "I agree with Mr. Kenney. You are in a euphoric mood and present decisions may be regretted later. I recommend a mild sedative."

Beltane's gaze on him was quizzical, whimsical, the gaze of a player in control of the board.

Nguyen turned towards the door. "There are medications in the security wardroom."

Beltane said mildly, "I can do without them," and then, without raising his voice, "If you quit this room, Doctor, you will be arrested before you can leave the Manor. The only equipment you need is the instrument I asked you to bring. You have it?"

Nguyen remained calm. "I have it." He returned to his chair and seemed attentive to what the premier might say next.

So I had got one thing right in these sorry couple of days—Nguyen was no innocent consultant. The threat of arrest indicated activity more serious than mere urging.

"I was saying that there are several possible views of the uses of the culling tool—how it should be used and to what numerical effect, but more importantly, on whom. These questions are neither new nor recent; they are what many have considered but few voiced until the Biophysical Institute made discussion mandatory. You don't create a weapon just to mothball it.

"The first suggestion was that our possession of a practical culling weapon should be made secretly known to all governments, with the recommendation that they take harsh, effective birth control measures or have measures forced upon them. This was voted down. Knowledge of the weapon would concentrate scientific effort and the attention of a swarm of intelligence services upon it; very soon it would be duplicated by other powers and an outbreak of racial stupidity might sterilize the planet. There are times when I contemplate humanity and conclude that this might be a proper solution, allowing evolution to turn to the development of a less truculent species."

Gus said, "Balls!"

"It's an opinion and I am not alone in it. The next suggestion was that it should be used heavily on the most congested areas, less heavily on more lightly populated countries, maintaining a rough parity of ratios with today's figures. This I take to have been the last gasp of the once-British ethic of fair play—to give all poor benighted beggars an equal chance, as it were, with all still on the same footing as at present when it was over. At this juncture the real nature of the discussion became apparent. Fair play was not on the agenda, not on anybody's agenda. The question, the only question was, Who's to rule the ruins? It was an exercise in power."

"Of course." Kenney ticked off his fingers. "Attila, Batu Khan, smallpox for Red Indians, Imperial Britain, Auschwitz, Babi Yar. Nothing changes."

"Quite so. It would be expedient—now there's a word that explains most of parliamentary history—to open up for rescue and redevelopment the most fertile but overused and choked ecological areas of the planet. That pinpoints half of Asia, half of Africa and the bulk of South and Central America. Also, of course, all of Western Europe and the Ukraine—save that nobody seriously considered striking Western Europe and the Ukraine. Those were civilized areas, preservers of the great Western traditions of art and science and philosophy. To be conserved at all costs. Just a light touch of the cull, perhaps, to thin them out a little."

"Besides," Nguyen said with only the gentlest of sneers, "they are homes of the white races."

"Yes. I was surprised by how long it took for anyone to say, *Why not a white man's world?*—but once the dam was broken it became easy to speak the unspeakable. There was some talk of preserving carefully monitored numbers of nonwhites for the sake of the gene pool, but it seems that most Western societies have been so infiltrated through migration that this is not a factor. A more useful suggestion was that reasonable numbers be preserved to form a serving and laboring caste."

"That happened," Kenney said, "to the black branch of my ancestry; they are only recently out of repression. Hitler had a similar idea in the early years of the last century. Others have shared it. Ah, well, power corrupts. What did *you* say, Jem?"

"I said nothing at all; I took the coward's way and cried for my father. I got him, too. All for nothing. You'd never believe what he said to me."

Gus cackled like a delighted schoolboy. "What if he said to scrap the whole lousy idea and let the world rot any way it likes. That'd stop you with a bloody nose, wouldn't it?"

Beltane seemed astonished, eyeing the innocent face and possibly wondering what he had chosen for a bodyguard. "You are an extraordinary man. It is very much what he said, and it made the first crack in our relationship. When I ask advice on how to act I don't care to be told to do nothing. Think of this: There are seven nations involved; three favor one plan and three another. Australia has the casting vote. Our seven states are also three and three on each plan, which leaves me to come down one way or the other. It is my privilege to decide who breeds and who is never born. No small decision, I think. That old man whom I returned to life treated me with contempt for being unable to make it. So much trouble and nothing for it. So, this morning we will do what no politician in his right mind would dream of doing—we will put the question to the people. We have only two here but they must suffice. Mr. Kostakis, on his own admission represents the gutter; Detective-Sergeant Ostrov possibly imagines he represents the thinking stratum of the masses, all astir with morality and good sense. We will discover what they think. Or what they think they think."

Kenney murmured, "For Christ's sake, Jem, are you out of your mind?"

"Possibly. Or at last in it."

"You can't possibly mean that you will make your response contingent on the ideas of people without . . ."

Beltane topped him while he searched for expression. "You mean, without political sophistication? Why not? They elect us and we treat them thereafter as vote fodder. Let them for once have a say in their own destinies."

Kenney relaxed with a fresh thought. "You talk like an autocrat, but cabinet will decide what answer you take to Canberra."

"That would be proper? Parliamentary? According to the rules? Wait and see, Dick. Mr. Kostakis!" Gus cocked his head, all interest and expectation. "Which of the programs I have outlined would you suggest be implemented?"

Gus eased himself off the wall. "You mean, like speaking for the gutter?"

"For yourself."

"You think that's the same thing, don't you? It may be, but no gentleman would have said it."

"I apologize. Are you angry?"

"A bit, maybe, but you're the top man that can say what he likes."

"Then now's your chance to say what *you* like."

"Then I reckon you're shit. No mind of your own."

Even with permission to speak, that was pushing directness too far, and I was surprised that Kenney laughed aloud. "Oh, Jem, you cried out for it!"

Parliamentarians are remote from us, pictures on a vidscreen, open mouths delivering ghost-written speeches; at close range their lapses into common humanity smell of deceit, as though the screen figure is truth and the real man a poorly made fake. Respect is hard to maintain. Yet, although I had traded some blunt words with the premier, Gus's open insult was more than a sense of fitness could approve.

Yet Beltane ignored Kenney and said to Gus, "That's straight speech and whether I like it or not it's what I require of you. Now, please, your opinion on the cull weapon options."

Gus looked peculiarly gangling and helpless, but I knew better than to think he was rattled, and after a moment he asked, "Didn't nobody suggest a killing bug instead of the sterilizing thing?"

"No. Sudden plagues striking certain areas and not spreading to others would identify plague-free countries as the aggressors. Sterilization, carefully administered, would delay identification for a long period, and a small leakage of the bacterium into the aggressor areas would make positive identification difficult. Propaganda would be used to suggest equivalent suffering all round. You couldn't count the victims because they would show no symptoms, for many years, beyond a forgotten cold."

"You bastards have got it set up right, eh?"

"Planned, yes. Your opinion?"

"Dump it. Don't do anything except close the institute and destroy the bugs. Drown them in acid or whatever."

"And let the planet rot under its rising heap of living bodies?"

"Yeah. Let it rot."

Beltane seemed not to believe him, but Kenney appeared charmed by this oddity; only Nguyen smiled like an idol with a secret.

"Your profile identifies you as a sentimentalist, but your suggestion is for long-drawn suffering over decades, perhaps centuries of starvation and squalor."

"I'm not all that sentimental, but I like seeing everybody get a fair go; none of this pickin' off the shit and keepin' the chosen people. The people have to suffer whatever way it goes, so they ought to choose their own way. You blokes with power are always itching to use it instead of watching which direction the fair chances point. But when the people start fighting for space to breathe you'll be some of the first to go, because you'll be useless then. How's that for an answer?"

Beltane shook his head, I couldn't decide whether in admiration or disbelief. He said, "A good answer but simpleminded, off the point and loaded with class contempt. We should test it for truthfulness."

Gus bridled like a good boy accused of dirty habits. "How's that? I don't tell lies."

"We all say less or more than we mean. Dr. Nguyen?"

Nguyen produced from an inner pocket an instrument I had seen before, shaped like a small hand-gun, blunt nosed to rest against the skin and force a drug clear through it to vein or area as desired. A transcutaneous injection syringe.

I said, "Don't let him, Gus!"

Nguyen grimaced irritably at me, and Beltane said, "It's a truth drug and quite harmless. Hundreds of people have taken it in clinical tests."

"I'm one of them, Gus, and I say don't let him."

Nguyen said, "The sergeant was caught in untruth."

Gus was puzzled, undecided; he had trust in Nguyen and his probity had been challenged. Nguyen said, "It ensures only the telling of truth, Gus."

I said as forcibly as I could, "Too much bloody truth! Truth right out of your guts!"

I couldn't have chosen a clumsier warning, delivering a straight jab to his pride, but my thinking was cluttered with personal resentment. Gus colored with very real anger and protested, "I'm honest. I don't have to be afraid."

It left in the air an unspoken, *Even if you do.*

Nguyen told him to open his shirt and, when he did so, pressed the injector nozzle under his sternum to deliver the dose into the main artery from the heart. "Four minutes," he said to Beltane. "Then ask again."

The surface of my mind was muttering murderously that I would not let this be done to me again, that under no circumstances would I permit a second humiliation at Nguyen's hands. Behind that was a curiosity, almost an eagerness to hear what belched out of Gus when his defenses melted away; Nguyen, who had given him self-respect with his training, would leave him with a new wound in his vision of himself. I had had the mental strength to withstand and absorb the new truth of my feelings, to rock back to an even keel, but I doubted that Gus's grasshopper mind would be able to bear with himself stripped mentally naked.

The minutes passed in expectant silence save when Gus said, "I'll be all right, Harry." He was trying to make peace with me, so I nodded, OK.

Time ticked by.

Nguyen gestured to Beltane, and the premier asked his question.

Gus said, "Like I told you, the proper way to go is to close up that institute and kill all the bugs. Let things go their way. When life gets too hard to handle, the poor buggers that have to live it will look for their own answers. It won't be nice but it'll be fair."

Nguyen's eyes were on mine and he was stifling laughter. He turned to tell Beltane, "A man honest on two levels. A rarity. Simplicity of mind or deep self-knowledge? It is something to be investigated."

Gus winked at me and I couldn't respond.

Nguyen said, "There are greater depths of truth—the reasons behind the truth."

He gestured with the injector and Gus said, "Try me!" walking proud on the edge of the pit.

The dose went into his midriff and we waited.

There was physical change this time. His eyelids narrowed and his shoulders drooped; he leaned heavily on the back of Cranko's chair, and the surgeon squirmed nervously away from him. Gus's eyes roamed through slits as if seeking a target, but I knew from experience that his conscious mind was out of contact with its depths; the surface man knew nothing of what stirred down there.

The minutes passed as though time had slowed. We were silent before the unusual and bizarre. Only Nguyen had any idea of what might be expected from the dregs of the mind, from areas that I guessed might touch on intuition, self-preservation and the snake's nest of repressions. At last I warned, "He could be violent," but Nguyen shook his head.

"His attention will be wholly fixed on the questions asked."

We waited.

It was almost shocking when Nguyen broke silence again. "Mr. Kostakis, what use should be made of the cull weapon?"

Gus's head moved on the pivot of his neck as though he looked for the source of the sound.

He said, with a faint blurring, "Kill them all. Don't sterilize. Don't wait. Kill them all."

The tone was at odds with all my idea of him—harsh, vicious, vengeful.

"Kill which people?"

"All of them. Everybody. What good are they? Selfish. Who cares what happens to anybody else?"

"Why do you say that?"

"Because and because. I know." The next words rushed up like vomit, fast and sour. "Who's killing the world? People. Can't stop eating, can't stop fucking, can't stop living, can't stop anything. Everyone says it's the other man's fault so kill *him* but leave *me* alone to do as I like. You got to get people out of the world to let it live." His voice changed to a saccharine whine as sickening as his hatred. "Let the wild things live— the tigers and eagles and sharks and all the beautiful strong shapes."

His subjects of beauty were startling.

Nguyen asked, "Should you die with the rest?"

Gus's face fell apart, out of control. Tears rolled down and splashed on Cranko, who heaved himself out of the chair to sit on the floor, refusing to look round.

Gus said in the cracked voice of a lonely boy, "I want to die."

"Why?"

"Why live? Who wants me? I try to do the right things, and they think I'm mad. I'm not mad, I'm just lonely. I want to die."

I had a moment's shamed vision of all the world of the lonely, the retarded, the God lovers, the deviates, the bearers of private internal visions and all the unwanted whom we try not to see or accept or understand.

Nguyen asked, "Because you want to die the world must die with you. Is that it?"

"No. Nobody dies with anybody. Everybody dies alone. Nobody cares."

It was eerie. I saw him in the prison of his mind, naked and skinny and shivering in an unrelenting cold, solitary in a vast echo chamber clanging with his own sad thoughts.

Nguyen broke the spell in the practical tones of a lecturer. "His conscious mind is not aware of these miseries save in flashes which it buries to save itself. It is not easy to will yourself to die. The need surfaces also in dreams, calming itself with symbols disguised and unrecognized. Sergeant, would you seat him in a chair? He will experience a certain shock as he recovers." He flashed me a smile. "Remember?"

I remembered. I approached Gus cautiously, not wishing to encounter a sudden outbreak of total muscular concentration. Nguyen understood, said, "He will not be aware of being handled."

He was no more than a heavy doll to be plumped into place.

Kenney said, "The voice of the gutter doesn't help, Jem. You've picked a solitary, a psycho sport, not the voice of the people."

"Did you expect that?" Nguyen asked. "The premier asked me to provide gut reactions and I am doing so, but there will be no consensus from the gutter. In spite of the good John Donne, every man is an island."

I don't think Beltane listened to him. "I want to hear from the sergeant."

It was the moment, and I was prepared for it. I stood up, ready to move. "My opinion is the same as that of Kostakis. The entire setup should be destroyed and the world left to worry its own way out of starvation and failing resources. Other species face drought and famine and survive; so shall we. I suggest also that these secret political talks be made public so that the rubbish in the gutter may experience at firsthand the care and solicitude of the guardians of its well-being."

I tried to say it in the level tone I used when giving evidence in the courts, but my voice shook a little with anger and disgust.

Beltane seemed pleased. "I incline to agree, but I wonder what basic drives lie behind the conscious thought."

I told him, "Wonder and be damned." I could no longer pretend respect for him or his game playing when my inner integrity was at stake. "I've had Nguyen's treatment before and I'm not playing a second round. I'm not baring my belly for him. Good morning, sir."

There's no fool like a dramatizing fool seeking to make a big exit. To walk from the room like a self-respecting police officer, I turned my back, confident that Nguyen would not be able to reach the main artery without my concurrence. He must have come after me like a slender cat because I felt the cold shot in the side of my neck.

Raging at him and at myself I turned about, took the injector from him and threw it onto Beltane's desk, grabbed his right forearm and broke it across my own.

He reeled back, gasping and pale. Resting the arm in his left hand, he retreated until a chair caught his legs and he sat heavily down.

He spoke, and I felt a kind of involuntary admiration for his fortitude and control, "There's no point in trying to leave now, Harry. The cocktail will be a little longer taking effect from random injection, but you would not want to be roaming outside with the levels of your mind disconnected, would you? Who knows what might be asked of you and what you might reply?"

I could not argue with that. I sat down again, miserable and frightened. "Nguyen, you said that this procedure was useless to the premier. So why did you do this to me?"

"Curiosity. I am a scientist." He let the words hang like an echo in the air before he continued, "I am also a human being. I know your mask of self-inflicted rectitude and I know the welter of unimportant little shames that makes it necessary to you. It is almost worth this—" he moved the broken arm slightly "—to know what at bottom fuels the pride of such a counterfeit of virtue." He turned to Beltane. "Would you please use your vid to summon a doctor?"

Beltane said bluntly, "You will have to wait. Keep the arm still and no harm will come to it."

That was heartless enough to penetrate my self-absorption and panic at what was to come to me. Come *from* me.

Beltane continued, "I don't give a damn for your suffering, Nguyen. When you leave here it will be for a prison cell, along with Cranko. Each of you knows why. You will be able to go fairly soon, but you must see the play out first since both of you had a part in setting it up. If you try to leave before I permit it you—or any of you—will be apprehended in the corridor and returned to this room."

The Small Office seemed to brace itself against further surprise. Or, perhaps, that was an illusion of my wandering senses as the cocktail began to take its first effect. I recall staring at Kenney and wondering how all this affected his consciousness of racial past and divided present. Then I heard Beltane ask a question and my mouth started to open and shut and make sounds that had nothing to do with my awareness of self. . . .

10

Kostakis:
The Facts of Life

From Commentaries; *The Social Complex: "It is difficult to refrain from conjecture, admittedly futile, as to what manner of man Kostakis might have been, given education and guidance. The twenty-first century must surely have seen, in its unregarded masses, the greatest waste of human potential in historical time."*

For quite a bit I didn't know what they were talking about, it was that much mixed up with stuff about satellites and experiments, all over my head. Truth is, I wasn't listening too hard because I was thinking about the things Beltane had said about him and old Gerald.

I know a few blokes—some women, too—who get their kicks doing things that to me just don't seem interesting. I don't have any moral ideas about off-course sex, except for pederasty because that can leave a kid bleeding and damaged. So I was knocked sideways when I heard Beltane talking about pederasty like a love affair. As if there were kinds of love I knew nothing about.

It started me thinking about love on my own account, as if he had opened up a whole country I never knew existed, where perhaps everybody had his own ideas about it and two people getting it right together might be . . .

I knew, just like somebody hitting me with it, why love and Gus had never really worked together. It was because I thought my loving was the only kind and when people didn't respond to it I got puzzled and thought there was something wrong with them.

I knew my wife thought I was some sort of a clown. When we got married she thought I was a real breakup, a joker to make life one long laugh. Somewhere she stopped laughing. Got tired of laughing. She changed.

That's how it seemed to me.

And the kid, the little boy . . . When he was little we was the greatest friends. We played together as if the laughing would never stop. But it did. He changed as he got bigger. He started to think I was a ratbag, and wouldn't bring his friends around when I was home.

I loved Belle and the boy, but I couldn't get close to them any more. And I'd been thinking all this time that it wasn't my fault, but it was. Beltane had been saying, under all his stupid confessing, that there are different kinds of love, and all the time I'd been satisfied mine was the only kind. My family . . . I thought they loved me still, or they wanted to, only I wouldn't go their way about living and behaving and I blamed them for handing me off.

What it come down to was, I'm selfish, too selfish to see I had to make the effort to meet them, to be what they called "normal" instead of chasing interests and ambitions that couldn't come to anything because I haven't got the knowledge or the talent or what it takes.

I felt as if my whole life had been wasted in the lies I told myself. Worse than that, I didn't know how to change . . . or which part was the lies. . . .

I had to stop muddling about in my head and try to make sense of what was going on. It come through to me slowly that they were talking about the cull, as if it was something real. They were dead serious about it and had got round to working out who had to go. At first I couldn't believe they could sit there talking it over like a club fixture the boys had to agree on.

But they could. They did.

Harry got hot about being called "gutter," but Harry has a big opinion of hisself. It didn't worry me much because I always knew what Minders thought about Wardies; still, I gave Beltane a serve when my turn came. He had no call to look down on anyone; I come off of a scrap heap and knew it, but he wouldn't know if old Gerald had picked him off of a trash recycler.

When he asked me what to do about the cull, I told him just what I thought and he seemed to like it. His trouble was that it didn't matter what he liked; in the finish he'd do what the strongest told him. I wasn't joking when I said he had no mind of his own; I thought it might put a bit of starch in his spine, but that Kenney only laughed like I'd scored a bull's-eye, and I knew it was only chitchat like a couple of comics on the vid.

Then they got on to this business with the truth drug and that was insulting. Harry tried to warn me off, but I know he's got a weak streak under that copper's hide and I felt like showing them how an honest man doesn't shift his ground, so I let Dr. Nguyen use his little drug gun. I know I answered the same under the detector because that was how I saw it and it was a better idea than their cold-blooded picking over the heap. I felt a bit vague about then, but I'm dead sure the words come out right. They must have because Dr.

Nguyen wanted to go deeper and I didn't see no reason to stop him; he'd only get more of the same.

But this time was nasty. It was like being split in two or like one of thooo dreams when you're outside yourself but can't hear what you are saying. You know you've got to find out, but you can't and you get that frightened that you wake up.

Then it *was* like waking up because I was sitting in a chair, when I knew I had been leaning over that bastard Cranko. I couldn't remember anything about being questioned, but that didn't worry me right then because it was Harry's turn, and he acted up bad and I was concerned about him. Apparently he'd had the gun before and got caught out in some way and didn't want a second lot. There was things I liked about Harry and I didn't want to find out that he's a liar. Still, I supposed, police have to keep some things to theirselves.

But first he said the same as me but with more reasons, but he tried to run out on the check test and Nguyen sapped the back of his neck and paid for it with a busted forearm, too fast for me to interfere. I wasn't ready, pumped up for rough stuff. It needs warning.

Once he knew the shot had gone in Harry didn't try anything else after that one bit of temper but just sat down and waited. I had time to think then and was trying to remember the dream, if that's what it was after I took the second shot; it was important if only I could place it. Maybe I had said something different the third time. I might have dug a better idea out of my deep mind and told them that; if the drug freed your brain up for truth, that was just what might have happened.

I was really shocked when they asked Harry the question for the second time and he went right away from his first idea. He talked in an ordinary voice as if he was talking about the weather or whatever, but what he said was, "We should make a white man's world.

No slaves, no servants; just us. We can talk to each other; we understand the same things."

Mr. Kenney said, "Listen to the racist behind the mask of professional virtue!"

Harry said, "No, no; I don't care what color they are. Not even dirt-digging Minder shit like you. It's just that there's no peace because Asiatics and black Africans and the South Americans that seem to come all colors don't have the same ideas we have or the same ideas as each other." He sounded so reasonable, as if this was obvious stuff anybody could follow. I suppose it was, really. "They're troublemakers, all of them, always wanting what they haven't got as though we should give it to them. That means trouble, all the way into the future, so why not stop it now? The future's for the fittest. One world, one white world of people that get on together. Dick Kenney, here, he's all right. He lives like a white man and he thinks like us. We don't have to be, to be—what? We don't have to be indiscriminate. We can keep a few good ones. See what I mean?"

Nguyen said, "I see very well," and Harry tried to spit at him, but his body seemed to be out of control and the gobbet dribbled on his chin. He looked nasty.

I got worried then whether I'd said what I thought I'd said. Harry had said, first up, what he thought fitted the picture of him he wanted the world to see, the good bloke all for fair play; now it sounded like he was saying what he really thought, how he felt about the world. What really made his idea stink was the way he invented a sort of reason for wanting it that way. Then I wondered, Did he invent the reason? After all, this was like having truth dug out of him like the muck out of a cesspit and this could be what he believed.

I got really scared then about what I couldn't remember.

Mr. Kenney said, "My maternal ancestors could teach you a thing or two about how well white men get on together. The greatest wars in history have been yours."

Harry waved a finger at him, admonishing. "That was the fault of different languages. Take them out, too. A white, English-speaking world is what we should have."

The premier had been watching and listening with a sort of disgusted fascination as if he was cornered by a snake. Now he said, "Three nations and three Australian states agree with that plan. Some of them follow the sergeant's reasoning, some find other justifications; only one is honest enough to hate what he calls the black and yellow scum. Scratch an educated man and find his ignorance; scratch a logician and find a sophist. On the whole I prefer Mr. Kostakis, whatever hell he lives in."

That frightened me, because I didn't know what he meant about me and hell.

He picked up the drug gun that Harry had tossed on his desk. "We'll have to excuse Dr. Nguyen on ground of incapacity." He held out the gun. "You, Dick? I feel we should know what lies behind the sergeant's nonsense."

Mr. Kenney said, like the gentleman he seemed to be, "Not I. The whole business is repellent. I don't know what has got into you, Jem. All this playacting!"

The premier came round to the front of the desk. "Then I must do it myself. The purpose is to look at some aspects of the world as they are, in spite of what we may imagine they are. Do you think any of us would emerge from the test smelling any sweeter than these two? Different, perhaps, but scarcely better. And if one of us turned out to have the mind of Christ himself, how we would hate him!"

He hefted the little gun and asked Dr. Nguyen, "Under the sternum, dead center, and squeeze the trigger?"

The doctor said like an automaton, still supporting

his arm, "Squeeze once. It delivers a metered dose." He must have been in horrible pain.

The premier moved up to Harry, who didn't look at him, and stood there, unsure of what to do next. The doctor said, "Sergeant Ostrov, open the front of your shirt."

Harry did what he was told like a vidplay zombie, and the premier jammed the gun into his middle and shot in the dose.

We waited for the longest minutes of my life while I tried and tried to think of what I said under the second dose. It began to seem it must have been something pretty bad that I didn't want to remember, the sort of thing that makes you afraid ever to look in a mirror again. Yet I had to find out.

When the time was up the premier asked, "Sergeant, what use should we make of the cull weapon?"

And Harry said, "Forget about it for now. Keep it for later. Clean our house first."

He had slumped forwards on his chair with his head just about on his knees, and his voice was hard to hear because he was talking somewhere down between his legs.

"Old people," he said. "You know how many old people there are, useless old buggers like old Gerald? No, not him. He's got some life in him. I like old Gerald. But the rest! Forty percent of the population over fifty! No jobs, no use to anyone. Eat and take up space and cost money and give nothing back. Start up euthanasia! You've talked about it enough, haven't you? Think the Wardies don't know what you talk about behind the doors? We know. Do it. Off at fifty! Knock off two-fifths of the world at one smack! No waiting!"

He slipped further forwards till he was nearly off the chair. The premier said, "That would have me pronouncing my own death warrant."

"You? Who'd care? No guts to do the wrong thing

and no guts to do the right thing! Tell me what to do, Daddy, but make it something nice that won't frighten me! It needs people who see straight to take hard decisions."

That should've busted Boltane, because it was true and he knew it was true, but he didn't show anything. I could see Kenney was hating it, but Dr. Nguyen was laughing fit to kill, without any noise, bending over his broken arm and shaking with the joke. It was the first time I ever seen him laugh and it wasn't nice. He was having some sort of revenge by digging the dregs out of Harry.

Beltane asked, as if this was a real king-hit of a question, "How old are your father and mother, Harry?" and Dr. Nguyen made a little clapping noise with his good hand on his knee, as if he knew what was coming and couldn't wait for it.

Harry made a chuckling sound, then I thought it was more like a snarl. "Old enough! Get them first. Get them out of my way."

That stumped the premier, but Nguyen asked, "How are they in your way, Harry?"

Harry slipped off the chair onto his hands and knees. I think this disconnection thing wasn't letting him have any physical control and his body couldn't hold itself up. (Holy Jesus, had I been like that, spilling all my deep dirt onto the carpet?)

Harry said with the sort of contempt you'd give to a queer's pimp, "You know that, Nguyen. Ian Juan Ivan John! I told you before. Ian! Know right from wrong! Juan! Always respect the law! Ivan! Obey your lawful superiors without question! John! Be upstanding for truth! Little boy being prepared to face the world foursquare for the right! But what for Harry? What is there for Harry? Them and their damned love round his neck like a rope till Harry's too old himself and it's too late for Harry. I wanted to kill them but I couldn't. You

can't kill love. It hounds you. Besides, murder's wrong
and Harry knows right from wrong. The law says no
and Harry is the law! Make a law that says, *Kill them,*
and set us all free."

He fell flat on his face as his hands slid away from
under him. He kept saying into the carpet, "Ian Juan
Ivan John," like a nursery rhyme and made gulping
noises trying to be sick.

Beltane ran out of being stone faced. "That's enough,
for God's sake!" He said to me, "Are you sufficiently
recovered to pick him up, Mr. Kostakis?"

Yes, sir, of course, sir. He couldn't ask another Minder to do it, could he? Bad protocol!

I picked him up and shoved him back into the chair.
It wasn't easy because he's a big man and I'm not all
that strong when I'm not pumped up to it. I felt sorry
for him with all that childhood stuff standing between
him and all his natural feelings. Whatever they were.
Most natural feelings need a bit of reining in, but his
were plain stuffed up.

I heard Dr. Nguyen saying, "Note the essential dichotomy at the heart of mankind. He loves his parents
dearly, otherwise their prohibitions would not be so
supinely obeyed. His righteousness is simple fear of
offending the adored, just as his vengefulness is his
inability to free himself from a beloved constraint."

Kenney said, "What an unpleasant calling yours must
be," and then I wasn't paying attention to anyone but
myself because all my questions were getting answered
in my head. The drug must have worked off because I
started to remember those missing minutes, a little at
a time, like a fog lifting from this bit and that bit until
the whole thing was clear.

It didn't matter about wanting to die; that come up
like something I always knew but never come to grips
with because I never let myself look straight at it. What
hit me was sick shame at being naked right through to

the bone in front of these heartless bastards that pawed
through my skull just to make points in a frightened
game the premier played with hisself.

Then there was another shame, at how the world
saw me, at what other people thought about me, at
what I knew all the time but pretended that I was
proud to be just what I was and to hell with what
the world thought . . . when all the time I cared and
cared, ashamed because my wife had married somebody that didn't fit the world properly and my kid put
up with me and wished he didn't have to—and what
really drove me all the time was wanting to be things
I never could be. Like that one that challenged the god
to music and all he got was the skin stripped off him.
That's really having nothing to live for.

I don't know how long I sat there like a sick dog,
thinking I would never be the same again and wishing
I didn't know about what drove me. The next thing I
remember clearly is Dr. Nguyen standing over me, still
holding his arm, and saying, "Don't worry too much,
Gus. The mind has its defenses. In a little while it
will heal over revelation like a scab over a wound
and you will draw new strength from the knowledge
of weakness."

That sounded preachy, and I was nearly crying when
I said, "What about you? What goes on behind your
yellow face?"

I shouldn't have insulted him, but I was upset. He
only shook a bit and said, "Some fear goes on there
because I am found out."

Beltane interrupted, with anger boring like a gimlet,
"You surely are, Doctor, and I have to thank Sergeant
Ostrov for that. He alerted me to a possibly sinister
interpretation of your guidance of my mental welfare;
it took the combined intelligence services just twenty-
four hours, once the suspicion was voiced, to pinpoint
you as a source for field agents of the Southeast Asian

Federation. It remains only to be discovered what you have reported and when and to whom. Your own drug will tell us."

Dr. Nguyen said, "At least the police will give me the medical attention you deny me. I am safe from interrogation; biochemistry has its uses and it has been seen to that a truth drug will kill me quickly. That will leave your decision makers in Canberra with a dilemma on their minds: Does the enemy know what you have or does he not?"

Beltane seemed to have cards in his hand that he kept to hisself. He said, "It won't come to that. In any case, Cranko probably spilled what beans he possessed some weeks ago; the network that snared him would certainly have contacts among enemy agents."

Cranko didn't like that and tried to protest that he was only locally political. Kenney gave him a tired smile, the sort you give to a kid who hasn't cottoned on yet to what the old folks do in bed.

Beltane checked the time and said, "It doesn't matter." He went back to the desk console and killed the room's sound screen. It was like being put back into a suddenly bigger world as all the noises of the Manor spattered into the room. I heard a big laugh raised up in the wardroom and wondered what the joke was.

Then all the insulated windows went up and the noise of the whole world burst in. Most of it was the racket of copters overhead, as if there was dozens of them up there.

Kenney thought they'd be channel copters and asked couldn't they be kept out of close range?

Beltane said, "The Air Force shepherded the channel machines away an hour ago. Those are Air Force fliers."

"For what?"

"Like me, they are waiting for one-thirty."

Kenney opened his mouth, ready to be indignant,

then must have decided he was dealing with a man off his balance. He shut up.

There was five minutes to go. I watched Harry come to life. He looked across to me and nodded without meaning anything and put on a smile without any fun in it. I reckoned he hadn't started remembering yet and his bad time was still to come. I felt better about Harry now than I had felt about anyone since I asked Belle to marry me and she buggered her life by saying yes. It was the feeling of recognizing somebody else's rock bottom is just as hard as your own.

The copters must've been circling because they began to fade away towards City Center. They got fainter and fainter and then stayed at the same level of sound as if they had gathered over one spot.

Cranko woke to it first. He screeched—really screeched—"You bastard, there are hundreds of people in there!"

"There are none. They were herded out an hour ago on pretense of a bomb scare. Not altogether a pretense."

Cranko stammered and made no sense for a bit. Then he was crying out about, "Years of work! Brilliant work by brilliant people. Irreplaceable records. Elegant, beautiful experimental procedures . . ."

Beltane pretended to clap. "So much beauty for such beautiful ends! At last I hear you concerned for something other than yourself."

Then the bombing began.

It lasted maybe a minute, in patches as if a pattern was being worked out.

Then it stopped, and it was as if silence had dropped on the world except for a long, long rumble that went on and on as if the institute would never stop falling. Then it did stop, and for a bit we were all quiet.

I didn't really give a bugger about the institute because somebody was sniveling out his self-pity, and it was me.

11

Ostrov: Coming to Terms

This drugging had been different from that first large-scale experiment; I wasn't sure, but I thought so. I thought that this time there had been a second shot, a booster, because there was a definite hiatus wherein I didn't remember talking or being questioned, much less what I had said or if I had said anything.

I felt sick and sore throated as though I had been retching, but there was no stinking mess on the carpet. The first thing I heard was Nguyen speaking of dichotomy and then, quite clearly, "He loves his parents dearly, otherwise their prohibitions would not be so supinely obeyed. His righteousness is simple fear of offending the adored; just as his vengefulness is his inability to free himself from a beloved constraint."

He was talking about me and he was saying something profoundly right, something I knew to be true though I had never thought about it—at any rate, not in those terms—in all my life. Or had I? Had it floated in my mind like a fact unnoticed? Or avoided?

He was trying to be kind. He was like most of us—repellent and remote or kindly and forthcoming by turns, with no knowing which turn would come next.

I saw Gus, in Cranko's chair still and looking like death, shaking slightly and paying attention to no one, wholly lost in himself and sniffing to hold back tears. I had a fair idea what was happening to him and could do nothing about it. Each man is indeed an island . . . consciousness is a desperate reaching for each other against ultimate loneliness, a need of community to hold at bay the territorial wild beast unexorcised from the foundations of the mind.

I lost track of passing time, self-absorbed to the point of seeing and hearing the people in the Small Office only when some word or movement caught my fleeting attention. I was absorbed in sickness and fear of the unrecovered minutes. A man should not be hit twice with terror of his true self. The mind suppresses with good reason. . . .

There was talk of Nguyen as a spy, seeming so obvious as to be irrelevant. I had known it. Or had I? Had it been one of those mental notes of possibility waiting for me to attend to it when there was time?

There was noise from outside the Manor as somebody cut the room's sound screen. Copters. A swarm, as if all the channels had converged on their prey at once. Somebody, Beltane I think, said "Air Force" and they went away. I heard the bombs—you can't mistake that sound—and thought at once that the advice of the gutter had been taken and the plague spot destroyed.

Then the gap cleared from my memory with smooth menace and the continuity was complete.

I stood aside from me while the bombs fell on Bill and Arlene, burying them and setting me free to blow with the wind, to be Harry at last and never again Ian Juan Ivan John, the puppet of a rhyme. Simultaneously my heart burst with grief and longing and a horror of unfettered hatred, and the bombs fell between the two halves of me.

They stopped and the world stopped with them.

I remembered what Nguyen had told my returning mind and knew that all my contradictions and brutalities could be resolved—not now but later, in solitude. In the grateful silence I thought of the fool who said that to understand all is to forgive all. I wasn't going to forgive myself anything, only to . . . what? Look about me with new knowledge?

Only minutes before, I had felt an almost hysterical ecstasy as I broke Nguyen's arm. Yet he had begun setting me free while he stifled his pain. Who knows what hides in us, for good and bad, waiting to get out, obeying no morality, only need?

I felt a pang for Kostakis whom I had taken up as a useful oddity and delivered to the torturers. There something must be done. . . .

I set myself, for sweet sanity's sake, to attend to what went on around me.

"You have seen that I followed my father's advice after all—and anticipated the voices of the gutter." That was Beltane explaining, like a teacher to his class. "With the institute sitting on the edge of City Center and close to several National Heritage buildings, the drop required delicate preparation. The tubular construction of the institute allowed a pattern of drops causing the whole structure to collapse inwards into its own central space in a pyramid of rubble. Followed by high-temperature incendiaries. What's left, Mr. Cranko, will be a pool of lava. Think of it! All your finely manufactured mutating bacteria boiled and incinerated in their culture media! All those minutely calculated chaos-ordered records reduced to ash and atoms! That's payment for treachery."

Cranko was stunned speechless, and I think it was the scientist in him that mourned for what he would have seen as great art destroyed.

But Kenney exploded, "Jem! You couldn't order the

destruction of a state building on your own authority!
You haven't the power for that."

"I haven't and I didn't order it. In the small hours of
this morning I told the Southern Area Services commander what was in there and why and what I felt
could be done about it. He agreed with me on the score
of necessity. Have you ever noticed that the armed
services don't favor cold-blooded genocide? It takes
politicians to order that. So he saw to the action, and
it would be interesting to see, once the tale is told, if
any fool tries to have him disciplined for it."

"You're going public to the country, Jem?"

"To the world. Names, dates, plans, arguments, every
little nastiness, every monstrous selfishness."

Can you imagine manic serenity? We were hearing
it.

On his desk a crypter beeped, and he picked up
the strip of extruded paper. "I usually leave encrypted
messages to the secretarial staff, but I can decode this
one for you. It is from Southern Area Command. It says,
*One hundred percent evacuation; one hundred percent
demolition.* There you have it—not a life lost, not a bug
spared."

Kenney had seen the wastefulness and the weakness
at once. "Now it all remains to be done again. You have
settled nothing, simply deferred decision."

"Referred it to the people."

"My ancestral *kadaitja* man would have known better. Do you expect rational discussion? You'll get panic,
fear, terrorism, war, revolution."

Beltane frowned at him like a thwarted boy, and
barked suddenly at me, "Ostrov! What will the people do?"

I had to shake myself together though it didn't much
matter what I said. "You mean, what will the gutter
vote be? Will the sewers drown in apathy or run with

blood? Either. Both. How would anybody know? But in the long run you haven't killed knowledge; it's all there in scientists' heads, waiting for reassembly."

That didn't disturb him. "Reassembling the weather column will take years; its microcircuitry was unique. By the time another can be ready the future will have been discussed, weighed, thrashed out round the planet. It will be a time for fresh ideas, new alternatives."

What can you say to a man who wishes on the world an atmosphere of terror in the hope that fear will generate a miracle? I said, "Here's one humane idea: Get some help for Nguyen."

The bland Asiatic face relaxed in brief acknowledgment. Of what? A kindness, a relief, a gratitude?

Beltane told him, with no kindness at all, to get out. "The security chief has her orders; she will attend to you."

Nguyen bowed slightly, courteously, to Gus and myself. "Knowledge sets you free to think real thoughts; it removes basic contamination." He nodded to Kenney. "You will find that the way of the honest man is impossible; it leads to the nuthouse." The word was strange in his usually precise mouth. "You, Mr. Premier, have spent your life in a nuthouse created for you by a confused and selfish man, and now you want to bring the whole of humanity inside with you. Bring their repressed fear of the cull to immediate reality and you will see the planet go down in blood as each nation seeks to inherit the ruin. Do not make your confession to the nation; stop the mouth of the area commander; invent any fiction you please but do not broadcast the truth about the institute and its contents."

He went to the door, and Beltane called after him, "The truth will be told."

Nguyen paused, looked back. "I am in no condition to kill you. I hope one of these capable gentlemen will do it before your stupidity sets the nations at each other's throats."

Beltane said in the calm voice of reason, "My speech was dispatched by courier to all channels as soon as the bombing began. It could be on the air by now. It possibly is. My blackmailer has not called for his answer; I suspect he is hearing it in the public domain."

Nguyen's face showed his pain. "I'm told that a butterfly beats its wings in the jungle and originates a train of effect that may burst in a typhoon in the China Sea. A sexually aberrant man is enthralled by a boy's face and half a century later the planet is given the conditions for a bloodbath."

Holding his arm, he went down the corridor to the wardroom and arrest.

Beltane stabbed at his console. "Listen to my own chip of the speech. You have earned the hearing."

His voice—calm, ministerial, practiced—came like political cream into the room. He addressed the country—in fact the world—as smoothly as he had for years addressed the House. The world knows what he said, is sick of hearing the farrago of confession run and rerun and analyzed. We four—Kenney and Cranko, Gus and myself—would have been the first to realize that we listened to the unemphatic, matter-of-fact, precise words of a man who if not actually insane was, at best, beyond rational thinking.

The hair-raising opening, "The seeds of this speech were planted half a century ago," warned us that he was about to shred his private history on the airwaves, and we listened in dumb, astonished discomfort as he made public the story of his relationship with Gerald, the medical and surgical dealings with Cranko (sitting there like a statue, with a rictus grin) and the previous night's appeal to the father who berated and disowned him. Having stripped his own life naked, he spared nobody, exposing the political information networks

with a completeness that made a joke of the simple
popular suspicions, naming names on both sides of the
House and in the public service (including the police
force) and naming go-betweens who ferried knowledge,
threats and deals for money. He told the story of the
Canberra discussions, naming this time not only people
but countries (and setting the planet's communications
in an electronic jam of denial, excuse and accusation)
and at last of the destruction of the institute. His final
words were as elegantly political as the people were
accustomed to hear from him, and they were designed
to set a match to the pyre: "It was not to be thought of
that decision in such a matter should be forced upon
us by racists, elitists and selfish men. Now the people
will see their leaders as they are and will be able in
future to do their own thinking in spite of them."

There was nothing for any of us to do; Beltane had
upset the board and tossed the pieces to the Wardies
of the world for rending and destruction.

It was Cranko, on his way to arrest and imprisonment,
who had the last word of the morning. "You'll see
democracy in action, Mr. Premier—just for a moment
as its boots smash your face."

Beltane did not answer him. Alone at the desk as we
retreated, his lip jutted in petulance. Misunderstood,
misunderstood . . .

We left him there. The secretaries would have to set
in motion whatever was to be done with him. Kenney
walked swiftly ahead of us, wanting only to be spirited
out as he had been spirited in and not be connected
with the debacle; Beltane had, for whatever reason (recognition of basic political honesty?) left his name out of
the listing of the damned.

The last I saw of him, he was being escorted towards
the parking area by a security man for an undignified
exit in some anonymous van. But who around here had
any dignity left to flaunt?

Gus plucked at my sleeve to hold me back while Cranko went on to the police waiting for him with a Secrecy Act warrant.

I'm not psychologist enough to guess at Gus's state of mind; it must have been damnable, even with Nguyen's word of encouragement. He looked shocking. The innocent face that could ape manic rage had little capacity for the reality of puzzled misery; he looked unpleasantly like a beaten child, and what he wanted to ask was whether or not I considered suicide wrong—as though my trust in right and wrong had come through the morning unscathed.

I could only regurgitate old convictions. I told him, "It would be wrong for you."

"Why for me?"

"It would be cowardice, fear to face facts."

He stopped dead, mouth open and jaw dropped, again like a kid but with the beginning of the raging mask that had terrified Cranko, and this time it was real. He screamed at me like a drunk who sees a single mad vision of all his hatreds and failures, "You sanctimonious bastard! How you fuckin' love yourself!"

I had heard that so often, spoken in cold blood in the past few days, that it had lost power to wound, and now, hurled at me in howling outrage, it started me on a bout of helpless laughter. I suppose I was, at bottom, as worked up as he but more practiced at suppressing feeling; what caught me was probably deep hysteria forcing itself into the light. I know I leaned against the wall and choked and hawked and spat with laughter.

In anyone's logic that should have driven Gus to mania, but it could be that both of us had taken the sort of beating you want to leave behind you; the mental first aid is to grasp at any attitude that frees you from pain. I didn't know what he might do; I was shaking and helpless and gasping for air, and I knew he was looming over me though I couldn't get my head up to see his face. I expected to be hit by a madman.

Instead, he slapped me sharply on the cheeks, saying, "Stand up, Harry; snap out of it, man!" Then, like an exasperated nanny, "You'll make yourself sick."

He waited while I shuddered back to normal, and we continued to the wardroom.

I must have got something right, however much by accident, because I have known Gus for many years now and I have never again heard him mention suicide.

In the wardroom was the quiet of stunned unbelief. Nguyen and Cranko sat apart, nobody speaking to them. Treachery has no friends. In that stillness there could be no privacy, but I had a question for Nguyen.

"Why did you give me that cruel second shot instead of letting me walk out of the room?"

He said steadily, "Because, like you, I am a professional with a conscience. It was necessary that your crux problem be resolved."

"Conscience brought you a broken arm."

"It brought you some understanding. As for the arm, that will be superseded by bullets against a wall. Old-fashioned but final."

"You did spy?"

"The premier used my name in his foolish broadcast and in the public mind that will be sufficient evidence. The intelligence agencies will surely find an execution expedient to help quiet Ward discontent."

That was pretty certainly how it would go. No comment could be adequate. I mumbled that I was sorry about his arm. He had done what he could for me in lunatic circumstances.

He said, "I should have taken more care."

That sounded like forgiveness.

*   *   *

Nguyen was a good man; his tenets were not mine but I could recognize and respect them. But—can a good man be a traitor? Or can a traitor be a good man? Is it honorable to recognize a loyalty higher than the one you have served all your life and which has, as your country, served you? Has a person the right to a judgment beyond the loyalty that supported him while he grew to a mature capacity for judgment?

Would not, for instance, loyalty to the planet's future take precedence over all others?

Or, was loyalty itself a political ploy, a trap to bind the sucker hand and foot and turn thought into a despicable treason?

My country, right or wrong?

Round and round, yes and no. Self-confidence had been sheared from under me. The vision of oneself as a quarreling dichotomy leaves few certainties, but I clung to the thought that Nguyen was, at base, a good man—he did duty as he saw it and in the welter of loyalties found a moment to attend to me whom he owed nothing.

It is not easy to pin down my state of mind just then, but there is a placidity, a sense of relief in seeing all the rigid structures of morality crumble and vanish.

Gus was nudging my ribs. "Here's Mrs. Beltane, Harry." Mrs. Beltane and Melissa stood in the wardroom doorway, dressed for the street and ready to leave, but Jeanette was expostulating with Ivy, trying to make her understand that security took orders only from the first secretary or from the premier himself.

Mrs. Beltane tried to push past her, and Jeanette stood in her way, physically capable of dealing with three like her but not sure that she dared risk using force.

Melissa stood back, puzzled and frightened by the

reality of anger between adults who were, according to her training, supposed to control their emotions.

Her mother called out to me, "Sergeant! Get this woman away from me!"

I had to explain as peaceably as I could, "This is her area of command, ma'am."

"To hell with her and her command! I want to know what I am to do. Now that Jeremy has made a publicly criminal fool of himself, am I to be pushed off home to face four damned channels interrogating and snooping until they are in possession of every secret of our lives? What's to be done?"

I made a spur-of-the-moment decision. "You'll have to stay a while longer. The channels can be stood off here. Later we'll find some out-of-the-way place for you."

Jeanette was stubborn. "It has been arranged that Mrs. Beltane and her daughter will leave the Manor. Only the premier can countermand that."

"Very well, I'll talk to him."

"Not yet you won't." She waved at the com-board where the green light was steady in the top right-hand corner. "He's reinstituted the sound screen. That means no interruption until he signals for it."

"Can't he be interrupted for emergency?"

"Not by you." She meant it. She had had enough of her command being pushed and stretched and ignored. I wasn't going to put her out of my way, physically, in order to reach the com override, damaging her dignity while her men looked on. In that case they might have ganged up on me.

I said to Mrs. Beltane, "I'll go to him," and started down the corridor with mother and daughter hurrying behind me and Jeanette yelling, "You go too damned far, Harry!" But she wouldn't risk physical arrest with all its administrative investigation and snarling any more than I would. She called to Gus, "Go after him

and see what happens. Report every word. I'll not be
blamed for this."

The door of the Small Office was still open, which
was peculiar in itself when the green privacy light
was still showing. I could see without going in that
the soundproof windows had been closed.

Beltane was not in sight and there seemed to be
nobody else in the room. The strong social taboo
against breaking a sound screen held me in doubt
(though all you need do is walk through it) until the
black splotches on the gold curtain behind the desk
decided me.

He was flat on his back behind the desk. He had
stood up to do it, and the force of the old, large-bore
round had flung him back and down like a doll. He had
done it the dramatic, senseless, disgusting way with the
muzzle in his mouth to blow brains, blood and shards
of skull over everything behind him.

I heard Melissa tiptoeing behind me and saying faint-
ly, "Daddy!" and her mother telling her to go out of the
room.

Gus came to shake his head over the corpse, brooding
and angry. "What good does that do? He's out of it and
everybody else is left to swim in the shit."

I had another puzzlement. "Why did he do it? He
could have made himself the hero of the affair, played
the one honest man in a dirty world, standing up for
his Wardies. He had a life to live."

Gus had found something on the desk. "Look here."

"What is it? Not poetry, for God's sake!" The note
was scrawled in short, single lines, like verse.

"No. Well, a sort of a prose poem, maybe."

He remembered not to touch it, and we bent over it
together with Mrs. Beltane peering between us.

> *I am nothing, I am nobody.*
> *I am a construct.*

I am a botched artifact, another man's
desire for creation.
I am nobody, I am nothing.

"Lousy verse," I said because the silence was too holy for the idiotic event. "Not even a good reason."

Gus disagreed. "I don't know about that. Old Gerald gave him the emotional heave-ho last night, told him he didn't have a mind to think with or something like that. You and me didn't make things any better. Maybe worse. So he did what we all said and blew the institute to stop the politicking and then took himself off."

"After talking his head off to the channels and telling things he should have kept to himself."

"I reckon he wasn't responsible by then."

I had forgotten Mrs. Beltane. She said sharply, "If I understood that horrible speech correctly, he never was. He was a puppet until the doll master became senile; then he was left dangling on the strings." She turned her back on the desk and the mess behind it. "I make no concessions to deviance, but Jeremy was seduced in adolescence and badly treated by his monitor. That paper says it: 'I am a botched artifact, another man's desire for creation.' So what did he have to live for? He had been discarded and derided."

Jeanette came, asking what nonsense Melissa was crying about, and stopping short, knuckles to lips, when she saw what the nonsense was.

Mrs. Beltane said, "I wonder if he left a will," and we stared at her, thinking, *So hard, so selfish, so soon.* "You think I'm heartless? I have Melissa to think of besides myself. The lord of the Manor is dead in a Manor he inhabited only by courtesy of the state, so this is no longer his or my home."

Gus snorted at her, "You got your own house."

"The house, yes, but no money of my own. House and I were supported by an allowance paid monthly.

That has, I'd say, just ceased, so I am interested to discover if there is any provision in a will."

I wasn't sure of the protocol but I said, "You'll have to stay here a while. There'll be a period of grace while things are sorted out."

Jeanette said, "The first secretary is the man for this," and made for the desk console.

Mrs. Beltane collapsed without signal or warning. She did not fall but shrank. Abruptly her clothes no longer fitted as she dwindled within them; the lines of her face, so fine and unnoticed, became in a moment lines of age; her mouth relaxed in helplessness. She sat slowly down on the couch where Kenney had sat through the morning and her voice murmured in a fog, "I hated him but I wouldn't have wished his awful death on him. Or his awful life."

Jeanette came from the desk to sit beside her, and her glance told us to get out of the place. We left, shepherding Melissa from her spellbound post by the threshold. In the passage she took Gus's hand, like a child, and he was terrified, but by then he had become part of a past in which she was no longer interested.

The first secretary came bustling along, a harassed official to whom emergencies were tantamount to lèse-majesté, and she flung herself on him, crying out, "Oh, Phil, Daddy's shot himself!"

Phil protested, before he took it in, "Don't be silly, girl!" and then, "Oh, sweet Jesus!" and began to run.

12

Ostrov: The Last Loose End

From Commentaries; *Ostrov: "For all of his vague conversion to emotional values, which may have been little improvement on his 'righteousness,' he was in the last analysis only a man of his time, little interested in the great questions to which he gave lip service but wholly immersed in the narrow ambit of family and friends. 'That's how the world became the way it is,' he wrote. Quite so."*

That seemed to be the end of my commitment to the Manor, with the paymaster lying dead. Of course it was not. My secondment was to old Gerald, to Jackson. And he was sitting at home with my parents, who would only minutes ago have listened to Jeremy Beltane's cold-blooded relation of the obscenities of his political life. I would have to take him out of there before accident or deduction announced to them who he was.

I would have commandeered the most easily available work truck in the garages if two detectives from

Center Station had not come through the back door as I reached it. I knew them both.

They had come for Nguyen and Cranko, so I took them to the wardroom where they solemnly charged them with enough crimes against the state to be sure of catching them on some of them.

One of them said to me, "The super says you're in charge of old man Beltane. Right?"

"So?"

"So you bring him along to the station and come in with us."

What charge could be laid on him? Burglary of time? Larceny of youthfulness? "He isn't here."

"Where is he?"

"I'll tell the super where."

They didn't like that, but I outranked both of them and so I sat in the back of the paddy wagon with Nguyen and Cranko and left the Manor without farewell or regret.

In the parkland surrounding the house some kids played football. I said to Nguyen, "The world's troubles don't concern them. They can't alter anything so they keep on playing. Sensible."

"The troubles concern you, Harry?"

"I'll have to help control our corner of them when the rioting starts. If it hasn't already started."

"I think not. There will be small outbursts and then a vast, uneasy calm, a placid film over alarm and despair and hatred of government everywhere."

"That pleases you?"

"No."

"But you did your bit to create this situation."

Unwillingly, he agreed. "But who could know that the disordered man would make public confession?"

"He was beyond reason."

I recited to him the lines left on the premier's desk, and he saw them as a plea for sympathy. "A vidplayer to the end. The actor believes in his histrionics and the histrionics become the man. 'A botched artifact,' indeed! Still, the old man must have wounded him unbearably to cause such an outburst of public pleading—crying out, 'It wasn't my fault; I was driven to it.' "

"Yet he spared the old man. He told secrets galore but not where Gerald is hiding."

Nguyen glanced at the detectives in front, shook his head very slightly and with his lips formed unspoken words: I will not tell them.

Oh, yes, he would when they took to him! I hoped to have the problem of Gerald under control before some fool photographer made his new face public. He was illegality incarnate as well as a sure subject of sniggering jokes and political grandstanding from the Opposition.

We left the park and moved along the road to City Center. This was not a residential area and at this hour only bicycle traffic moved; nothing attested strong reaction to a world-shaking revelation.

We moved into the top of Elizabeth Street, at the Center's edge, and at last there were people on the footpaths. They stood around in gesturing, excited groups, but I could see no hint of rising ugliness; there would have been more animation for a football final.

"I expected more reaction."

"It will be slow at first," Nguyen said. "It is, after all, only an old fear breaking the surface of reality at last. Later there will be gatherings and outbursts. Politicians might do well to leave town."

Cranko gave a barking laugh but did not speak.

A few weeks later, law and vengeance shot both of them. As though it mattered any longer.

The station superintendent was grim, his mind fixed on immediate duties, keeping the impact of world shock at a distance. "Your Manor secondment will be over when you have turned Gerald Beltane in to us. Where is he?"

I suppose it was the habit of obedience that made me answer automatically to a direct question, "In my home." Yet I was wondering whether I *should* hand the old devil over. He needed protection, not bullying. As a delaying tactic, I said, "He's done nothing wrong; what was done to him was not by his will."

"With the premier dead"—Jeanette had been in duty bound to pass that information to the police—"the older Beltane becomes an essential witness. And his own legal position is uncertain." For a moment he looked human, even likable. "I'm surprised that you should have involved yourself personally—and your parents— when you could have stowed him safely in a police cell. It isn't like you."

"My brief was to protect him, sir."

"Against the police? Definitely not like you. I've always thought you too cool for compassion." His moment of humanity passed. "You can have a car. Get him."

When I commented on the orderliness of the streets the constable driver said, "We won't get much trouble in Center. It's the Wardies'll kick up." He homed in on his own particular puzzlement. "I don't know what to make of the racist stuff. How can we be like that when three Australians in four are brown or yellow or black or some sort of brindle?"

"Old ties. They dangle down the generations."

"Bloody stupid. The people don't think like that."

"Politicians do when they're looking for overseas friends."

In Port Melbourne, that warren of apartment blocks and lodging houses and dwellings crammed with aging, extending families with no space to spread, the people were in the streets. Where else to go? Yet the air was not tense. There were groups, a few arguments, even a couple of loudmouths trying to be rabble-rousers, but no sign of mob instinct. They had come into the daylight to see each other, feel each other's nearness and be not alone in anger and apprehension.

They had lived so long with the cull threat as an undercurrent to life that the sudden reality struck no sparks from old fears. After all my tensions of the past forty or so hours (all that had elapsed since I set out for the Manor on Friday night!) it was hard to credit an atmosphere of simple talkative concern. I felt there should be mobs marching and burning, blood warnings flashing across the world, murder in the air.

Well, there would be time for those while the race bred like maggots across the carcass of the earth.

At the house I told the driver to wait while I went inside.

Gerald was not in sight. Dad put down his book and looked questioning but not disturbed; Mum put her head out from the kitchen to say, "I didn't know when to expect you back."

"I didn't know either. I'm hungry."

She did the housewife's split-second calculation of food. "I'm saving the meat for tonight. There's cereal and some fruit."

"Anything. Is Jackson still asleep?"

Dad supposed he was, since they had heard nothing from him. I waited until Mum put the food on the table before I asked, "Didn't you hear the premier's speech at one-thirty?"

Dad nodded. Mum said as she poured the tea (whenever I saw her she seemed to be pouring tea), "How could we miss it? The channels used the priority flash signal." She passed me my cup. "Even if all the things the premier said are true, he should have been prevented from saying them. Couldn't you have stopped such foolishness?"

"The speech was recorded long before I got back to the Manor. Neither of you seems much bothered by it."

Dad asked, "Should we be? What good would agitation serve? A pack of fools was set to be more than usually inhuman, and the premier blocked them, but he should have kept his good deed to himself. The world was reasonably balanced in misery; now there will be enmity and suspicion."

Mum took over. They seemed often to work as a double act. "The dark peoples of Asia and Africa and South America will not forgive that Anglophone alliance. Their share of the land surface is far too small for their numbers and now they have a fine reason for pushing harder into the European and American territories. One can't blame them, but it will be brutal and unpleasant."

The primness of her speech was the telltale sign; she was appalled by events. She was as artificial as any Minder, but at that moment I loved her for it, for keeping feeling at bay while she got on with feeding her son. Her behavior made sense of Nguyen's human dichotomy.

Dad's secret service fantasy peeped out in an eagerness he could not quite suppress. "Why did the premier call you back? Are we allowed to know?"

A day earlier I would have ducked around the question; today I didn't give a damn for discretion or the closed mouth of responsibility. Like suicidal Beltane, I felt free to do and say as suited me. "He wanted to lay truth on the table, no matter who got hurt, and watch it throb. He wanted to speak his own unaided mind for the first time in his adult life. He was mad."

Mum reproved, "You shouldn't speak like that. He was unwise, certainly."

"I mean mad. Insane. Out of his mind. Trash for the looney bin. And when he'd finished doing maximum damage he shot the back of his head out. He's dead. I found the body."

They were suitably horrified for the moment that horror lasts in a violent world, until Dad said, "There's been no vid announcement."

"They'll hold it until they set the deputy premier in control and work out a smart lie to cover the facts. They'll say he was out of his mind and spouting garbage, but too many people around the world know that he told truth. Including the Southeast Asia Federation. Still, don't go putting it round the neighborhood yet."

Mum said, "You know I don't gossip," and Dad, "We know how to keep quiet."

Their awful equanimity pierced my calm. "Don't you care? Aren't you afraid of the future?"

Dad said, "We have always been afraid of the future. Our world fell apart in the thirties, but we survived. Life became less livable, but it still went on."

"Perhaps not this time."

Mum was admitting nothing. "You worry too much. I suppose it's in the nature of your work."

If the hordes of Asia poured in overnight they would find my parents drinking tea, quietly affronted by noisy invasion manners, preserving the masks that helped make empty existences bearable.

I told them that I had returned for Jackson. "I have to put him under arrest and take him in."

Dad wanted to know what he had done. "Or should I not ask?"

"Protective custody only."

"He has enemies? In the Manor?" For once in his life his romantic notions paid a dividend as he made the intuitive leap: "Visiting politician? With the new face the premier spoke of? That one?"

"Yes. I'll get him out of here. You won't want him hanging around."

Mum surprised me. "Do I hear morality speaking? Be gentle with him."

I marvolod, "Nothing shakes you two, does it?"

They made that lightning communication of eyes that comes with time and love, and Dad said, "Many things shake us, but even fear becomes commonplace, like noises in the street. Small compensations are one's life, not the large despairs. So do what you have to do with the man and come back to us when you can."

It had never before occurred to me that they missed me during my absences, that their son was one of the compensations for despair. I thought of Nguyen leaving his family without farewell and of Gus unable to be at one with his, and was ashamed.

Gerald (there was no point now in thinking rigorously of him as Jackson) rose a little from the pillow when I entered. He was in glaring mood, bear savage.

I tried with, "Were you able to sleep?"

"With that damned thing squawking in my ear?" He jerked his head at the tabletop vid I kept for long nights when shift rotation left me awake while my parents slept. "It nagged at me to listen to a special bulletin."

"So you don't need me to tell you what has happened."

He snarled at me, "Were you looking forward to telling me?"

"No." I had dreaded it.

"Don't pity me!"

"I must. I'm human."

"You are? What other wonders do you bring?"

He was hiding behind his game of get the copper's goat, and I had no urge to explain my changing heart to him.

He sat up and put his feet to the floor. "Made a fool of himself, didn't he?"

"Of you, I think. You taught him and wrecked him."

That was cruel, but there had to be an end of his playacting. He folded his hands between his knees and bowed his head and said quietly, without any tremor, "Leave me a little dignity, Harry. Last night my disappointment and wounded vanity exposed the fact that love had foundered long before. Can you listen—before the psychiatrists get at me and tear motive and intention to falsified pieces?" He fumbled at openings until, baldly, "Are child molesters still hated?"

"Yes. People don't give a pimp's curse about sexual preferences—I don't think most ever did—but pederasty has always been the unendurable perversion."

He said in a wondering tone, "Pederasty? I never thought of it like that. Jem was the only time for me. I bedded women all my life but never loved them as I loved the boy. I wanted a son, but there was a congenital defect and the new laws banned IVF; if you couldn't, you didn't. Do you know why I wanted a son?"

He needed an answer, to be comforted that another could understand him. I made a stab at it: "To carry on when you would have to leave off. To leave a continuing mark on our history."

He was pleased with me. "Yes!"

"Well, you've surely done that." There was no point in letting him wander among his dreams.

"I know I spoiled it, Harry. Or did I? Was it just the luck that ran against me, the senility and the Alzheimer years? You can't say I didn't train him well; he went up through the ranks like a bullet. Oh, I was proud! And then there was a more personal pleasure . . ."

He paused to consider that. I suggested, "Of running the show from behind the curtain. Dealing and manipulating."

"Yes, Harry—the vanity. It clouds the vision more than hate or love or despair; nothing warns you when to stop or to try to see straightly what you are about.

Jem and I didn't last long as lovers. That was a side issue, an excuse I made to myself for choosing this intolligont, malleable son. I never did such a thing again. Truth is, I suppose, that I gavo all my love to myself. No matter. I taught him well, and when I faded out he went on to become premier, without me. I came back from the dimness to find him head of the state, and that was some justification for it all. If I had been there to steer and advise he wouldn't have been premier of Victoria but prime minister of Australia.

"I knew something was wrong when he visited the ward. An uncertainty. A lack of strength. I didn't see yet that all his certainty and strength in the past had been my certainty and strength. If he had had any of his own I had knocked them down and imposed mine. I failed to see that he became only a speech-making extension of myself. Then I retired into incompetence, and he ran for years on borrowed impetus until he came to the problem he couldn't solve. He skidded to a helpless halt, crying for the father who had deserted him. So he called me back, and last night he told me how he had let himself be maneuvered into the hands of political blackmailers and a spy. You know all that."

"Yes."

"I let myself be disgusted with him. Vanity ruled. He had broken the first rule of confrontational politics: Trust nobody! Now he was in an impossible position that he wanted me to see him out of. That's where the end began."

He stood to stretch his arms and legs as though he ironed out creases in himself, but I have the impression that he needed to be on his feet to say the rest without whining.

He bared his teeth in what should have been mockery, but there was no mirth there. "Two lifetimes of devotion ended where every divorce begins, in recrimination and name-calling and the exposure of feelings concealed under years of habit. I raged at his stupidity and found myself berating an empty vessel labeled premier, while he resented being talked down to by an old fool he had rescued from doddering senility. He wanted a comforter and got a contemptuous scold. I wanted pride in my creation and got a puppet that had lost its strings. At some stage he yelled that all his mistakes were mine, that he was what I had made him—and that was where both of us realized that true affection had died when we had become a ruthless team where I planned the strategies and he kicked the goals. The end of love is cold dislike on both sides.

"At some stage I told him that any fool could see that the institute must be destroyed and the whole situation brought to a halt. He said that would finish nothing, but I made him see that it would get them all a breathing space. Some fool said that politics is the art of the possible. It isn't; it's the art of the stopgap. We parted in anger, but at least he did what I told him; he had the foul place destroyed. I suppose he could think of nothing better. Then he had to tell the world about it! He must have been out of his mind."

"He was. He shot himself. He is dead."

He looked at me for a long time without speaking. His face changed gradually, rumpling like paper crushed between the hands, and silent tears edged out of his eyes and down the wasted reconstruction of his cheeks.

He felt aimlessly at his pockets for a handkerchief, then took the one I offered him to scrub at his face like an angry child. He said in a voice like stone grinding, "Pay no attention. It's only self-pity."

He sat back on the bed, all pride gone out of him.

Someone knocked.

Mum called through the door, "Your driver is asking how long you will be. He says the station keeps vidding him."

I opened the door a little way. "I'll be with him in a few minutes."

She peered past me to Gerald with frank curiosity in a sudden celebrity, however tarnished.

Gerald recovered aplomb with a public performer's agility and closed one eye to her in a conspiratorial, meaningless wink. She giggled like a schoolgirl as she shut the door, and I reflected that I had never before heard my well-conducted mother giggle. Or, perhaps, I hadn't noticed. In God's name, where had my eyes been all these years? Fixed on myself?

I said, "We'd better go," and opened the wardrobe to get my uniform. It was time again for professional harness; secondment really was over.

"Go where?"

As I laid out the jacket, shirt and trousers I told him I had to take him in.

"I thought I was to stay here."

"That was a good idea, but a dead man's orders no longer run. The commissioner wants you and I have to deliver you. I'm sorry." I meant it; I saw no humane future for him.

"I have committed no crime."

"Not recently, but there was once a falsification of records, contribution to the delinquency of a minor and later on a fraudulent imposition on Parliament. If they want to get you they'll rake up charges from history if they must."

"From half a century ago!"

"But with ongoing consequences. And your right to life will be questioned."

He sat back on the bed. "That's a poor ending."

They might, I thought, find some circuitously legal way to invoke the euthanasia provisions. That would be kind though kindness would not be the object. I picked up the braided cap and shepherded him before me into the lounge room. The mid-afternoon was brilliant in the front window and Gerald gestured angrily at it.

"Look there! I've scarcely had opportunity to see the daylight and they're ready to close me in." He swung on me. "Is an old man's detention so urgent as to deny him an hour's walk in the sun?"

I started to tell him not to be so damned silly and in mid-sentence changed my mind. Without thinking it through I said, "Walk in the sun if you want to. The commissioner can wait that long."

He hadn't really expected that. "Do you mean it?"

"Why not?"

At this late hour in his affairs he still couldn't resist a dig. "Where's my Ape, my dutiful orders man?"

"It's a day of changes for me, too." He could make what he wished of that. "My father might like to take the walk with you."

Dad looked suitably startled until he decided that subtle planning lay behind my words and was at once ready to take his part in intrigue.

Gerald asked, "To keep an eye on me?"

"Company. Where could you run to?"

He shrugged and said to Dad, "It will be a pleasure to spend an hour with a cultured gentleman." So composure was to be the stage direction; he would carry it well. "I recall that as a boy I used to walk out along the jetties on the beachfront. Some were dismantled when the water level rose. Do any remain?"

Dad said, "There is one, preserved by the National Heritage Foundation."

"Good. I should like to stand there in sunlight and look over the sea. It should be not too far from here."

Dad matched him, olde worlde hospitality for total self-control: "Some ten minutes, but the UV is strong and you have no hat. Allow me to loan you one."

"A kind thought. Thank you."

The exchange of gents' club courtesies had to be

brought back to this day and age; I told them, "Go out the back way; there's a policeman in front."

From the back door Gerald said to me, "Thank you, Harry. I trust this will cause you no embarrassment."

"Who cares?"

He permitted himself a theatrical raised eyebrow. *Is my Ape a human in disguise?* At the laneway he put on Dad's hat, which was a trifle too big for him, and gave a brief wave. The expression on his face was pure mischief; we two had made our deal. The pair of them ambled away together.

Mum said, "I hope you know what you are doing?"

"What am I doing?"

"Risking your career."

My career. She did not mention the consequent descent into poverty for herself and Dad. I didn't deserve them.

She asked, "What's come over you? Why did you send your father with him?"

"To be a witness." That is, if Gerald's nerve held.

She began to gather up the cups and saucers. "You've changed overnight, become somebody else. What has happened?"

"I was given my life to look at and I didn't like it."

I went out to the driver and told him to take the patrol car back to the station.

"What about the prisoner we had to pick up?"

"He isn't here."

"Is that all I tell the super?"

"That's all. I'll see him later."

I watched the time edge slowly by until, after just fifty-three minutes, Dad came back, alone and shaken but still buoyed at having played his little part on the fringe of great events and asking wonderingly, "Did you know what he intended?"

"More or less."

"You should have warned me."

"And spoiled it for him? He liked an unexpected twist. How did he do it?"

Dad searched for a word. "Formally. Like the gentleman he seems never to have been in fact. We walked to the end of the pier while he expounded his rather cynical view of the immediate future; then he said, apropos of nothing, 'Tell Harry: *Vanitas vanitatum*—and there's an end of it.' He handed me my hat, thanked me for the loan and stepped off into six or seven meters of water. I watched the bubbles rise as he emptied his lungs. I imagine he gulped water and drowned at once." He gave me the undercover look of a back room boy making his report. "There was no one near us to help and, as I told the desk officer when I reported the accident, I can't swim."

Dad must have done some thinking on the end of the pier; he swims better than I do. However, in these days we don't interfere gratuitously with the choice of life or death. You don't get thanked for it.

Later in the evening I told the superintendent what I had done and even gave a nonsensical account of feeling sorry for the old man (which may have been the truth, or some of it) as a reason for my action.

He heard me out in grim disbelief and vidded the commissioner. He believed still less in the texture of reality when the commissioner called me to the screen, dressed me down very mildly for taking the case into my own hands and decided that under the circumstances it was as useful an outcome as any. The deputy premier had got to him, I guessed.

The super, balked of a hapless victim, could only order me to report for duty to my suburban station in the morning.

I went home.

*   *   *

Public numbness wore off quickly; there were mob-bings and manhunts and street brawls in the night, fired by the cynical outrage of the vid releases from the colored nations who saw whitey delivered into their insulted hands.

I was called out to do my professional job of mob control in the streets, but my thoughts were elsewhere—with my empty mind, shorn of easy morality and stupid certainties and the thoughtless habit of belief in my own probity . . .

With Gus, who needed someone to stick by him while he struggled for balance . . .

With my father and mother and the long, long job of getting to know them . . .

The horrors to come meant little while I battled with the problems of the here and now.

That's the human fashion. Tomorrow is always a long way off. Something will turn up, won't it? We'll muddle through.

Won't we?

Won't we?

That's how the world became the way it is.